This book is dedicated to my children.

Without their love and support,
I would not have kept my promise to go to the trapline.

And

A very special thanks to my husband Gordon.

It was only because of him that I experienced the beauty and the wonderful
life the Yukon wilderness offered.

Thank you Darling

I would not change a single day.

*To Mary
Love always
Lois*

A Promise Fulfilled
– My Life on a Yukon Trapline –

◆

Rose Toole

To Vic

*Enjoy
Rose Toole*

TRAFFORD

Canada ▪ UK ▪ Ireland ▪ USA

Note for Librarians: a cataloguing record for this book that includes Dewey Classification and US Library of Congress numbers is available from the National Library of Canada. The complete cataloguing record can be obtained from the National Library's online database at: www.nlc-bnc.ca/amicus/index-e.html
ISBN 1-4120-2055-7

TRAFFORD

This book was published *on-demand* in cooperation with Trafford Publishing.
On-demand publishing is a unique process and service of making a book available for retail sale to the public taking advantage of on-demand manufacturing and Internet marketing. **On-demand publishing** includes promotions, retail sales, manufacturing, order fulfilment, accounting and collecting royalties on behalf of the author.

Suite 6E, 2333 Government St., Victoria, B.C. V8T 4P4, CANADA
Phone   250-383-6864   Toll-free   1-888-232-4444 (Canada & US)
Fax   250-383-6804   E-mail   sales@trafford.com
Web site   www.trafford.com
TRAFFORD PUBLISHING IS A DIVISION OF TRAFFORD HOLDINGS LTD.
Trafford Catalogue #03-2634   www.trafford.com/robots/03-2634.html

10   9   8   7   6   5   4   3   2

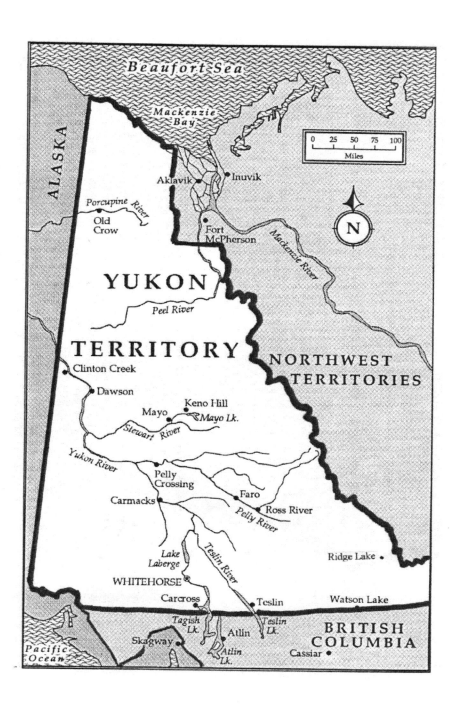

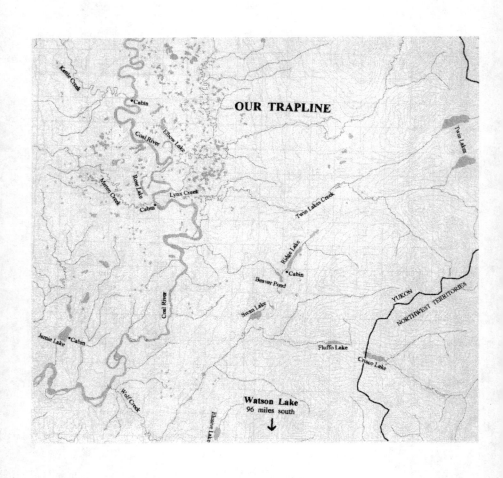

OUR TRAPLINE

Kettle Creek

•Cabin

Coal River

Elbow Lake

Martin Creek

Rose Lake

Lynx Creek

•Cabin

Twin Lakes

Twin Lakes Creek

Ridge Lake

•Cabin

Beaver Pond

Coal River

Swan Lake

YUKON

NORTHWEST TERRITORIES

Jamie Lake •Cabin

Puffin Lake

Cisco Lake

Wolf Creek

Elusive Lake

Watson Lake
96 miles south
↓

– Contents –

– MY FIRST YEAR AT THE TRAPLINE –

Saturday – September 28th

I can't believe it, the long awaited day has finally arrived and I'm actually here, watching as the Yukon slips by beneath the wings of the Otter floatplane flying my husband Gordon and myself, to a small remote lake in the mountains – a hundred miles north of our home in Watson Lake, and, a hundred miles from the nearest neighbor.

After months of nail-biting and days of hectic packing, trying to make certain we'd have all the supplies we'd need for the next four months, we're on our way and surprisingly, I'm enjoying the flight. With the cool mid-September temperature, the air is smooth – not a trace of turbulence. With mountains clothed in their vivid, multi-hued fall attire, the ever-changing view is spectacular as mountains then valleys with their winding streams, interspersed with occasional beaver ponds, sweep by beneath us.

We're headed for Jamie Lake and the small log cabin nestled on the ridge above its eastern shore that will be our home for the next four months. Since it's my first venture into the wilderness for a lengthy stay and despite reassurances from my husband, I've spent many sleepless nights worrying whether I'll adapt to life in the wilds, giving up all the accustomed comforts of our home in town.

It's a beautiful, sunny day, a smooth ride thank goodness, or I'd probably have tried to get off and walked. It's hard to believe an hour has passed and just ahead in the Coal River valley, Jamie Lake appears. After circling the lake to check wind direction and most importantly, make certain the cabin hasn't been demolished by bears, the pilot makes a smooth landing. A few minutes' later finds us tied up to the makeshift dock, busy unloading the supplies and gear we'll need for the coming months.

All too soon, after bidding the pilot, Derek Drinnan, goodbye, we watch as the plane takes off. Shortly, the only sound heard is the faint throb of the engine receding in the distance – then absolute silence. Gordon and I are alone except for our dog "Murky". Completely on our own! No neighbors – no sound of vehicles – just total silence. How traumatic for a city bred girl!! Now I understand the meaning of the saying – "Silence is Deafening"

Next, it was time to get to work packing all our gear up to the cabin. Besides, I'm hungry and its past three o'clock. I was too nervous to eat lunch before we left home so right now I'm ravenous. Gordon tells me we'll have a bite just as soon as we pack the first load to the cabin so we get moving! Sounds easier than it turns out to be. The trail up the slope winds in amongst balsam and a few spruce. Really not all that steep but when you're not used to a pack-board or carrying rather large boxes in your arms for any distance, it seems a lot further than it actually is. Maybe it's that I'm not in as good shape as I thought I was. Anyway, after a few short rests we reach the top and I have my first look at the cabin, our home for the next few months.

The cabin is actually a bit larger than I thought it'd be. It's built of logs with walls on three sides banked with earth. At first glance, snuggled against the ground, it didn't look very high with its flat, sloping roof. It should be easy to keep warm during the cold months ahead. When Gordon opened the door and I got my first close look inside, it appeared smaller than I'd expected it to be. It actually is twelve feet by twelve feet square – but didn't look that roomy. Two bunks line the back wall while the table is located along the south wall next to the stove. Shelves along the walls provide some cupboard space. Windows, badly in need of washing, are located in both the north and south facing walls.

Actually not too bad. With a few changes here and there and a bit of paint to brighten up the interior, it should be quite cozy. First things first though and as Gordon heads down the trail for a bucket of water, I get busy outside building a fire to heat tea water. Digging through one of the boxes, I soon located bread, peanut butter and cookies for a quick snack. It only takes a few minutes for water to boil and soon, sitting around the fire, we're busy drinking tea and munching on bread and peanut butter. My first meal on the trapline. Don't think anything I've had before ever tasted so good. I was starving!

A short lunch break and then back to packing supplies up from the lake. It seemed to take forever but finally the last load reaches the cabin and I collapse on the ground. It's taken us just over three hours to get everything moved. Gordon "promised me" that today's many trips from the lake would be the hardest work I'll do here. I found climbing the hill from the lake tiring on my back. We now have enough supplies for six months. While we were packing the last load from the lake, Murky started barking and carrying on. I then spotted a big fat porcupine climbing a tree near the cache. Gordon chased him away as we were afraid he'd tangle with Murky or get at our grub. Murky, even after several tangles with porcupines resulting in a face full of quills, still goes after them.

After completing a few chores, we decided to take a break and make a quick trip to check out the meadow east of here, hoping to spot a moose or caribou. We'll need one for our winters meat supply.. Gordon led the way down the trail he'd cut through the spruce years before – about a ten minute walk. No moose and no caribou, so back to the cabin. We were both hungry again so while Gordon got a fire going in the stove I was busy picking through the boxes for supper supplies. It wasn't long before we were sitting at the table enjoying potatoes, cauliflower and roast beef with fresh tomatoes and tea. My first meal at our Jamie Lake home.

The cabin is rather cute – at least it will be when we sort our stuff out. Gordon's already busy painting the ceiling white – at least part of it will be finished this evening. It should sure brighten the cabin and look super when it's all done. I'll wash the windows and then hang the orange colored drapes Gordon's sister, Eileen, made for us. That should make it even more homey. There's no snow yet and its quite warm – the stars are shining and a full moon. Real romantic. Radio reception is great. I know I'll never replace John for company or his Apricot Cobbler but I'll sure do my darndest to make this trip as enjoyable as possible. Instead of dragging the months out – time will fly by.

John Grant is an RCMP buddy who'd been going to the trapline with Gordon for several years. His famous "Apricot Cobbler" was one of the gourmet delights he produced one summer trip. Seems they were cooking outdoors over an open fire. One evening after eating, just sitting, relaxed around the fire with it's bed of glowing coals, John came up with the idea that he'd like to make an apricot cobbler and bake it by means of reflected heat from the fire. Great idea!! John's an excellent cook.

Anyway, the cobbler was made and placed in a pan beside the fire. A large piece of tin was bent and propped behind the baking pan to reflect heat downward to facilitate baking. By then, since it was getting quite late, John decided to leave his masterpiece to bake, retrieving it early morning. This would give it ample time to bake before the coals cooled off. He'd be up at daylight before the birds located it. Excellent planning so – off to bed. Sure enough, next morning John's up with the first hint of light and out to admire his masterpiece. Gordon soon heard muttering and a few bits of profanity so he's out in a flash to see what the problem is. Looking, he can't stop himself from bursting out laughing, seeing John digging through drifted ashes, trying to locate his prize cobbler. Seems the wind had come up during the night, blowing all the ash that had accumulated from many previous fires. His reflector was a perfect backstop for them. Anyway, they did try the cobbler but the ashes had given it a rather unique flavor.

Later, lying on my bunk, reflections on past events that had led to my being here in this little cabin in the Yukon wilderness paraded through my mind. Gordon had always enjoyed time spent in the bush, away from the lifestyle the majority of people have. Years before, he had received the trapping right to the Jamie Lake area from the Yukon Government. Since then he'd had many enjoyable seasons trapping, often accompanied by our youngest son, Jamie, or John Grant. They all seemed to enjoy it so much that I, in a moment of weakness, mentioned I'd like to try it too – when the kids were through school. We have six children so I figured I was pretty safe making this promise. But finally the day came when the last fledgling left the nest and I had to live up to my promise. So here I am, hoping I won't disappoint Gordon by not enjoying what is so dear to him.

Sunday – September 29ᵗʰ   First morning – enjoying coffee after a fitful, moon-lit night. A gorgeous, sunny – not a cloud in the sky morning.

The only cloud was when Gordon tried calling Watson Lake Flying Service, our radio contact with the "world" and found the radio dead. A few minutes of panic but after checking and changing batteries, we got it working but signals were out. Then I wanted to check the temperature and found the thermometer's tube on the ground, thankfully unbroken. Sure hope things go wrong no more than three times. Next, deciding to have bacon and eggs for breakfast, we realized we'd left the box of eggs out in the open porch. Seeing Murky's water dish covered with a good half inch of ice, our hearts stopped – but the eggs were Okay. Not a good way to start our first morning here.

Painted ceiling and sorted groceries until noon and then, after listening to wolves howl – went for a walk to the second lake which lies just to the north of Jamie Lake. Curious to see what the wolves had been carrying on about. About a thirty minute walk but no sign of wolves or the moose they might have been after. Gordon had thought the wolves might have chased a moose or caribou into the lake. Unable to tackle it in the water, they'd take out their frustration by howling. The trail along the lakeshore went past the spot where a Beaver floatplane had crashed in August of the previous year. A father and son from Vancouver had for some reason, landed on Jamie Lake but on takeoff, hit the tops of three large spruce – killing the father and seriously injuring the nineteen year old lad. Several five gallon plastic gas cans were left scattered about the site. Either a bear or wolverine had tried sampling a couple of them, as indicated by teeth marks through the plastic. There must have been a real strong wind this summer. Many large spruce have been uprooted and of course, invariably fell across the trail. Gordon removed the smaller ones on our way back to the cabin. Later this afternoon we took another walk southeast of the cabin until we reached a high lookout point overlooking the Coal River. Gordon, with his binoculars, glassed for moose or caribou for quite some time but wasn't able to locate any.

Tonight we had dinner by candlelight – real cozy. Not dark enough for propane lights so thought we'd conserve our propane supply and use a candle. After supper, tried calling Northwestel on the radio but signals were out. Gordon painted more ceiling – now we have three quarters of it painted white. Sure looks good and brightens up the place. I painted the two window casings. You would not believe the difference that made!

Monday – September 30th +2C   Another nice day – sunny and clear.

After breakfast got busy strapping gear on our packboards since we're planning on heading to the Coal River – a few miles east of here where Gordon cached his semi-freighter canoe last season. We'll be using it to go up river to the Rose Lake cabin. The cabin is actually located on the bank of the Coal River and not on Rose Lake. The lake is another two miles up and about a mile back from the river. We finally got away at eleven o'clock with loaded packboards containing a few items of clothing, sleeping bags, two radios – SBX11 transceiver for radio transmissions as well as a small receiver to listen to in the evenings plus groceries – very few. We also have two rifles – a. 270 Winchester in case we find a moose plus a .22 rifle for grouse and rabbits. It took us over two hours of packing over a very rough trail before we reached the river. The trail was very rough and the packs, especially mine, seemed to get heavier with every step I took. Since I had never had a packboard on before, I found it very tiring on my shoulders. Rather pleased that it didn't bother my back. I carried about thirty pounds – Gordon's was about sixty. I also carried the .22 rifle slung over my shoulder while Gordon had the .270 over his shoulder and carried the chainsaw by hand. He was very surprised that I was able to carry my load all the way. Murky really enjoyed the run. He stayed between us all the time. Sissy!!

After a few minutes rest getting the kinks out of our shoulders, we got busy skidding the canoe down the bank to the river. The canoe is a seventeen foot, aluminum, semi-freighter canoe that is ideal for use on the river according to Gordon. While I went back up the trail to the nearest trees to retrieve the paddles hanging there out of the reach of porcupines, Gordon brought down the 31/2 HP outboard motor from where it had been stored beneath canoe. Before he completed clamping the motor on the stern of the canoe, I finally managed to retrieve the paddles but couldn't help wondering what the set of holes through the blade of one paddle were for. Soon got that cleared up. Previously, the paddles had been hung from tree branches so they'd be about six feet above ground. No porky could reach that far but instead, a bear had come down the trail and decided to try sampling one. It appeared that after one chomp on the blade he found it not to his taste. He did leave a nice, neat row of holes through the blade though. Since then the paddles have been slung over higher branches, clearing the ground by a good ten feet. Those grizzlies do get big and can reach. It wasn't long before we had the motor refueled and running, loaded Murky and our gear aboard and shoved off into the current. The Coal River, this far upstream and at this time of year, is quite shallow in parts. The water is crystal clear flowing over a sandy, gravelly bottom. It turns and twists in loops along its course, frequently speeding through boulder fields. I, in the front of the canoe with paddle, was to direct the route between boulders lying submerged just below the surface. Sure enough, a few minutes later as we were navigating through an extra fast, narrow section with water tumbling between huge rocks, I got us hung up on a large boulder. We were stuck fast and, of course, I near panicked. Shoving with paddles we finally worked our way loose with no damage done but had to paddle through shallow, rocky areas for the next few hundred yard to avoid another rough stretch. One section of river was very wide and very shallow so we ended up getting out and pulling the canoe until we hit deeper water. I was thankful rubber boots had also been cached with the canoe. Further on, it didn't help any when the weather closed in on us with cold rain which threatened to change to snow. Luckily, there was a tarp in the canoe that I covered myself with. Gordon had coveralls on and insisted that he was quite warm. We ran out of gas at one point when crossing over a shallow stretch of river but, since we had extra fuel along, were soon on our way.

It was a wonderful surprise, rounding a bend, to finally spot a cabin perched on the riverbank. A few minutes more and we were pulling our canoe up on the sandy beach in front of Rose Lake cabin. First out was Murky — anxious to run and stretch after the two and a half hour river trip. Wow, up close the cabin left much to be desired but I'm sure when we get it organized it won't be so bad. It's just nine feet wide by fifteen feet long – inside. It has no floor, just sand, but does have four tiny windows. At that moment of inspection the clouds overhead parted and all of a sudden sunshine streamed through the southern window pane. Hope it's an omen for the weeks ahead. Nearby is the first cabin Gordon built here. It's called 'The Black Hole of Calcutta". It's very tiny, six by eight feet and was originally built as an overnight stop. It's also built of logs, chinked with moss. A pole roof covered with a couple feet of moss to keep the heat in and, over all, a plastic tarp to keep rain and melting snow out. It also has a tiny wood heater that can only take wood about twelve inches in length. Gordon spent a few winter nights in it when he couldn't make it back to Jamie Lake cabin but says it's not something he ever looked forward to. You spend more time shoving those tiny chunks of wood in the heater to keep warm than you do sleeping. Compared to this cabin, the one we'll be using looks like a palace. We've got a gorgeous view right in front of the main cabin. A wide, sandy beach extends from the cabin door, both up and down river for several hundred yards. Further exploration will have to wait – it's time we got our gear inside the cabin. The rain clouds seem to have moved over along the mountains to the southeast and now the sun is shining. The sun's warmth sure feels good after the chilly canoe ride.

While I was busy cleaning shelves and bunks in the cabin, Gordon was getting pots, pans, groceries and other gear we'd need down from the cache. The cache, about fourteen feet above ground, looks like a little cabin sitting atop a log platform that's supported by four posts. The four supporting posts are peeled logs, set solidly in the ground. About six feet above ground, tin is nailed around the legs for another three to four feet. The tin prevents animals from climbing to the platform and into the cache since their claws can't get a grip on the tin for the purchase they need for climbing.

After getting things pretty well sorted out in the cabin and stored away and with the sun still shining, decided it'd be a good idea to go up river to where Lynx Creek enters the Coal. Gordon guarantee's we'll catch a Dolly Varden trout for supper. Says it's a certainty at the creek mouth or in the river riffles just below. So, back into the canoe with fishing rods and on to Lynx Creek – about a fifteen minute run. The river is quite low at this time of year so sandbanks and sandbars extend all along it. The main channel divides and subdivides as it flows along, resulting in many shallow channels but usually only one deep enough for our use. It took a bit of navigating to keep in the deeper water but no real problem since the water is crystal clear, making it easy to see rocks, log snags and even the occasional fish as we moved along. Also noticed many fresh moose tracks along the sandbars. Our fresh meat supply is nil so hope to get a moose fairly soon. This time of year the meat, if properly dressed and looked after, will keep indefinitely. We reached Lynx creek, beached the canoe and fishing rods in hand walked about twenty feet back down river. I insisted Gordon take the first three casts into a section of riffles and then I'd try. Since we'd just passed over that spot with the canoe, I was certain any fish that might have been there would be disturbed and not strike right away. Bad mistake, on the second cast a fish struck and a few minutes later we have our supper wriggling on the bank – a five pound Dolly. I didn't even try a cast since a fish that size was plenty big enough for the two of us and to catch more would be a terrible waste. Next time though, I get first cast.

By now the sky had started clouding over and with the wind picking up, we figured it might be smart to head back to the cabin. Got there just a few minutes before rain really started coming down. We quickly got a fire going and it wasn't long before the cabin was nice and warm. Gordon cleaned the fish while I was busy sorting through the canned goods we'd brought down from the cache, trying to find something that would be filling and complement our trout. Finally success and not too much later we were sitting at the table enjoying dinner. The first meal for me at Rose Lake and actually the first real meal since we'd left Jamie Lake. That trout, accompanied by pork and beans did taste good. After supper Gordon hooked up the antenna for the radio. I hadn't realized we were so far out – the first station picked up was Radio Moscow!!

Tuesday – Oct. 1ˢᵗ +3C   Foggy out this morning. Hard to tell if it's cloudy or not. Can't even see across the river.

Murky has certainly been good on this trip – no barking or howling. Even with the patchy fog, from the cabin door we have a gorgeous view. The river is about fifty feet from the cabin across a wide sandy beach. The crystal clear water flows over a sandy bottom and occasionally, right from the cabin, you can spot a fish swimming by. It would be a dream of a place for a summer cottage. The river here is on a "U" bend and we're located at the bottom so have a view up and down river. Mountains on both sides with fresh snow on their peaks shining in the morning sun. It's just beautiful. But, the smell of fresh perked coffee tells me it's time I got busy making breakfast. After breakfast there was cabin cleaning to be done – then mixed up a batch of bannock. Bannock is a type of bread that's baked in the frying pan on top of the stove. It's very good and tasty. You can add raisins or blueberries or just about any kind of berry for variety. And what's most important, it takes the place of bread. Most cabins don't have stoves with an oven suitable for baking conventional loaves. While I'm busy inside, Gordon was out with his chainsaw getting a start on our winter wood supply. Luckily there is a good stand of dead, dry spruce just a short distance behind the cabin. It's almost essential to have your wood cut and stacked before snow comes, otherwise it's a time consuming, miserable job cutting and packing the wood out – wading through a couple of feet of snow.

Mid afternoon we went upriver, stopping at Lynx Creek to catch a couple more nice Dollys – my fish – and then on for another couple of miles. Pulled up to the bank, tied the canoe and then quietly walked the short distance to Rose Lake, hoping to find a moose. No moose but lots of tracks, many real fresh. We walked back to the river then sat and watched the shoreline for quite awhile before heading back to the canoe, then drifting down river to our cabin. No wind, just patchy clouds – scenery was great, a nice afternoon. Later, while I was preparing supper and Gordon was on the riverbank cleaning the second fish, he suddenly rushed in for his rifle.

He'd heard a bull moose calling from somewhere down river. With rifle in hand, he ran along the riverbank a short distance before stopping and crouching behind a large spruce. He then let loose with the plaintiff, wailing "HERE I AM, HONEY", call of a very lovesick cow moose. I had to cover my mouth as I started to laugh. But – his call sure brought results. Down river about half a mile, a large bull suddenly appeared, running from the timber to stand atop the high river bank. It stood for a few seconds until Gordon repeated his seductive wail then jumped over the edge and down the steep bank – landing with a splash in the water below. He quickly crossed the river and climbed out onto a sandbar, trotting along it until he was directly across from Gordon. Gordon shot and the bull took off. He fired again just as the moose ran out of my view. I thought he'd got away and was really disappointed with Gordon's shooting. I should have known better. Gordon saw him fall at the end of the sandbar.

We took the canoe and paddled over to the sandbar and down to the moose.

He was a good sized animal and would provide us with our winter's meat. We felt very fortunate getting our meat so soon and at such a handy location. There would be very little packing required getting the meat to the cache. Getting our winter's meat home usually meant at least two to three day's work with packboards. We quickly dressed the animal out and propped it open before leaving. It was getting too dark to do anything further. Tomorrow, we have our work cut out for us – cutting him up and hauling the meat back to the cabin. We'll then have to erect a meat cache sturdy enough to withstand the assault of a wolverine or grizzly trying to get a free meal. Fresh meat will certainly be a welcome change from the canned variety, Spork and Prem, we'd otherwise have had to depend on. Not getting meat was one of our biggest concerns but now, with it lying in front of us, we both have a feeling of real relief. We're set for the winter. John Grant would certainly have enjoyed this day.

Wednesday – Oct. 2ⁿᵈ "0"C   Light rain and snow overnight and still snowing – a dull day but it's cozy in the cabin.

Breakfast of oatmeal and bannock. Afterwards, it was out to our moose. We cut it up and hauled the meat home. It took several hours but finally got it all stashed up in the meat cache we'd built a short distance behind the cabin. We didn't build a little house on the platform. Instead, fairly large poles were laid across the cache floor to lay the meat on. This way it has space for air to circulate around and will keep indefinitely – especially as temperatures will soon remain well below freezing. A tarp is suspended above the meat to keep the rain and snow from it. The meat cache is just a platform mounted on four legs. Really rustic compared to our supply cache but it does work well. The moose was about a twelve hundred pound animal with only small horns. The horns had several broken points. He must have done a lot of fighting since one front shoulder was very badly bruised, making the meat inedible. One rib section was all bruised and also a good part of the second shoulder so it didn't leave so terribly much meat. It hadn't helped matters any with Gordon shooting him in a hind quarter when he thought the moose might be getting away. First shot was in the chest so he wouldn't have gone far but Gordon wasn't taking chances. The damaged meat won't be wasted since we're saving it for Murky. He'll be well fed for a good part of the winter.

Cleared up nicely this afternoon. Mountains all covered with snow but it's pretty well melted around the cabin. Got a good fire going this afternoon just a short ways down from the cabin where Gordon's planning on boiling traps. He rigged a tripod over the fire to suspend a five gallon pail of water to boil traps in. A few wood ashes are added to the water. The traps are placed in the pail and boiled for ten minutes or so. During boiling, the ash acts as lye, removing any rust that might be on them. After the traps are boiled this way, water is dumped and replaced with clean water and put on to boil again. This time though, he adds the short ends from green spruce boughs to the water. When the boughs have boiled for a good half hour, the traps are replaced in the pail and left for a few minutes. They're then slowly removed from the pail and placed on a pile of boughs to cool. The boiled spruce boughs produce a waxy substance that coats the traps so they rarely rust. Also, all human scent is removed. The traps we use are the quick kill type. The old leghold traps haven't been used for years and are unlawful to use in Canada. When an animal steps into one of the modern traps it is dead within 15 to 30 seconds This humane type trap is the only kind we use.

After we'd finished boiling traps it was back to cutting more wood for our winter supply. Also later on, went back for the lower parts of the moose legs and further down river, hung them high on a dead snag – hopefully out of reach of wolverine. Not much in the way of meat on them but Murky will love to chew on them this winter. Later, we also enclosed the back and sides of the "World Trade Center" (John Grant's christened name for the biffy) with small spruce trees then covered all with plastic sheeting. We also looked for a watch that John had forgotten and left on his spruce bough bed when he and Gordon were camped here a couple of years earlier. The boughs had decomposed so much that it was impossible to find anything.

Thursday – Oct. 3rd -1C Foggy and a few flakes of snow falling this morning.

Not a good night for me . Started thinking of bears and got nervous. All that meat up near our cabin and the remains of the carcass on the sandbar in front. Then I got a terrible pain – I won't say where. It turned out spruce trees are even against me. Outdoor biffys are for the birds. I got some spruce gum on my underclothes and you can guess the rest.

Gordon doesn't trust the weather so we're not going further up river to our Kettle Creek cabin. It's a good three hours by canoe. We'd originally planned on going and getting the cabin ready for winter but now it'll have to be done after freeze-up and snow . We'll then go by skidoo. Instead, we're packing up and going back home to Jamie Lake. Gordon's making breakfast. Coffee and bacon sure smell delicious and pancakes just about ready. . Finally left Rose Lake at eleven and canoed down river, running the motor in the rougher stretches but paddling most of the way. It was enjoyable and kept us warm despite a cool breeze. This time we pulled in to shore a short distance upriver from where the canoe had previously been cached. From here, we don't have to go through the section of river with all those big boulders where we'd hung up on our way upriver. Instead, we'll have to pack about half a mile further before reaching the Jamie Lake trail. It was a great trip down river but was cloudy and foggy so didn't get many pictures. It only took us about an hour, traveling with the current.

We cached motor and the paddles beneath the canoe and then, pack boards on our backs, headed up the trail to Jamie Lake. We did a bit of trail clearing as we went and got back just after four. It was a good hike over a rough trail and it was nice to sit down again. Right now we're enjoying a drink and playing cards. We noticed moose sign all the way along the trail and also a lot of marten tracks showed in the skiff of snow. Gordon has gone bonkers. He says it's only seventeen more days until he can ski for free at Panorama. Panorama is a ski resort in British Columbia where we've previously skied. They have a policy that allows for free skiing for anyone sixty years of age and older. His birthday's on October twentieth. REALLY, I don't know what two old???? are doing here – one hundred miles away from nowhere. Thank goodness our daughter Patti claims that age is only a number or it would really have me worried. Dinner tonight of fresh moose tenderloin, fresh potatoes with dilled butter, carrot sticks and fresh tomatoes from Grandma Toole's garden. Sure tasted good – really roughing it!!

Friday – Oct. 4th 0C   Started snowing early this morning – looks nice.

Had a late, lazy breakfast at ten-thirty, omelettes, toast and coffee. Played cards then Gordon cleaned and straightened out the porch while I re-arranged the inside of the cabin. We do have a large porch extending along the front of the cabin which is handy for storing our wood, tools, traps and other supplies. Especially appreciated when the snow comes. Later, inside the cabin, had Gordon remove the top bunk. There'll be less storage room but it'll be much easier getting into bed with no heads banging into the top bunk. We'll also have more comfortable sitting space. Hung one window drape – looks great. Gordon also finished painting the ceiling. Later, we got a fire going outside, adjusted more new traps and boiled them in spruce tips, all ready for the opening of trapping season, November first. Supper was baked beans with bacon and potatoes and bannock. Gordon said the bannock was my best effort so far – really good. The sun shone awhile this afternoon and melted snow off the trees – very mild out. Gordon has definitely gone bonkers – claims this is like a second honeymoon.

Saturday – Oct. 5t -6C   Clear, little fog. Will be a glorious day.

We had quite a rude awakening. The cabin was shaking and first thought – a bear is trying to get in. It was a relief to finally realize it was an earthquake. It certainly shook the cabin and our nerves. The radio antenna outside was really dancing. Later, we got word by radio that the quake was centered to the east of us in the Northwest Territories. The cabin is much brighter inside with the ceiling, as well as window frames, painted white. I even painted the inside of the door – looks great. Next year we'll get linoleum for the floor – easy to keep clean. The stove certainly heats the cabin in a hurry. We don't keep fire going at night, for now. Mornings, Gordon's up first to light a fire in the stove and put the coffee on. A few minutes later when the cabin's nice and warm, I'm up to wash in a basin of warm water Gordon always has ready for me – talk about service !! During breakfast we decided to work around the cabin doing some of the jobs that should be completed before the snow came. I was delegated the person responsible for boiling traps so they'd be ready for use in another few weeks. While I kept busy keeping the fire burning under the ten gallon drum full of boiling water and traps, Gordon was working nearby with his chainsaw. He cut down a number of dead spruce and then sawed them into stove wood lengths. By the time I finished my job Gordon had a good start on our winter's wood supply. By the time we finished stacking wood in the porch it appeared that another three sessions with the saw would pretty well look after our winter's requirements.

After lunch we went for a leisurely walk along the ridge to the north of here just above the lake, hoping to pick up some grouse. No luck – didn't see any birds but spotted fresh moose and caribou tracks as well as a few sets of marten tracks. Dinner tonight was roast moose with potatoes, carrots & onions with Grandma Toole's squash. Hadn't used the oven before so was sure hoping it worked. It's just a metal box with a hinged door on the front that Gordon had made. It sits on top of our stove which is manufactured from a hundred pound propane cylinder. It's a first rate stove for cooking and heating and I've now found the oven, with a grating to keep the roaster off the bottom, also works surprisingly well. The oven is also equipped with a thermometer which really isn't needed. Supper turned out really well, even better than I'd hoped for. Everything considered, it's been a really super day..

Sunday – Oct. 6ᵗʰ -8C   Sunny, not a cloud in the sky.

Murky barked during the night. Gordon got up to check but couldn't see anything. This morning he did find marten and rabbit tracks near the biffy. It's located about seventy-five yards behind the cabin. Later, he also spotted fresh caribou tracks over by the old tent frame – about two hundred feet to the north of the cabin. That's probably what upset the dog. Guess Murky didn't appreciate all the company. Also too bad it was too dark for us to see. Tried the oven again this morning and baked a scrumptious cherry pie. It turned out great. I'm really amazed at his little oven. Later – went for a walk to the big meadow that's about three miles northwest of us to pick up traps and, hopefully, a caribou. No luck with caribou. The view from the edge of the meadow is tremendous, mountains all around with snow-capped peaks shining in the sun. We sat on hummocks for quite a while enjoying the beauty. Picked up a few traps and then wandered back home.

We had moose tenderloin smothered in mushrooms, baked squash, peas, coleslaw and garlic toast, for supper. Really roughing it!! Too full for pie so will have it later. The cabbage was one I sent out but hadn't been used by Gordon when he was here on a trail cutting trip in August. It kept very well in our little root cellar under my bunk. He had cut out a small section of flooring, removed earth below and then lined the hole with boards and "Presto", a root cellar. With the section of flooring replaced, vegetables remain nice and cool and keep for lengthy periods. Later, tried the transmitter but again failed to raise Northwestel – a bit disgusted as we'd just purchased new crystals and antennas for their frequencies. Finished the day by remodeling the table, painting the legs and putting new oilcloth over the top. A big improvement in here from the day we arrived. Will hate to leave.

Monday – Oct. 7th *-12C* Another sunny day. Got a little cool in here towards morning.

Fire sure felt good and coffee – even better. One big "Woof" from Murky last night – checking, tracks indicate a marten had gone right past his house. Mid morning we headed up "Ridge Run" with chainsaw, axe, tea pail and lunch, clearing and widening trail for our skidoo. Saw lots of sign along the way, especially porcupine. Lots of grouse but no twenty-two rifle. Stopped for lunch after a couple hours of clearing trail and built a fire to boil tea water. It wasn't long before we were contentedly sitting with backs resting against a spruce, sipping tea and eating toasted sandwiches. Sun was shining, warming everything. A few short days and I'm already starting to understand why Gordon enjoys this lifestyle. All too soon though, it's back to trail cutting for another three hours and then back to the cabin. The trail we're working on, "Ridge Run", follows the high ridge above the lake that's located to the north of Jamie Lake. We noticed it had frozen over whereas Jamie Lake only had a skiff of ice along the edges. On the radio tonight, Calgary was reporting – 4C while we are – 3C. Stars shining here whereas Calgary was receiving snow. Peaceful and quiet at Jamie Lake – what a contrast to the city.

Tuesday – Oct. 8th -8C   Cloudy but warm, another nice day.

After breakfast headed down the Canyon Run, clearing and widening trail where necessary. This run heads southwestward from Jamie Lake and follows the high bank paralleling the Coal River. The trail is several hundred yards back from the river and for most part follows an old game trail With our clearing, it's now like a super highway for the skidoo. Saw marten sign all along the way. Fixed up cubbies (box-like affair for traps) and brought traps back for boiling. Ran out of oil for the chainsaw so will have to finish trails tomorrow. It took a lot more chainsaw work than Gordon had expected . Started snowing lightly this afternoon just as we got back to the cabin. Tried calling to Northwestel and also Watson Lake Flying service. No answer. Took the Northwest antenna down as we've made no contacts. Think we must be too far away in mountainous country for their frequencies to work. We're very disappointed in this.

Wednesday – Oct. 9th "0"C   Cloudy but pleasant, another good day.

It will be another nice day for cutting trails – no fresh snow other than for the few flakes we received yesterday afternoon, making it easier walking and cutting. Finished breakfast and with tea pail and lunch, headed out to complete the Canyon Run. We finally finished the trail, all the way down to the creek that flows from the chain of meadows to the northwest of here. We didn't cut the brush along the trail leading down from the ridge to the creek – about half a mile. It will take at least an hour and a half to clear that section since the willows are really thick, completely overgrowing the trail in places.

Gordon did three hours of steady cutting, enough for one day. Trail clearing is especially hard work for the chainsaw operator. He's bent over most of the time since brush and trees have to be sawn off as close to the ground as possible. Cutting higher would produce stumps that you'd run into with the skidoo. My job is to throw all the debris off the trail. Gordon used six and a half tanks of gas in the chainsaw during yesterday and today. We did a good job though and walking back, thought it looked great. We were gone seven hours in addition to our forty-five minute break for tea. Saw lots of marten sign. I'm bushed from all that walking, clearing and packing. While he cuts trail and I'm removing debris, I'm also packing the lunch makings, the .270 rifle (in case we meet an unfriendly grizzly), plus the packboard loaded with extra gas and oil. Sort of reminds me of that TV show – Ma and Paw Kettle. Jamie – you'd never believe the improvements on the trails plus the changes in the cabin. It's so nice and bright and cozy in here.

Thursday – Oct.10th -1C   Its another sunny day.

After breakfast we again tried contacting Watson Lake Flying Service but again, no luck. Guess signals are still out. We'll have breakfast and try again before heading out for more trail clearing. Finished up a few odd jobs and tried the radio again at ten-thirty. Couldn't believe it when we received an answer. We reported everything fine here. It was good to finally make contact as Gordon was beginning to think that something was wrong with our radio. We then, with the usual lunch and gear, started down our Jamie run heading southwards towards the river. From the cabin, we first begin following the higher ground that eventually turns into a ridge and, a couple of miles further on, to a high bench that overlooks the river. This was the old trail with the last section suitable for snowshoe use only – not skidoo. Today we're hoping to find a way down from the ridge and across the narrow creek below to the large meadow stretching along the river. The problem was in finding a way down that ridge where it wasn't too steep since we'd be traveling both up and down it once snow arrived.

It took a lot of hiking and checking of downward sloping ravines before we finally found a route we could use. We blazed it all the way to the creek before taking a break, building our tea fire and having lunch. Sure nice to have a rest after more than four hours climbing up and down that slope. The new route looks good, although there are some fairly steep parts that may give us a bit of trouble with the skidoo if we don't keep the snow well packed. Took a total of five hours climbing up and down then blazing the route before we took time out for lunch. We then decided we'd had enough exercise for the day and will finish clearing the trail tomorrow and headed back the relatively short distance to the cabin. For supper we had baked stuffed tenderloin, baked potatoes, squash, fruit and cake. Really roughing it, eh!!

Friday - Oct.11th -2C   A little bit cloudy today.

This morning we found fresh wolverine tracks around the cabin. The wolverine didn't even wake Murky – some watchdog!! Right after breakfast, with the usual gear, we headed back to finish clearing the trail we'd spent so much time locating and blazing the day before. Turned out not to be as much work as expected. Mainly small balsam along the new route – they're easy cutting and don't grow close together. Best of all, hardly any willow until we reached the creek below. Even then it wasn't bad with only short patches of willow to clear. Gordon cut a number of dead spruce for a makeshift bridge across the creek. It's not elaborate but certainly will support the skidoo. After crossing the creek, we found ourselves in a section of very large willow that took a while to cut through. From there on it was past a stand of open pine, no clearing required, and we were in the open meadow. HURRAY! We can see open meadow, dotted with occasional patches of pine, for a couple of miles – all the way to the river. Believe it or not – we don't have to slash trail any further. What a heartbreaker!! All the packing of extra gas and oil was for nothing.

We then left our gear, except for the packboard that held our axe and lunch gear and hiked over to the river. We followed the sandy shoreline for a couple of miles upstream before stopping under a big spruce where we built our tea fire and had lunch. It was an enjoyable break from the trail clearing we've been doing. We've opened a lot of new country for trapping where we can use the skidoo. A lot of fresh caribou tracks around here – all through the meadow and along the river. Later in the afternoon on our way back Gordon was telling me to be careful crossing a small creek or I'd get wet feet. So what happens – he thought the ice was thick enough but it wasn't so he, not me, ended with a boot full of ice water. Some Guide!! Further on he decided to cross a small, shallow channel of the river to reach a sandbar where walking would be easier – Murky following. I stayed on higher ground, walking along the river bank. It wasn't long before Gordon crossed back to me. While the sandbar was nice and flat with no obstructions and appeared easy going, walking in the loose sand was hard work. Murky decided to continue down the sandbar, investigating the occasional driftwood pile while we continued along the riverbank. Finally, the sandbar ran out and he couldn't find a dry way back to shore. The shallow channel that separated him from us had changed to a sizeable and deeper stream. Poor dog panicked – running back and forth while we stood on shore laughing. He finally took the plunge and came across in the icy, cold water. He got his revenge though by immediately rushing to us and shaking the water from his fur. Surprising how much water a dog's coat can hold. We were surprised to see the Coal River was freezing over – some areas right across – other places just a small open channel remaining. Walking home, we both felt pleased with finishing the trail plus the extra bonus of time spent along the river. It's been another good day.

Saturday – Oct. 12th -1C   Cloudy with a few snowflakes falling.

We've been here for two weeks and can still look at each other without woofing our crackers, to use our daughter Patti's expression. Actually, it's been a very enjoyable two weeks. We had snow last night, about an inch. After breakfast we'll be out again to cut more trail. We hope to get most of the trail clearing completed before we have more snow.

We ended up cutting trail for another four hours to reach the beaver meadows west of here. Must have covered a good seven to eight miles round trip. It was cloudy with snow showers during the entire day. It wasn't until after we returned home that the cloud cleared it off and the sun started shining. Murky just would not leave us today. He must have gotten the scent of something that bothered him, perhaps a bear. We didn't spot any tracks though. Think we'll be taking tomorrow off. We're both tired of trail cutting and need a change. We must walk between six and ten miles a day in addition to clearing between four and ten thousand cut willows and trees from the trail. At least it seems that many. Jamie Lake has completely thawed with most of the ice patches around the shoreline disappearing. The second lake has frozen completely over but the ice is not strong enough for walking on. The creek also has ice along its edges – winter's coming. Gordon pulled a muscle in his groin so we're forced to ease up for a day or two. I certainly hope it clears up soon as I worry so much.

Sunday – Oct 13th -3C   A little cloudy but blue sky showing in areas so think it will be a nice day.

I was up first this morning and got the fire going. Brrr – it was coooool. The cabin heats up fast, thank goodness.   It's usually only a short while before the windows are opened so it won't get too warm. Gordon feeling better this morning. He may have also gotten chilled yesterday as it was cold out. The damp cold went right through him, especially since he got soaking wet from snow falling on him from the brush he was clearing. Gordon's feeling much better this afternoon and is out boiling more traps. I took advantage of a "day off" and baked an apple pie. Turned out great. I pretty well have the heat figured out perfectly for baking pies – really pleased. Also made three pans of cinnamon buns. Burnt first ones – put too much sugar and butter on the bottom and they really burnt. The other two pans, I baked halfway through then turned them over and they were Okay. Now I'm making cabbage rolls for tomorrow. We're having roast moose with veggies for dinner tonight. We played a lot of cards this afternoon and I was the big winner. My opposition's a dumbhead in playing solitaire – almost as good as in crib. Just before supper Murky started barking. Gordon ran out and checked down the trail past the tent frame until finally spotting signs where a wolf had been sitting and watching. Will have to get him one day soon before he makes a meal of Murky.

Monday – Oct 14th -4C   Little cloud this morning, another nice day.

Last evening Murky again acted up but it was too dark to see anything. Checking this morning, Gordon found tracks where a wolf had circled the yard. He was smart enough to stay below the knoll where the cabin sits so he wouldn't be seen. Big Bad Wolf – I'm definitely not going out alone in the dark. Finished knitting the back of my sweater yesterday. Hope to have it finished this winter. Had my first instruction in chess but I'll reserve my opinion of the game until later. Jamie Lake still not frozen over, only a few ice patches – even have two ducks swimming around. They'd better get a move on and head south.

Gordon says we've had a very rewarding day. We went to the beaver meadows again – walked across the washed out beaver dam where it was undercut by the outgoing water. What a deep hole beneath the dam – hate to fall into it. While walking across the meadow, Gordon found tracks of a lynx. He was so pleased as lynx are very scarce around here. We blazed a new trail through the brush, across the meadow to the beaver houses, then off to the far end of the meadow where we had lunch. Tea with bannock, corned beef and peanut butter. Sure filling. We then walked further on and were happy to find more beaver houses and a new dam that flooded much of the upper meadow. When it's all frozen it'll be much easier going with the skidoo and, a real bonus – no trail cutting. Fixed up marten houses on our way. We saw all kinds of tracks today – lots of moose, caribou, wolf, lynx, marten, mink, weasel, beaver and even tracks of a mouse.

Returned home on another old trail where I spotted a trap box. Gordon checked it out, puzzling over it until he found the sprung trap with the drag all overgrown with moss. Must have been there for years. While we were at the meadow, Gordon tried calling moose. It was rather funny to watch Murky cock his head as if he knew what was going on. He always stands right behind Gordon and except for his head moving side to side, never moved a muscle – not even his tail, which is usually wagging. No moose, so back to the cabin. Bath night again. Gordon's heating water outside on another stove. For privacy I have a shower curtain which is hung to partition our palace. It works very well.

Baking cabbage rolls for dinner tonight with apple pie for dessert. Lots of meat in the rolls – real tasty. Feel tired now as we must have walked a good ten miles in our rubber boots. Walking in them is very tiring but the meadow country, still not frozen, was very wet so they were needed. Cleared up late afternoon – was gorgeous with the sunshine and sparkling mountain tops. We'll sure be in condition for skiing this winter! The second lake is frozen over but ice still not hard enough to walk on. We saw where a moose had walked out on the ice and broke through. It was lucky as it was able to break ice back to shore and get out. Most times when moose and caribou break through the ice on lakes or rivers they're not able to break a path to shore and die. A terrible, lingering ending.

Tuesday – Oct. 15ᵗʰ -15C   Beautiful, not a cloud in the sky. Jamie Lake has frozen over – wonder what happened to our two ducks??

We decided last evening that if it wasn't snowing in the morning we'd head back to Rose Lake via the Ridge Run trail. Got away at eleven-fifteen with our loaded packboards plus the chainsaw and rifle we carry by hand. In a straight line it's only about seven miles to Rose Lake but by the trail we have to take it must be about twenty – at least it sure seemed like it. Cleared more trail on the way but didn't finish it all. We were getting tired by mid-afternoon and wanted to reach the cabin before it got too late. We finally arrived just after four in the afternoon, not even stopping for lunch.

We found everything was fine, even the meat in the cache that we were so concerned about. No clouds all day, it's still sunny and beautiful. The scenery is really spectacular from here – especially with the sun shining. We saw lots of fur sign on our trip. More lynx tracks than Gordon has ever seen around here before. He reported a maze of tracks from mink and marten around the meat cache. Thankfully, they had no luck climbing the cache legs that he'd wrapped with tin. It's actually quite breezy at this location. It's quite open with the river and sandbars stretching in front of the cabin.

This cabin isn't near as "homey" as Jamie Lake but with a lot of work could be made comfy. After snow arrives we'll travel by skidoo – haul lumber from Jamie Lake and put a floor in. Paint for the door and drapes for the windows would be nice. Also if he brings that large window, originally planned for the Kettle Creek cabin, and uses it to replace the little window over the table, what a difference it would make!! The view would be great. My drapes wouldn't match, as Gordon's sister Eileen and I had planned, but I'm sure it won't matter. This cabin won't be used as much as Jamie Lake or Kettle Creek cabins. Gordon, in rubber boots, managed to cross the river to the sandbar where we'd got our moose, hoping to find a bone for Murky. No luck, every scrap and bone was gone. River is quite low with some slush ice running. This evening we started peeling bark from the log walls in the cabin. It should help to brighten them up.

Wednesday – Oct.16th   -6C   Real surprise when we got up this morning. It snowed during the night and a few flakes were still coming down.

With a good chance of more snow, its back to Jamie Lake for us before it arrives. We aren't prepared for plowing through a lot of snow. We only have our hiking boots here and they're quite low. Definitely not suited for wading through a foot of snow. We heard cranes flying over during the night. Think they've got their seasons mixed. Hope they get to where they're going before it freezes up too much more. Last night was the first time since our arrival, other than for my initial shock at being alone on the dock when the plane left, that I felt sorry for myself being out here. I was so COLD. The floor of packed sand was damp and my feet felt frozen. I knew Gordon was warm – lying on the top bunk reading, so I didn't complain. After I got into bed and warmed up, the feeling left. We had planned on flooring the cabin today – Gordon cutting floor boards from spruce logs with his chainsaw but now that's put on hold.

We left Rose Lake around ten-thirty and got home just after three. On our way back we slashed trail in a few of the worst places so figured our actual walking time was just a bit over three hours. It was a bit slippery with the fresh snow but we still moved at a good pace. Saw several sets of marten tracks along the way as well as a real fresh set of tracks by the cabin. Had French onion soup with cheese, garlic toast and tea for our late lunch. Making a stew for supper.

Thursday – Oct.17th   -7C   Overcast with a few snowflakes falling – sort of a dull looking day.

Snowing lightly so maybe we'll get to use our skidoo soon. I've been getting rather worried about Gordon's ability as a trapper. We had a mouse getting at our bread supply – chewing holes through the cardboard box it's stored in. Gordon decided to set four different traps inside the box but caught nothing. Then we noticed the mouse had also got into the box of bread out in the "breezeway" or front porch. Gordon had left a trap baited with cheese when we'd gone to Rose Lake. Still no mouse when we got back – just more holes through the box. My trapper got mad then and moved the bread into a large, sturdier box and placed a trap on top of it. He was determined to catch that mouse – especially since we'd brought a bottle of wine that was to be opened in celebration of our first fur catch. Before going to bed, full of anticipation, he made one last inspection of his trapline. From the muttering I was pretty sure the mouse was still on the loose. Sure enough, Gordon found the wrapper from our French bread had been pulled through the box opening and really chewed up. The mouse must not like French bread since it wasn't touched. Now Gordon was really desperate. He set four traps – three on top of the box that were baited with bread and the other, placed alongside the box, baited with cheese. This morning, faith in my trapper has been restored. He got his first fur for the season. (But, I have news for him. I'm keeping the wine for bigger and better things – like a lynx!). Really, is it that hard to catch a little mouse!!

After the past strenuous days of trapping, we're taking the day off and I'm making home-made soup. Gordon's busy locating small, straight pine trees to cut and then split lengthwise with the chainsaw. The half sections are then peeled and nailed over the moss chinking between the logs. Sure makes it look better – a great improvement. Before long we'll hate to leave this place. Jamie and John will think they're in the wrong place when next they come out here because of the many changes. Later, noticed more fresh wolf tracks around our grocery cache that must have been made during the night. A huge raven here also, teasing and terrorizing Murky. Gordon says the trees he's cutting down are like the Nabob coffee bean advertisement, "Many are picked but few are chosen". He needs small, straight trees and they're few and far between. While he was busy with the saw, I finished up the laundry. Always something to keep you busy.

Friday – Oct.18th -4C   Overcast with a few snowflakes to accompany the trace of snow that fell overnight.

This morning I asked my ex-weatherman what it was like outside and he said, "Its cloudy and sunny and a few fluffy flakes". Now that's giving conditions intelligently. It's almost on a par with me asking for a certain card while playing and asking for a black – red. Wonder who's getting "bushed". I had a splitting headache yesterday and during the night. It was so bad that even my teeth hurt – enough for me to think they might fall out. Thankfully, this morning the headache's gone and my teeth still seem to be where they should be.

Saw tracks where a rabbit had sat right outside our "Dining room" window during the night. We tried calling Watson Lake Flying Service but signals were still out. Gordon finished nailing the split sections he'd cut yesterday between the logs in the cabin and then put up more shelves for me. Place sure doesn't look the same as when we arrived. Even a step has been installed by the door. Later, we went for a walk up the old "Jamie" run to see if any traps had been left from last winter but found they'd all been brought in. Occasionally, towards at the end of the season when you're springing traps, one will be dropped in the snow and lost. Right now we have about two inches of snow on the ground. When we got back to the cabin, I built a big fire in the garbage pit to thaw the ground while Gordon was busy digging a new pit alongside it. All our garbage is emptied in a pit and burnt. Later, when the pit is pretty well filled, the burned out trash is covered over with the soil dug from the new pit. In all the years Gordon's been out at Jamie Lake, not once have the cabins been bothered by bears. Leave trash and garbage about and you'll always have trouble with bears breaking into cabins.

Saturday – Oct. 19th -5C   Not nice – overcast, snowing and windy.

Snowing. Radio reception is still out – very annoying and worrisome. Playing cards this morning. We don't want to leave in case reception picks up. Wondering how Patti and Jamie and the rest of the family are doing. Twelve more days to the start of trapping. Called the flying service again – no answer. We had planned on going down River Run to do a bit of slashing but weather's not nice, snowing with a cold wind. Instead, Gordon's boiling up wolf snares and getting more firewood. I'm baking up a storm – got brownies made in place of his birthday cake for tomorrow. They turned out excellent – made from my pre-mix brought from home. I baked them in double pans so they wouldn't burn. Also baked a pie shell for a lemon pie plus a pan of buns for our lunch to accompany the tomato/macaroni soup. Also baked two pans of cinnamon buns – everything turned out great. The double pans are the answer to ensure your baking doesn't burn. Went for a walk this afternoon and did a wee bit of slashing. We also cleared a bit more along the trail from the cabin to the lake. Gordon then brought the second skidoo up to the cabin. Time goes by quite fast – we've been here three weeks now.

Sunday – Oct. 20th -8C   Snowing – beginning to look more like winter every day.

It's Gordon's sixtieth birthday today so I got up first and made the fire – warmed up the cabin and made coffee. I still think we should take alternate days starting the fire but he says, NO!! I tried a match from the ones I carry in my jacket pocket but it wouldn't light. Then discovered they are the type you have to strike along the original box or they wouldn't ignite. After I got the fire going, checked the ones I had in the waterproof match container I always carry with me in case of emergencies and found they were the same kind. I would have been in one heck of a spot if I had to get a fire going out on the trail and couldn't get the matches to ignite. I changed those matches in a hurry. Both Gordon and I carry matches for emergency use in waterproof containers. The container is about the size of a twelve gauge shotgun shell, made of two aluminum sections that screw together. It's called a "Marble's Waterproof Match Holder" and is, in Gordon's estimation, a real life saver. When he was trapping along the Yukon's White River in nineteen forty-six, he broke through the ice when the temperature was minus sixty-five below. He went in up to his neck. He said he got out just about as fast as he went in and managed to get a fire going. The waterproof match box kept his matches dry and saved him from freezing to death. He was up river with his dog team checking traps and about ten miles from any cabin or help when it happened. It took him over three hours, rotating around the fire in his Stanfield's woolen longjohns before they and the rest of his clothing, propped on poles, were dry enough to wear. Since then, he's always carried his match container when he's in the bush.

In the afternoon we went for a walk up our Ridge Run – about an hour away, hoping to get a couple of grouse for dinner but saw none. Wonder where all the grouse we'd seen sitting along the trail when we were clearing it are now hiding ?? Gordon did get one grouse near the cabin earlier this morning but we should have at least two for a good meal. During our walk we counted twelve different sets of marten tracks that were made since last night so prospects look good. One marten had come right up to the cabin. For dinner tonight, we had cabbage rolls, grouse, squash and brownies for desert. Later in the evening, got through on the radio again – a real relief.

Monday – Oct. 21st -10C   Overcast and dull out. A bit cooler – should help freeze the river and streams.

Snowing lightly but still not enough to run the skidoos. We must have about three inches on the ground. After breakfast we went up River Run as far as the big meadow. From there it's only about a mile further to the river. The trail from the meadow to the river is pretty well cleared but we still had a short section that was a real jungle of trees that had to be cut and removed before we reached the meadow. It took us a couple of hours of clearing brush before it was passable for the skidoo. We hitched Murky to the little toboggan so he could haul the chainsaw, gas, oil and lunch makings. It was certainly easier than having to pack them. The toboggan slid along with little effort and from his expression, I think he enjoyed pulling it. Saw at least seventeen sets of marten tracks that were fresh, plus several that were older, so looks good for fur. By three o'clock it had started to snow heavily so we're hoping that next time we go out on the trail we'll be able to use the skidoos. We were pretty wet from slashing with heavy snow falling so decided to head for home and get dried out.

Tuesday – Oct 22nd -16C Clear out this morning and nippy. It didn't snow much overnight – must have cleared off right after we went to bed.

By the time we finished breakfast the sky had clouded over again and started snowing, plus, fog rolled in. Not too nice but we decided to go out and do some exploring anyway. Went across to Beaver Meadow Run, following the meadow to where it forks and then continued up the left arm scouting for fur sign. We saw between ten and twelve sets of tracks but in the poor light tracks were hard to see so possibly there were more. Further up the meadow we got into an area where beaver had dammed a little stream and discovered a large, active, beaver house. Checked around a bit more before deciding it was time to head home.

By the time we returned, we'd been gone over five hours. On the way back we walked for a short distance along the ice of the second lake but found it wasn't all that safe so finished by following the shoreline. As soon as we reached the cabin we got a hot fire going in the stove. Almost immediately, sparks started falling from around the chimney. We found a bunch of pine needles, etc. that we hadn't noticed previously, lodged against the chimney. The stovepipe, hotter than usual, started them burning. Gordon got up on the cabin roof and cleaned it out PDQ. Thankfully no damage was done.

Later, while packing in wood, Gordon found a set of fresh marten tracks right under our window. Must be keeping track of us. I made chili for supper tonight – nice and spicy to go with fresh bannock. It was very good. I don't know whether my cooking has improved but everything seems to taste so much better here. Could it be all the fresh air and exercise we've been getting?? Did up my Christmas cards tonight but will have to write notes to go with them later.

Wednesday – Oct.23rd -10C Light snow falling again. Wish it would decide to either snow or quit altogether.

We need snow for skidoos but sunshine for scouting. After breakfast we headed up our new Super Highway – Jamie Run to the river. We wanted to cross the river to check the Wolverine Run on the other side. Tried crossing over along a back eddy of the river but the ice wasn't safe. We then decided to try further up river. Checked ice thickness every few feet with the axe until we finally hit a section that was judged safe and tip-toed across. A little intimidating hearing the river rumbling beneath your feet, knowing you're separated from an icy plunge by only a few inches of ice. It's hard to describe our feelings as we followed the river canyon. It was awesome with its walls rising several hundred feet above us along both sides – unbroken except for occasional narrow branching fissures further upstream.

We decided to try climbing one of the banks that I'm sure was equal to Mt. Everest and look for tracks along the ridge above. Going was tough – think Gordon was preparing me for the mogul ski run at Smithers, B.C. We finally climbed to the top and finding no sign, slid down. We then followed the shoreline as far as a back eddy where he'd had a trap set the previous winter. Ice on the back eddy was quite safe so we followed it for quite a ways. It was super going and saw lots of tracks. Built our tea fire and had lunch, totally enjoying being by ourselves. It's a feeling that's hard to describe – complete contentment and a sense of belonging. People who haven't been fortunate enough to be alone in an environment they totally enjoy would have no idea of my feelings and what I'm talking about. Guess I'm starting to realize why Gordon enjoys being out here.

This new area is going to be a great Run with the skidoo – it goes for a long way. We must have walked a good seven miles or more. Saw wolverine tracks on this Run – hence its name. Clouds cleared off this afternoon and it was lovely and sunny for us while we hiked back home. The snow is dry and powdery but not packing yet.

Thursday – Oct. 24th -11C   Light snow. We were pleasantly surprised this morning. I had expected the temperature to be away down since it was – 17C last night with a clear sky – moonlight making it so bright.

My first glimpse of Jamie Lake cabin – needs a woman's touch

Packing supplies up from float plane – seemed further with each load

Fall view along the Coal River – spectacular scenery

Alternative to the skidoo – much quieter and doesn't run out of gas

Gordon got through on the radio to Patti. Later, he decided to take the skidoo and go as far as the Ridge Run on the trail to Rose Lake. The skidoo would pack the snow and at the same time he'd clear the willows in the ravine and widen the trail for easier travel. He expects to be back before two o'clock. I would have liked to have gone along, especially since it turned out to be a beautiful, sunny day. He wanted to go alone on the first run in case he ran into problems. Anyway, I had a bath and later baked a lemon pie for supper. Also baked buns which turned out really well. I can't get over this oven!! Also did a large batch of laundry.

Gordon got back at two-thirty – overflow on the lake so skidoo got "slightly" iced up. After lakes and rivers freeze over, water levels usually drop. The layer of ice, no longer having support, cracks and drops or the weight of the heavy snowfalls pressing downward causes the ice to crack. As the ice is forced downwards water wells up along the cracks and floods over the ice often to a depth of ten or more inches. The layer of snow above keeps the water from freezing even in temperatures of minus thirty and colder. The only indication there's overflow beneath the snow is when the snow cover, usually over the deepest overflow area, drops into the water leaving a black hole in the snow. They're hard to see, especially if it's snowing. You always have to keep an eye out for overflow since it'll quickly build up freezing slush on your skidoo and bog it down. Then you have real fun wading around in water and snow, trying to clear your skidoo so you can drive it out of the mess. Anyway, he didn't get bogged down, just slightly iced up. He got to the ravine and did a lot of slashing. Also saw lots of marten tracks. He found there really wasn't enough snow for the skidoo so we'll have to wait for more snow before using it again. Had stew for supper – very good.

Friday – Oct. 25th -8C Snowing but quite pleasant out – no wind.

Was just thinking today that one thing I'm going to miss when we leave Jamie Lake is the soft water. Using it makes my hair and skin feel so good.

During breakfast we decided to head for Rose Lake and left about eleven-thirty. We reached our Rose Lake cabin around three forty-five. Not too bad a time on the trail considering the amount of snow on the ground. We hitched Murky to the toboggan so he was able to haul a lot of the gear, chainsaw, naptha for lamp, paint, etc. Made the load on Gordon's packboard a lot lighter. Made it much easier for us and Murky didn't seem to mind, trotting along with his tail wagging. We fixed up ten cubbies along the way – all ready for the start of trapping season on November 1st.

We counted forty-two sets of marten tracks from Jamie Lake to the ravine that runs into Marten Creek but gave up after that. There were lots of tracks everywhere. We walked down Marten Creek since the ice, thankfully, was plenty thick enough from the ravine to Rose Lake. Marten creek flows into the Coal River just a couple of hundred feet north of the cabin. Many marten tracks all the way – including lynx, so it looks good. When we neared Rose Lake cabin, the creek was like a highway with so many tracks of marten, wolf and lynx. We were so pleased with all the sign. Tracks were all along the creek and right up the river to our cabin. Very many tracks around the cabin, the Black Hole and around the meat cache. But what a shock – somehow the little beggars had gotten into the cache and devoured a good half of the meat. We are pretty disgusted but if nothing happens to the balance, will have enough for our stay. We'll make certain they don't get at the meat again because if they do, it's back to canned meat.

Had lunch at four-thirty and then went across to the sandbar where we'd got our moose. Remains have been all cleaned up except for a few scraps on the head. Animal tracks all over the area. We then went to check the two legs that had been hung for Murky and found something had chewed part of the meat off. We'd hung them from a tree overhanging the riverbank so it wouldn't have been a problem for just about any animal to get at them. What had remained of the legs was pretty well all tendon and muscle so it's no real loss. Figured Murky would be happy chewing on them though. Instead, came back with the intention of giving Murky a different bone we'd left on the roof of the Black Hole but discovered it was gone. Only thing left on the roof was a maze of marten tracks in the snow. A wolverine must have climbed up earlier and made off with it. Later when checking the meat cache, I found it hard to believe a little animal, the size of a marten, could eat so much in ten days. Must have had all its Uncles, Aunts and cousins helping out. We're still trying to figure out how the marten got up to the meat. The cache legs are wrapped with tin which should have made them impossible to climb.

Heavy snow shower just now so I can just barely see the mountain tops. Gordon's getting another dry tree for firewood to keep our supply up. We figure we have enough plywood here for flooring about a third of the cabin. After finishing his wood project he's planning on using the chainsaw to cut two by four inch floor supports from a couple of spruce for floor supports. We plan on starting the flooring project tonight. We also have a small, green color, indoor-outdoor rug here which should cover a third or more of the floor. It will greatly improve the area around the table and especially the bunks, having something to put your bare feet on in the morning. Later, I decided to try the new oven we had made for this stove by baking a pan of brownies. They turned out just great – the oven's a success.

Saturday – Oct. 26th -17C   Clear – promises to be another nice day.

The sun's just starting to shine on the distant mountains. Just their peaks illuminated in a rosy glow. The trees along the riverbank are dressed in white, covered with sparkling hoarfrost – just lovely. There's still a little open water in the river in front of the cabin. When we were getting ready for bed last night, temperature was minus twenty so were really pleased to find it hadn't turned colder. At least I was while Gordon was hoping for colder temperatures to freeze ice on the creeks.

This morning he was busy making oatmeal porridge for breakfast. Did you ever try pouring oatmeal out of a three pound box that had two bags in it?

Suddenly, I heard a "Help Quick"!! While pouring from one bag, the other had fallen into the pot of boiling water. I came to the rescue before it got too wet – just a wee bit through a small hole in the corner. After breakfast Gordon got busy with his chainsaw, cutting and splitting a bunch of green spruce poles. We nail them over the moss chinking that's between the logs. What a difference – looks so much brighter. I also hung one set of drapes we'd brought from Jamie Lake.

Later, hitched Murky to the toboggan and went over to the moose kill to haul the head back for him to chew on. Is he ever possessive of it!! After lunch went for a walk up river to Lynx Creek. then followed along it for quite a ways. Saw several lynx and marten tracks. It was a glorious day for a walk. While writing my notes this evening the pen ran dry so now I'm using a pen Gordon found when he was here in September. Michael Asselin from Martinique, a hunter Gordon had here several years ago had lost it. Surprised to find that after all those years lying in spruce needles it still writes. This evening Gordon's putting more flooring down and has about two thirds done. Will sure make it more comfortable. Without a cover, the dirt floor is damp and cold. While he was busy with the floor, I painted the door, the headboards above the bunks as well as the bookshelf. Also hung another drape. The place is taking on a homey atmosphere but still not like Jamie Lake.

Sunday – Oct 27th -18C   Got quite windy for awhile during the night – the wind really howling. It also snowed a little. The wind has completely died down and now it's even a bit foggy, especially over sections of open water along the river.

Visitor at the meat cache again and Murky didn't even let us know. It was sure nice to wake up to a place that is so much brighter. Hard to believe what a difference the "little" work we did on it makes. After breakfast we went for a walk up Marten Creek to the ravine. Wanted to finish clearing a short section of willows in the ravine to make it easier for the skidoo. Also wanted to figure out a new trail from the ravine and down to Marten Creek. The old way was too steep as you came down off the bank from the ravine to the creek. You could get down OK but getting back up with a skidoo wasn't so good. Gordon ended up cutting a new trail through the bush and around one bend of the creek to a section where there's a gentler slope. We had Murky hitched to the toboggan so he could haul the saw and our lunch. He really likes being in harness – just stands patiently while being harnessed but raring to go. On our way back Gordon built a few more cubbies – two for lynx and three for marten. We'll set them on the next trip here after November first, after we complete setting out all the Jamie Lake Runs. Five more days to wait – I'm anxious to see how trapping's done. Murky sure is enjoying his moose head. Cleared up nicely this afternoon and right now at five-thirty in the afternoon, the sun's still shining on our mountain tops. Took a picture of the scene. It's down to minus seventeen already and clear. Will get a little nippy tonight.

Monday – Oct. 28th *-24C*   Foggy and snowing a little but the sun is starting to show through thin patches of cloud. Perhaps it will clear and be another nice day.

Temperature dropped to minus twenty-seven just before we went to bed. Gordon was up during the night to put wood in the stove. This cabin does get chilly at night if there's no fire so I really appreciated him doing that. I told him that when I get home to Watson Lake I want the waterbed all to myself for one night so I could twist, turn, jump, roll over, etc. to my heart's content. I hate these mummy type sleeping bags. I'm such a restless sleeper and this bag is so restrictive that I have to fight in the morning to find my way out from the liner twisted around me. We've been here a whole month and I'm still sane – but just, Gordon says. We're going back to Jamie Lake this morning.

It was good walking back to Jamie Lake. Once the sun started to shine it really warmed up but was a little chilly at first while we were in the shade traveling up Marten Creek. Once we hit the trail through the timber going up the ravine it was fine – much warmer. It was certainly easier coming back now that trails are all cleared out. While following the trail around the second lake we ran into a mass of caribou tracks – very fresh. A herd must have just gone by. We also noticed wolf tracks following right behind them. Also found several more sets of wolf tracks on Jamie Lake. After we were back, both commented on there being a lot more snow at Rose Lake than Jamie Lake. After lunch Gordon took the skidoo down to the meadow to pick up the big toboggan that had been left there. He decided there's almost enough snow for skidoo travel – just a couple more inches would be great.

Tuesday – Oct. 29ᵗʰ -10C   Snowing. About two inches fell overnight, so pretty soon we'll have enough for good traveling.

Its one of those "dull" days that Gordon and Jamie found so depressing when they were out here but don't appear that way to me. Really, it's not any duller than at Watson Lake when we had a day like this. After breakfast, we decided to take the skidoo and pack Canyon run but only got about half of it completed. The shortage of snow made for very rough going so I ended up doing a lot of walking. At one point the skidoo tipped over and I got a wee bruise on my leg from landing on a sharp willow stump. Finally decided to give it up and came back to the cabin for lunch. Afterwards, Gordon headed back by himself to finish packing that run. I stayed home and had a bath, after which I got busy cutting and grinding meat for hamburger. I'm making a big batch of spaghetti sauce. Days are getting shorter but even now at five forty-five in the afternoon it's still not terribly dark. We just have the candle lit at this time. We've been having dinner by candlelight every evening. We don't usually turn the propane lights on until around seven.. Romantic – or conservative???????

Wednesday – Oct. 30ᵗʰ -10C   Clear – looks like a nice day ahead.

We're going to pack the trail down to the Meadow run and then try and find another route back so we'd have one big loop rather than returning on the same path. What a laugh!! Just got going and then the sky clouded over and within minutes there was nothing but snow and fog. We went anyway and of course, while crossing the second lake, got into overflow. I ended up walking from there, all the way across to the meadow. Crossing the meadow was tough going for the skidoo because of all the willows, hummocks, etc. Finally got to a section where we could travel in the timber but soon, because of thick underbrush, had to turn back and try the meadow again. Guess what happened? We got into so much overflow that Gordon ended up getting his feet soaked. There just wasn't any ice at all – just water covered with snow all through the grassy areas. Finally got out of the mess and decided to heck with trail packing and headed home. Had some skidoo problems as well. Gordon thinks the belt just needs changing. Hope he's right. Murky sure told us off when we got home. Should use him instead – no getting stuck in overflow – no problems.

Thursday – Oct. 31 -8C Dull and foggy out. Can't tell if there's cloud up there or not.

Halloween tonight- wonder if the goblin will come here?? It's the last day of October and trapping season starts tomorrow. We've tried to reach Watson Lake Flying Service for the past three days but no luck, signals were out. Not a nice looking day – foggy this morning. By eleven the fog started to lift and it started to look like another great day. Gordon worked on the skidoo and test ran it out and back as far as the meadow on River Run. It ran fine so he decided to make a trip to another meadow just beyond the second lake north of here. From there he'll have to walk. He's trying to locate a small lake we've seen from the air. Pretty heavy timber with rolling hills so he'll be lucky to find it. If he does locate it he's planning on connecting a trail to the second lake and then onwards to the Beaver meadows west of here. It would replace our present trail which is terribly rough with high hummocks most of the way – hard on the body and harder on the skidoo.

While he's away I'm making pies and a big pot of homemade soup. During our last trip to Rose Lake on October twenty-fifth, I got a slight ache in one of my teeth. I though it was probably from the cold air. Ached every day for awhile but at night it cleared up. The last couple of days it's ached a lot more. Think I'm getting an abscess on my "eye" tooth – it hurts way up towards my nose. I sure hope I'm wrong. Originally, I bit on a tiny piece of walnut shell (I think) and it hurt then so we'll just have to wait and see. I didn't tell Gordon as he'd have panicked and probably had me flown out of here. Gordon got back by one o'clock reporting he'd found a new route to Beaver meadows – easier to get to and much smoother. We went back this afternoon to pack it with the skidoo. He'd only walked it in the morning while slashing and clearing, figuring out where it should go. After we finished trail packing, returned to the cabin for coffee. During coffee we decided to spend the rest of the afternoon snowshoeing, packing the trail through the meadow east of here on River Run. Make it a lot easier for the skidoo when it's packed. My first snowshoeing lesson here – I've used them on level ground a few times before but never on the type of terrain we covered today. I did fine except, on the way back, had problems climbing a big hill we'd packed on our way to the meadow. I kept sliding back down time after time so, totally disgusted, ended by taking my snowshoes off and walking up.

Friday – Nov. 1ˢᵗ -12C   Nothing but fog – completely fogged in.

Trapping season opens today. After breakfast we headed out to the Meadow Run via the new trail we'd found yesterday – setting traps along the way. The traps we use are called a "Conibear" trap, named after the inventor. They're considered a humane trap since animals entering them are struck by double bars closing around them that produce an immediate deadly, lethal blow. The old leghold traps that were used by trappers for centuries are no longer used and are illegal. Gordon places most of his marten sets up in spruce trees about six to eight feet above the ground. He uses wooden boxes that are built before season. They are a four sided box about six inches square and fourteen inches long. The one end is left open but the other, the back end, is covered by wire mesh. The box is nailed or wired to a tree with the open end, where the trap is placed, facing to the front. The bait, usually smelly fish scraps, is placed in the back of the box and the trap is set in the opening at the front of the box. Animals smell the bait, climb the tree and try to enter the open end of the trap box to get at it. They usually shove their head into the opening and are caught. Most often they're dead immediately, struck on the head and neck by the double bars snapping shut around them. The sets are placed in trees so that mice won't be as likely to chew on the fur and destroy the valuable pelt. It's a real learning experience for me.

Most of the day the sun couldn't decide whether to come out and for the most part didn't. The result was that our valley remained fogged in. I did a lot of snowshoeing over the really rough areas, especially over the hummocky sections. Once we get more snow these sections will smooth out and be fine. Still a lot of overflow on the lakes and creek but managed to stay clear of it as we came over our trail this morning. While we were having lunch under a couple of big spruce on the edge of the meadow – big fire going, tea delicious – we suddenly found ourselves in the midst of an avalanche. We'd built our fire too close, beneath the spreading boughs of the trees. The warmth of the fire caused the snow load above to slip and plummet down on top of us. We had just made our second pot of tea which, fortunately, was placed to the side. It was just showered with snow while the major portion landed right on top of our fire, putting it out. What a way to start the first day!!

Another major catastrophe after we got home – I went to clean my glasses and the frame snapped at the nosepiece. From now on I'll have to wear my sunglasses all the time when I'm indoors since I can't do anything without them. Thank goodness my sunglasses have prescription lenses so I can still use them. Unable to reach the Flying service on the radio so hope Patti and Jamie aren't too concerned yet. It's been eight days since our last radio contact.

Saturday – Nov. 2ⁿᵈ -16C Sunny – should be a great day for setting out traps.

Sure wish we could get hold of Watson Lake Flying – still no contact. Planning on going up Jamie Lake Run today. Our old, wooden toboggan has a couple of breaks, so Gordon is trying to fix it with tin from a five gallon pail to make do until we get to Rose Lake and retrieve our skimmer. The skimmer is somewhat like a toboggan except that it's made of heavy gauge aluminum, has sides along its full length and curves upwards at both ends. Slides along like a dream. We want to set out all the Runs from this end before going to Rose Lake. Our Run down Jamie way enroute to the river was good until we got to the creek – sun shining and not a cloud in the sky. We'd hoped to get across the river to Wolverine run and then proceed further up river to check another creek for fur sign but things didn't work out that way.

Gordon, without first checking the ice thickness with the axe (something he'd warned me to always do) boldly walked out onto the creek ice. He was sure it was more than thick enough to hold both him and the skidoo. He didn't bother taking the axe from the box at the back of the skidoo but strode ahead, periodically stomping the ice with his foot to prove it was safe. Sure enough, just before he got across, there was a cracking sound when he stomped, the ice gave way and he was dumped into the drink. Of course he had to pick a spot to break through that was just above a deep hole in the creek. The water was waist deep but then, trying to get up the slick, muddy sides of the hole, he lost his footing and plunged in deeper. I was just out of my mind – I panicked. But he did get out in a hurry, although it seemed like ages to me, turned the skidoo around and we headed for home. He said he wasn't cold.

Anyway, I have decided today that trapping is not for me. Too many hazards where I'm concerned and I do not want to come out again. In fact, I'm ready to go home right now – I'm going to be a nervous wreck by the time we do get home. Another problem is the lack of radio communication with signals being so poor – ten days since we've made contact. Gordon's fixing my glasses tonight, using a bit of snare wire and tape from the first aid kit. Sure hope they hold as wearing my sunglasses in the evening is the pits. And so ended the second day of the trapping season!!

Sunday – Nov.3rd -14C Patches of fog and cloudy.

Foggy this morning but it eventually cleared up quite nicely. In fact, by four this afternoon the sun was really shining. We've tried calling Watson Lake Flying about a dozen times or more and still no reply. We hope Patti and Jamie aren't too upset and we do get a message through to them before they send a plane to check on us. They advised us, when we were leaving, that if they didn't hear from us over a ten day period a flight would be sent out to check on us. We can't leave the cabin for long as we want to make sure we're here when signals do pick up. We did make one fast trip to the east on River run but only put out seven sets. So far, that makes ninety-five in total. We have all the runs starting from here done for short distances only. We'll extend them when we start check-ing traps. At least we have a start on setting out our lines. The river where we crossed was Okay, only having a little overflow in areas. We saw about a dozen ptarmigan along the river, first one's I've seen since we've been here. Overall, there's not much fur sign since we returned from Rose Lake. Earlier, there were tracks everywhere. Coming back from Rose Lake on the twenty-eight, we spot-ted a few tracks on the Ridge Run closer to Jamie Lake – since then, very few. We've had lots of snow the last while so sign would have been covered quite quickly. Be interesting to note if the full moon has anything to do with their travel. Gordon says they travel a lot when the moon is full – we'll see.

Had a lovely dinner tonight and afterwards, believe it or not, we got through on the radio to a miner employed by a Company working out of Yellowknife. When we explained our problem, not being able to get through to Watson Lake, he got on his phone and tried calling our home but no answer. Patti and Jamie weren't at home. He said he'd try calling Patti at the bank (where she works) in the morning to relay word that we were OK. He promised to give us a call tomorrow evening and relay any news. Talk about a considerate person. Bet

Patti and Jamie will be surprised when they realize the round-about route our message took to reach them.

Monday – Nov. 4ᵗʰ -19C   Just heard that Watson Lake is colder at minus twenty-one. Nice out here – sunny – should be a gorgeous day.

We're going out on Jamie Run again. Murky won't be happy since he'll be left behind. Still no communication with Watson Lake Flying, which seems very strange. Jamie Run is in great shape for the skidoo so we made good time getting to the creek at the base of the hill and on to the river. Only took about forty-five minutes instead of the hour and a half it usually takes. Gordon managed to keep out of the creek this time. We crossed over on thick ice, only about ten feet above his wading pool of yesterday. Surprised to see him actually use the axe to check ice thickness today!! Further on, we crossed the river – no overflow – and up Wolverine Run and onwards for another couple of miles to the end of the channel. Really good going, just the right amount of snow covering the six inches of ice. Most places we followed sandbars as they're safer than ice and sure don't have any overflow. We set traps out on the way back. Also stopped for awhile to make tea and toast sandwiches over the fire. What a great way to enjoy a day!! On our way back, while crossing the river, we decided to try exploring further upstream since there was plenty of ice for safe travel. We'd only gone a couple of hundred yards before running into, you guessed it, overflow!! Took a few minutes to get the skidoo turned around and the ice knocked off before we could head back to our trail and straight home. About five minutes from the cabin, on our way back, I spotted a red aircraft flying by. Just hope they weren't looking for us.

Tuesday – Nov. 5ᵗʰ -18C   Foggy in the valley but the sun's now shining on the mountains to the south.

We packed up and headed up Ridge Run, on our way to Rose Lake. Murky pulled the small toboggan which was very lightly loaded. We figured he'd stay on the trail if he was in harness and not romp around while we were putting out sets. It turned into quite a long day with baiting and setting traps along the trail. Sure glad we had our trap boxes in place before the season opened. We wouldn't have been able to set near as many traps today if we also had to put up the trap boxes. It was quite exciting to see marten tracks crossing or following our trail, sometimes climbing right up to the boxes. Next time it will be even more exciting, knowing we just might have a marten in the trap ahead. I know it will sure build up my anticipation. Setting out "our" traps did make for an informative and interesting trip. We took a break at our usual lunch spot for a cup of hot tea and toasted sandwiches. Our stopping-place is under a big spruce that has its lower branches about eight feet above ground. Lots of head room underneath and there's never any snow on the accumulation of dry spruce needles around the trunk. The tree grows along the top of a ridge that slopes down to a lake in front. Nice dry spot for lunch with a lakeside view – what more could we ask for!!

Even with only a light load on his toboggan, Murky was getting played out by the time we reached Rose Lake cabin. The last section of trail down Marten Creek was quite fast with just a trace of snow on the ice. The skidoo just slid along but it was slippery footing for the dog. Set a few more traps along the creek so he did get a few rest breaks. On our way down Marten Creek, just before reaching the Coal River, we passed very many marten tracks – regular trails. When we got here we noticed tracks all over – around the cabin and even tracks in the snow on the roof. We found the beggars had gotten into our meat cache again but hadn't made off with very much. With the snow, we were able to figure out how they were able to get onto the cache. There was a tall spruce growing just over a hundred feet from the cache. They were smart enough to climb to the top of the spruce which was about thirty feet higher than the cache – then make a flying jump for the cache. They didn't always make it, as marks in the snow indicated, but with perseverance got their free lunch. Anyway, Gordon spoiled their fun by cutting down that tree.

When we checked the supply cache we found a visitor. A marten had taken up permanent residence. When Gordon opened the cache door, facing him was a hissing, teeth-gnashing marten. Gordon wasted no time closing the door and running back to the cabin for his .22 rifle. When he got back, the marten was gone – guess looking at Gordon's face from close range had really scared him!! We found the meat that had been stored inside was eaten up but what was worse, he chewed up and totally destroyed one of our foam mattresses. He generally made a real mess of things. Luckily, he couldn't locate a can opener or all our canned goods would likely have been sampled. Again, it was a tree quite a distance from the cache that was the launching platform. Smart animals but, if he sticks around, we'll catch him.

I got busy starting a fire in the cabin while Gordon was chopping through the river ice for water. Didn't take much chopping as the ice still isn't very thick. Hooked up the transmitter and tried getting through to Watson Lake Flying but again, nothing. We didn't get through to Yellowknife last evening as planned since signals were very poor – not even a good grade of static!! Soon had tea water boiling and a quick lunch. After lunch, took the skidoo and skimmer and went up to retrieve what was left of the two sections of moose leg we'd hung in a tree for Murky. They'll keep him happy most of the winter, having something to chew on. A few chores to complete and then into the warm cabin. Days are getting much shorter now and really dusky by five in the evening. After supper we tried the radio again – nothing from Watson Lake Flying. We then called Yellowknife as the plan had been for them to relay messages to us from Patti and Jamie. At first nothing except heavy static but when we tried later, was a real relief when Yellowknife answered the second call and advised us they'd gotten hold of Patti and everything was fine at home. Really appreciate the assistance of that Yellowknife operator. Looking around the cabin, it's hard to believe how much brighter the interior is because of the work we did on it last trip. Now that the skidoo's running, we'll bring more materiel up next trip to complete the renovations.

Wednesday – Nov. 6th -22C Its very foggy this morning but at least it warmed up a bit from last night.

Checked the thermometer before going to bed and found it down to minus twenty-eight. Stars shining from a clear sky so thought we'd probably be in the minus thirty range by morning. After breakfast, headed back up Marten Creek. Planning on setting traps along it for another six or seven miles past the ravine where the trail branches off to Jamie Lake. But it wasn't to be – about a mile past the junction we found a large spruce had fallen across the creek, completely blocking it from bank to bank. It was firmly lodged about two and a half feet above the creek ice. Since the tree was around two feet in diameter and we didn't have the chainsaw with us – our highway was blocked. The creek banks on both sides were too steep for the skidoo to climb so thus ended our jaunt up Marten Creek for today. We'll head up this way again tomorrow but for certain, the chainsaw will be with us.

So, it was back to the cabin for a quick coffee and upriver to Lynx Creek, then following along it and putting out more sets. Got a few miles up the creek but not as far as we'd planned. We were forced to head back after running into overflow. Gordon was busy the rest of the afternoon cutting more firewood while I baked a cake. I went for a walk in the late afternoon and found a marten in one of our lynx sets so ran home for Gordon. We returned with the skidoo, removed the marten and reset the trap. On our way back to the cabin, found another marten had wandered into a set we'd just passed a few minutes earlier. Two marten for him to skin this evening but he's not complaining. Just before going to bed, he went out to check the traps set around the meat cache. You guessed it – got another one. Three today from right around the cabin. Pretty darned good. He skinned the marten this evening. While he does the skinning, I assist by fleshing them – removing bits of flesh or fat that may still be on the inside of the pelt. Hope we have a good season this year. We have a total of hundred and twenty-five sets out right now so, here's hoping!!

Thursday – Nov. 7ᵗʰ -19C   Real miserable out – cloudy, windy and cold.

We'll not go up river as we'd freeze while traveling in the open with the wind blowing the way it is. Decided to change plans and go back to Jamie Lake instead. Gordon figured if the weather turned really cold and not having our heavier, warmer clothes, it might be a bit uncomfortable. Also, our gas supply for the skidoo was limited at Rose Lake. Now, bringing the skimmer back to Jamie Lake, we'll be able to haul gas and more groceries, etc. when we return. Also when we return next time, I'll be driving the second skidoo so we'll have two machines when we head up to Kettle Creek. Gordon feels it's too far to go up to Kettle with just one machine in case we have mechanical problems. A long snowshoe trip home if your skidoo packed up. Kettle Creek is only seven twisty miles up river from Rose Lake but we plan on going at least that far again up the creek.

On the way back to Jamie we picked up another three marten. Murky had quite a workout coming back. It only took us a bit over two hours of steady going to cover the distance. Murky followed right behind, pulling his little toboggan. He got off the trail once when the toboggan got hung up around a tree and was one concerned dog until I went back and untangled him. Spaghetti tonight – with that bottle of wine Gordon's been so worried about, thinking it might freeze. Our fresh stuff, vegetables and fruits as well as the eggs, didn't freeze while we were away. They're stored in the little cellar beneath the bunk. Since we had time on our hands this afternoon, Gordon decided to clean out the cache. Sorted out pots and more pots to take to Rose and Kettle on our next trip. We also placed a complete set of warm clothes in the cache for each of us, available for emergencies such as a fire. Also packed a set to take to Rose Lake for storing in that cache.

Friday – Nov. 8ᵗʰ -22C   Cool, broken clouds with sun filtering through occasionally.

After breakfast, headed up Canyon Run to check traps. We took both skidoo's and left Murky at home. He was not happy with our decision as his howling laments indicated. Quite a lot of sign, marten tracks pretty consistent all the way to the creek. We picked up another eight marten in the eighteen sets we'd made – purty good, eh! The bad part was when we found two of the marten had been eaten with just the head of one and the tail of the other remaining. We were not happy with that!! Marten are very cannibalistic and make a meal of anything that opportunity presents. Gordon has seen tracks indicating two marten were traveling and hunting together, probably litter mates. Further on, when one of the pair was caught, his buddy made a meal of him. So much for brotherly love!! We traveled with the skidoo's to the end of the trail we'd previously cleared – to the top of the ridge overlooking the creek below.

We put on snowshoes and headed down the old game trail, slashing willows as we went. Willows were pretty thick so it took a lot of time and axe work to cover the three quarters of a mile to the creek. Finally got there and crossed on rather flimsy ice, setting a couple of traps on the other side. A couple of hundred yards ahead there was another creek we had to cross if we were going to do any exploring further on. Took a while to find a safe crossing but finally we found one and started up a draw into new territory, heading southward. After covering more than a mile and only seeing one marten track, we decided not to set any traps there and headed back to the skidoo's. The snowshoeing sure did me in. It was tiring on my back blundering over rough terrain covered with thick willows, plus the climbing that was required while going up and down hill to the creeks. I was just played out by the time we got back to the skidoo's. Saw lynx sign again – must be a lot around. Sure hope we catch a few. It was good to get on the skidoo and ride all the way home – no more snowshoeing, at least for today. After we got back to the cabin and had the fire going, tried contacting Watson Lake Flying but again – no reply. It will be six weeks from tomorrow since we arrived here. Time sure has flown.

Saturday – Nov. 9th -34C   Baby, it's cold outside!! A clear day with the sun shining. Really beautiful over towards the mountains where the light gives the peaks a pinkish glow.

After breakfast Gordon went to check the Meadow Run by himself. With it being so cold, he didn't want me to come along. It wasn't that hard to convince me that staying home would be a wise decision. He was quite concerned about using the skidoo in these temperatures. Metal gets pretty brittle and that is a very rough trail. I kept busy in the cabin doing odd jobs and making soup for lunch. Gordon was back by early afternoon and reported no problems – skidoo ran like a top. He only got four marten and one weasel. I was disappointed after the luck we'd had on Canyon and Ridge runs but that's trapping. Next time we could pick up double or triple that many. He did appreciate the hot coffee I had ready when he returned.

Sunday – Nov. 10th -33C   Just a few patches of cloud and cold.

Gordon got up early to get the fire going and heat up the cabin and noticed it was minus thirty-three at that time. A bit later the sky started clouding over so hopefully it will warm up a bit. Still no signals from Watson Lake Flying. After breakfast we put our warmest clothes on and went down Jamie Run – nothing. We then headed up Wolverine run where we finally found a marten in our last trap. Not a great day for the fur harvest. After we got back to the river, decided to head up it for about three miles to where a creek runs in from the east. The section along the river where Gordon got into overflow last time was frozen solid all the way to the creek mouth so travel was easy but chilly. We left the skidoo's there and walked up the creek for a good mile. Looked very good with lots of fur sign and what's even more attractive, skidoo travel should be fairly easy since there's only low, sparse willow along the way as well as a lot of open country.

We followed along the creek for quite a ways. Further on we ran into sections with numerous boulders projecting through the ice. The creek ice was fine for walking but wouldn't be good for skidoo use. We'll have to route our trail through the meadows instead. Tomorrow if it's nice and not too cold, we plan on coming back and setting traps further upstream. We only put out five new sets before turning and heading for home. Good to be back to the cabin again with a warm drink. You get chilled right through while riding the skidoo but don't realize it until you're back inside a warm cabin. Then it seems to take forever to get warmed right through. Murky was glad to see us back. By the amount of frost covering his face it looked as though he'd spent the day curled up in his house with tail wrapped around his lower jaw. Listened to Yellowknife calling us tonight but they couldn't hear our return call so will try again tomorrow.

Monday – Nov. 11th -16C   Very nice out and not so cold.

Tried calling Watson Lake this morning and Yellowknife answered instead. We were so surprised as their transmission was very clear. The operator said he would phone this morning to Patti, at the bank, and let her know everything is OK with us. We can't believe that signals to Watson Lake Flying could be out since October 24th. Wonder if something's wrong with their antenna.

After breakfast we headed out, returning to the creek we'd followed for a short distance yesterday. The country along it does look interesting. Mainly open, grassy meadows with the occasional patch of willow for the first couple of miles and then sections of fairly heavy timber, interspersed with more meadows. Followed along the creek bank for the first part, beyond where we'd gone yesterday and then turned back onto the creek Good going since there were no more boulders protruding through the ice. We ended by setting eight more traps. Most of our time was spent exploring the country for fur sign and finding a good trail into it. Snowshoeing, exploring the new country has been quite enjoyable. The snow is not too deep and blessedly, willows are quite small and very patchy, making pretty easy going.

Had lunch about one-thirty under another big spruce. Its spreading branches had kept the area beneath completely dry and free of snow. With heat from our fire reflected from the tree, we enjoyed a warm and very comfortable lunch break. We took our time sipping tea, gazing at the mountains and enjoying being out here. And at the same time – feeling just a bit sorry for all the people who'll never view and enjoy what we, most often, take for granted. All too soon it was time to get moving. I could've spent another hour or so under the spruce. It was so cozy but Gordon said we'd better get going if we were doing any more exploring. Late afternoon we turned around and finally headed home. Murky was there with a big welcoming "Woof". Later that evening while snug in the cabin and mentally reminiscing over the past hours, I had to admit that life in the bush has a lot more to offer than most people realize.

Tuesday – Nov. 12th -14C   Cloudy and not so cool – looking like another nice day.

Just after breakfast was totally surprised to hear Stan's voice answer when we called Watson Lake Flying Service. Stan is the Chief pilot and a partner of the Company. He explained the lack of communication over the past weeks. Seems they were relocating their radio equipment from the float base to the hangar at the airfield. Something went wrong with the equipment and they finally ended up having to install a new transmitter and receiver. So all is explained but it sure had us concerned. You never knew when something might happen, perhaps an accident requiring communication with a doctor and an evacuating aircraft. That's a concern that's always in the back of your mind while we're living out here. Just have to be extra careful.

Again headed out for the river and onwards to the creek we'd been following yesterday, intending to go still further upstream. We got fooled though. After leaving the skidoo, we followed the creek for a short distance and then, rounding a bend, ran into overflow. Found that beaver had built a really large dam, flooding the entire area along the creek and even into the surrounding meadows. In order to avoid the flooded area we climbed to the timber covered higher ground. We had to slash a trail for quite a distance through the timber until we were past the flooded area, then back to the creek. A real mess in the timber with blow-downs crisscrossing everywhere so it took a terrific amount of chainsaw work to travel even a little ways. After getting back to the creek, we found the creek ice was unsafe. Warm mineral springs seeped into the creek resulting in ice only a couple of inches thick. As a matter of fact, there were even quite a few patches of open water. Because it was so tough going through the timber, we decided to call it a day and turned for home.

Set out a few marten traps along the way back and also snares for lynx and wolves. A lot of wolf sign here. Noticed where they'd been chasing a moose – the moose breaking through the ice along the creek. Patches of moose hair and splatters of blood on the snow showed they weren't just fooling around. Further on the moose tracks headed up into the timber with wolf tracks following. Gordon was pretty certain, had we followed, we'd have found a wolf kill not far ahead. Instead, we turned around and headed for home.

Not as nice a day as yesterday but warmer. Sky clouded over with snow starting to fall just as we got back to the cabin. The trail was good and solid from all the skidoo travel the past days so I decided to walk about half the distance back. Boy, am I getting in shape. Yellowknife called again, loud and clear. Will be calling us every night in case we have problems getting through to Watson Lake and also just for a chit-chat. It's really nice of him and we do appreciate this additional contact.

Wednesday – Nov. 13th -3C   Warm, snowed all night and it's still coming down. Right now we have an additional two inches on the ground.

Gordon took off this morning with the skidoo and skimmer for Rose Lake. He's got a heavy load of gas for Rose and Kettle as well as the plywood needed to finish the interior of Rose Lake cabin. With this extra snow the skimmer should be easier to pull than it was last trip. The plan is to offload at Rose Lake then turn around and return to Jamie Lake. Sure hope he doesn't have any problems. This fresh snow is quite wet so should pack into a good, hard trail which, if our plans go according to schedule, we'll be using tomorrow. Plan on the two of us heading back to Rose Lake tomorrow if he doesn't have any trouble today.

To keep myself occupied while he was away I decided to do some baking. I'm busy with buns, cinnamon rolls, brownies and have already made a batch of chocolate oatmeal drop cookies. I'm also preparing a dish of scalloped potatoes to go with ham and squash for our dinner this evening. Purty good, eh kids!! Bet you thought we'd starve up here because I didn't cook up a storm during the month prior to coming out. Gordon got back just after two this afternoon, reporting the going was tougher than anticipated with the sticky snow. He also picked up one marten. Later this afternoon we measured the ice on Jamie Lake and were surprised to find it's now nine and a half inches thick.

Thursday – Nov. 14th -4C   Lots of fresh snow since yesterday, kept on steadily falling all night. It's the heavy kind, not the fluffy, powdery stuff we had before. Water started dripping from the roof at night and I thought it was raining.

There's now too much snow over the trail for us to go all the way to Rose Lake without first packing part of the trail. Gordon took the skidoo and headed out to pack the trail up the big hill on Ridge Run. Sure maddening. Our trails were all well packed before this snowfall. When Gordon got back later, he mentioned he was having problems caused by the heavy, wet snow packing around the rollers on the skidoo. Made for real heavy going and figured he spent as much time clearing rollers as packing trail.

Regardless, after a snack, he refueled the skidoo and loaded the stove destined for our Kettle Creek cabin on the skimmer and headed out for the Coal River. He thought it would be the better choice since there weren't any big hills along it to climb with the heavy load. With the amount of snow we have, rough sections shouldn't be too bad. Sure hope he's right. He planned on stashing the stove when he reached the river then set traps on his return trip. If we're not able to haul the stove to Kettle Creek this winter by skidoo then at least it'll be handy for transporting by canoe next fall. It was getting pretty dusky by the time Gordon finally got back, tired after a long, hard day. I had been getting really worried and when at last I heard the sound of the skidoo, nothing could have been more welcome.

Friday – Nov.15ᵗʰ -14C   Clear now but lots more snow overnight.

Hear Watson Lake is minus twenty-one and Old Crow is down to between minus thirty-five and forty. That's cold!! This morning we hooked Murky to his toboggan, hopped on our skidoo and with the skimmer lightly loaded, took off for Rose Lake. It was very tough going with all that fresh snow. We even had to pack and break trail up to the crest of Ridge Run before the skidoo could make it. Gordon said he's never seen as heavy a snowfall over such a short period. I also ended up doing a lot of snowshoeing, helping over the tougher areas. We finally reached the section of the trail that follows the ravine to Marten Creek with expectations of relatively easy going along the creek for the rest of the way to the Coal River and Rose Lake. A few minutes later when we reached the creek, we couldn't believe what we were seeing.

There was at least a foot of overflow covering the creek from bank to bank, slowly flowing along. Gordon snowshoed downstream through the timber for a good half mile, hoping the overflow wouldn't extend so far, but no luck. There was still a good foot of water stretching downstream as far as he could see. No possible way to get around the overflow and therefore no way to get to Rose Lake. Darn It!! Nothing to do but unload supplies from the toboggan and head back to Jamie Lake. We did take a short break to make tea and have a bite to eat. Murky especially appreciated the rest as the soft snow was tiring for him. Sure hope the Coal River isn't flooded like this. We're now planning on going down our River Run to the Coal and then up river to Rose Lake tomorrow. At least that's the plan we came up with during our tea break. The trail from Jamie to the Coal should be in pretty good shape since Gordon was over it yesterday when he hauled the stove across to the river. Just before starting back, he cut down a couple of eight foot tall, well branched spruce trees. The butt ends were looped together by a short section of rope tied to the back of the skidoo. Trapper friends of ours, Leo and Mabel, had told us to try this method of grooming trails once there was enough snow. We were surprised at the excellent trail the dragging trees produced. The branches dragged snow into the dips while scraping it off the high points and at the same time scraped snow from the trail edges to widen it. Just like a superhighway now.

Saturday – November 16ᵗʰ -24C   Sunny with just a skiff of snow overnight.

After breakfast we took off with the skidoo and Murky for Rose Lake and Kettle Creek via the River Run trail to the Coal. Got to the river without too much trouble other than for having to break trail with snowshoes over a couple of the steeper sections. Took a little longer than expected. The Coal River looked fine with good ice and no overflow but quite a depth of snow. The going was tough, tougher than we had expected because of the deep snow. We'd only brought the one skidoo so as to cut down on gas consumption. Gordon thought travel on the river would be a lot easier than it turned out to be. I ended up doing a lot of snowshoeing, following along behind on the skidoo trail.. Some sections, windswept, were excellent and I could ride but most of the time I snowshoed. Gordon wanted me to drive the skidoo and break trail while he snowshoed but I declined. Balancing that machine while plowing through two and a half to three feet of snow wasn't that attractive. I'd probably have ended up spending most of the time digging the machine out. I just haven't skidoo'd enough for that challenge. To top it all, coming around one of the bends and almost halfway to Rose Lake, we ran into overflow. Not too much at first so were able to skirt it by crossing over and onto sandbars then back on the ice for another hundred yards or so. But, the overflow kept getting worse so we decided to cache our load – gas, groceries and even Murky's toboggan.

I'm beginning to wonder if I'll ever get to see Kettle Creek cabin or even Rose cabin again. So we turned around and returned over our trail, back to Jamie Lake – too disgusted to even stop for tea. Ah well, there's always another day and that blasted overflow's just got to freeze pretty darn soon in these temperatures. But – it was such a gorgeous day, sunny with not a cloud in the sky, not even a chilling wind. We did pick up another two marten on our way to the river this morning. Just after four-thirty, we got back to the cabin and right now I'm thawing out homemade soup for lunch/supper. Nice to sit back and relax. Its been a pretty strenuous day. Later, talked to Watson Lake and Yellowknife – signals nice and clear. Yellowknife now calls every night, great.

Sunday – Nov. 17th -39C   Man, that's getting cool but it's starting to cloud over so hopefully it will warm up. This temperature should certainly freeze the overflow.

I stayed in bed until ten – first time ever, I think. After a late breakfast and despite the temperature, we took off on snowshoes to check traps along our Canyon Run. I snowshoed as far as the end of the ridge where we'd left our skidoo last time and then walked down through a horrendous jungle of willows to the creek. Today, I turned around and headed back while Gordon carried on to check the three sets we had by the creek below. I've never done as much snowshoeing before in my life. I was completely played out by the time I got home. I broke trail for quite a ways today on the way out, my choice, while Gordon was checking and rebaiting traps. Plowing through the deep snow had taken a lot of effort.

Just after I got the fire going really well and the cabin warmed up, Gordon came in and reported we'd caught nothing in the traps by the creek although one was sprung with the bait missing. Probably a mouse – they're a real pain when it comes to springing traps. They're small so can easily get at the bait in the back of the trap box and clean it up within a short time. Sometimes they'll inadvertently rub against the trap trigger while climbing in and out, springing it. Very rarely is one ever hit by the closing trap jaws. We did pick up one marten and a rabbit on the section I'd been over so it wasn't a complete failure. It was just too cold for the skidoos today and we would have certainly been chilly riding them. At least we kept warm snowshoeing. Surprised when I first got back just after three and saw the temperature had warmed up quite a bit – a mere minus twenty-six. An early supper tonight and then I'm stretching out, relaxing in bed while Gordon does his reading.

Monday – Nov. 18th -21C   Cloudy and a little foggy. Light skiff of snow overnight.

After breakfast we packed up, loaded the skimmer and headed for Rose Lake via the Ridge Run. A short ways down the trail from the cabin we were surprised to find fresh marten tracks and then, in our next trap, a marten. It wasn't frozen so must have been caught only minutes earlier. Not too much further along the trail there were more marten tracks and in the next trap, another marten. A real surprise!! With the packed trail, the skidoo had no problem climbing to the top of the hill on Ridge Run. We found more marten tracks along the crest. It was turning into an exciting trip for me going down the trail, watching for marten tracks. We'd see tracks coming onto and then following along the trail, hoping they would continue onwards to the next trap just ahead. Quite often tracks followed along the trail to a trap but there was no marten. Either it didn't like our bait or had some other business to attend to. Then other times, there would be a marten waiting for us. Gordon can't figure out where they all came from and wonders if they're crossing from the hills and mountains to the west of us to the range just east of here. Be interesting to know. Anyway, by the time we reached the ravine leading to Marten creek, we'd picked up twelve marten. Hard to believe!!

Travel was excellent with the dry snow we now had because of the cold temperatures so we made pretty good time even with the stops for resetting and rebaiting traps. When we reached Marten Creek we picked up the groceries and supplies we'd cached there last time. Sure pleased to find the overflow was frozen solid, giving us a real highway all the way to the Coal River and Rose cabin. Only took us a bit over three and a half hours from Jamie Lake, even with the resetting and digging out of some traps we found buried in the snow. Picked up two more marten in sets along the creek. It's been a great day!!

Once we reached our Rose Lake cabin it didn't take long to get a hot fire going, warming it and heating water for tea. After finishing lunch we decided to go up river to Lynx Creek and check the few sets we'd put out there. Going was good along the river. Overflow which had caused us so much trouble before had saturated the snow causing it to drop into water below. The cold temperatures of the past few days had then frozen it solid. It was also easy going for the first mile or so up Lynx Creek until we ran into overflow which forced us to turn back. We only were able to check one trap but it produced a lovely marten – not bad! When we got back to the cabin and while Gordon was chopping a hole through the river ice for water, I went and checked the two traps we'd set at the cache. Sure enough – another marten. Don't think he's the one responsible for chewing up our foam mattress though. The one we caught is quite light in color whereas the guilty one was very dark, almost black.

After completing a few necessary chores and with the fire safely dampened down, we headed down river. Planned on breaking and packing trail along the river for a few miles but we'd only gone a short ways before we ran into overflow. The extreme cold had caused the ice to shrink and crack and then, because of the heavy weight of snow on top, it drops and water wells up through the cracks. The snow's a good insulator so water floods over the ice beneath the snow and spreads – sometimes for miles and can often be from six inches to a foot deep. It's only when the snow becomes pretty well saturated, losing it's insulating quality, that it will again freeze. The heavy snowfall and cold temperatures of the past days were ideal conditions for overflow – as we're finding out. Anyway, we turned around and headed back to the cabin.

Still clear and sunny by late afternoon but its sure starting to cool off. Soon as the sun starts going down the temperature drops. Checking later, we found it was already down to minus thirty-two at five o'clock. Gordon hooked up the propane light to replace the kerosene lamp we'd been using in the cabin. It gives a nice even light unlike the kerosene lamp which fluctuated a lot of the time. Also nailed a couple of pieces of plywood over the log walls behind the bunks to make it a little brighter. Later on Gordon stepped outside to check on the temperature before going to bed. When he came back in a few minutes later and reported how beautiful it was in the moonlight, I had to see for myself. After putting on my parka, I stepped outside. It was beautiful beyond description – full moon shining, snow capped mountains glowing in the distance and above all – northern lights dancing across the sky. I had gone out for a quick look but stayed until the cold forced me back inside. The beauty of this moonlit winter night was something no one could properly describe, least of all, I.

Tuesday – Nov. 19th -37C   Cold but sunny – the mountains look gorgeous. Gordon thinks it would be great for skiing out there.

The weather sure seems to be against us. First, not enough snow or ice, then too much snow all at once with overflow and now pretty darn cold. We did snowshoe across and up river a ways to the first bend where we put out some lynx sets in a bit of a willow-covered back channel. Lots of rabbit tracks and a few lynx tracks to indicate they occasionally hunt for dinner there. Later, Gordon took off for the mouth of Twin Lakes creek. It enters the Coal about three to four miles down river. He hopes to pack trail up the creek for a few miles and set out a few traps if fur sign is favorable. We'd like to go further up Twin Lakes Creek when temperatures warm a bit and put a few more sets out. He got back late afternoon reporting a good part of the trail packed. No overflow and quite a lot of fur sign – everything from wolves to weasels. Just before going to bed we again looked outside – clear and beautiful, the same as the previous night. A bit cooler though at minus forty-two, Brrrr!!!

Wednesday – Nov. 20th -44C   Clear out – not a trace of cloud. Yup, guess winter's not fooling and it's really here.

This is getting a little cold and at these temperatures I'd rather be anywhere but Rose Lake. There's nothing much I can do other than keep stuffing wood into the stove but it does keep the cabin nice and warm. Later, we decided to walk to Lynx Creek and check that run but soon came back and took a skidoo instead. It had warmed up to around minus thirty-five by then. Ice on Lynx was fine – overflow all frozen. We managed to pick up another two marten but also found two other traps had been sprung. No sign of mice stealing bait so it's a bit of a mystery. Soon turned around and headed back to our warm cabin. I have to figure out what we'll have for dinner this evening. Later, another clear, moonlit evening with temperature dropping steadily. Time for bed.

Thursday – Nov. 21st -45C WOW – that's equivalent to minus fifty Fahrenheit. This is getting ridiculous – but the fire is cozy and the coffee's great.

It was just too cold to do anything today. We skinned and placed the two marten pelts on stretchers. Then after lunch, about two-thirty, we snowshoed from the cabin through the bush to try and find a way that would connect with the ravine we've been following to Marten Creek. A route that avoids following the creek so we'd be able to miss all it's lovely overflow. We hoped to locate the route for use next season. It really didn't take us all that long and Gordon thinks, after several hours of axe and chainsaw work next fall, the new trail will be the way to go. Walked back from the ravine to Rose Lake via the creek. With just a trace of snow on the ice it made for an enjoyable stroll. Then it hit me, it's ridiculous – I'm already planning on "next year". I have enjoyed being out here except for the cold spell we've had but not yet sure if I want to come back. Depends on many things. I'll have to give it a lot of thought before I decide.

Friday – Nov. 22nd -32C A little warmer. There's a bit of cloud up there so hopefully it warms up more.

Yellowknife called us again last night and we had a bit of a talk – nice. Later this morning Gordon took the skidoo down river to bring back the groceries, gas, toboggan and plywood we'd cached last week when we weren't able, because of overflow, to get all the way to Rose Lake. This time the going was great and he got back in just under an hour and a half. Overflow all frozen and not much snow on the ice. The plywood he brought up will finish off the floor in the cabin – a big improvement. Too bad the temperature isn't a little warmer. It's lovely out, sunny but cold.

Finally decided to have a real quick lunch, pack the skimmer and head back to Jamie Lake via Marten Creek. Skidooing up the creek a short while later, we found a lot of seepage from the creek edges and banks running onto the ice. Slowed us a bit working our way around them but, even so, it only took a bit over three hours to get back to Jamie Lake. With a good fire going and the cabin warmed up, we opened the lid covering our storage cellar, expecting to find everything frozen solid. It was a pleasant surprise to find our fresh stuff, eggs and vegetable were not frozen. We had forgotten and left our Seven-up and ginger ale on the cupboard shelves where they had frozen solid – popping their tabs. Later while having supper of chili and bannock, I discovered I'd lost the crown on a tooth, the one that ached so badly three weeks ago. I'd bitten on a piece of bannock (they were not that hard) and it just broke off. Now it's a trip to Whitehorse and the dentist as soon as possible.

After supper we talked for quite awhile before deciding the best arrangement would be to close down our trapline for the season. The other option was for me to fly to Watson Lake by air charter then drive to Whitehorse for dental work. When it was completed I'd return to Watson Lake and fly back to Jamie Lake. This suggestion I vetoed. I don't like flying, especially without Gordon being along. The other factors to consider were the cost of the flights and the relatively short time we'd have left before closing if we were to be home at Watson Lake for Christmas. Another consideration was the amount of fur sign – marten tracks were few and far between since our heavy snowfall. The marten we'd picked up lately, with the exception of our last run to Rose Lake, had been caught earlier. The main food for marten is the mouse. Early in the season when there's little snow, mice will travel on top of the snow when going from the base of one tree to another or between downfalls, etc. Later, when snow is deep, they travel under the snow. The marten pretty well follows the same pattern, out in the open when snow depth isn't so great but once you get depths of eighteen inches and over, they generally remain for long periods under the snow hunting mice. They do come out periodically for a short spell but if it's really cold they just seem to disappear, remaining underneath for long periods – no tracks anywhere. That was happening to us – marten sign everywhere before the heavy snow and cold temperatures, but now rarely seeing a track. On our last trip to Rose Lake when we had such good luck, there were marten tracks everywhere. On the way back today, not a single fresh track!! It's disappointing after the way we started the first week of the season. But the marten are still around, cozy, with a couple of feet of snow overhead keeping them warm. And most important, those nice fat mice are right under there with them – dinner's handy.

Saturday – Nov. 23rd -23C   Cloudy out and looks like a pretty nice day.

Got through to Watson Lake Flying and talked to Stan, one of the pilots. He phoned our home but no answer so will have to advise the kids later on about our change of plans. Gordon headed out to check and close our Meadow Run. That Run is extremely rough and with all the snow, thought it would be better to go alone – not even taking the skimmer. I shampooed my hair as the water here is just great. Water at Rose Lake, which we get from the river, has mineral in it that leaves a black, almost greasy residue on the basins that's hard to remove so I don't like washing my hair there.

Gordon got back later from closing the run – no fur and no sign, hard to believe. Later, started taking inventory and packing groceries to take to Rose Lake to have on hand for next year. If we come out again we'll be spending a lot of time at Rose Lake and Kettle Creek. Hauling supplies over with the skidoo will save a lot of heavy backpacking next fall. Snowing lightly this afternoon. I'm working on my sweater and have it nearly finished – hope it fits. Also, made a lemon pie for supper.

Sunday – Nov. 24th -18C   A decent temperature for a change. Snowed a bit overnight but is clearing up.

Today, we skidoo'd down Jamie Run to the river. Lots of heavy snow over the trail making it very tough going. Finally reached the river and traveled up it about a hundred feet, then into overflow – what a wet mess. Took a long time to get ourselves out and ice cleared off the machine. After that we snowshoed, trying to find a way across the river to the sandbar on the other side. Finally located a way across and from there, headed up river along the sandbar through very deep snow. I snowshoed as the snow was so deep and heavy. It was hard breaking trail with even one person on the machine. The skidoo was frequently bogging down. Gordon finally reached the end of the sandbar and back onto the river and yes, you guessed it, back into overflow again. What a day!! When I caught up to him and after helping get ice and slush out of the tracks and rollers on the machine, we decided it would be smarter to snowshoe across that channel and leave the skidoo behind. Again, a bit further up, the entire river – shoreline to shoreline was covered with overflow which extended all the way to the creek and our new Wolf run. Despite the overflow, we packed a good trail with snowshoes which should, we hope, freeze hard enough overnight to be useable tomorrow.

It was a relief to finally turn around and head for home. We were both thoroughly soaked, from the mukluks on our feet to the moosehide mitts on our hands from wrestling the skidoo and clearing slush from the rollers. By the time we got to the cabin we were covered with ice from our feet to the mitts on our hands. Took a while in the warm cabin to melt enough ice off our outer clothing to switch to something dry. It wasn't long before nails along the walls were draped with drying clothes. Mukluks are hung far enough from the stove to dry slowly. If you get them too close to heat, the native tanned moosehide they're made from shrinks and shrivels, ruining them. They're always well looked after since we're so dependent on them for warm feet during the winter. They're light and when worn over a couple of pair of heavy wool socks are always warm and comfortable.

All the plans we'd made last night are dashed. We had hoped to close the Runs from Jamie Lake by Monday afternoon then go to Rose Lake on Tuesday, closing traps on the way. From Rose Lake, we'd shut down the Lynx Creek Run. Trail would be excellent since we'd just come over it a couple of days ago. Then back to Jamie Lake on Wednesday and possibly home to Watson Lake on Thursday. But, because of conditions we'd run into today with the overflow, we'll be at least another day closing Wolf Run, darn it!! One thing though – I'm sure getting experience with overflow. Gordon says, "Look at the bright side – it's good for the waistline with all that snowshoeing exercise." He admits it was sheer stupidity on his part getting into that overflow and I certainly agree. He was so certain the river ice was OK and just didn't bother to check.

Monday – Nov. 25ᵗʰ -32C These temperatures are getting a little out of hand but we're not the only ones in cold air.

Radio reported Grande Prairie, Alberta is minus thirty-three. Brr-rr!! As soon as breakfast was over, Gordon took off to check, hopefully, both the Wolf and Wolverine Runs. He went by himself since, with all the snow, I'd have had to snowshoe most of Wolf run once we'd left the river. That would have taken an hour longer so we decided it would be smarter for me to stay at home. It's now dropped down to minus thirty-four, clear and bright sun. It will be just beautiful on the river and up Wolf run – now I do wish I had gone along. Instead, I'm reading a boring book right now but plan on baking a pumpkin pie later on. The ninth pie in nine weeks, even better than the number I bake at home. Tried calling Watson Lake Flying but reception poor – Stan can hear me but I can't make him out.

Late afternoon Gordon got back with five marten, four from Wolf Run but only one from Wolverine. Animals are just not moving in these temperatures. It took him over four hours to check the Runs and he agreed, had I been along, I'd have been snowshoeing all of Wolf Run through very deep snow. Next, heading for Wolverine Run, he'd found overflow on the river where he usually crossed. He ended up snowshoeing the entire Run rather than take a chance with the skidoo. He really got his exercise. Makes me glad I stayed home.

Tuesday – Nov. 26ᵗʰ -42C That's what it shows on our thermometer but could be much colder since mercury-filled thermometers are only considered accurate down to minus thirty-eight, near mercury's freezing point.

Doesn't look as though we'll be going anyplace today. It was so bright during the night that you could have read by moonlight. With these temperatures, I doubt we'll get home Saturday. Don Taylor, who operates a fishing camp at Stewart Lake, called us this morning when we weren't able to get through to Watson Lake Flying. Don relayed a message to us through another bush camp at Grave Lake advising us that Watson Lake is minus forty-six and there would be no flying until temperatures moderate. We've had the radio on and just heard that Calgary, at noon, was down to minus thirty-four with a gusty thirty-five knot wind. That would be a heck of a lot colder than here – we have no wind.

We heard a great tearing boom this morning and were really puzzled as to the source. It wasn't until later in the day, after noticing a dark, irregular line appearing in the snow across Jamie Lake that the puzzle was solved. The initial cracking of the lake ice had caused the boom and the following tearing, splintering sound resulted from the crack ripping from shore to shore. Water then welled up all along the crack and seeped to the top of the snow where it's now showing as a dark irregular line across the lake.

Gordon's been busy putting out small spruce trees, about a hundred yards apart, to mark the runway he's packed with snowshoes. Bit of a job packing an area about twelve hundred feet long by fifty feet wide but it is necessary to ensure the ski-equipped aircraft gets airborne as quickly as possible from our small lake. Also, any overflow that overruns the packed runway will quickly freeze. I was out giving him a hand this afternoon – just have to get my exercise. He's also getting things ready for the plane to relay a load to Rose Lake from here. We have just too much stuff to haul over by skidoo.

Wednesday – Nov. 27ᵗʰ -35C   Not much letup but perhaps there's hope since a bit of cloud is showing, over towards the mountains.

Gordon took off after breakfast to close Canyon Run. It was too cold and too hard on the skidoo with both of us so I stayed home. It didn't take him very long. Trail was excellent since it had been packed after our big dump of snow. He didn't catch anything and reported seeing just one set of tracks in all that distance. Hard to believe the turnaround in the marten movements. After lunch he hauled a bunch of gear to the runway for Stan to relay over to Rose Lake. Also packed up most of the remaining supplies, ready for the cache, in case we fly out soon. Tonight the moon is so bright and beautiful – but it's clear and cold again.

Thursday – Nov. 28ᵗʰ -34C   Not much letup yet – a bit of cloud over the mountains to the west, much the same as yesterday morning.

Tried calling out but again, no signals. In fact, none for the past three days. Gordon went to the Coal via River Run with a load of plywood for Rose Lake. At least, next year, we'll have lots of plywood to finish off the interior of Rose cabin and also for the extended porch roof he's planning for the Kettle Creek cabin. He'll stash the plywood well back and above high water mark at the river where, next fall, it'll be handy for hauling the rest of the way by canoe. By one o'clock the temperature had warmed up to only minus twenty-six and the sky had pretty well clouded over. Hopefully it stays warmer for us – at least until we complete our last Rose Lake trip. We've changed our agenda a bit – now planning on getting picked up by plane at Rose Lake rather than here. Before we leave for Rose Lake we'll close the cabin and put everything in the cache, ready for next year. The runway on the river will be longer and the approaches up and down river are much longer and better.

Gordon mentioned this has been the worst winter weather he's ever experienced – very heavy snowfall, extreme temperatures and terrible overflow. He was late getting back from the river because of skidoo problems. Afterwards, worked on the machine until he thought he had the problem fixed. Had lunch and then down to the lake with the skidoo for more runway packing. After that chore was completed and we were heading back to the cabin, the skidoo quit. Gordon thinks the problem is with the coil and since we have a spare one – should be easily fixed. Hopefully, he's right. We need the machine for that last trip to Rose Lake. Our other skidoo is already hung in the trees since we figured we'd not need it again this season. Safe storage for the skidoo's was a problem until he got the idea of getting them up in the air out of the reach of animals. He ties a pole between two trees, about twenty feet above the ground, with a pulley attached. Light cable is run through the pulley and attached to the skidoo bumper. Then, with a lot of pulling on the other end of the cable, the skidoo is raised out of harms way.

Friday – Nov. 29th -28C   Clear, not a cloud in the sky and a littler warmer.

Packing up to leave for Rose Lake. It's clear and real sunny – another gorgeous day. Finally got everything stored away in the cache, said goodbye to the cabin and we were on our way. It was quite a feeling, leaving the cabin. I've really enjoyed the time I've been here – all the good memories. To think I may never see it again was pretty sad. Shortly after climbing up the big hill on the trail to Rose Lake the skidoo started acting up so Gordon turned around and headed back for Jamie Lake, planning on getting the other machine. After he'd turned back, it ran perfectly all the way to the lake. So – turned around again and once more headed for Rose Lake. In the meantime I'd kept going down the trail, determined to walk all the way to Rose Lake if I had to. Trail was packed hard enough for good walking so I just carried my snowshoes. Gordon finally caught up to me as I was starting down the ravine leading to Marten Creek. Nice to get on the machine and ride again. The creek was fine, it had flooded a bit but was again frozen hard, so had no problem getting to Rose Lake. It wasn't long before we had a fire going and tea water heating.

After lunch, Gordon took off for Twin Lakes Creek to check and spring the traps set there. Returned late afternoon, rather disgusted. He ended up doing a lot of snowshoeing because of overflow and then to cap it, didn't catch a thing. Not a single track all the way down river and up Twin Lakes Creek. Hard to believe that since the heavy snowfall and our cold temperatures, we haven't seen any fresh tracks – not even rabbit. Tried calling Watson Lake Flying and also Yellowknife but no luck, signals have been out the past few days. Cabbage rolls for supper, along with moose steak and then, for dessert, chocolate squares with fruit and of course, hot tea. It wasn't long after dishes were done that we filled the stove, closed the dampers, took a quick look outside and crawled into our sleeping bags. Certainly no trouble getting to sleep out here.

Saturday – Nov. 30th -40C   Brrrrrr – Baby, it's COLD outside!!

It was even colder when we first got up this morning and now at ten-thirty, it's still pretty darned cold. This is unreal – at these temperatures we won't be home, even for Christmas. Also, still have Lynx Run to close down. Again, no signals. Not even able to contact Yellowknife but we did manage to reach one of his radio contacts who'll relay a message to Watson Lake Flying that we'd like a flight on Sunday. Really don't know if he got our message correctly as his reception was poor but we could hear him, loud and clear. After finishing breakfast, Gordon got busy packing a runway on the river ice – no overflow but loads of snow to snowshoe down. Later, with packing completed and after a quick cup of coffee, he went up river to check and close Lynx Run. I stayed home taking inventory and getting things ready for the cache – just in case. Looks like I'll have to wait until next year to see Kettle Creek cabin – something more to look forward to if I do come out again.

Sunday – Dec. 1ˢᵗ -37C   Fogged in and still cold. Sure hope it lifts because,"I wanna go home".

Last evening Gordon completed putting the flooring down in the cabin. Now it's all finished except for trim around the edges. Sure looks nicer. A short while after breakfast, we finally got through to Watson Lake to find they're also fogged in so will have to try again tomorrow. Gordon's been cleaning up things outside and now is busy manufacturing more planks from our spruce trees. That chainsaw does a good job but it looks like hard work. By one o'clock the fog had cleared completely and a brilliant sun was shining. Not much heat from the sun though – still minus thirty-six. Definitely no flight today.

Monday – Dec. 2ⁿᵈ -42C   What can I say ? It's cold but sunny and gorgeous.

After breakfast, went outside to feed a few scraps to our dog. Murky was all curled up with his tail around his nose, in the doghouse Gordon had built for him under a nearby spruce. He was covered with hoarfrost but appeared to be quite content. He was ready to run after us – ready for play, even in these cold temperatures. But we "chickened" out and went back into our warm cabin. A quiet day, sticking close to home, listening for the sound of an airplane engine – just in case. Signals were out again – couldn't raise anyone on the radio so didn't want to go too far. We very likely wouldn't have anyway with this temperature. All the chores are finished so we're doing a lot of card playing and reading. Occasionally, checking the thermometer, we're thankful we have a snug, warm cabin. Gordon did go out for a spell to cut more planks. Just sitting around is definitely not his thing!!

Took one last look outside before going to bed. It's really impossible to describe the overall beauty of the scene that met my eyes. Overhead, a full moon was beaming down from a sky filled with twinkling stars. In front, the frozen, snow-covered river appeared to be covered with millions of sparkling diamonds reflecting moonlight. Shadows from trees along the river banks stretched in narrow bands far across the snowy surface. Watching, it's almost as if I could see movement in their shadowy depths but it was probably only imagination. Aurora danced across the northern reaches of the sky, a fitting crown for the distant mountains that stretched far below. Above all, a complete, perfect stillness. Not even the rustle of the wind. Finally turning and seeing smoke drifting upwards from the stovepipe, the spell was broken. Suddenly I realized I was cold and it was time to return to the warmth of the cabin and my bed but, it was hard to leave.

Tuesday – Dec. 3rd -40C   Clear, another chilly morning!!

This is unbelievable – this stretch of cold weather. Got up, wondering if Stan will show today. There is a bit of cloud up there to the west. Maybe it'll start clouding over and warm up. We're going to start cutting down on our groceries since we have very little left of some things. Only seven tea bags and a half a pound of coffee – the essentials! We do have lots of meat so no concern about going hungry. Most of our other supplies were left at Jamie Lake for Stan to relay here by plane. Gordon completed more of the finishing touches to the cabin – looks great. I read "The Other Side of the Mountain " for the second time – a great book.

Gordon finally got hold of Watson Lake Flying Service at noon. They reported Watson Lake was having light snow and the Hyland River valley was fogged in. Weather's good here so it's exasperating. We're to check back in an hour in case weather's cleared up sufficiently for Stan to take off. If Stan can't make it, Gordon's planning on hitching Murky to the toboggan and heading back to Jamie Lake for a few supplies. He'd rather do the hiking than take the skidoo down from where he's got it hanging, out of the reach of bears. Right now he's back out cutting more planks to finish the floor under the bunks and even planking for a step out front.

Just finished getting through to Watson Lake Flying and – Hurray!! Stan and the Beaver are on the way. Rushed to tell Gordon and then got busy packing the last of our gear into the cache.. It didn't seem to be any time at all before I heard the sound of the aircraft engine and soon spotted the Beaver circling to check our runway. Minutes later, the plane landed and Stan taxied to a stop right in front of the cabin. He reported the weather was good all the way after he cleared the Watson Lake valley. Before flying here, he had landed at Jamie Lake and off-loaded the gear, mostly gas, onto the dock, picked up the stuff we'd left by the strip and here it was. Sure good to have it flown over – saves many skidoo trips. His arrival was about two-thirty. My first human contact, other than for Gordon, in nine and a half weeks.

It only took a matter of minutes to unload and transfer everything from the plane to the cabin and even less time to load ourselves, Murky, our bag of fur plus assorted gear we're taking home, into the aircraft. Minutes later, after taxi-ing to the end of the runway, we were in the air. Looking out the side window and seeing our cabin below, a wisp of smoke still drifting from the stovepipe, I had a feeling of sadness. It looked so forlorn sitting there all by itself – .almost like deserting a friend.

It took me a few more minutes to return to the present and the anticipation of flying home to Watson Lake. Just under an hour later we were landing at Watson Lake, being met by Patti and Jamie. I really had missed them and it was so good to see them again. As soon as we had all our gear and Murky trans-ferred to our vehicle, we were off for home. It wasn't until I was actually inside our house, seeing the furniture, pictures on the walls, the view from the window that I felt, YES – I really am home. Patti made us a beautiful dinner – barbequed T-bone steak, baked potato with crab and cheese, fresh green beans, cauliflower and broccoli with a lovely salad and garlic/cheese bread. Just about the same type of meal we'd been having at Rose Lake!! Loads of mail to go through, most for the fire.

Sleeping that night in a king-sized bed with loads of room, even with Gordon alongside, wasn't as restful as I'd anticipated it would be. I'd doze off, only to be awake a few minutes later when the furnace or the freezer or the refrigerator came on. Little sounds I'd never noticed before kept waking me. Not at all like the unbroken quiet we had out on the trapline. After turning the TV on – it was only minutes later before it was off. What seemed entertaining before now seemed not worth watching. I began to wonder if being out in the bush had really changed me.

Wednesday – Dec. 4th -35C

When we got up this morning it was a surprise to find the temperature had risen and it was snowing heavily – sure lucky we got home yesterday. Later, over coffee, we both started reminiscing about the past months and how much we'd enjoyed them, even with all the overflow, deep snow and cold temperatures. I especially felt a sense of self-satisfaction, knowing I had been a real help to Gordon. Our fur catch wasn't that great, only forty-nine marten, but we're not complaining. We had been surprised at not catching any lynx but, once the snow arrived, hadn't seen another track. Wonder what next year will be like???

YIPES!! I'M ACTUALLY GOING BACK –
I CAN'T BELIEVE IT.

*F*riday – *Sept. 11*th

I can't believe this!! Here I am, back at Jamie Lake for another season. I had done a lot of thinking about not coming back this fall but, remembering how we really enjoyed last year, decided to give it another try.

We had a very hectic summer with our hay operation – such a wet season. It seemed to rain every second day at Watson Lake. We worked hard, especially Gordon, getting our hay crop off. He's only had a couple of days off so it'll be great out here, just relaxing and working when we want to. Gordon finished work on the farm about seven last evening. It took us until eleven-thirty to close the house up – draining the water system and removing all plants and groceries we don't want frozen. Patti was also busy packing and removing her belongings – and she had lots, since she's being transferred to a position with the bank in Whitehorse. She's moving in with her brother, Jamie, until she leaves. We'll sure miss her and Jamie too – he's also thinking about moving to Whitehorse for the winter. Our home will be vacant so we had to make sure it was properly winterized.

We were to leave with Watson Lake Flying Service at nine-thirty this morning. We had the Otter aircraft all loaded and were strapped in our seats, waiting for the pilot to start the engine. Nothing – the thing would not start – dead battery. Not a great way to begin, especially when I'm such a nervous passenger. We finally did get away at ten-thirty and had a real nice flight. It was a gorgeous day – not a cloud in the sky. The lake here, Jamie Lake, was like a mirror – not a ripple. After landing, the first thing I did was run up to see if the cabin survived the winter. It did – but a marten or some other animal had been in the porch scattering all our pails and traps about. Luckily, nothing got inside the cabin. Flying here, we had a full Otter load – two thousand pounds. Lots of groceries, roofing paper, plus a new skidoo. Gordon was not pleased with the John Deere "Spitfire" machines we'd been using so bought a Tundra long track machine, made by Bombardier. It's a larger machine and made for work whereas the Spitfire is more of a recreational machine. We sent one Spitfire back to Watson Lake on the return flight

After waving "good-bye" to the pilot of the departing Otter, we each grabbed a box of supplies and headed up to the cabin. After tea and a quick lunch, the next few hours were spent packing the rest of the supplies to the cabin. I swear, the distance from the lake has doubled and also gotten steeper than it was last year. My better half say's NO – we're just not in shape. Another break for tea, roast beef sandwiches and cookies. Later, while Gordon did a few odd jobs, I decided to pick blueberries which I made into jam this evening. Our radio signals are not good tonight – no music – a disappointment.

Saturday – Sept. 12th +3C   Our first morning here. We woke up to a nice sunny day – no clouds.

Gordon got up first and put the coffee on. While we were waiting for the water to heat, Murky started to bark. Gordon looked out and there was a "Big Bad Black Wolf" watching us. He rushed for his rifle and from the porch fired one shot, killing the wolf. Gordon figures it was this year's pup but, because of its large size, looks more like a two year old. The wolf is jet black and probably made the tracks we'd noticed yesterday down along the lakeshore. We're glad we got him since there was a good possibility he'd keep hunting around this area, just waiting for Murky to make the mistake of going too far from the cabin. Then the wolf would have had him for dinner. While we were checking him over, heard more wolves howling from the meadow east of here. Probably other members of the pack.

A short while later while finishing up breakfast and drinking coffee, Gordon tells me he sprained the index finger on his right hand yesterday while starting the Spitfire skidoo. The finger does feel better today but is still swollen. What a way to start our season!! We had planned on leaving today for the Coal River and then upriver to Rose Lake. The next day we would have continued up the Coal to our second cabin, located on the riverbank across from the mouth of Kettle Creek. We'll have to delay our plans for a day because of the wolf. It has to be skinned and the hide placed on a stretcher. With the other jobs that have to be done before leaving we'd really have to rush and, even then, probably not finish everything. Gordon spent all morning skinning and looking after the wolf hide while I cleaned and sorted gear in the porch.

This afternoon I went and picked two cups of low-bush cranberries. Not many around here. Also picked about five cups of blueberries – will make more jam or possibly a pie for tomorrow. After returning from berry picking, I helped Gordon start putting a new roof on the cabin. This cabin has a flat, sloping roof – not a gable type roof. He's placing two by fours on the old roof to support the plywood nailed over them – like a new roof over the old roof. We'll only be doing half of the roof since we don't have enough plywood to cover it all. The other half of the plywood was flown to Rose Lake last winter for use over there. Anyway, the worst part of the roof will be done. With new grey roofing paper covering it, will look super.

Sunday – Sept. 13th +5C Cloudy and drizzly – not nice, especially when our roof wasn't finished yesterday.

I'm making coffee this morning while Gordon's out on the roof closing off the ends so rain doesn't run under the new roof we started yesterday. Gordon talked to Don Wilkinson later this morning. He's at Twin Lakes guiding a hunt and hopes to visit us at either Rose or Kettle. We hadn't been able to raise Watson Lake Flying or Don Taylor on our radio so it was good talking to Don Wilkinson and learn our radio transmitter does work. Guess signals are out at Watson Lake.

It's now eleven-thirty and just got through to Watson Lake Flying. We requested they contact our neighbor, Sheila Frank, and let them know everything is fine out here. Also received a message from Patti advising her transfer came through and she'll be going to Whitehorse by the end of September. We'll sure miss her but then Whitehorse isn't all that far away – only a bit under five hundred kilometers. It must be a relief for her, knowing where and when she leaves, after waiting months for the decision. At noon it started snowing – sure hope it doesn't last long. The weather has certainly changed our plans for today and for our trip up river to Rose Lake tomorrow. Heard several flocks of cranes as they flew over – guess winter isn't too far away. I sorted groceries today, listing contents on the sides of the boxes. This way it'll be much easier finding what you're looking for – saves a lot of awkward digging through boxes when they're up in the cache.

Baked a cake in my new oven. We had a new one made for us, slightly modified from the one we had last season. Gordon installed a thermometer on the door and checking, found it registers 100 degrees lower than the inside thermometer. When it's showing two hundred and twenty-five degrees on the outside it's about three hundred and twenty-five inside. It will be handier as I won't have to keep opening the oven door to check my baking but will have to remember its lower reading. Later in the afternoon we went for a walk to the second lake and up the trail on Ridge Run, hoping to find grouse – none. Also did a little trail clearing – stuff that had fallen down since last year. Cleared up nicely late evening, just before going to bed.

Monday – Sept. 14th 0C It clouded up again overnight but looks as though it'll clear up. Hope so since we need warm temperatures for finishing off the roof. Have three more sections of roofing paper to tar and tack down.

We have fresh "chicken" for tonight's dinner. About seven-thirty this morning, Gordon heard grouse feeding near the cabin. He went out and got three – one was on the cabin roof busy pecking away at the sand. We heard and then spotted the Beaver aircraft flying over later this morning, probably taking hunters to Twin Lakes where Don Wilkinson is guiding. Twin Lakes are about eighteen miles north-east of here. After breakfast, went for a short walk to the meadow on River Run way to see if we could spot any game. Nothing, so returned to the cabin for the axe and chainsaw so we could start clearing winter blow-downs from the trail. Closer to the cabin, Gordon cut up three dry trees for firewood then split the blocks while I carried and stacked them in the porch. As soon as Gordon has the roof finished we're going up another trail to check for moose. I have supper all prepared, ready for us when we return – fried grouse, potatoes and turnip with cranberry sauce. The grouse should be super since they were young birds. The cranberry sauce, as well as a quart of blueberry jam was freshly made on Saturday.

Later in the afternoon we headed up a trail Gordon and the boys had made when they packed the canoes to the river. The first part of the trail was along the old Jamie Run that pretty well follows the high ground southward from here. Further on, it branches off along a ridge that extends all the way southwards to the river. The high ridge provides an excellent lookout point. From it you can see quite a ways up and down the river as well as the entire meadow that stretches for a couple of miles towards our Wolverine run. After waiting and watching for about an hour and a half, Gordon finally spotted a cow moose. We watched it for a long time until it wandered off, disappearing into timber along the river. Too bad cow season isn't open. Even so, it was so nice just lying in the sun watching the river. On the way home we again spotted the Beaver flying by.

Tuesday – Sept. 15th   Not a cloud, beautiful – although the ground looks frosty.

We're getting ready to walk to the river. From there, we'll take the canoe the rest of the way to our Rose Lake cabin. We had coffee with eggs and bacon plus fried left-over oatmeal porridge for breakfast. I made breakfast yesterday and slightly miscalculated our needs so couldn't throw the surplus oatmeal away. Guess if you're real hungry it would taste great but I wouldn't recommend doing it often. When you're a hundred miles from the nearest store with a flight charge of one thousand dollars for a return trip, you don't throw too much away. Gordon said it wasn't bad with blueberry jam – Yuk!!!

We left Jamie Lake at ten-twenty, finally reaching the river where the canoe was stashed at about one in the afternoon. It was such a nice day – hot really. We dragged the canoe down the bank and into the river, then mounted the motor on the transom. Next, Gordon filled the gas tank and gave the starter cord a yank. On the second pull, it started. HURRAY!! I was really surprised and think Gordon was too, that it started so easily after lying on the cold, damp ground under the canoe for ten months. We loaded our gear and then Murky and I climbed in. Gordon gave the canoe a shove, hopped in and we were away – headed up river for our Rose Lake cabin. On the way up river, we had a few minor problems finding the right channels to run through with the canoe. The Coal River changes its main course so often that you never know where the shallows will be. After you pass through the first section of boulders, the river bottom is nothing but sand, always shifting with the current. Sections that were three and more feet deep last year now only had six to eight inches of water running through them whereas last years shallow sections now were the deep channels. Makes for interesting navigating.

Anyhow, we got to Rose Lake late in the afternoon only to have the cabin greet us with a real mess inside. Guess the river had again flooded this spring and water got into the cabin, floating the benches, a few logs and the pail we'd left behind to new locations. They were scattered all over the floor – what a welcome!! First off, we cleaned up the mess in the cabin then had a belated lunch. Later, we brought all our supplies down from the cache. After finishing that chore, we figured it was about time to head up river to our special fishing spot. I caught a nice Dolly Varden trout which we're having for dinner tonight. We also spotted a real big greyling but he wouldn't take any of the delectable lures we threw at him. He did strike at one of Gordon's lures but after a few seconds, threw the hook and was gone. Later, Gordon tried calling moose and thought he heard an answer. We have had a grand day canoeing on the river. Quite a change from last year when it rained so hard. We now have a beautiful evening with not a cloud and a full moon rising – wonderful.

Wednesday – Sept. 16th -5C Another gorgeous day – no cloud – no breeze – just sunshine.

Should be great going up river. Gordon and I both think it's colder now than it was last year when we came out on September twenty-eight. The mountains are beautiful with the sun shining on them. We have such a good view of them from the cabin window. It'll be even more beautiful when we install the larger window.

We finally started upriver at eleven o'clock, heading for Kettle Creek and our second cabin along the river. The canoe was loaded with a stove, plywood, groceries, pots, etc. All the necessary supplies for setting up housekeeping. Also made sure our sleeping bags, in plastic bags, were on board. I then climbed in and took my seat at the front of the canoe since I'm the lookout who's supposed to spot the snags, rocks and shallow channels before we run into them. Murky climbed in next, lying down at the back end of the canoe. Gordon shoved the canoe away from shore, hopped in and we were off. It was another gorgeous day for traveling on the river. We again found the river bottom and main channel had changed so much from the previous year. We frequently had to cross from one side of the river to the other in order to keep in the deeper channel. Even then we found it tricky getting across some sand and gravel bars that we just couldn't avoid. Several times we had to paddle our way back then try a different location for crossing. Lots of fun, especially with a full load. It took us over three hours to reach Kettle Creek. In a straight line it's only about seven miles from Rose Lake but, following the river with all its twists and turns, it must be at least fourteen miles. It really is an enjoyable trip, especially when the weather's nice. The river is crystal clear so you can see right to the bottom, irregardless of whether the bottom is six inches or ten feet below. Clean, white sandbars all along the way. The river banks are covered with spruce and pine – quite open in parts with no underbrush, almost like parkland. Lot's of great places for berry picking or just stopping and relaxing with a cup of tea. Moose tracks all along the sandbars, often intermingled with those of wolf and bear. And nowhere any sign of man. No axe cuts, no old campfire signs – just our wonderful new country.

Coming around the last bend, I finally spotted the cabin located high on the river bank across from the mouth of Kettle Creek. A few minutes later we pulled up on the sand bar below the cabin, glad to get out and stretch – especially Murky. We each grabbed a box of supplies from the canoe and headed up to the cabin. The cabin is much larger than the one's at Jamie and Rose Lake but needs a lot of work. It was built in nineteen eighty-five by Gordon with the help of a couple of his buddies, George Porter and Gerry Quebec. The cabin is sixteen feet long by twelve feet wide. It has nothing in it so far. No floor, no stove, no table, bed or chairs – just the four walls, roof and the door. There is one small window on the north wall that overlooks the river. We brought a good stove for the cabin as well as plywood for the floor with us in the canoe but everything else will have to be manufactured from local trees. First thing, we installed the stove and got a fire going to heat tea water. While Gordon finished unloading the canoe, I got lunch ready. It wasn't long before we were sitting on a log eating sandwiches and drinking tea.

We decided that since there was so much that had to be done, we'd work for a couple of hours and then head back to Rose Lake. We especially needed the large window and more plywood for the floor that we'd stored at Rose Lake. We'd also have a much more comfortable night at Rose Lake in a cabin with beds. First thing tomorrow morning we'd return with the required supplies. After lunch, Gordon got busy with his chainsaw, manufacturing two by fours for floor joists that we'd need to support the plywood flooring. It would be really great to have the floor completed by tomorrow. The cabin only has the one small window. Jamie had made us two large picture windows, three feet by four feet in size. We're planning on installing one here and the other in the Rose Lake cabin. The larger window will be a great improvement, especially after I hang the red drapes I've made for it. They'll go with the red and white table-cloth I also brought along – will look super. That's the first thing I've done in each cabin – hang the drapes – makes it homey. Our trip back down-river was great – only took us about an hour and a quarter, floated a good part of the way with the motor shut off.

Thursday – Sept. 17th -1C   A bit of cloud but its clearing so should be a good day to go back up river.

First thing this morning, Gordon went to one of the meadows behind the cabin and tried to call in a moose. No answer. Got through on the radio to Don Taylor this morning. It's good to contact someone and let them know we're okay. After breakfast we packed all the plywood and one large window as well as a bunch of odds and ends in the canoe and started up river for Kettle Creek. We got about half way before running into problems with sand bars. Then, after getting clear, the motor wouldn't start. After Gordon had worked on it for several minutes and changed the spark plug, it came to life with the first pull and we were on our way again. We made better time today since Gordon knew where to cross over most of the submerged sandbars. With my help on the paddle, poling over about eight different sandbars, we managed to get through without hanging up on any of them. The trip to Kettle Creek only took us a bit over two and a half hours.

After lunch, Gordon was back cutting two by fours while I was busy picking blueberries, enough for nearly a pint of jam. I also hauled up most of the plywood and other supplies from the canoe. After Gordon completed manufac-turing a sufficient number of two by fours, we started on the floor and managed to install two thirds of the floor joists and half the plywood flooring. Oh, what a difference!! Since we don't have a bed, we'll have to sleep on our new floor tonight. It's sure not like my waterbed!! Tomorrow will see a lot of work done on this place.

Friday – Sept. 18th +2C   It's cloudy out but nice – looks like another good day.

First morning at Kettle Creek. It's not the Hyatt Regency in Hawaii but next to it. Our closest sandy beach is directly across the river. Gordon says, "What can you expect for twenty-five dollars a night – the Hyatt charges twenty-six!! Mid-morning, we heard the sound of a small motor and minutes later a canoe came around the bend from upriver. Sharon Robey, from Minneapolis, Minn. and Don Wilkinson, a guide for Caesar Lake Outfitters came down by canoe from their camp which is located about six miles (in a straight line) up-stream. By river, it's closer to twelve miles because of the river's twisty, wind-ing course. Their hunt, with horses, had originated at Twin Lakes which is lo-cated around fifteen miles east of here. It was good to have some company for a change. They stayed about three hours while we all had lunch – soup, tea and bannock plus a sausage that Don had brought along. They were traveling the river in hopes of getting a caribou or moose.

This morning Gordon took out the small window that was originally in the cabin and replaced it with the three foot by four foot window we'd brought from Rose Lake. It just did wonders for the cabin. It's so much brighter inside, plus, we now have a great view of mountains to the north. We next finished off the floor and after that installed the small window in the west facing end wall. It allows the afternoon sun to shine into the cabin. Just beautiful!! Later, we'll put a third window in the side wall above our bed. We didn't have time to get our bed and cupboards made – probably tomorrow. Late afternoon, we hiked to a high lookout point about a mile down river. It's a knoll, about two hundred feet high, sitting a short distance back from the riverbank. It's an ideal location to glass for game in the meadows and along the river. Not our day – no game spotted. Back to the cabin for dinner. We were both getting pretty hungry. Tried the radio but again no contact made. This afternoon the cloud had cleared away and with the warm sun, temperature climbed to the plus fourteen range – very enjoyable.

Saturday – Sept. 19th -7C   What a change!! Its sure getting cold, clear sky. Hope the weather changes soon and we have some more mild temperatures.

Gordon got up early and went to one of the meadows to check for game. When he tried calling moose, our stupid dog answered with a number of barks. If any game was in the area they'd not reply but head for the hills. Gordon was a bit disgusted. It's sure good to be able to look out our big window and see the mountains in the distance. They're about four to five miles away but, showing above the heavy spruce growth across the river, they look much closer. No snow on them yet but colors of the foliage on their slopes are changing, mostly red's. Signals are poor although we did manage to get a message through to Watson Lake Flying, relayed by the operator of a hunting camp at Tuya Lake.

Again at lunch time, just as we were ready to sit down and eat, there was the sound of an outboard motor. Sure enough, a canoe appeared around the bend upriver bringing Fabian Porter, a native guide for Caesar Lake Outfitters and his hunter from Switzerland, Hieni Nusseli. Hieni is one of the two Swiss men that had bought our hunting operation. We managed it for them for a few years before stepping out completely. They sold the operation to the Wilkinson's a year later. It was nice to visit with Hieni again. He even remembered how I love Swiss chocolate and had brought me some – a very thoughtful gentleman. After our visitors left, Gordon got busy constructing our bed. He built the supporting frame out of chain sawed lumber then covered them with boards he'd also manufactured with the saw. In place of a mattress, we piled the ends of small, green spruce boughs over the boards, to a depth of about eight inches.

Next, a light tarp was placed over the boughs and then the sleeping bags were laid on top. You end up with a comfortable, springy bed plus the aroma of green spruce needles makes it all the more inviting. Super – and it looks great!! There's so much room in this cabin compared with our other two. Next, Gordon cut a bunch of slats from the small, straight spruce he'd located just across the river. Managed to nail up slats to cover about a quarter of the spaces between the logs. It covers the moss chinking between the logs and really brightens up the cabin. Afterwards, we gathered a bunch of moss for additional insulation for the roof. This cabin is warm. Still no moose and we sure need meat.

Looked like rain for a while this afternoon but cleared up nicely and a short while later, with the warm sun, temperature again went up to plus fourteen. We did manage to get through to Don Taylor and set up a schedule with him. This evening we talked to Jim Close at Watson Lake Flying so at least we know our radio is okay to reach Watson Lake.

Sunday – Sept. 20th -3C   Nice morning – just a few clouds.

Caesar Lake camp called this morning to advise us to come up river to their camp for a load of moose meat. They didn't have as many pack horses as they needed to haul all the meat back to base camp and, knowing we hadn't gotten any fresh meat, called and offered it to us. Nice of them and really appreciated. We'll go tomorrow morning since we won't have time to get up and back today before dark. No fun navigating the river in the dark – especially with a loaded canoe. I just hope a bear doesn't get at the meat during the night. They asked us to come and overnight with them but we declined. We'd have to haul all our sleeping bags, foam mattresses and dishes. With the river being so shallow up-stream, we decided not to haul all that extra weight. The mountain they've been hunting on has an old forest burn that we can see from our cabin. In fact, it's the only mountain we can see from our newly installed window.

We got the cabin roof all finished today – lots of moss on it for insulation. The ceiling of this cabin is made from planks that Gordon cut with his chainsaw. He did a great job of it, all even thickness. After finishing with the roof we chinked the log walls, both inside and out, where new chinking was needed. Out in the bush, away from a hardware store, chinking is done with green moss. You tamp it between the logs with a piece of wood shaved to resemble a dull chisel. Afterwards, on the inside of the cabin, slats are nailed over the chinking. They help hold the chinking in place as well as keeping anyone from brushing against the dried moss – it's itchy. Gordon nailed more slats in place but ran out of nails before he finished. Have to complete that job on our next trip. We worked steadily from ten in the morning until three in the afternoon, completing all we could before coming in for lunch. After lunch, Gordon was back to cutting more two by fours, sufficient for the framework of the outhouse. Later, he finished his workday by cutting enough slabs to enclose it. We're out of nails so will have to nail it together on our next trip. Time for supper – the clouds had cleared again after a little shower this afternoon. Hope it stays clear for good canoeing tomorrow morning.

Monday – Sept. 21ˢ -7C Sure frosty this morning but looks gorgeous with not a cloud nor breeze.

We left at ten-twenty to go upriver to the Caesar Lake camp, much to Murky's unhappiness. The trip was beautiful – sun shining and warm. We reached their camp at about twenty to two after navigating around innumerable boulders, snags and about fifty shallow stretches of river. Got hung up a few times, trying to cross over some of the bars. The meat was right at their campsite under cover and looks delicious. We had tea and lunch, then loaded the meat into the canoe – a good hundred pounds. Gordon decided the location where the guides had left their canoe was too close to the riverbank. If the river flooded in the spring, it would be washed away. We moved it further inland under the protection of the trees. Also, he was not too keen on where they had built their cache. It was a good twenty feet up in between three very tall trees. The three cross-braces, from tree to tree, were nailed on. He thought that, if there was any amount of wind, the swaying would loosen the braces and the cache would collapse and fall to the ground. They had stored the outboard motor up there with a folded tarp lying over it. He got some rope and lashed the cross-pieces to the trees. If the nails pulled out, the rope would hold (he hopes). He also tied down the tarp so it wouldn't blow away from the motor. He hated to interfere with their setup but said he felt it should be done. They'd also left a bag of empty cans against the meat. We figured they wanted us to dispose of them. We loaded them in the canoe to take back to Kettle. Gordon will then burn and bury them. They mustn't have had a spade and couldn't dig a pit for their garbage.

We finally got away at twenty to three and got home just after four-thirty. A lot faster going down river, especially when you have an idea of where the shallow stretches are. It was not as nice coming home. Sky had clouded over, a wind had sprung up and temperature dropped. Hard to see the stumps, etc. in the river with the wind-rippled surface. Murky was sure pleased to have us back home. As soon as we'd finished unloading and storing the meat, Gordon went out and cut another load of spruce tips for our bed. Placed under our foam mattress, will make for even more comfortable sleeping. The sky had really clouded over while we were coming down river and, shortly after we reached home, started to rain. Within a short time the clouds were right down on the mountain tops.

Tuesday – Sept. 22nd +7C   Milder out but wet. It rained all night and looks like it will continue all day. The mountains are covered with snow this morning.

This cabin is very warm . We didn't put much wood in the stove at night and had our door open. Should be good for this winter. Our new mattress is now very comfortable. I had never slept on spruce boughs before coming here. Heini Nussli had named our cabin, "Hotel Rose". By eleven the temperature had dropped to plus three. Much cooler with a gusty wind – not pleasant. Gordon is outside building the outhouse while I'm making vegetable soup from of our meager supplies. We hadn't planned on staying here very long so didn't bring much with us. The bulk of our groceries, as well as all our fresh stuff, is at Jamie Lake. They will surely taste good when we get back there. Gordon used to tell me how wasteful his guides and the hunters could be. Take a can of fruit or beans or meat and after a spoonful or two, throw the rest away. I used to find that hard to believe but now I don't. When I went to dispose of the bag of cans we brought back, right on top was an opened, one and one-half pound can of ham with just a small chunk taken out – the rest thrown away. A large chocolate bar, broken in half and put in the garbage. How wasteful!! Guess who's getting a treat tonight – Murky. He'll enjoy that ham. Rather have Murky get it than a grizzly. Sure hope that Gordon's lashing down of the poles at Caesar Lakes camp yesterday will protect the cache. Trees are really swaying back and forth – it's really windy out.

Tonight, we're having moose steak done up in mushroom sauce and vegetables. The meat surely looks good and we're very happy Don left it for us. It probably was a help to them also since Yukon Game regulations require guides and hunters to save all meat that's fit for human consumption. They can't just leave it behind. With Don not having enough packhorses to bring it out in one trip, he'd have ended up making a second long trek. Still very miserable outside at bedtime.

Wednesday – Sept. 23rd +1C   Light snow – wind has died down but it's very dull out.

First decent morning, we head back to Rose Lake. Radio signals have been out for the last few days. Fantastic radio reception in the evenings. Had an Edmonton station on last night playing all the old-time hits, Bing Crosby, Guy Lombardo, Patti Page, etc. Great listening. The only drawback is that good reception starts late in the evening and is best when it's time for bed. We play cards a lot of the time in the evening. Since we had to backpack from Jamie Lake to the river, we didn't pack reading material since its heavy and we needed so many other supplies. I did sneak in a Readers Digest so that's helped a little.

Time goes by quite fast, even on miserable days. Always something that can be done. Gordon cut a bunch of slabs today and has the porch nearly enclosed. The porch is twelve feet wide by ten feet long – lots of storage for wood, etc. Keeps everything nice and dry. I built a big fire outside and burnt a lot of the branches left from last year's cabin building.

I tried my hand at baking without using an oven. Made a "Prune Torte" – for lack of a better name. I used bannock mixture, placing it in a pie tin which was then covered with a one and a half inch high lid. Shortly after, I placed a layer of pre-cooked prune mixture over the bannock, replaced the cover and let it cook on the stove. Turned out surprisingly well! It was the first baking we've had since leaving Jamie Lake. Not too sweet, tasted good with afternoon tea. Think it would be even better made with pre-cooked apricots. We did up a bunch of firewood later on – stacking it in the porch. Temperature's about plus one this evening and still not nice – wet snow coming down.

Thursday – Sept. 24th +2C   A miserable morning with a cold wind. We have snow on the ground but it should melt off as soon as the sun shines – I hope!!

At noon, heavy snow showers with a wind – real nasty. Gordon says we're going back to Rose Lake tomorrow. Later, got through to Watson Lake Flying with a message they'll relay to Patti. Thankfully, radio signals came in clearly for a very short time. Gordon finished enclosing the porch this afternoon. We then cut and hauled in a bunch of firewood, both dry and green stuff. Lots of dry wood around here but can't say that for Rose Lake where good, dry wood is scarce.

About five o'clock, Gordon decided our radio antenna should be raised to a higher location. He figured the easy way to get a rope higher, with antenna attached, would be to throw the hammer with rope tied to it, up and over a higher branch. Good plan – great idea. After many repeated attempts, he finally got it just where he wanted it. The only problem was – the hammer got stuck high up amongst the branches!! He used his "short" ladder and, with a long pole in hand, tried to knock the hammer loose. No luck. Next, his plan was to climb the spruce but I objected. Finally, he did manage to knock the hammer down and proudly pulled the antenna up to its new, higher location. By the time everything was finished, we were both soaked and cold. Our reception just better be good after that ordeal. At six forty-five this evening, still windy and snowing lightly. Hope its better by morning.

Friday – Sept. 25th 0C   Can't believe this – still snowing. Solid overcast.

We have between eight and a half to ten and a half inches of snow on the ground. There's ice forming on the shallow edges of the river and a lot of icy slush is floating down. We're going to rush through breakfast and head back down river to Rose Lake. We have warmer clothes there, as well as warmer boots and mitts.

We left Kettle Creek at eleven o'clock with all our meat and what was left of our supplies stashed in the canoe with us. There was a lot of slush floating all across the river but even so made good time, reaching Rose Lake in a little over an hour. I had to paddle just once but only for a very short section. Gordon probably would have made it without my help but I wanted to do my share. Spotted four greyling in one of the back eddies – nice to see. The motor just purred along, no problems whatsoever. About halfway back, Gordon suggested we pull up on shore and build a fire under one of the big spruce so I could warm up. I said no, I wasn't really all that cold. It didn't seem very cold although my hands were a bit chilly since I only had a pair of leather gloves on. I did stick a pair of wool socks in my jacket, thinking that if I needed more on my hands, I'd slip the socks over my gloves. By the time we came around the last bend, it was sure good to see Rose Lake cabin.

After pulling up on shore, the first thing I wanted to do was get a fire going.. That's when I realized I was cold. I had a hard time holding and striking a match. Not much feeling in my hands and I had a hard time to keep from shivering. Gordon was right. We should have stopped for a warm-up. Next time I'll know better. If I'd been much colder or it had taken a bit longer getting here, I don't think I'd have been able to light a fire. With a good fire going, it didn't take long to take the chill off the cabin. Put tea water on as well as a pot of homemade soup that I'd brought from Kettle Creek. After getting thawed out with our hot lunch, we felt much better. There's not quite as much snow on the ground here as there is at Kettle. The sun's even trying to shine but still a lot of low cloud and fog that keeps blocking it out. The mountains northward are nearly all in sight so everything looks a lot brighter. We'll overnight and if the weather does stay good, remain here for a couple more days, getting some work done in preparation for winter. Really doesn't look like it's that far off. We'll have to install that larger window in the cabin and then get in a lot more wood.. Right now, Gordon's outside putting meat up in the cache while I'm making a batch of bannock and a pan of brownies.

Late this afternoon we finished installing the thirty-six by twenty-four inch window in the north wall of our cabin. Now when we're sitting at the table we have a great view of the river and mountains. It also makes it so much brighter in the cabin. Also, I've finally been able to hang the pair of red drapes I'd made. Looks real cozy. Gordon's tired tonight but we both think it's more from mental strain than otherwise. He does get very uptight when the weather changes rapidly from good weather to the really miserable days we've been having lately. We've even been considering, should really wintry weather start this early, that we might go back home since it's a long time to wait until trapping season opens on November first. We had hoped to go after beaver up Kettle Creek but guess not this season. We found the creek had already frozen over in places. We also wanted to cut a few trails from Kettle Creek cabin, especially upriver through the timber and alongside the numerous meadows but guess they'll have to wait until later. If the weather should warm again, we may take a day's jaunt upriver and do some clearing. Sure hope so!! The way the river's starting to freeze, we don't dare take the chance of overnighting at Kettle. One cold night and there'd be ice over most of the shallow stretches, making getting back here by canoe very questionable.

Saturday – Sept. 26ᵗʰ 0C   Its very dull, dismal and foggy out and the start of our third week.   Time has gone by so fast. The day started with some excitement. We'd slept in until nine-fifteen. Gordon was up, just putting the coffee on when Murky started barking. He grabbed his rifle and ran outside to see what was bothering the dog and immediately spotted a bull moose standing on the sandbar just across the river. One shot and we had our winter's meat. From inside the cabin I couldn't see what was happening since there was a number of small spruce blocking my view through the window. Gordon rowed the canoe across to make certain the moose was dead, then bled it and removed the entrails before crossing back for coffee and breakfast. Guess we stay here for at least another day as it's going to take some time butchering the animal and packing the meat to the cache. Murky has sure earned his keep so far – first a wolf and now the moose. Gordon reported it's a large bodied animal – lots of meat. Too bad a plane can't land here so we could send some home for the freezer.

It was mid afternoon before we finally finished cutting up the moose. I even helped skin the animal. My first time!! What a bloody, gory operation – although I'm sure I was of great assistance to Gordon!! We found the moose had one side of his rib cage all bruised from fighting. He wasn't very fat – not like the meat we got from Don. For a "Thank You", I had three ribs cut off and then presented them to Murky. Is he ever going at them – the first bones he's had to chew on since we left Watson Lake. He's really enjoying them. The moose scraps and bones will sure help with our dog food supply, although we do have lots of dried food at Jamie Lake. Until skidoo time, we'd have had to backpack his food whenever we came to Rose Lake. Now he'll have bones, etc. to work on. It will sure be quiet around here in the evenings from now on, not hearing Gordon's lovesick moose calls anymore. My husband, the hunter, just informed me that you "row" a boat – and – you paddle a canoe. He read my notes from this morning where I'd stated, "he rowed the canoe over to check on the moose". Sure picky.

Later this afternoon Gordon installed a three by two foot window in the cabin wall directly across from the window we'd installed yesterday. It's a big improvement over the tiny one that was there before. The new one is great, lets a lot more afternoon sunshine in. While Gordon was hauling meat from across the river with the canoe, I decided to wash the newly installed window. It just didn't come real clean after the first washing. Jamie, you did a first class job of constructing the windows for us but unfortunately, in your haste, you put the dirty side of both panes of glass to the inside. Tomorrow, Gordon's taking it apart and reversing the panes so I can wash them. The other two windows you made for us, now installed, are fine but on this one – You Blew it Jamie!!

Sunday – Sept. 27th 0C   Foggy out – but clearing.

A lot of the snow has melted off and sandbars are nearly all clear. Since the day we returned from Kettle, there hasn't been any slush coming down river. After breakfast Gordon got busy looking after the meat, placing it on poles beneath the cache to cool. We'll be putting it in the cache in another day or so, depending on weather. He's also got repair work to do on the ladder before climbing up it with a moose quarter draped over his shoulder. I helped as much as I could. Fog finally cleared up and just after lunch, sun was shining out of a clear sky. Lovely!! We worked on the interior of the cabin, really re-doing it. Took out the bunks and the little cupboards from the end walls and then finished putting in the floor under the bunk section. I also peeled the logs in that area. They were wet beneath the bark since plywood tacked over them had kept them from drying. Should dry out and be warmer now. In place of the bunks, one above the other, we're putting in one bed – about a queen size. The bed is made in two parts and will make up into a chesterfield. It will be so nice and comfortable to be able to sit back and relax. Plus, the lighting will be much better – especially for reading. Previously, the bottom bunk area had been dark for reading and not handy for sitting since the top bunk didn't allow any head-room. Next trip we'll build cupboards along the end wall.

About four-thirty, took a break from our jobs and headed upriver to Lynx Creek and our favorite fishing hole. We'd only been fishing for a few minutes before Gordon hooked a beautiful Dolly Varden, large enough for two meals. Sure tasted good tonight with Rice-a-roni and peas, then canned fruit with our tea. With the weather clearing up so nicely, we may stay here a couple of days longer. We still have our winter's wood to bring in. Radio reception is fantastic this evening.

Monday – Sept. 28th 0C   Light sprinkling of snow overnight and overcast this morning.

After breakfast we got busy finishing the jobs that should be done right away – especially if it kept snowing. I dug a three foot square by three foot deep garbage pit out back, where we can burn and later bury our refuse. While I was digging, Gordon was busy getting the moose hind quarters ready for hanging under the cache. He looped a rope over one of the base logs atop the cache then tied one end to a moose quarter. Next, grasping the other end of the rope and with a lot of pulling, yanking and slipping managed to haul the quarter up and tie it above the reach of animals. After we'd hoisted up the two hind quarters they were covered with sacking to keep birds away. The two front quarters were suspended from a tree leaning out over the river. When the river freezes, they'll be a good twelve feet above the ice surface, well beyond the reach of bears or wolves. After that job was done, Gordon was busy installing new asphalt roof-ing on the cabin. While he was nailing it down I was busy checking and replac-ing chinking in the cabin walls – especially around the newly installed win-dows. A lot of the old chinking had fallen out where it hadn't been tamped in properly. We got through to Watson Lake Flying at noon and were advised that Patti is moving to Whitehorse on October 4th. Also were advised that the whole country is fogged in.

While having tea, about four-thirty, we looked out the window and saw it had started to snow. I casually remarked to Gordon that it would be wet walking to Jamie Lake tomorrow. His reply was "Let's go now" The next few minutes were a mad rush – getting essentials loaded in our packs, deciding how much meat to take, disconnecting the radio transmitter, etc., etc. It wasn't long before we closed the cabin door and with packs on our backs, rifles in hand, headed down the trail for Jamie Lake. Checking my watch, I was surprised to note it already was past five o'clock. We'd tried to keep our loads reasonable but Gordon, just ahead of me, had a pretty good load. Besides his pack, loaded with backstraps from the moose and other gear, he had the radio transmitter – a heavy thing, as well as his .270 Winchester rifle. I had my hiking boots, the moose tenderloins plus other odds and ends in my pack in addition to the .22 rifle slung over my shoulder.

The first part was tough slugging since we had to go through brush – no real trail – to reach the ravine. We do plan on cutting a trail through there eventually. Beyond the ravine we had to cross several swamps. When it started snowing heavier, Gordon remarked he was sure glad we decided to head for Jamie Lake. My pack kept getting heavier and heavier and finally, about three-quarters of the way, I gave in and handed the .22 rifle to Gordon. My back was aching from a lot of uphill going. The climbing was hard on me, even though it was a gentle incline. With the sky clouded over and snow falling, darkness fell quite early. Footing was treacherous with snow covering the tree roots. At one point I slipped into a hole with one foot, right up to my knee, then couldn't pull my foot out without first removing it from the boot. Then I had to yank to get my boot out.

The snow kept getting deeper the closer we got to Jamie Lake. Gordon was becoming concerned about the cabin and cache after spotting wolverine tracks in front of us heading right down the trail. If a wolverine got inside the cabin it would make a terrible mess of our winter supplies. We finally reached the cabin about eight-thirty. It had taken us a good four hours of tough hiking. I don't think I could have walked another step – at least it seemed that way. We turned on our propane light, got the fire going and just rested for awhile. Later we had hot tea with bacon and eggs – first fresh eggs in two weeks, then to bed. Dirty dishes can wait till morning.

Tuesday – Sept. 29th -1C   Believe it or not but I lived through yesterday. I didn't sleep all that well – my body was just so sore but feels better this morning. And guess what – the sun is shining and it's a beautiful day!!

It's especially good to be back "home" to more supplies. Even so, while having breakfast this morning, we both decided that we like it better at the river. It's much opener and the scenery is so much nicer. We're just going to relax today. We've worked steadily since arriving eighteen days ago, actually haven't had a break since finishing haying on our farm. I think we deserve a day of rest. When we were walking back yesterday in the dark, the though that entered my mind was "And we have two more months of this". Would you believe, after all that, this morning we're already discussing next year!!

Took things real easy today – we're both tired. Gordon boiled traps and cleaned up the porch, then covered the cache with a new tarp. I puttered away inside the cabin – baked buns, cinnamon rolls and a big pot of vegetable soup – this time with fresh vegetables.

Wednesday – Sept. 30th -2C   Clear and sunny again – another lovely day.

Snow has pretty well all melted so we decided at breakfast to take our lunch, hike over to the big meadow west of here and spend the day just loafing around, glassing for game. About an hour later we took off, much to Murky's disgust. Gordon had his pack with our lunch and tea pail plus his ever present rifle. Never know what you may run into out here. At this time of year there's the occasional bad-tempered bear wandering around. Not enough fat on their bodies for hibernating and little chance of putting more on with shrubs and berries pretty well finished. Anyway, we hiked over to the meadow and up to a knoll that overlooks miles of open country. Under a couple of big spruce, we piled pine needles for comfortable seats, sat down with backs against the trunk and just enjoyed the view. With the sun beating on us, it was warm and so very comfortable. Gordon did a lot of glassing with his binoculars and spotted three small herds of caribou. No moose showed. We made a small fire for tea and toasted sandwiches at lunch time. Then we both fell asleep. Relaxing in the warm sunshine, it was impossible to keep your eyes open. Just after four in the afternoon we headed back to the cabin and Murky. A really restful and totally enjoyable day.

Thursday   Oct. 1ˢᵗ -4C   Another sunny morning although a bit cooler. No wind so it's really not cold and with the sun, will warm up quite rapidly.

After breakfast, we packed our lunch and with rifle and chainsaw, took off up Jamie Run for our Super Highway, then past the creek and on to the Coal River. We decided to cut a skidoo trail through the patches of willow and buck-brush to connect with Wolf Run so we could avoid traveling on the river ice for about two and a half miles. That stretch of the river had given us so much trouble with overflow. Seems we were always getting the skidoo stuck. Trail cutting turned out to be surprisingly easy. There wasn't much cutting required to connect one open area with another. After it was cleared, we found it only took a few minutes to cross the new section and reach the river. We then decided it was time for our lunch break. Gordon built a small fire on the river bank beneath the spreading branches of a very large spruce. A short time later we were stretched out on the ground, backs against the spruce, enjoying tea and toasted sandwiches. It was gorgeous out – sunny and warm.

On our way back and just a couple of hundred feet from where the trail crossed the creek, there was a heavier stand of willows that we had to cut through in order to join up with our old trail. Sure enough, just about finished when the chain jumped off the chainsaw bar. Then we discovered that my "Dear Hus-band??" had forgotten to bring along the chainsaw tools. After a lot of work, he finally got the chain back on the bar but it was far too loose. Rather than take a chance on wrecking the saw, we felt it was better to leave the saw, oil and gas under a tree and finish that section another day. We then headed for home.

We had a scrumptious dinner tonight. Tenderloin of moose smothered in mushrooms, potatoes and carrots and a bowl of coleslaw with radishes, apple, carrots and onion. It was delicious. Tonight we're just sitting back, listening to the radio and reading – relaxing. Nice!!

Friday – Oct. 2nd +1   Snowed during the night and it's still coming down. Winter seems to be upon us early this year.

About ten-thirty, we were back down Jamie run to where we left the saw yesterday. A couple of minutes with the proper tool and the saw was running. It only took another ten minutes to finish clearing that patch of willow to connect up with our old trail. On our way back to Jamie Lake we rerouted the trail in a couple of places – cut out a couple of sharp turns. It was cloudy and very wet – not a bit nice working outside. By the time we got back to the cabin, three and a half hours had elapsed and we were both soaked. But now, we do have a great trail leading to the river and on to Wolf Run. After lunch, while Gordon was outside cutting more firewood, I baked a delicious cherry pie and a pan of bran muffins.

Saturday – Oct 3rd +2C   Woke up during the night to see stars shining from a clear sky. Cloud must have moved off after we'd gone to bed. This morning we awoke to another surprise – heavy snow coming down.

Sure looks like winter – almost enough snow in some places for the skidoo. Last evening I went to bed with a sore throat and sniffles and I'm still all stuffed up this morning – not pleasant. Just as the coffee started perking, Gordon raced out of the cabin saying the dog was loose. Instead of the dog, he was met by a large, bristly porcupine in the porch. Wonder who was more surprised!! Porky ran out, dog barked like mad while Gordon was trying to get his boots on. By the time he got outside, the porcupine was half way to the lake – still going strong. He'll be safe enough if he keeps away from here. Murky has a habit of trying to take a bite out of porcupines and always ends up with a mouthful of quills. Not a happy time for him while they're being yanked out with pliers. What a way to start a morning. Later, talked to Watson Lake Flying. Today is Patti's last day of work in the bank at Watson Lake. Snow is very wet so we'll be doing things around the cabin today. It's much too wet to check trails or do any cutting. Gordon did go out and cut more wood – he likes to keep the supply up. Much easier cutting it now than later when there's three feet of snow on the ground. I was busy doing laundry and just lazing around.

This afternoon is still very wet with more rain than snow – a real slushy mixture. Gordon's now making cubbies (trap-boxes that are set in trees) out of pieces of scrap plywood that were lying about. He had made up a bunch of them, about fifty, before leaving home but the plane was so loaded that they had to be left behind. These cubbies really work well and are easy to set. After finishing up, he came inside where we drank tea and played cards until suppertime. Signals are good this evening, really excellent reception so we listened to a program of old-time music.

Sunday – Oct. 4th +2C   Solid fog – and I mean solid fog!! You can't see a thing. Hope it clears so we can go somewhere today.

Today is Patti's last day at Watson Lake and I miss her already. It cleared up a little by lunchtime so decided to go to the Beaver Meadow to see what the beaver had been up to. When we got to the meadow we found it all under water. The beaver had built a high dam across the creek, flooding the entire area. There were several active houses we'd hoped to take a couple of beaver from today but the weather said – NO!! After the fog cleared off, the sky clouded over, it got real windy and then the rain poured down. We turned and headed for home over that rough trail, soaked through. Not a pleasant trip. With all the meadow flooded and hopefully freezing later, it should be good for skidooing. Because of the dam, water in the creek is very deep this year.

By the time we reached the cabin we were soaked through from head to toe and pretty chilled. Was sure nice reaching a warm place and changing into dry clothes. Later, we again had tenderloin, potatoes and vegetables for dinner. We also had a delicious dessert tonight. This afternoon I tried creating a new dessert using my blueberry jam. I added a bit more water to the jam and placed it on the stove to heat. Next, a half cup of bannock mixture was added, along with a little sugar. The new creation was left to steam for a few minutes. Shortly after, we tried my new masterpiece. It was good, so good that we've decided not to use the blueberry jam as jam but keep it just for these desserts. We don't have too many varieties of dessert out here – especially ones that can be made so easily on top of the stove. I now wish I'd had more time earlier to pick more berries.

Monday – Oct. 5th *+5C*   After a rainy night it looks as though we'll have a gorgeous day. Clear and sunny.

We had planned on going to Rose Lake for a few days but Gordon changed his mind a short while later. He didn't trust the weather when the sky began to cloud over. Instead, we went up Canyon Run and fixed cubbies. Walked down to the river at one place, hoping to get a beaver or two but found the houses and dam had washed away. Had a leisurely lunch under a big spruce and then came home. On the way back, we managed to get one grouse. During our jaunt the cloud had cleared off and it turned into a very nice day. So much for predictions!!

Later, while enjoying our dinner, Murky started barking and whining again, the third time since we'd returned. Gordon grabbed his rifle and stepped outside. Facing him, only a few steps away from the cabin, was a big bull moose. Several minutes passed while they stared at each other. Finally, the moose turned and trotted off, heading towards the meadow east of here. Gordon took off running down the trail, just reaching trees bordering the open meadow as the moose walked out in the open, grunting – calling for a lonely female. Gordon grunted back, imitating another bull, whereupon the bull started threshing his horns against the brush, preparing for a fight. Just about then Murky, back at the cabin, and hearing the moose call, started whining. Anyway, that scared the moose off. He turned and sauntered across the meadow and into the trees on the opposite side. Gordon figured that if Murky had kept quiet, he probably could have talked that bull right up to the cabin and in for dinner. While all this was going on I had remained inside the cabin. I thought it was another wolf causing all the excitement and missed it all.

Tuesday – Oct. 6th -3C   A bit cooler than yesterday and a little cloudy. It rained during the night so should have melted some of the snow.

Mid-morning, we went for a walk to the meadow, curious as to where that moose had gone yesterday. We must have covered at least three miles of rough going, tracking him, before finally returning to the cabin around eleven-thirty. We had decided to head for Rose Lake and so, after a quick lunch, with packs on our backs headed down that trail. Took us a bit over three hours of steady going to reach the river and Rose Lake cabin.

Shortly after getting here, it got very windy, clouded over and started snowing – just showers. Nonetheless, snow soon covered the ground. First off, we checked our meat and were pleased to find that nothing had bothered it. Gordon did discover the meat Don had given us had started to spoil. They had de-boned it for easier packing on horses but, being all cut up, it just wasn't keeping well. Also, temperatures were still relatively warm when we got the meat from them. Will have to trim it tomorrow and save what we can. Nothing other than ravens had visited the remains of our moose on the sandbar. Next, we got busy cutting and stacking wood since there wasn't much on hand. Dry wood has to be cut quite a distance from the cabin since there just aren't dead trees anywhere nearby. Later, after supper, Gordon built cupboards.

Wednesday – Oct. 7ʰ -3C   Ground is white this morning. Wind died down overnight and a bit foggy.

Poor radio signals this morning. We were able to hear Jim, at Watson Lake Flying, but he couldn't read us. Did hear that Watson Lake weather is down in rain and snow. We have fog but its lifting and the sun's shining above – may yet be a nice day. After breakfast we headed out, hoping to find a trail from here to the string of sloughs just past the ravine, on the way to Jamie Lake. We'd like to find a route that would be good for winter skidoo travel. Travel along the creek ice from here to the ravine is often impossible when it's covered with overflow. We eventually did find a route for our trail, after a lot of wandering about. The sun didn't appear and with a low, foggy overcast, it was hard to keep directions straight. We also checked out a series of swamps in the area, hoping they could be connected with the meadow just to the south of Rose Lake cabin. We followed a lot of different swamps, where going was tough, before Gordon finally decided we'd better backtrack and finish another day. With no sun and that kind of terrain with no landmarks, it would have been easy to get confused. We finally ended up blazing a trail from the ravine to the cabin. It's a lot shorter than the old way, following the creek. Tomorrow we'll come back and clear the brush from it. We're pretty certain we know how to connect up with those swamps we were checking today but will wait for a sunnier time before blazing a trail to them. A route through the swamps, avoiding the creek and also the ravine, would be especially good for a skidoo trail.

After we got back to the cabin, Gordon took the Spitfire skidoo down and got it all ready to go. This afternoon and evening were beautiful. Cleared up completely but the temperature is sure dropping fast – down to minus nine when we checked, just before going to bed.

Thursday – Oct. 8ʰ -4C   Fogged in overnight. Must have clouded over since temperature is warmer this morning.

A lot of slush coming downriver so it's definitely the end of our canoe travel for this year. Later in the morning it started snowing lightly, just as we were leaving to clear the trail we'd blazed to the ravine yesterday. It didn't take us all that long to clear the trail since there were only a few willows and not too many small swamp spruce to cut and throw out of the way. Sure will be a lot easier traveling, either walking or skidooing now that we don't have to travel along the creek. Snowing very heavily this afternoon. After finishing the new trail, we returned to the cabin for hot coffee. Later, while Gordon was out cutting more wood, I sorted supplies in the cabin and started preparing supper. Late evening, were surprised to see how the weather had again changed. Temperature had warmed up to plus two and it was raining.

Friday – Oct. 9th -2C A gorgeous, sunny, not a cloud in the sky morning. A lot of warmth in the sun – feels nice.

Slush and ice still coming down river. After finishing breakfast, got through to Watson Lake Flying. Really surprised at how good signals are this year. Trees and brush are all covered with beads of water from snow melting on their branches. When you touch a branch, you're immediately doused in a cold shower so we're waiting until they dry a bit before going exploring. We've decided to stay at the river for another day even though we're short of coffee. Just have to tough it out!! The mountains, covered with snow, are especially beautiful with the sun shining on them. Had a visitor on our antenna pole – a raven. He wasn't the least bit afraid. Sassy, squawking after he finished feeding on meat scraps across the river.

At three-fifteen, our thermometer read plus twelve. It's just a gorgeous day. No more slush coming down river so we're still able to use the canoe. After finishing with our tea, we took the canoe and went a short distance up river. We wanted to check out the possibility of clearing a trail across a big bend on the river. If a trail was feasible, it would shorten our winter route by close to a mile. As it turned out, we didn't reach the opposite side of the bend where we wanted to so will have to try again later. While checking for a shortcut, we did find a number of small swamps and sloughs we could follow part way, reducing the amount of trail clearing that would be required. On our way back down river, tried fishing at our favorite spot but no luck. We had also brought along a big chunk of moose bone with hide still attached, which we stashed in the brush along Lynx creek – hoping that marten will be lured to that site. After getting back to the cabin, Gordon cut more wood and then boiled a bunch of traps in readiness for the coming season.

Saturday – Oct.10th -8C Br-r-r, cool this morning. Just a few clouds so looks like a nice day.

Gordon thinks it was much colder during the night because it was completely clear at bedtime. Sky had clouded over a little by this morning. Lots and lots of ice and slush on the river this morning. Marten creek froze over during the night. Definitely no more canoe travel. Going back to Jamie Lake this morning. Talked to Watson Lake Flying – they reported weather is good all over, clear skies. It's now been four weeks since we arrived on our trapline and everything is going great.

We got back to Jamie Lake about two-thirty. Had Murky pull the small toboggan loaded with a bunch of meat. Saved us doing a lot of back packing. He was starting to get played out by the time we reached here. Poor Pooch. He actually likes being in harness. When he spots the harness being taken down, he starts jumping and whining until you put it on him – then it's just tail-wagging. He's a good dog. On our way back, Gordon fixed up a number of cubbies along the trail. The new trail we'd cut to the ravine was great, only took us half an hour to get there instead of the hour it used to take us, following the creek. The weather was gorgeous – sunny, making an altogether enjoyable trip.

When we first entered the cabin, I was horrified when I spotted a real mess by the cupboard. We'd left a quantity of cheese and mixed pie dough in dishes on the floor since they'd remain cooler down there. Guess a mouse had decided my pie dough was great. It had shredded all the wax paper covering the dough, then nibbled on it – the beggar!! When Gordon was putting on his low rubbers that he uses for slippers, he found more dough stored in them. Further checking also revealed pastry dough stashed in his high-top rubber boots. That wasn't the end. Checking his pillow, he found more dough under and in it and also caches of pie dough inside his sleeping bag.

I can't figure out why it was all in his belongings and not mine. Perhaps it's because he's always saying my pastry is the greatest. The soft-hearted mouse had saved it just for him to enjoy rather than eating it. Talk about a sacrifice!! Gordon's first remarks when reaching the cabin were – "We're back to the land of groceries and goodies". It's too bad a floatplane can't land at the river so we could have a good supply of groceries at the Rose Lake cabin. We can backpack so little from here because of the distance. Once we get snow we can haul more over with the skidoo. If we do decide to return next year – meaning, if we decide before leaving here this winter, we'll radio out and have the supplies flown to Rose Lake when we're picked up in December. That way we'll have supplies waiting there for us next fall, saving a lot of packing.

We've had several discussions regarding returning next year. Gordon was much more vocal than I about the possibility of trying out different ways of spending our fall and winter seasons. One idea was to go to the Okanagan area, picking and doing up some fruits. At the same time we could visit relatives and friends then return to Watson Lake to spend more winter time at home. He claims he has a very guilty conscience about having me here – away from everything. I do miss our home with its conveniences – especially contact with the family. I miss that very much and am forever thinking of the kids, wondering how they're doing. But, it was more my idea to be here than Gordon's. I know how much he enjoys this life and I'm glad I can now help him enjoy it even more. I do have a guilty feeling about his having to do so much heavy work alone. Even now when I'm here, there are times I can't help him or he just won't let me.

Trapping can be a very lonely life at times with quite a lot of heavy work.

You're always busy getting trails ready, cutting winter's wood, winterizing cabins, scouting for fur sign, but – it's also a very rewarding life and never boring. Pure air – no contamination of any kind, quiet and peaceful and most times relaxing. Most important, a chance to just be together again, enjoying each other's company. You're all alone in the wilderness, completely independent from outside resources but at the same time, completely dependent on each other. It makes you realize just how much your partner means to you. Which life is better?? I don't know. I'll just have to wait and see. Guess we'll have to try a trip south someplace and then perhaps we'll have the answer. Oh, oh – just found pie dough in Gordon's new winter boots – those mice sure favor him.

Sunday – Oct.11ᵗʰ +3C   High cloud and a col-l-l-d wind.

Finished breakfast and decided to wander over to Beaver Meadow – maybe get some grouse. We found most of the creek and pond the beavers had dammed were frozen over. Even so, it was great just sitting under a spruce tree with a fire going, tea water boiling and lunch – hamburgers made from moose tenderloin. Were they ever good served in bannock. A while later we walked further up the creek to check two other beaver houses and discovered that some animal had pulled them apart – undoubtedly killing the beaver. Gordon thinks it was done this past spring, likely by a wolverine. We couldn't get to the other side of the meadow because dams had flooded the entire area and so headed back home.

Really warm tonight. At eight in the evening it is still plus eight, the stars are shining and the snow is just mush.

Monday – Oct. 12ᵗʰ +3C   It's a month ago that we arrived here. This morning is just beautiful – warm and sunny – not a cloud to be seen.

After breakfast we went up Jamie run to our Super Highway leading to the river. Instead of branching off down our new route, we left our packs at the junction and followed an old trail further up the hill that Gordon and Jamie had used five years previously when they'd trapped using snowshoes – no skidoo.

He wanted to pick up the traps that were left hanging in trees all these past years. After collecting traps, we climbed down to the river and just sat in the sun – the scenery was so nice. Afterwards, hiked back to collect our packs and walked down to the creek in the meadow below, made a fire and had lunch. Later, Gordon climbed to another high point, hoping to spot caribou. No luck so we headed for home, reaching the cabin just after five. We were both very tired. We've come to the conclusion that high- top rubber boots are not ideal for long walks. They have played us out and, besides, wearing them bothers my back.

Tonight we're having leftover spaghetti from the large batch I made last night. Just hope it gets colder so the rest will keep. Must have warmed up to at least five Celsius or higher today. Not the greatest temperature for keeping meat.

Tuesday – Oct. 13th -2C   Thanksgiving day. A gorgeous day again.

We're taking the day off to just do odd jobs around the cabin – after we finish our leisurely breakfast and an extra cup of coffee. Later, Gordon worked outside while I did a bit of laundry and a bunch of baking – apple pies, bran muffins and brownies. Gordon got the new skidoo all gassed up, ready to go. Then he replaced a window in the cabin with a larger, forty-two by thirty-six inch one – nearly double the size of the previous one. Gives us more of a view and lets in a lot more light. It's too bad we don't have another one of that size to replace the one in the other wall.

Beautiful full moon tonight – northern lights dancing across the sky. Quite a sight!!

Wednesday – Oct. 14th +4C   After such a beautiful evening, the sky had to cloud over and rain most of the night.

Still cloudy this morning and damp outside. After installing the window yesterday, the cupboards were full of sawdust and chips so we busied ourselves washing all the shelves and dusting off the canned goods. Then I lined the shelves with oilcloth – sure a great improvement. Gordon cleaned the wall logs behind the stove and then sprayed them with fire retardant. He has enough retardant to do the wall behind the stove in one more cabin but not enough for both Rose and Kettle. Later after lunch, went for a walk up Jamie run to our lookout point overlooking the river and meadows, hoping to see caribou. No luck – seems they haven't yet started coming through this fall. Most of the snow has melted – just the odd patch left in shaded areas.

Thursday – Oct.15th +3C   Can't believe the change in our weather from the latter part of September.   Rained all night and very dull looking this morning. Be nice if we were up river again, finishing jobs at the Kettle Creek cabin. Murky isn't feeling well – something seems to be bothering him as he just lies in his house. Hope it's not serious – poor pup. After breakfast Gordon dug a garbage pit and then later, we went for a walk to the lookout point overlooking the river. Basically a lazy day. Raining again tonight.

Friday – Oct. 16th +5C   Overcast and warm. Great temperatures but not for trappers. We need the ponds, meadows and creeks frozen over for easier hiking.

This morning we went for a walk up River Run to the small meadow, about half an hour away. We brought the chainsaw along since we wanted to do a bit of re-routing of the trail. Right now the trail goes straight up and over the top of a steep hill. After clearing brush and small trees, we managed to reroute it around the hill and rejoin the old trail on the other side. A big improvement but sure took a lot of work clearing the way. Last time over the trail, when we were heading for the river and Rose Lake, we discovered a very large tree had fallen across the trail, completely blocking it.

The spruce had an unbelievably large root system which had also been uprooted, along with the earth and moss covering it. The moss-covered root system now stood upright, large enough to supply the wall for a good-sized cabin, if you were to build there. Anyway, we had to reroute our trail to avoid that blockage. Naturally, we had to cut the trail around it through an area with lots of willow but finally got it completed. Great!! While there, we also found the remains of a caribou that wolves had killed. Only thing left was a good-sized piece of hide so we don't know if the kill was made there or in the brush further away. Murky did find a part of the leg which he proudly carried over to us for our examination before chewing and eventually burying it. We couldn't find any other remains, which is not unusual. The leftovers are usually worked over and carried off within a very short time.

Saturday – Oct. 17ᵗʰ 0C Cloudy and a little cooler today.

We're pleased the temperature has dropped a bit as we were concerned about our meat. With it being so damp and warm, we worried it might spoil. Meat keeps quite well at temperatures above freezing but only if the air is relatively dry. It's been five weeks, today, since we arrived. This morning I finished one side of the sweater I've been knitting. Looks good. Also have half of the other side done. Gordon's busy working on our wood supply this morning. Afternoon, we went for a walk up to the second lake to check the ice – still patches of open water. This evening we played chess and I finally beat Gordon. I think he set me up to win but he claims not.

Sunday – Oct.18ᵗʰ -1C Light snow overnight and still coming down – very lightly.

We had some excitement during the night. When Murky started barking a second time, Gordon was up like a shot to check on what was bothering him but couldn't see anything in the dark He was sure there must be a wolf prowling around. When it got light this morning, he found tracks showing that a caribou that had been chased by a pack of five or six wolves. The caribou had detoured to pass the cabin by about forty feet whereas the wolves had kept right on the trail and passed within a couple of feet of us. From tracks in the snow, you could tell where the wolves had stopped, then sniffed the cabin walls before urinating on them. Tracks indicated that the wolves had each taken a turn splashing sign on the wall while we were lying in our bunks on the other side. We were a maximum distance of eighteen inches from them. Talk about contempt for humans!! After examining the cabin, the wolves continued following the caribou down the trail to the meadow east of here. After breakfast, Gordon is going to follow their trail to see if they caught the caribou. Later, when he checked as far as the east side of the meadow, there were no signs to show they'd caught up to it. Just hope they don't pull it down but chances are pretty good that they'll have a caribou dinner whenever they feel like it. I wouldn't want to be that animal.

After lunch we took off for our Canyon Run, backtracking along the trail the caribou and wolves had followed during the night. Good to get out for a walk, even though it was very damp. Snow on the trail hadn't melted so tracks made by animals really showed up. Followed the trail back for a couple of miles to where the caribou and wolves had first reached it, then turned around and headed back to the cabin. Quite chilly with it being so damp. Next time I'll wear something warmer.

Monday – Oct. 19th -1C Foggy – but the sun is trying to break through.

First thing after coffee, tried calling Watson Lake Flying but signals out. Then we took our time over breakfast. We've finally reached the point where we can relax – take things easy until trapping season starts. Mid morning, fog had dissipated and the sun was shining out of a cloudless sky. We packed a lunch and went for a leisurely hike up Ridge Run and then kept on going for a few more miles, as far as the swampy sections of the trail. It was gorgeous out. Saw lots of wolf sign along the way. We were surprised and disappointed to see all the ice had melted off the other lakes but should have expected it, being so warm. With all the snow and rain we've had, low areas on our trail were full of water and the ground was just so soggy. Later after reaching the spruce, actually three of them, where we usually stop for a break, we got a fire going and put the tea pail full of water on to heat. Before, when trail clearing, we'd always wanted to stop at this particular spot for a break but never seemed to have the time. Always seemed there were other priorities. We did take a small swede saw along today for clearing any small trees that might have blown down across the trail but the chainsaw was left at home. It turned out being a very relaxing and enjoyable day.

Tuesday – Oct. 20th +1C We're fogged in this morning but a bit of a breeze blowing so hopefully it will clear.

These temperatures sure aren't doing our "ice making" any good. Everything has thawed again. At this rate we'll not be using the waterways for skidoo travel. Still no radio contact. Today is Gordon's sixty-first birthday. Later in the morning, got through to Don Taylor at Stewart Lake to relay a message through to Watson Lake for me. Just before noon the fog cleared off and we had lovely sunshine again. It turned into such a beautiful day that right after lunch we decided to go for a walk up Jamie Run, all the way to the river. We were hoping to see caribou but lack of sign showed they haven't come through this area yet. We did see occasional tracks from stragglers so one day soon the main herd should be on the move. It'll be quite a sight. It was very wet walking, ground is super-saturated.

Had a nice birthday supper for Gordon. I shed a few tears at supper when presenting him with a gift and cards from Patti and Jamie. It was touching. Made me so homesick and lonesome for the family. Gordon was surprised to receive gifts, trying to figure out how I'd kept them hidden all this time. Sky remained clear this evening and later, with a full moon, was just beautiful.

Wednesday – Oct. 21st -2C Didn't get as cold as we'd hoped it would with the clear sky last night. The sky clouded over by morning and right now we're having light snow.

Shortly after breakfast the snow stopped falling, sky partially cleared and the temperature climbed to plus four. Not good for making ice. Jamie Lake only has a little ice around the edges and none over the rest of the lake. Went for a walk up Canyon Run just to see if we could spot any tracks. All we found was one marten and one squirrel track. We'd come looking too soon after the snow-fall this morning. By the time we headed back, most of the snow had melted. Oh well, it was a nice walk. At the rate the snow has been accumulating, we'll never be able to use our skidoo's. The weather has really been super for every-one except the trappers. We decided that if the weather is decent tomorrow with a below freezing temperature, we'll head for Rose Lake in the morning to check that everything's OK. On our return trip, we'll bring back more moose meat..

Thursday – Oct. 22nd +2C   Something is wrong – we got cold and snow in September and now that it should be colder, with snow – it's pouring rain.

The ground is cold enough that the rain doesn't melt the snow. Bet it will be very icy out. I can just picture the highways in this weather, probably solid sheets of ice. There's certainly no trip to Rose Lake in this rain. Thank good-ness we're snug as a bug in a rug in this cabin. Just have to relax, drink coffee and read or play cards. Don Taylor tried calling us last night on forty-four-forty-one frequency. We could hear him clearly but he couldn't read our trans-mission. Called him this morning on the Watson Lake channel, forty-four-forty-six, and got through. Rechecked our other channel and again found it not work-ing. Must be a faulty crystal. We won't be able to call in each evening and report on the regular sched he's set up for people in the bush or even call and talk to other trappers. Some of the conversations and comments are very interesting and informative. It's nice to learn how other trappers are doing

Friday – Oct. 23rd 0C   Surprise, surprise – it's sunny out and after we finish a quick breakfast we're heading for Rose Lake.

I got my sweater finished last night – all that's left to do is sewing the pieces together. Looks nice! Before we left, Gordon went to retrieve his heavy mitts from the box under the bunk where his extra heavy clothing is stored and

– guess what?? More pie dough!! Those mice sure favored him – thank goodness.

We reached Rose Lake about two o'clock. A great trip, sunny and warm and altogether gorgeous – really enjoyed hiking along our trail. We were astounded to find the river free of ice – none at all, not even any slush. There wasn't even any snow on the sandbars. Temperature, in the sun, was up to plus sixteen Celsius – just great. And last year, on the twenty-third of October, it was minus ten. Such a switch-around from the last part of September. Coming over, we saw lots and lots of wolf tracks following our trail on Ridge Run. Come November first, we'll have to get snares out and catch a few. Across the river on the sandbar, nothing was left of our moose kill. Everything had been eaten or dragged off, with the exception of the hide. Some animal had also been able to pull down a piece of meat we'd left hanging beneath one of the caches. Wolverine tracks all around so pretty sure who's responsible. Gordon can't figure out how they could reach the meat – a real puzzle.

Saturday – Oct. 24th +1C   After such a beautiful day and evening, we couldn't believe it – awaking during the night to the sound of pouring rain.

Still pouring down when we got up and had breakfast – not much reason to rush this morning. It kept on raining all day so we just worked around the cabin finishing up the small jobs that had always been put off for another time. It was just so wet outside, we'd have been soaked within minutes if we tried cutting wood or doing other outdoor jobs. A lazy day with lots of reading and relaxing. Still raining when we went to bed. What a change from yesterday.

Sunday – Oct. 25th +1C   Fogged in solid – rather depressing but at least it's not raining.

Nothing more to do at Rose Lake so after breakfast we packed our gear and headed back on the trail for Jamie Lake. Just as we were leaving, the fog started lifting and the sun broke through. Even so, it was wet out – everything from the needles on the spruce to twigs protruding into the trail were covered with water droplets, waiting in anticipation for an unsuspecting soul to brush them. Looked lovely, like hanging jewels shining in the sun. But, brush them ever so gently and immediately receive a cold shower. The ground was completely saturated, water lying in every depression. Should make for good skidooing if it ever freezes up.   The rivers, creeks and lakes have all risen from the snow and rain. Some meadows we'd walked through during the early part of September had been totally dry but now it's hard finding an area you can cross without getting your high-top boots filled. Gordon noticed that Marten Creek had risen more than two inches overnight. It was like a skating rink outside the cabin at Rose Lake this morning. Very treacherous walking. When we'd gone to Rose Lake two days previously, we'd noticed the four lakes on our route had ice on them. They were totally clear of ice today. We sure hope it freezes and snows before the start of trapping, November first. We've seen very few marten tracks but without snow, you just can't spot them.

Got back to Jamie Lake mid-afternoon after a slow trip. We did stop around noon to build a fire and make tea to go with our sandwiches. Even after all the rain and the wet snow we've had, it was still dry at our favorite stopping place. Our fire's built beneath the spreading boughs of a very large spruce. The boughs shed the rain and snow, always keeping the piles of pine needles we sit on, dry. A real nice, comfortable place for a break. Most of the way, the brush was so very wet. You had to knock water off the branches with a stick or barge ahead, taking showers of ice-cold water. Gordon opted for the stick – Sissy!! Even so, we were both soaked by the time we reached the cabin. Nice to get inside, get a fire going, warm up and then change into dry clothes.

Monday – Oct. 26th -2C   Drizzled last night but turned to snow by morning.

This morning we discovered we have between one and two inches of snow on the ground. After breakfast, went for a walk down Jamie Run to the river to see if we could catch a couple of fish but never even got a bite. Ernie Leach, another trapper, had reported last night via radio that he'd been catching fish in the Hyland River. He must be a better fisherman than we are. We noticed, crossing the creeks, that they're all very muddy. You'd never make coffee with that water!! Even the river water was not clear but definitely not as cloudy as the creeks. Must be why we never caught a fish?? Good excuse anyway.

Tuesday – Oct. 27th -8C   Got colder this morning – that should help freeze up things. It's not nice out though – a nasty wind.

Nice and warm in our cabin – especially with that last cup of coffee. Today everyone in Canada is supposed to turn their clocks back one hour. We're going to be different and remain on the old time. We feel we lose an hour of daylight if we make the change. We hitched Murky to the toboggan and went for a walk down River Run. He's so out of shape that we have him pull a bit heavier load each day, trying to get him in shape for work he may have to do later on. It will also make it easier for him when running behind the skidoo. It was good walking. Trail was firm underfoot since all water-soaked leaves, etc. had frozen.

Once we crossed the meadow and entered the timber where we were out of the wind, it was quite pleasant. Reaching the river, we found a lot of ice floating downstream – quite a change from yesterday. About half way to the river, we noticed where a small band of caribou – only five or six animals had gone by, crossing our trail. Looks like they're on the move so hope we're lucky enough to see the next group. Hiked back home mid-afternoon. We all enjoyed the outing – even Murky. This evening the temperature started dropping and by five o'clock, it was down to minus ten. Half an hour later it was sitting at minus twelve. Tonight, it's finally going to get cold, we hope!!

Wednesday – Oct. 28t -20C   WOW – what a change in temperature – but it's beautiful out – sunny with not a cloud in the sky.

This temperature should sure help freeze things up. Hope it doesn't get too much colder this year – last years minus forty-five was a bit much. Because it was such a gorgeous, sunny day, we decided to go for a walk up Canyon Run with Murky and his toboggan. All the water-filled dips in the trail were frozen and the dry snow made for easy walking. Murky's toboggan needed little help sliding along. When we reached the creek flowing through the meadow at the end of the run we, rather Gordon, decided we wanted to cross the creek. The ice wasn't solid enough to support us so he cut down a spruce tree, threw it across the creek and away we went. We fixed up a few, actually four, trap cubbies over on the other side. Another four days and we can set them – I can hardly wait. Still not many tracks to be seen but with our getting snow just a couple of days ago we didn't really expect to spot many. Jamie Lake finally froze over last night – about two weeks later than last year.

Thursday – Oct. 29th -25C   Temperature has certainly dropped – hope it's not a repeat of last year's minus forty temperatures.

Despite the temperature it's gorgeous outside, especially to the west-south-west where the mountains, lit by the rising sun, have turned a lovely pink. After breakfast, we plan on going scouting towards Beaver Meadows. We're pretty certain that water in the ponds and throughout the area should be frozen by now. The creek ice would still be questionable, especially after remembering a couple of very deep holes around the dam. Up to now, we've not been able to cross the creek and check the meadow beyond because of flooding around the dam. About an hour later we were on our way, accompanied by a happy, tail-wagging Murky. With the ground frozen solid, the going was great. When we reached the creek and even though the ice looked safe, we dropped a couple of small spruce across – just in case. Crossed on the trees with no trouble then continued up the string of meadows for a long way. We saw many tracks made yesterday plus a couple that had just been made. With the tall grass in the meadow, there's good cover for marten or mink.   It was lovely out with not a cloud in a bright, blue sky. Midday, we walked over to a clump of spruce, built our fire and had lunch. It was totally enjoyable and relaxing in the sunshine. Don't know how many miles we walked, probably more than ten. We made a complete circle with our wanderings, fixing a few trap houses, getting them all ready for setting in another day or so. By the time we got back, it was starting to cool off. Sun had already sunk behind the mountains to the west – time for supper and then to stretch out in bed. Altogether, an unforgettable day.

Friday – Oct. 30ʳ -23C   Temperatures like these are sure building up the ice. Beautiful out, sunny.

It should be a great day for walking over to Rose Lake. We're going there to check on the cabin and our meat cache. Gordon's uneasy with that wolverine hanging around. We took off right after breakfast and after a real nice jaunt, arrived at Rose Lake two and a half hours later. The frozen trail made for excellent walking so we made very good time. Saw only a few tracks until we got close to Rose Lake and then, a lot of wolverine sign. Luckily, nothing got into the meat cache we were so concerned about. It's gorgeous here with the sun shining on the mountains. The river has frozen over, now covered with five to six inches of ice. We walked across the ice to check our old moose kill. It was completely cleaned up – even the hide was gone. We then hiked a short distance up Marten Creek. The ice was very slippery, treacherous for walking. I did a three-point landing, knee, hip and elbow – it hurt. That decided us not to go very far.

We found Rose Lake cabin very frosty inside – everything covered with hoarfrost. After we lit the stove and the cabin warmed up, the hoarfrost melted and water began dripping from the ceiling. Gordon was kept busy wiping it down until it had all dried. Next year we'll have to insulate the ceiling. Didn't take long before the cabin was nice and warm and dry. After lunch we kept busy for a couple of hours getting in more wood then finished up with a few other chores before dinner. Tonight we'll be trying out a new, king-sized blanket that we brought with us today. Should be toasty warm.

Jamie Lake cabin by moonlight

Looking up river from our cabin at Rose Lake

A rewarding day on the line – a good catch of marten

Our winter's fur catch

Saturday – Oct. 31ˢᵗ -26C   It's been seven weeks from today that we arrived. Clear, sunny skies and gorgeous but I do wish it would warm up.

This morning Gordon got the skidoo down from where he'd hung it in the trees last winter. We then decided to test run it. We took it out on the river ice and headed up river to the mouth of Lynx Creek. It just purred along so went up the creek for quite a ways. Eventually, seeing open water ahead, we turned around and came back to the river. Travel on river ice was so inviting, we couldn't resist heading up river for another three to four miles. Noticed one spot, a side channel, where there was still open water but most of the river was covered with lots of ice – black ice and clear. With not even a trace of snow on it, you could see clear to the bottom of the river as you traveled along. It was really fun!! We stopped for lunch on the shore of "Horseshoe Lake". It's a "U" shaped lake that's only a couple of hundred feet back from the river. By the time we got home, it was late afternoon and the temperature had warmed up to minus fifteen. Gordon took another short hike up Marten Creek but found the ice was still too slick.

Sunday – Nov. 1ˢᵗ -25C   Trapping starts today. Not as nice as yesterday, dull and cloudy.

Right after breakfast we headed up river to Lynx Creek and set out our marten traps. After that was finished, we returned and set a number of traps around the cabin area and also a few up Marten Creek. By then the sky was completed clouded over with low clouds and it looked as though we'd be having snow shortly. We packed up and headed back to Jamie Lake, setting traps along the way. It did snow but not enough for the skidoo. When we left Rose cabin, there was only one to two inches of snow on sandbars along the river and we found about the same amount when we reached Jamie Lake. It would be good if it snowed more so we'd be able to use the skidoo when setting traps. We could cover a lot more country in a shorter time as well as making it easier for us.

When we were up Lynx Run this morning, we reached a section that had two big beaver houses – side by side – on the creek. Really unusual to have them that close together. There was also a huge feed bed of poplar, willow and aspen right alongside. They're all set for a long winter. When we were upriver yesterday, we spotted tracks made by a large wolverine. They were in the same general area where Gordon had seen them in past years so it must be his home range. This year we're going to try and catch him. On our way to Rose Lake on Friday, we saw quite a number of caribou tracks along the Ridge Run section of the trail. We've been disappointed in the number of marten tracks that have shown. There have actually been very few marten tracks this year – not like last year when they were all over. We haven't had snow this year and tracks are harder to spot so perhaps that's the reason.

After we returned and got the fire going, we just took our time over lunch – talking about which runs to set out next. Later, Gordon got in more wood – all neatly stacked in the porch. I'm sure we've got more than enough to last till spring.

Monday – Nov. 2nd -7C   No snow overnight and its much milder, nice. Bit foggy out this morning so don't know whether we have cloud up there or not.

Right after breakfast we were out, heading down Jamie Run on our way to the river. Since there was enough snow for the toboggan, Murky was in harness – trotting along behind us. He had a very light load, our lunch makings, swede saw and a few spare traps. We set traps along the way to the river, then crossing to the other side, set traps along Wolverine Run before taking a lunch break. We're pleased at having such a good start setting out traps along this line. Weather has been excellent. During the morning the fog cleared off letting the sun shine down on us from a clear sky. Another gorgeous day – really warm in the sun. Mountains are beautiful with the sun shining on their peaks.

After we got back to the cabin, I decided to bake a pie and a batch of muffins while Gordon took the Tundra Skidoo out for a test run on the lake.

After he got back he reported that it sure handles better than the Spitfire. It's geared much lower than the Spitfire and walks up the hill so effortlessly compared to the other machine. We're really looking forward to using it – once we get enough snow. Later, Gordon did take the Tundra out on River Run for a short ways, setting a few traps. He just had to try it out!!

Tuesday – Nov. 3rd -3C When we first got out of bed this morning, it was fog and more fog – visibility only a couple hundred feet. Can't tell whether there's cloud above or not.

By the time we'd finished breakfast, fog had pretty well cleared away and within another half-hour, cleared completely. Really great in the warm sunshine. After breakfast we headed up Jamie Run, following it to the creek and onwards across the meadow section to the Coal River and the start of our Wolf Run. There wasn't enough snow for the Tundra but also not enough snow to make for tough walking. Really gorgeous day – almost like early spring. Wolf Creek with thin ice was not safe to walk on. Instead, we followed along on the higher ground, mostly meadow interspersed with willow clumps but rough going, hummocky. We saw quite a lot of marten sign and set out a number of traps. We walked quite a long ways checking for sign and setting traps before deciding it was time to turn back. Besides, our side of the creek was getting extremely rough. We couldn't find a place to cross to the other side for better footing. A strong, cold wind had also started blowing – not nice.

We hadn't even stopped for tea. A big mistake since we would have been rested a little. While we were setting the second last trap, the sky rapidly clouded over, wind came up and minutes later we were in rain showers. The showers didn't last very long but the air sure cooled off. I was beat by the time we reached home, with soaking wet feet.

Wednesday – Nov. 4th +2C What a change in temperature. Our snow is just about gone. It's cloudy and a little windy this morning.

While eating breakfast we decided it would be a good day to finish setting out our River Run, all the way to the Coal. We could finish setting that line and at the same time check the traps we'd set a few days earlier. When we started down the trail a short while later, I couldn't believe it when we got our first marten. A beautiful, large, dark male in the first trap. It was soon followed by two more in the next sets. Our first catch of the year. The first marten was caught in the set we'd made just down the hill from the cabin while the other two were from sets across the meadow. Sure glad Gordon had time to set those traps the other day. Later, after reaching the Coal River and setting traps along the way, we found our plan to cross the river wasn't feasible. We had planned on crossing the river and then following up a small creek on the other side, hoping it would connect with Wolf Run. The river changed our minds. The ice was all flooded and halfway across was an area of open water. We were disappointed at not being able to cross and explore new country but pleased that we'd completed setting out our Jamie Run.

Thursday – Nov. 5ᵗʰ -4C   Clear and sunny and a little bit cooler.

A good day for a walk up the Canyon Run so right after breakfast we took off down the trail. It was nice walking in the warm sunshine. Most of the snow had melted and by this afternoon the last patches will likely disappear. Along the way we picked up three marten from the few traps we'd set previously. Finished setting out traps as far as the meadow then crossed the creek and headed up into the hills on the other side. Because thick stands of spruce covered the hillsides, we'd thought the shaded ground would still have a blanket of snow. We wanted to check for marten tracks but were disappointed to find only a few patches of snow and no tracks. With the temperature changes over the past days, snow was frozen hard so tracks just wouldn't show. The creek section ,where we'd laid a couple of spruce atop the unsafe ice in order to cross last time, had frozen then flooded several times, building ice a good two feet thick. One trap was flooded over and frozen in. Took Gordon quite a while to chop it free. I wish I'd brought the camera today to take pictures of the ice. Some places it was built up so high and yet, right beside the ridges in canyons below, there were open channels of water.

We finally stopped for lunch on our way back, building our tea fire atop the ridge that overlooked the meadow below. It felt good taking a break after all the walking we'd done. Hot tea and toasted sandwiches sure hit the spot. Later on our way back, we spotted fresh wolf tracks. During the day the sky had completely clouded over and a wind had sprung up – looks like it might snow, we hope. I've been after Gordon, ever since we've been married, to get me a rabbit so I could try wild rabbit stew. He'd finally decided to set half a dozen snares for rabbits a short distance from the cabin. Upon checking the snares on our way back – Success and Hurray!! He had two rabbits so I'm stewing them for dinner tomorrow.

Friday – Nov. 6ᵗʰ -17C Temperature has really dropped again – should freeze up all that overflow.

Glad we were inside last night. It got really miserable, very windy and then started to snow. The wind finally died down by mid-morning. It would have been miserable out hiking with that wind so we stayed in bed later than usual and then decided to take the whole day off.

After we got up and had a late breakfast, I started on my baking – a lemon pie and buns, some plain and some with cinnamon. Gordon decided to try his new Tundra again and headed over the trail to the second lake and onwards to the Meadow Run. He set out a few traps along the way. He really likes that new machine. Had our rabbit stew for supper but did not enjoy it. It was good and tender but had a gamey taste. Think it's too late in the fall – rabbits are eating willow by now.

Saturday – Nov. 7ᵗʰ -33C Getting cold. Sky is clear so will be a nice, sunny day.

I told Gordon that if it gets as cold as last year I'll not come back another year. Last year's temperatures were too cold for us to be out in the bush alone. Besides, animals don't move in those cold temperatures anyway.

Right after finishing the breakfast dishes, we headed out to check the rest of the traps on Meadow Run. We got two more marten and one mink. Also walked a lot further up the meadow and set more traps, even though we didn't see any marten tracks. It's only been one day since the last snowfall so didn't expect to see much sign. Sure wish there was more snow, enough so we could use the machines!!

Before going to bed, we took one last look outside. No cloud, sky was full of shining stars. Just a few bands of northern lights above the mountains in the west. It had been a gorgeous day with not a cloud to be seen. There was real warmth from the sun during the day, even at minus thirty. Gordon says – Are we ever going to be in shape for skiing !!

Sunday – Nov. 8^t -32C   Clear but cold – be nice when the sun finally appears.

Heard on the radio that Edmonton is in the minus twenties but also has a real strong wind. That would be cold!! Signals have not been good for the past few days. Ordinary radio reception is pretty good though. Can just barely make out Don Taylor's schedule for the past few nights but he can't read our transmissions. By the time we finished breakfast, the sun was up and it was quite nice out.

Gordon took the Tundra and went up Ridge Run and onwards with a load of gas for Rose Lake. Murky, with his toboggan, followed along behind. They went about three-fifths of the way with the skidoo, then cached about half of the fuel. From there, they continued on foot to Rose Lake with Murky hauling the other half of the fuel on the toboggan. We plan on walking to Rose Lake tomorrow, picking up the rest of the fuel on the way. The balance of the trail beyond the fuel cache is so rough that Gordon didn't want to take the skidoo over it without more snow. A lot of our terrain is very rough, nothing but hummocks –

not even the easiest walking. There really wasn't enough snow to use the Tundra today but we need gas at Rose Lake. It's required for the Spitfire so we can travel on the river. If we do decide to return next year we'll have the Beaver aircraft, that's picking us up in December, deliver a barrel of gas to Rose Lake. We'd then have fuel on hand for the canoe and skidoo – no more packing it over in little containers.

Gordon and Murky finally returned late in the afternoon. Sure glad to see them. He reported everything went well on the gas haul, thanks to Murky. Everything fine at Rose Lake. While I stayed home, I made up a pot of homemade soup and baked cabbage rolls for supper.

Monday – Nov. 9th -33C   This is ridiculous, being here in these temperatures. Sky is cloudless.

It's cold but beautiful out so decided to head up Ridge Run and onwards to Rose Lake. Left right after ten o'clock with our packs and Murky with his toboggan – arriving at Rose Lake just after one. We only brought five gallons of gas from the fuel Gordon cached yesterday. It would have been just too hard for Murky to pull a heavier load over that rough trail. On our way, we did pick up ten marten. We got five on Ridge Run, one on Marten Creek and four around the cabin. Not bad, eh!! But – we did not see a single new track that was made since the last snow. That was very disappointing. Had lunch at the cabin and then, late afternoon, went back up Marten Creek setting out another seven traps on the way to the ravine. While I was getting supper ready, Gordon chopped a hole through the river ice for water. Reported ice thickness at about fourteen inches.

Tuesday – Nov. 10th -20C   A little milder and a bit cloudy this morning.

After breakfast we bundled up in preparation for our trip upriver with the Spitfire. Riding is nice but can be pretty chilly if you're not properly dressed. The trip to the mouth of Lynx Creek didn't take very long, even with our frequent stops to check animal tracks. On the way up Lynx Creek, we picked up a marten in the first trap then – nothing more. Disappointed!! We went a long way up the creek but didn't see a single marten track. At one point, the Spitfire stopped on us and Gordon had a heck of a time getting it started. We finally got back to the river. I was hoping he'd turn back to Rose Lake and then head for Jamie Lake to pick up the Tundra. Wasn't to be – Gordon decided we should go further upriver to check the traps we'd set and then go on to Kettle Creek and do some scouting. We had traveled around the first long river bend before Gordon decided it wasn't such a smart plan. Instead, we'd go back to Rose Lake, have a quick bite and then head home to Jamie Lake.

On the way back, got as far as the mouth of Lynx Creek before that D——D machine went BANG and stopped dead. The coil had blown. There's definitely something wrong with this machine – the coil has been used for less than ten hours. It's the third one that's gone with less than fifty hours of use on the machine. Thank Goodness we didn't go to Kettle. We had to leave the Spitfire on the river and walk back to Rose Lake.

After a rushed lunch, we headed back up Marten Creek on our way to Jamie Lake. We've decided, come "Hell or High Water", we're going to bring the Tundra to Rose Lake. It'll be done very slowly and carefully since the trail, with very little snow, is really rough right now. We need that machine at Rose Lake if we're going to do much trapping along the river. It had been great up until today, traveling with the Spitfire along the river and creeks once they were frozen. Right now that machine is completely useless. The Tundra, when we get it to the river, should work even better. Got back to Jamie Lake just before dark – glad to be back to the cabin and something warm to drink.

Wednesday – Nov. 11th -28C   Another beautiful sunny day for us – if you can call minus twenty-eight beautiful. Watson Lake is reporting minus thirty-four so guess I can't kick. I'll need my head examined next year if I decide to come again – ridiculous in these temperatures.

Right after breakfast, we packed the Tundra. We're taking Gordon's large, down – filled sleeping bag, five gallons of gas and a box of groceries. Gordon drove the Tundra while I followed behind. Murky, pulling his little toboggan, lightly loaded with more supplies, trailed along behind me. On the way, Gordon stopped to pick up the ten gallons of gas he'd cached the other day while Murky and I kept on going. Gordon slowly made his way over the rough area with the skidoo, finally reaching the ravine and Marten Creek where he caught up with Murky and me. I rode on the Tundra, with him, for the rest of the way to the cabin. It was very easy going along the creek, smooth ice and just a skiff of snow. Gordon reported the Tundra was operating just great – didn't overheat like the Spitfire always did when it had to exert a little effort.

We reached the cabin just after one o'clock, a bit over three and a half hours on the trail. While I was making lunch and heating up the place, Gordon went upriver and towed the Spitfire home. He'll work on it when and if the temperature warms up. After lunch we went back and up Marten Creek, past the ravine to where that fallen spruce blocked further passage. With the chainsaw we'd brought with us, it didn't take long to clear the obstructing tree, opening the creek for further upstream travel. That job finished, we turned and headed back to the cabin where there were chores that had to be done before dark. At seven-thirty the temperature had dropped to minus thirty-two. When we went to bed a short while later, it had dropped to minus thirty-four. Glad to be in this nice warm cabin with a good, big woodpile.

Thursday – Nov. 12th -25C Don't know how much colder it got during the night but it is a pleasant surprise to find it's warmer today.

When we were out checking the temperature before going to bed last night, we noticed how bright it was outside. A full moon was shining overhead while across the northern and eastern sections of the sky bands of northern lights rippled and danced as they moved across. Really lovely. We've had some very spectacular displays of aurora this season.

It was a nice surprise this morning to find the temperature had warmed up a bit. Sky clouded over early this morning with a little snow coming down. Radio signals were good and Gordon had a long chat with Don Taylor and Hans Jensen. We hear most trappers are experiencing the same slowdown we're having. Very few marten have been taken and a definite scarcity of sign this year. Would be interesting to know whether it's the lack of snow, cold weather or if it's their low cycle. Also heard Watson Lake has a foot of snow while we only have an inch out here.

After breakfast we went up Marten Creek. The Tundra worked great, what a change from the Spitfire. Further upstream, the creek had a lot of seepage along its sides but the main channel was all frozen. We only saw a couple of marten tracks but set out four traps. A bit further along, Gordon spotted a beautiful, tall, dry spruce tree which he just had to cut down and cut up for firewood.. We were able to load all the bone-dry wood into the skimmer and haul it home. Doing some baking tonight with the wood – great. Noticed before going to bed that the sky had cleared up so will likely be cold again.

Friday – Nov. 13th -35C   Beautiful out but cold. Not a trace of cloud. The mountains to the north and east even look cold.

We took our time over a leisurely breakfast this morning. Gordon still says, "It never gets cold here". I don't believe him!! Two years in a row and it's been very cold. Wolves howled all night, waking us at times. I was so surprised when I got up this morning (decided to let Gordon stay in bed – again) and went outside. There, on the sandbar across the river, sat a great big, black wolf. Murky was just watching him, not barking. Then I remembered Gordon had not brought his .270 rifle on this trip. It would have been such an easy shot for him. The wolf just sat in the open watching us – completely unafraid.. When I called Gordon out, he brought his twenty-two but it was completely ineffective at that distance. At the sound of the "pop" of the rifle, the wolf stood up and just sauntered off – showing complete disdain. Oh well, there will likely be a next time. He was a very large animal. After that excitement, we took our time over breakfast, hoping the outside temperature would rise a bit.

Last evening Gordon set a fishing line, baited with a chunk of moose, in the water hole. Upon checking it this morning- success. Seems trout also enjoy moose meat. We're now going to have fresh trout for supper tonight. It will taste really good, a welcome change from the steady diet of moose meat we've been having. Gordon has now decided to try a piece of marten for bait and is putting out a couple more sets. Be interesting to find out which, moose or marten, is most desired by our trout. Maybe we should even apply for a grant from the Government for this research project!!

At two o'clock we headed down river to where Twin Lakes creek enters the Coal River, then followed up the creek. The going was great until we came to a large spruce that had fallen across the channel. We didn't have the chainsaw and with steep banks along both sides preventing our going further, had to return downstream, setting traps along the way. Reaching the river, we decided to follow it down to where our River Run from Jamie Lake joins in. Travel was excellent with no overflow so it didn't take long to get there. Saw very few tracks along the way but later we set a few more traps along the riverbanks on our return to Rose Lake.

It was a quite enjoyable trip with the sun shining but as soon as it started setting the air cooled off – fast. It probably took us close to twenty minutes to come back by skidoo. Quite a difference from the two hours that's usually required when traveling by canoe in the fall. Temperature was already down to minus twenty-three by the time we got home. We'd been gone for about three and a half hours and were surprised at being able to cover that much distance in so short a time. We're both really pleased with performance of the Tundra skidoo. We did have a late start this morning with Gordon setting out wolf snares and then checking his fish lines. Besides, it was far too cold to leave before lunch. The Tundra runs like a dream and starts on the first pull. I can even start it whereas the Spitfire required a really hard pull that was impossible for me.

Gordon just finished checking his fish lines and, at the second hole, pulled out a huge Dolly Varden. Makes this mornings trout look like a baby.

Saturday – Nov. 14th -28C   Foggy this morning and a bit warmer.

The ice on the river was sure cracking and booming during the night – almost like gunshots. After breakfast we headed up river for our Kettle Creek cabin and this time, we made it. It was a good trip even though it wasn't sunny. We picked up two marten from the traps we'd set along the Coal River earlier. We also set a few more traps on our way up. We wondered what the interior of our cabin would be like since we'd been away for quite a lengthy time. Figured squirrels might have been making a mess of things inside and half expected to see hoarfrost on the ceiling and walls. When we opened the door, SURPRISE!! Everything looked super. With the fire going it didn't take long to warm the cabin. While the cabin was warming we walked across the river and followed up and around a couple of bends on Kettle Creek. Spotted a few sets of marten tracks and put out a few traps. Then it was time to head back to the cabin for lunch.

After lunch we took the skidoo and headed further up the creek – looks good. We plan on moving to Kettle in a day or two, then going way up the creek putting out more traps. Probably go further upriver as well. By mid-afternoon the sky had clouded over and looked like it might snow again. Kettle Creek country has double the snow that Rose Lake has. Anyway, it was time to turn around and head for home at Rose Lake. It took us less than an hour to return – little snow on the ice made for a fast trip. After checking the fire, first thing Gordon did was check his fish lines. Sure enough, he caught two more Dolly's. One was small but the other a nice size but not near as large as the one he got last night, but still nice. He's just so excited about catching trout through the ice.

Sunday – Nov. 15th -29C   Clear – will be a sunny day.

We've been at the trapline for nine weeks – the total length of time we spent here last year. After breakfast we loaded traps, axe and other assorted gear into the skimmer, started the skidoo and headed down river to where Twin Lakes Creek enters the Coal. We planned on setting traps along it for several miles but ran into overflow a short ways up the creek and had to turn back to the river. Reaching the river, we then decided to go further down, as far as the area above our Wolf Run. We'd noticed, when following and setting traps along Wolf Creek, that its general course was from the hills to northeast. If we could blaze and then cut a trail from the Coal River to connect with our Wolf Run the two runs would be combined in one loop and save a lot of back-tracking.

When we thought we'd gone far enough on the river, we left the skidoo and headed into the bush, blazing trees as we went. Two and a half hours later, we still had not located the headwaters of Wolf Creek. From there onwards, no more blazing – we just explored for fur sign. Locating a connecting trail to Wolf run will have to wait for another day. The numerous grass covered potholes we walked through all had marten tracks showing where they'd been hunting mice under the snow. We had hoped to reach Wolf Creek and perhaps more open meadows but only located another small creek. We were running out of time so headed back to the river, blazing trail as we returned. Next time we'll try branching off a little further on and again try to reach the meadows along Wolf Creek. We did set out a few traps today so did accomplish something. I was beat by the time we got back to the river from all the miles of walking. We got on the skidoo, turned it around and headed for home.

Monday – Nov. 16th -18C   Broken sky conditions this morning so perhaps we'll get snow within the next couple of days.

Just a skiff of snow fell overnight but not enough to make a difference. We still only have about one inch of snow and can't go anywhere with the skidoo other than for the river. After breakfast we're going to Kettle Creek and stay for a couple of days – exploring for fur sign and setting traps.

Had a great trip up river to Kettle Creek cabin. The sun was out and it wasn't too cold since there wasn't a breath of wind. Murky pulled the little toboggan, empty. Even so, we had to stop a few times for him to catch up and take a break. He's not the fastest dog, being a bit overweight, but is a real good companion and loves being in harness. Along the way we saw several signs of marten – tracks crossing and following along the river. When we reached the cabin, Gordon got the fire going so it would warm while we took off up Kettle Creek. Got one marten at our third trap. We continued quite a ways upstream until we reached a section where the ice didn't look so good. Gordon got off and walked ahead while I drove the Tundra. We finally reached an area where the creek was covered with layers of shell ice. You could hear the stream running, gurgling, beneath. It didn't build my confidence – a dip in that icy liquid was something I'd gladly do without. A short ways further along, we came to patches of overflow. Gordon was even less impressed with ice conditions just ahead so we turned around and headed back, setting out traps along the way. We sure saw tracks!! More fur sign this afternoon than we've seen in a month. Looks good.

Tuesday – Nov. 17ᵗʰ - ??   It's clear and will be another gorgeous day. But it is CHILLY !!

It was so bright out last night with a full moon. We don't have a thermometer at Kettle. The one destined for here is still sitting at Jamie Lake. I think the temperature's between minus thirty-five and minus forty but Gordon says it can't be more than minus twenty-five. I'm sure he's wrong. You can see the mountains from our big window. There's one high, pointy peak, all snow covered, that's all pink with the sun shining on it. The lower sections of the mountains, reaching down to timberline, are still pretty bare of snow.

After breakfast we took the skidoo and headed further up river, checking for animal tracks – especially those made by marten. We traveled for several miles without seeing a single track – pretty disappointing. It was also much colder than Gordon had originally thought so we finally turned around and returned to our Kettle Creek cabin. After warming up, we packed our gear and returned to Rose Lake, arriving just after one in the afternoon. It was still minus twenty-nine so guess my estimate of this morning's temperature was pretty close.

We headed down river right after lunch. This time we brought the chainsaw along since we plan on going up Twin Lakes Creek to clear that blocking tree. Only took a few minutes work with the saw to clear it out but just a short distance further on, ran into overflow – bank to bank. No way to get around it since both banks were high and steep. On the one side, the bank had slid right into the creek, bringing down a maze of trees which further blocked any access by skidoo. It would be one heck of a cleanup job to remove all the debris so we left the skidoo, climbed the bank and got around the mess. Further along, with overflow frozen, it was good walking. We went quite a ways further up the creek and, seeing quite a few marten and a few mink tracks, set several more traps. Without the skidoo, looks like we'll not be able to go very far on the creek. A short while later the sun dipped behind the mountains to the west. It was definitely getting colder, time to turn around and head for the skidoo and home.

Got back just after four-thirty and right away Gordon had to check his fish lines. Sure enough, two more fish, one a nice Dolly but the other was a big, ugly pike – not so good looking but still good eating. Early evening the view from our cabin was gorgeous. The mountains looked especially lovely – white tops silhouetted against a deep blue sky. A full moon shone above and down below its rays were seemingly reflecting from millions of diamonds strewn across the snow. It's already minus twenty-nine and will probably drop to minus forty by morning.

Wednesday – Nov. 18th -23C   Sure a pleasant surprise, warmer – but very dull out – cloudy. Looks as if it might snow. Last evening around ten o'clock, temperature was sitting at minus thirty-five.

After finishing breakfast and bringing a supply of firewood in for the stove, we packed our gear and started up Marten Creek with the skidoo, heading for Jamie Lake. Only got about half a mile before running into overflow – deep, no going through that, so turned around and headed back to Rose cabin. I ran in and put a heavier shirt on under my jacket. Then we were off again, down river to where River Run from Jamie Lake meets the Coal. Great going on the river with no overflow and only a little snow so we made good time. Heading over River Run trail for Jamie Lake was a bit different. It is very rough with one hummock after another so Gordon had to travel very slowly. Murky had his empty toboggan to pull while I walked the entire distance. Saw a few new marten tracks but nothing in the traps. Had to laugh at Murky. When we reached the hill above the big meadow just before Jamie Lake, Gordon drove the skidoo down by a roundabout gentler way. Murky followed right behind him while I decided to take a shortcut down the steep slope. I think Murky must have decided I was lost or something. He left Gordon, came across to me, then stopped and looked up at me, as if to say "Lady, you're off course". He then turned back to intercept Gordon's trail while I followed right behind him.

When Murky and I reached the cabin, Gordon was still behind us setting a snare. The first thing the dog did was go about halfway into his house and stop. Then his tail really started wagging. Upon checking, I found the two rabbits Gordon had caught for him were stashed inside. Guess he was happy to find them still safe where he'd left them. By the time we reached Jamie Lake, the sky had cleared and the sun was shining. So much for the snow we hoped to get!! Oh well, it's still a nice way to be welcomed home. After lunch we got through to Watson Lake Flying for the latest news. They advised us the forecast is for more cold weather.

Thursday – Nov. 19th -18C   Temperature not bad – especially hearing that Mayo and other stations were down to minus thirty-nine this morning. Watson Lake is a mere minus twenty-four. It's overcast with very light snow falling.

After breakfast and an extra cup of coffee, we decided to take the skidoo to the second lake, leave it halfway down the lake where our trail cuts through the bush, then continue on foot checking traps on Meadow Run. With so little snow, that run is terribly rough and hard on a skidoo. We ended up springing all the traps since there was very little fur sign. Not one fresh track. Gordon has also decided that this run, located between Canyon and Ridge runs, makes them all too close together and could result in over- trapping the area. This is also the longest run and the roughest. Gordon estimates we walk about twelve miles checking it. We were both disappointed at not getting any fur or seeing any sign.

Friday – Nov. 20th -23C Overcast this morning with light snow. Sure hope it keeps up. We could use a good foot of the white stuff.

After breakfast we took the skidoo and, with Murky and his toboggan, headed down Jamie Run to the river. About half a mile from the cabin, while I was riding in the skimmer with Murky following along behind me, I glanced back and saw that Murky seemed to be tangled in his harness. Then I realized – No!! It wasn't the harness that he was mixed up with. I shouted for Gordon to stop but he couldn't hear me so rolled off the skimmer and ran to Murky. We'd set a wolf snare on the old trail and Murky, instead of following behind us, decided to take that route and was caught in the snare. He was gasping for air but thank goodness, didn't fight. I kept hollering for Gordon but he couldn't hear me. He didn't realize anything was wrong until he turned to check on me and saw I was missing. Then he heard me yelling and ran back. I couldn't loosen the lock on the snare but Gordon soon got it released and Murky freed, apparently none the worse for his experience. Poor dog!! We were lucky – the locks on snares can't be released by the animal caught in them. With air cut off, they're gone within a couple of minutes.

After a short rest for Murky, we continued on. After crossing the creek at the bottom of the hill we continued on to the river rather than following the new trail we'd cut across the meadow to Wolf Run. Without snow, travel across the meadow would have been very rough going for the skidoo. Continuing up river and facing into a wind, we found it very cold traveling. Wind seemed to cut right through you. Reaching the mouth of Wolf Creek, we left the Tundra and continued on foot. Murky, with his toboggan, trotted along right behind us. We'd only gone a short distance before Gordon stopped and cried out – Oh No!! He realized he'd forgotten to bring along traps for resetting. What a Turkey!!

We continued onwards anyway and, sure enough, in our first two traps, we found marten. Third trap was empty, no sign of a visitor – bait untouched. Fourth trap also held a marten. Anyway, out of the eleven traps we'd set, we found one trap sprung by a marten who'd then made off with the bait, four traps had nothing, but – the other six traps all had marten. Pretty good catch. Unfortunately, two of the marten were damaged, one badly. Mice had chewed a patch of fur from one, but the other, a real beauty, had a large section of his body eaten away by another marten. What a shame. Marten are very cannibalistic and will make a meal of anything that presents itself, even litter mates. We went further on through the area and set a few more traps that had been left when we'd closed the line last year. Lot's of sign throughout the entire region.

The weather had turned really miserable with a gusty wind. Snow had started to fall so we turned and headed back. We'd only gone a few steps before Gordon stopped, exclaiming, Oh D— !! He'd taken another shortcut – forgetting to pick up one of the marten we'd left for our return trip. When we leave animals to be picked up later, we usually hide them under snow or tree branches, then pick them up on our way back. Gordon trotted back and a few minutes later returned with the missing marten. Upon reaching the river and our skidoo, we loaded Murky's toboggan as well as our catch in the skimmer. We then headed down river to Wolverine run. We picked up another marten there – also spotted lynx tracks. After completing the trap check on Wolverine, it was back to the river, then following it to the junction with Jamie Run and the trail home. Once we left the river, the trail was terribly rough so I got off the skidoo and walked the rest of the way home. Sure got my exercise today. It was nice to sit back in the cabin and relax for a while. Next, supper and bed. I know I'll have no trouble sleeping tonight.

Saturday – Nov. 21st -30C   Cool again but a little cloud up there so hopefully it will warm a bit.

Today, we hitched up Murky and went up Canyon run checking traps. As it turned out, we didn't see any new tracks and closed the run down. We've caught a total of seven marten on this run – not very good, considering the number of miles it covers. We could have taken the skidoo but decided the walk would do us good. It turned out to be another gorgeous day, cloud cleared off and the sun shone down on us. Temperature was minus twenty-three when we got back but it felt warmer with heat from the sun.

Late afternoon the sky clouded over and tried to snow a little. We received, grudgingly it seemed, about a dozen flakes. Temperature dropped to minus twenty-five by seven this evening.

Sunday – Nov. 22nd -21C   Will be a nice day – just a skiff of new snow. We must now have a grand total of at least three inches on the ground!!

Right after breakfast we started our skidoo, hitched up Murky and headed down Jamie Run to the Coal River. After reaching it, we followed upriver on the ice to the mouth of Wolf Creek, the start of our Wolf run. Two days previously, when we'd checked traps and found we'd caught six marten, we didn't have traps to reset at all our bait boxes (because some "Turkey" forgot them), so returned today to complete the job. We took the skidoo as far as the third set and left it there. Just too rough to go further with only a couple inches of snow on the ground. We walked the rest of the way, Murky pulling the toboggan with our trapping gear. Finally got beyond the beaver house, the furthest point we'd reached last year, cut through the timber and got to another large meadow. It was beautiful out and warm with the sun shining. There was lots of fur sign – tracks all over. Further up the creek we located three active beaver houses. The beaver had built several dams which flooded the entire meadow. The flooded areas were frozen so it made for easy walking. The creek, however, was not safe. We placed six more sets amongst the trees bordering the meadow and then turned back for the river and our skidoo.

Back at the river, we headed downstream – intent on checking Wolverine run. By the time we reached the turnoff for Jamie run I had persuaded Gordon to let me off there so I could walk back to Jamie Lake with Murky. Poor dog was tired and it would save him at least three miles of extra running. By the time Gordon got back to the cabin after checking Wolverine, I had tea and hot soup waiting. Really welcome since we hadn't taken time off for lunch. We'd left at ten-fifteen this morning and Gordon got back at five-thirty. It had been a long day. He was rewarded on the Wolverine run, catching a marten in the lynx set we had put out. The marten must have been caught just before he got there since it wasn't frozen. He didn't go to the other sets since they'd been checked just two days previously.

While we were up Wolf run this morning we'd noticed, after reaching the first beaver house, tracks of three otters traveling along the creek ice. We must have missed them by only a few minutes. Further on, we left the creek and cut across a small meadow where walking was safer than along the creek ice. When we eventually turned back to the creek, there was no sign of the otters – no tracks. They had to be somewhere between where we'd left the creek and returned to it. It would have been nice to see them romping along. You could see all along the creek where they'd played and slid down the banks – just having a good time. They'd even lain down for a rest under a big spruce in the middle of the meadow. We did set a marten trap in that tree. It certainly would have been a treat to see those otters playing. Had a late supper tonight. It's been a great day.

Monday – Nov. 23rd -10C Warm but dull out. Overcast with light snow falling. Not the nice, big, fluffy flakes – just light, little ones.

Gordon decided we were taking a day off so is sleeping in. Our last day off was November sixth when he'd taken the skidoo for a test run and set a few traps at the same time. It hadn't been much of a day off for him. He's just going to put a Teflon liner on the bottom of the skimmer and do nothing more today. At noon I checked our snow depth – a total of five inches around Jamie Lake cabin. Looked in on Murky, asleep in his house. Was rather cute to see him sleeping with his head resting on a rabbit. A rather unique pillow, I'd say. Later in the afternoon we brought the rest of the groceries down from the cache, re-packing most of them in preparation for hauling them to Rose Lake.

Tuesday – Nov. 24th -15C Clear and a little windy – looks like another nice day.

Had a good breakfast and then got busy packing Murky's toboggan with a box of groceries. The skimmer was next, loaded with three boxes of groceries, most of our clothes (in duffle bags), rifles and other assorted gear. I hopped on the skidoo seat with Gordon and we were off – headed for our Rose Lake cabin via River Run and the Coal. When we reached the first meadow a few minutes later, I got off the skidoo – just too rough with our little bit of snow. I preferred walking the rest of the way to the river rather than riding that bouncing skidoo. The trail had a good amount of snow but was still too rough for riding double on the skidoo. The skimmer had no room for me since it was filled with our gear. Once we reached the river, I rode the skidoo the rest of the way. With sunshine and no wind, was a gorgeous trip upriver to our Rose Lake cabin.

We had brought a lot of groceries and other supplies over from Jamie Lake. If we decide to come next year we'll have a good assortment of canned goods as well as dehydrated foods available. If we decide not to come again, we'll have them ready for our flight home in December. We still aren't sure if we want to come again – half thinking of not returning. We still have a lot of stuff to haul over from Jamie. We had picked up two marten this morning on River Run. One was caught beside or should I say, down the hill from the Jamie lake outhouse! Sure a surprise. Soon as he had the fire in the stove going , Gordon was out on the river checking his fish lines. Sure enough, minutes later he came in with a pail of water and a nice Dolly. After leaving the water for me, he was back out to check his second line. The ice on the river is between fifteen and eighteen inches thick and he found his second line had frozen to the bottom of the ice. Anyway, after a lengthy time chopping ice, he got it loose and found a good sized Lingcod at the end of it. Neither of us had eaten Lingcod but apparently it's very good. Will save it and try it when we get home.

After lunch we skidoo'd up Marten Creek for several miles setting out traps. The going was good – all the overflow had frozen and was now covered with fresh snow. Only saw a few marten tracks though. We had a sad experience this afternoon. Our skimmer had come apart all along one side where the weld broke. The trip this morning must have been just too rough for it. Sure too bad since it's a handy piece of equipment. Will have to use the toboggan from now on. Gordon thinks that when we have it back to Jamie Lake where there's more equipment, he'll be able to repair it by placing a two by four inside the seam – then bolting the base and side to the timber. We had the Dolly Varden for supper, really good. Nice to have a change from moose meat or the canned stuff we brought with us.

Wednesday – Nov. 25th -12C   Warmed up overnight – was minus twenty-eight at bedtime. Clouded over and snowed about an inch.

We headed up Lynx Creek this morning to check traps and picked up three marten from our sets. Lots of tracks all along the way. We also had a trap sprung by a wolf and another sprung by a Canada Jay or "Whiskey-Jack". Not much left of the bird. It had been eaten by a marten. After returning to the river, we proceeded downstream and then up Twin Lakes Creek, finally stopping when we ran into overflow. We left the skidoo on the creek ice after placing a couple of small spruce under it so it'd be clear of the overflow and not freeze down. We then finished checking that run on foot. Nothing in the traps and no new tracks – discouraging! By the time we got back to the skidoo, weather had changed – much warmer and snowing quite heavily so we headed for home and supper.

Thursday – Nov. 26ᵗʰ -33C Wow – did the temperature ever drop. Was down to minus thirty-five earlier. Quite a change from yesterday afternoon when we got back finding it was only minus six. Despite the cold, it's gorgeous out with the sun shining on the mountains.

It's just too cold to travel the river so we just took it easy and had a lazy breakfast. We had planned on going up to Kettle Creek and check our trapline there. After breakfast, Gordon decided he'd go up Lynx Creek and set wolf snares around the area where the wolf had sprung our marten trap. We've noticed a lot of wolf sign all along the creeks and rivers this year. He wasn't gone very long, reporting it was really pretty cool out in the open, especially traveling along the river. We just lazed around for the rest of the day, at least I did – reading and doing a bit of knitting. Gordon was busy skinning marten, hauling water and checking his fish-lines. Nothing!! He also worked for awhile on the carburetor from the Spitfire. We also played card games with me winning most games. We're having spaghetti with meat sauce plus lemon pie, for supper.

Friday – Nov. 27ᵗʰ -20C Milder but solid overcast. Maybe snow??

Right after breakfast we harnessed up Murky, got on our skidoo and headed upriver for Kettle Creek. Going was good on the river with the fresh snow and no overflow, excellent going. Kettle Creek ice was just the opposite, lots of overflow which finally forced us to leave the skidoo and walk the last half of the Run. We only caught one marten – very poor, so we shut down the Run. Because of so little fur sign, we decided to close down the entire Kettle Creek area. It was heartbreaking closing our cabin. We'd had high hopes of using it a lot this year and now we wouldn't be. I, being a softy, broke down and shed a few tears. We had planned on using Kettle as our main residence on the river. It's the largest, most comfortable cabin of the three and I'd really enjoyed being here.

On our way back on the river, we picked up one mink. Lots of wolf tracks all along the way, right up to Rose Lake. Not a happy day.

Saturday – Nov. 28th -22C   Foggy this morning, looks like it will be a real dull day.

Today we headed down-river, planning on checking our second Wolf Run. Travel on the river was excellent and it didn't take us long to reach the point where we had to leave the skidoo and continue on foot through the timber. We only picked up one marten, very disappointed after all the tracks we'd seen earlier. Gordon is convinced that after the early part of November, marten move to higher ground – their movements triggered by weather conditions, snow or whatever. They certainly must do something like that or else go into hibernation as all of a sudden there just aren't any tracks. Oh well, they'll be here for next year.

Sunday – Nov. 29th -7C   Nice temperature.

We're going back to Jamie Lake today. It was a beautiful day for our trip. No marten in our sets though. I rode on the skimmer for about two-thirds of the way but think it would have been easier to ride a bronco than the skimmer. With so little snow, it was very rough. Everything fine at the cabin, especially after we got a fire going and the place warmed up.

Monday – Nov. 30th -5C   Snowing and windy but still warm. Not a nice day

We finished breakfast and then took off down Jamie Run to the river and our Wolf Run. Great skidooing along the river. We walked Wolf Run, checking traps but didn't catch even one animal. Just no tracks at all. Gordon's more than ever convinced they must move to higher terrain. One day marten tracks are everywhere and then – nothing. They've gone. We sprung all our traps on the

return to the river and then headed back down to Wolverine Run. At one of the
sets on Wolverine, a wolf had dragged the trap and toggle away. The rest of the
traps were empty so we sprung them. Not a very productive day!!

Next, it was back up the river to the junction with Jamie run and the return
to Jamie Lake. A sad feeling, knowing we won't be out on these trails again – at
least not this year. When we returned to the cabin we took our time over lunch,
reminiscing over experiences of the last weeks. Also, already wondering what
it would be like next year. We have decided to haul all the groceries and a lot of
the other supplies to Rose Lake. We would then have our gear and groceries
over there should we come back next year. We even discussed selling our trapline
but nothing definitely decided as yet. We both like being out here so much.
Gordon can't get over the fact that I really enjoy being way out here – just the
two of us, knowing our nearest neighbor is over a hundred miles away. We have
today, rather, today Gordon has named the meadow on Wolf Run "Rose Meadow"
Quite an honor!!

Tuesday – Dec. 1ˢᵗ -10C   Gorgeous out – was windy during the night.

We're packing up everything today. Right after breakfast Gordon left with
the skidoo for Rose Lake with a load of gas and supplies. Rest of the supplies,
we'll take with us when we go tomorrow. It's too bad the floatplane can't land
at Rose Lake in the fall but the water is too shallow. If it could fly in there we'd
have all our supplies at a central location. We were up during the night. The
northern lights display was unbelievably beautiful. Gordon said it's something
he'll really miss – the bright nights with the aurora displays.

Wednesday – December 2ⁿᵈ -18C   Clear and in another hour when the sun
comes up, should be sunny.

Finished our last breakfast at Jamie Lake for this year, then packed everything we're not taking to Rose Lake in the cache. Finally, with everything packed
away, we loaded the skimmer and harnessed Murky, then took off up Ridge

Run trail, en-route for Rose Lake. The skimmer was heavily loaded so I walked along behind it while Murky and his toboggan brought up the rear. With so little snow, the trail was very rough – especially when we reached the meadow section with their hummocks. I had no trouble keeping up to the skidoo since Gordon was only able to creep along over some sections. Murky sure didn't want to come today. Don't know if he didn't want to pull the toboggan or if he's not feeling well. Maybe he sensed we were leaving Jamie Lake and knew he wouldn't see his house and his rabbit pillow anymore and was just sad. I know it was hard for me to say goodbye to the cabin, remembering how I've enjoyed being here. But, probably will see it again next year. We finally reached the ravine and a few minutes later Marten Creek. The trip had taken us quite a lot longer today since we were also springing traps along the way. I climbed on the skidoo behind Gordon and rode the rest of the way to Rose Lake.

After reaching the cabin, I got busy starting a fire in the stove while Gordon was busy unloading the skimmer and stashing boxes of supplies in the cache. We had a quick lunch, then after refueling the skidoo, started back up Marten Creek with the intention of closing the traps we'd set along it. Things didn't work out that way. Just a short ways past the ravine we ran into overflow – lots of it, bank to bank. Anyway, we turned around and came back to the cabin. Checking that line will have to wait for at least a couple of days when, hopefully, the overflow's all frozen.

After warming up over a couple of cups of hot tea we got on the radio and called Watson Lake Flying Service. Surprise!! Signals were very good. We called to request the Otter aircraft for Saturday for our flight home. We were advised the plane wouldn't be ready until at least Monday since it was in the process of being changed over from floats to skis. Disappointing for me, having to wait a few extra days. Now that we've pretty well completed closing our lines and are just about through for the season, I want to go home, badly. Oh well, a couple of extra days relaxing will be nice. Finished the afternoon by taking inventory of the groceries we have here.

Thursday – Dec. 3rd -17C   Very foggy out. The trees across the river are just a grey blur.

Right after breakfast we started the skidoo and headed upriver to Lynx Creek. We went upstream, checking and closing traps until, about halfway, we ran into overflow. No getting around it so we turned back and headed down river to Twin Lakes Creek. Following up the creek was a real surprise – no overflow – really good going. It was the first time we've been able to go all the way on this line using the skidoo. We only picked up one marten. Quite a let-down. On the way back as we were traveling along the river, the fog finally cleared off, the sun came out and it was beautiful. We then decided to try going up Marten Creek again. We were surprised to find the overflow we'd encountered yesterday was all frozen over, except for the first section. Gordon managed to drive the skidoo onto the bank and along it until we were past the wet section – no problem. Finished checking and springing traps – no marten, then turned and headed back for home. On our return trip we could tell it was cooling off rapidly, even with the sun still shining. It was gorgeous though. Part way back, I had Gordon stop so I could take another picture of the mountains with sun shining on them, just about the same view that we have from our cabin window.

This evening we finished revamping our bed. The bed mattress is made in two sections. Each section is composed of three, four inch thick, foam pads. We covered each section with floral patterned material. Does it ever look super – also brightens up the cabin. During the day, the bed acts as a couch with one section of the bed for the back and the other for the seat. Looks real neat too. Easier to make up the beds and no loose ends to tuck in. Another bonus – I finally found a place where I could use that material. I've had it for at least fifteen to eighteen years. Hurray!!

Friday – Dec. 4th -27C   Fogged in again this morning. Last evening at bedtime, temperature was minus thirty-two and with clear skies it must have dropped even further.

It turned out to be a rather lazy day with no traps to check. Took our time over breakfast and by the time we finished, fog had disappeared, sun was shining – giving us another cool but beautiful sunny day. I took more inventory and packed stuff away then painted the wall behind the stove as well as the grocery cupboards and the new corner cupboard by the bed. They're all painted white which certainly has brightened up the cabin. Gordon completed a number of odd jobs outside in addition to clearing away trees along the south side of the cabin. With the trees removed, we'll receive a lot more sunshine in the cabin. He also stored all the surplus groceries in the cache, ready for next year.

Tonight, signals are all from Europe – quite a number of stations come in real clear so we have our choice of music. Can't understand the various announcers though. Locally, Don Taylor called from Stewart Lake but the transmission was very weak so we weren't able to communicate with him. Communication has been almost non-existent the last while. We've only been able to get through to Don or Watson Lake Flying a couple of times in the afternoon. Temperature already down to minus thirty-two when we went to bed.

Saturday – Dec. 5ᵗʰ -33C   Looks like a repeat of last years temperatures. We're fogged in again.

Time to go home and sit in front of the fireplace. Did something to my back so am in agony the past couple of days. Either twisted it unknowingly or got a cold in it. Sure hurts. Gordon went up Lynx Creek this morning to check and close traps at the far end, the traps we couldn't reach last time because of overflow. After he got back without any additional marten, he was busy for quite some time marking out a runway on the river in preparation for the plane. Hopefully, it will be arriving on Tuesday. He used small spruce trees about six feet tall. He stands them in the snow along the edges of the runway – spaced about a hundred and fifty feet apart. They're a big help to the pilot, especially when the light is poor on cloudy or snowy days. When coming in for a landing on a white surface, it's hard to judge your height above the snow unless something is present that is in contrast to the whiteness. Later this afternoon, managed to talk with Bob Close at Watson Lake Flying.

Sunday – Dec. 6th -13C   Overcast with light snow this morning. To date, we have had seven and one-half inches of snow. We'll probably get loads now that we're through trapping.

Right after breakfast Gordon started the skidoo and headed for Jamie Lake to pick up another load of gas. Because of the rough section of trail he can't haul much of a load. We're pretty sure hauling heavy loads over that area was responsible for wrecking our skimmer. Just not enough snow to fill the holes between the hummocks. He returned early afternoon with more gas, reporting a pretty good trip with no problems. Everything fine at Jamie Lake and saw only a couple of fresh marten tracks along the way. We've been here for twelve weeks now – will be good to get back home. It's been a rather disappointing trapping season with so little sign of animal life but has been very enjoyable in a lot of other ways. Traveling the river by canoe and later by skidoo was totally enjoyable – especially on sunny days. Even enjoyed cutting trail when the weather was nice. It was especially interesting scouting for fur sign and the anticipation of setting traps later on. It's surprising how interesting a walk along a trail now is to me since I've learned to read the different animal tracks. We've decided that if we come back next year, we'll probably not stay as long. We'll come here late in September and probably go home earlier. We'll see!!

Monday – Dec. 7th -17C   Beautiful out this morning. Stopped snowing shortly after we went to bed. We now have about twelve inches of snow so must have received at least five inches over the last day.

After breakfast Gordon was busy getting everything that's going to Watson Lake down to the river bank, ready for loading on the plane tomorrow – if it comes. The rest of the stuff is stored in the cache. There are just a last few items left in the cabin for storing at the last minute. My back felt a little better today so about two o'clock, we took the skidoo upriver and then up Lynx Creek for a short distance. We then put on snowshoes so we could explore an area where there are a lot of potholes, little meadows, etc. Looks like an ideal area for marten and should be relatively easy going for the skidoo with just a little clearing required here and there. Should we come next year, we hope to travel more on the meadows and little sloughs rather than following the creeks, thus avoiding the overflow.

Tuesday – Dec. 8ᵗʰ -35C Cold out – a bit of cloud so possibly it will warm up.

Late last evening we got word, relayed via Don Taylor, that the plane will not be here until tomorrow, the ninth. It apparently will be bringing out a load of building material. We're sure curious about that because we did not order any. The signals were so poor that maybe Gordon misheard the message. It was eventually cleared up this morning when we got through to Don Taylor at Stewart Lake. Jamie – Bless his heart – is delaying the plane by a day in order to get a load of building materials and windows out to us. He figured we might as well utilize the empty plane coming here – smart lad!! But, we do not need any more windows and depending on what he's sending – perhaps not the other materials either. Now the weather will probably cloud over and we'll get snow or fog or?? that will prevent the plane coming in. I'll hang him by his little toes if that happens!! Oh well, Gordon pulled out a frozen Dolly last night so we'll have a feed of fresh fish for dinner tonight. Right now Gordon's outside, clearing snow off the roof of the little cabin. It has a flat roof so he intends storing the materials up there where they'll be safe if the river floods in the spring. When he's finished with that job he's going to put on his snowshoes and do more packing on the runway.

Wednesday – Dec. 9ᵗʰ -17C   Fogged in again – hope it clears. No radio signals this morning either.

Not much we could do except have breakfast and then sit around the cabin trying to get through to Don Taylor or Watson Lake Flying to find out if the aircraft was on it's way. No word until just after lunch. We were advised the plane had left and should be landing here about three o'clock. It was a mad rush then, getting the rest of the supplies into the cache, our gear packed and placed down by the runway. Just finished when the sound of the aircraft engine was heard. A few minutes later the Otter landed and taxied up in front of the cabin. The aircraft was really loaded with a lot of groceries, lumber, windows and a forty-five gallon barrel of gas. Took a while to get everything off-loaded and stored away. We took off at about four-thirty for Watson Lake.

It wasn't until we'd landed at Watson Lake that Gordon advised me that he'd have to go back within the next few days. He'd forgotten to take the ladder down from the cache. What a sneaky way to have an excuse for returning!!

1987

THIS IS SCARY – I'M REALLY
LOOKING FORWARD TO RETURNING

M onday – Sept.14th

A cold, blustery day at Watson Lake. We'd hoped to be away to the trapline by now but with so much still to do at home, we delayed our flight. Also, the Otter aircraft we'd planned on using is temporarily out of service with mechanical problems. The engineers are changing the engine so now we expect to get away about the twentieth, a week later than planned.

We had a very busy season with a tremendous hay crop. The weather was very wet so that also put us behind with our work. My garden was also a big job. I'm still busy putting away veggies for the winter – making mincemeat, jellies, pickles, etc.

I'm really looking forward with anticipation to our return to the trapline this year, especially to the Coal River. Gordon had flown out in April with a couple of helpers to build a larger cabin at Rose Lake. It still requires quite a lot of work to finish it off, another project that will keep us busy this fall. Near the end of August he also flew to another part of our trapline, to a lake we've since decided to name Ridge Lake. He was accompanied by three friends who helped with the construction of another cabin. We now have four fairly large cabins and one smaller one, all located in the northern part of our trapline.

Tuesday – Sept. 22nd

After a longer delay than anticipated, ten days total, we're finally here – back to our home at Jamie Lake. Sure a real schimozzle this year. We really required the Otter for flying out to the trapline since we had so much gear. Boxes of groceries, duffle bags of clothing, pre-cut but unassembled trap cubbies and our two dogs. But most important – two, five gallon pails of half decomposed fish scraps for trap bait. They are quite aromatic so enclosed them in double plastic bags, hoping they'd help contain the scent. We found they did help – somewhat!! We knew the Beaver would not be able to handle the load of supplies. But finally, because of more delays with the Otter, we had Watson Lake Flying Service bring us out with the Beaver. They'll fly the remainder of our supplies out in a few days time. We were to leave at seven this morning so got up at five-forty to make coffee and breakfast. Phoned our son, Jamie, and wakened him at six to come over for a quick coffee. Anyway, a few minutes later, all of Watson Lake was down in solid fog. Fog persisted and it wasn't until nearly twelve-thirty that we finally took off. My nerves were shot by then – I hate flying.

I do admit, it was a good flight to our lake. Air was smooth with no turbulence. Scenery was gorgeous. Leaves on the trees as well as foliage on mountainsides had switched to their fall colors, displaying a mix of red and orange hues – just beautiful. As we approached Jamie Lake, Gordon asked the pilot, Hans Jensen, to fly over our cabin to make certain that bears had not demolished it. It was fine. If the cabin been torn apart, we would have flown to our new cabin at Ridge Lake. A few minutes later, after landing, we quickly unloaded the Beaver and waved Hans goodbye. He had other flights to make and wanted to get away as quickly as possible.

After hiking up to the cabin, we found everything was fine except for the mess created by a squirrel that had taken up permanent residency. We found a huge pile of pine cones stacked under the bunks – enough to more than fill a five gallon pail. Heaps of cones were also piled around the foam mattresses.

One of Gordon's high top rubber boots was filled to the top while the other one was only a third full. Our new occupant had also stored and hidden, inside the cabin, a variety of mushrooms. It took me quite a while to remove our unwanted tenants winter larder, sweep the cabin clean and finally, wash and sterilize the dishes, shelves, table, etc. Meanwhile, Gordon was busy packing supplies up from the lake

After finishing lunch and unpacking the few things brought in, we headed up our trail – Super Highway, to the river. We hoped to shoot or at least spot a moose. A couple of minutes after we reached the ridge overlooking the meadows along the river and settled down, Gordon with his binoculars, spotted two moose across the river about two miles away. Turned out there were at least four of them. We quickly climbed down from our lookout point on the hill, reaching the meadow below. Crouching, darting from one patch of willow to another, we hurriedly crossed the meadow.

Several minutes later, we were crouched behind a lone spruce growing on the riverbank. Peering between branches, we could plainly see across the river to where the four moose, two cows and two bulls, stood. Gordon first tried getting their attention with the plaintive, low moaning call of a lovesick cow moose desperately needing a partner. When that brought no results, he tried the grunting, challenging call of a bull looking for a fight with any other male in the vicinity. We hoped the calls would entice at least one of the bulls to cross to our side of the river, eager to add another cow to his harem or take up the challenge from another bull. Nothing much happened. The bulls grunted a few times in response but appeared completely satisfied with their present partners. If we shot one of the bulls across the river, it would make an awful lot of packing for us. We were at least four miles from Jamie Lake, a long pack with a load of meat. We decided not to take one but would return the next evening, hoping to find them on our side of the river. It was still a very enjoyable experience – seeing moose at such close range. The bulls both had massive antlers. They were grunting and pawing the ground, defying any bull on our side of the river to try to come over and steal one of their cows. Should have had a movie camera!!

By the time we got back to the cabin, it was quite late. Both of us were ready for a break and something to eat. When we went to turn the propane on for our lights, we discovered the tank was empty. The valve must have been leaking. We'll now be using our gas lamp until propane arrives on the next aircraft. We have two new dogs with us this year, Katy and Celsius. They're both trained to harness so we're looking forward to trying them when snow arrives. They took the flight out really well and have settled down in their new home – no carrying on.

Wednesday – Sept. 23rd -4C Beautiful morning. Sunny and frosty.

I didn't sleep very well, even after our hike yesterday. It really surprised me that the two dogs did not fuss during the night. Not a single bark – really good. Gordon went to the meadow east of here to see if he could spot any game – nothing. Surprised me that the dogs didn't bark or whine when he left. Returning, he reported that, on the last trap box before the meadow, a marten had left his calling card. He used the top of the cubby as his bathroom. Some respect!!

About ten, we went for a walk to the second lake. Lots of moose tracks along the trail. We also brought back a couple of large plastic pails we'd cached there. They'll be handy as feed or water pails for the dogs. In the afternoon, Gordon was going to demolish the shower stall he'd built outside the cabin but I suggested he put shelves in and we'd use it for storage. He cleaned it out, installed shelves, manufactured a door and replaced the roofing. It makes a great storage area – safe from dogs, birds and animals. In the past we've had to bring things into the cabin if we went away for any length of time. Now we can just latch the door tight. At least our whiskey jacks won't be able to get at things.

Mid afternoon we again headed up the Super Highway to the river and our lookout point, to glass for moose. It got quite chilly towards evening after a breeze sprang up so Gordon started a small fire. Felt good. Later, just as we were about ready to leave, he rushed over and grabbed his rifle from where it was leaning against a spruce. He'd heard a moose grunt, sounded just below the base of the hill!! I got up and immediately spotted a moose across the river. Gordon kept making the calls of a love-starved cow as we crept down the hill and headed towards the river. The bull knew exactly where our calls were coming from. He jumped in the river with a huge splash, swam across, climbed up the bank on our side and rushed in our direction. He'd come a short distance, stop to listen for the next seductive, moaning call from Gordon then start running towards us again. Finally, he was in the open as he crossed a grassy section along the riverbank. Gordon fired one shot and the moose dropped. We had our moose – our winter's meat!!

When we walked up to the moose, the first thing we noticed was that his head was hanging over the edge of the riverbank. Directly beneath, the water was very deep. We're sure lucky he didn't end up in the deep channel where we'd have had one heck of a job getting him out. Gordon immediately got busy skinning and butchering the moose. The moose was real fat, in excellent shape. While Gordon was busy, I remembered that last winter we'd left a fishline and hook in one of the nearby trees. I found it, baited the hook with a scrap of meat and threw it in the water. A few minutes later a small Dolly Varden struck but soon threw the hook. I kept trying and, sure enough, the fish struck again and this time I landed him. Dolly Varden are very cannibalistic and it's likely the blood in the water from the moose had attracted him. Later, when we were finished with dressing out the moose, we took a section of ribs and tenderloin as well as my fish and headed for home.

Tomorrow, we'll return with our dogs and start packing the meat up the trail to the top of the ridge and then home. We have our work cut out for us. It will be a big job, all that packing. It'll probably take at least six trips. It's about a thirty-five minute walk from the cabin to where the moose is but the return trip, climbing to the top of the ridge with loaded packboards, will take much longer. Thank goodness the dogs are trained for packing and that we brought their packs out with us. They should be a big help. Now we can relax a bit – at least after tomorrow, when the work is done. We have our meat for the winter, our main concern. Getting the meat home won't be as easy as it was during the last two years but we're still very pleased. The moose was just a young bull with small antlers but the body is quite large.

After we got back to the cabin, Gordon trimmed the meat we'd brought home and gave the scraps to the dogs. They sure enjoyed them. We had beef T-bone steaks with mushrooms that I'd brought from home for supper. Surprised to find the steaks were still frozen when I brought them in from our storage cabinet. Also had a nice salad made from the last of my lettuce, together with cucumbers and tomatoes that Carol Pecconi had given us. Carol had also brought us about a three gallon container of green tomatoes. They're now slowly ripening, so should have fresh tomatoes for quite awhile. If they ripen too fast, I'll make soup from them. Carol had also given us another bunch of green tomatoes, about two weeks ago, from which I'd made five quarts of green tomato pickles using her recipe. Also had enough to make mincemeat for six pies. We topped dinner off with two pieces of Swiss chocolate each – a gift from our daughter Debbie. Chocolate she'd brought back from her trip to London and Germany in July. It was delicious – have to ration them.

Thursday – Sept, 24th -4C   Fogged in again but will be sunny once the fog clears.

Gordon's busy this morning fixing his packboard to use for packing our meat home. Somehow, a porcupine had managed to get at his packboard which he'd left hanging in the porch when we'd left last year. The porky had eaten all the leather straps so now he's busy improvising. Will be interesting to see how the two dogs act running loose, especially packing. We had made dog packs for them so they should be able to pack a fairly good load, we hope!! We got the dogs from Bill Thompson at Whitehorse. He races dogs. The dogs are purebred, registered Malamutes. The mother, Celsius, is eight years old while her daughter, Katy, is just four. They're large dogs but ever so gentle. They were trained for racing and haven't packed before so it may be an interesting day. Finally, packboard repairs completed, we put the empty packs on the dogs – they didn't really object, and headed for the river to retrieve our meat. At first we led the dogs since we didn't know how they'd act. They were fine.

As we were going down the trail in the fog, Gordon noticed Celsius suddenly stop and her tail drop. She didn't want to go further. It was an indication that either wolves or a grizzly had gone down the trail ahead of us. At first we couldn't see tracks in the pine needles covering the trail but soon bear tracks and fresh droppings told us who was just ahead. We wondered if a grizzly had claimed our moose. In the fog with poor visibility, it was pretty tense following the trail, knowing a grizzly sow and her cub were somewhere just ahead of us. We slowly, carefully, crept along the trail, checking every patch of brush along the way. The fog finally started clearing just as we were coming down the trail from the ridge. It was a real relief, finally being able to see more than a hundred feet ahead of us. We now branched off the trail, just a short distance from our moose. The final approach was made by Gordon, alone. He slowly advanced with rifle cocked and ready, stopping every few steps to minutely examine every clump of willow or grassy tussock that might conceal a bear. He continued on in this manner, taking a good bit of time covering the last couple of hundred yards to the moose. It was a great relief to find it untouched. Surprising how warm it suddenly seemed. The last few minutes certainly got our adrenalin flowing. We were really lucky since the bears had gone by within a few hundred yards. The light breeze blowing had carried the scent of our kill away from the trail. Otherwise, things could have turned out very differently!!

We got busy, skinning and butchering the moose, then sorted smaller pieces for the dog packs. Around noon the fog finally lifted to reveal a cloudless, sunny day. We strapped loads of meat on our packboards and were all set to go. First though, we thought it might be a good idea to see how the dogs would accept carrying their small loads. What a disaster!! They didn't even know how to stand up with their packs on. Eventually things got straightened out and we packed our loads over to the base of the hill. We tied the two dogs there. I removed their packs while Gordon climbed the hill with a hind quarter of moose. After he returned, we went back to the moose where he loaded the second hind quarter on his packboard. While he was packing the hind quarters, I was busy carrying his rifle as well as my pack which contained our gear and some meat, back to the base of the hill. I made tea while Gordon packed the second hind quarter up the hill and along the ridge a short distance. We finally had tea and toasted meat sandwiches. We were starving by then so they really tasted good. After lunch he carried the dog packs and then my load to the top of the hill. It was too steep, he insisted, for us girls!! We then completed relaying the meat back to Jamie Lake. It sure felt good to finally finish packing for the day.

The dogs actually were very good considering it was the first time they'd been packed and also the first time they'd been out with us. Think they'll work out really well and save us quite a lot of packing. Tomorrow we'll go back and haul the front quarters home – if the grizzly hasn't gotten there ahead of us. For supper tonight, we had spaghetti and meat sauce which I'd brought from home. From now on its moose and fish. Later this evening, Gordon got through to our radio contact, Don Taylor, for the latest news.

Friday – Sept. 25th -3C Sunny this morning – no fog, no clouds – a gorgeous fall morning.

After a breakfast of hotcakes, we put the packs on the dogs and headed back to the moose, hoping to get the rest of our meat. No problems with the dogs. We arrived at the base of the hill and retrieved a large piece of moose we cached yesterday, plus our tea pail, cups and Gordon's knife. From that distance it looked as if nothing had bothered the remains of the moose other than for the Whiskey Jacks(northern term the for Canada Jays) busily scavenging meat scraps. Just about seventy-five yards before reaching the moose, there's a small stream running into the river which we have to cross. What we saw in the mud along the edge of the stream caused us to come to a screeching halt. Fresh grizzly tracks!! After thinking about it for awhile – probably ten seconds, we figured it was too nice a morning to get into unpleasantries with the neighbors so turned around, picked up our gear at the base of the hill and headed home.

We felt it was the only sensible thing to do. Where the moose was lying, in the grass on the riverbank , the distance to adjoining stands of thick willow was only about twenty feet. When we'd walked through them the previous day, we'd noted depressions from eighteen inches to two feet deep between the clumps. Ideal locations from which a bear could watch the site. There was a very good possibility the bear was lying up in the brush, watching the kill. If we had pro-ceeded, it would undoubtedly have charged. At that close distance he would have had all the advantage and would have been on us before we could stop him. Gordon figured he'd be lucky to get off one hurried shot, definitely not enough to stop the bear unless he was very, very, lucky. Out here alone, we just can't take that chance!! As it is, we'll head back later this afternoon and check it out. If the bear is on the kill, we'll do our best to get him and then retrieve the remainder of our meat.

While waiting for lunch, Gordon started building a cache for the meat. We want to keep the meat away from the other cache and our supplies. For lunch, we had left over spaghetti and meat sauce, the trout and some moose tenderloin plus a fresh tomato. Really good. I'd also cooked up a pan of bannock to go with my homemade jam. Gordon continued working on the cache this after-noon while I just puttered around, hauling water and then doing a small amount of laundry. Chinked a bit of wall where squirrels had pulled the moss out from between the logs and then dug a pit for waste water.

Later in the afternoon the sky started clouding over and quite a breeze be-gan blowing. Sure hope the aircraft arrives soon with our roofing material and the rest of our groceries. We want to finish repairing the cabin roof before it gets too cold. We're hoping, seeing so many moose still around – fresh tracks everywhere, that it will be a nice late fall. Last year there was between eight and a half to ten inches of snow on September twenty-sixth, although it did melt off later. The dogs are really terrific, no noise, no barking – even better than Murky.

At about four-thirty, Gordon came in for tea and cake but before I had time to pour, was sure I heard an aircraft. Gordon said "No" but I said "Yes" and sure enough, a minute later the Otter was flying over us. Immediately, we were down to the lakeshore to meet it. Gordon helped tie the plane to the dock, then looked into the aircraft and remarked, "Where are the groceries" ? The pilot looked dumbfounded, since plywood, a few pieces of two by four lumber and a forty pound propane tank was all he had on board. Turned out that Stan, at Watson Lake Flying, had forgotten all about our groceries, snowshoes, chainsaw, etc. that he'd put into their storage building. Stan had helped load the lumber but forgot the rest. Now it's still a waiting game – "When will our groceries arrive"?? The worst is that the ginger ale, to mix with my scotch and the orange juice for Gordon's over-proof rum aren't here. Now we really have to rough it. !! At least we got our propane for lights.

We packed the supplies up to the cabin and weather permitting, will finish re-roofing the other half of the cabin tomorrow – after we finish packing the rest of our meat home. Just after we finished dinner and were washing dishes, the dogs started barking. Something was down the hill below the cabin. Gordon went out with his rifle but it was too dark to see anything. He did hear antlers rattling against trees so thinks a band of caribou had gone by.

Saturday – Sept, 26th "0"C   Sunny but windy. Tried calling Watson Lake Flying but no reception.

After breakfast, Gordon started re-roofing the other half of the cabin and while working, heard the sound of an aircraft. A few minutes later the Beaver flew over and landed. We ran down to the lake to meet it. Stan was the pilot. He'd brought in the rest of our groceries, lumber, snowshoes, odds and ends, plus the nails Gordon needed for the roof. We'd spent a good while this morning sorting through cans of nails, hoping to find enough to start the job. Stan must have felt a bit sheepish about forgetting the groceries since he didn't mention anything about it. He wasn't feeling very well, not his usual laughing self. He had such a sore throat that it hurt to talk. Too bad he had to make the flight today but we did appreciate receiving the balance of our supplies, especially since the weather had started closing in, turning cold and windy with a light drizzle – not nice.

Anyway, we finished the roof just in time. Gordon nailed plywood in place while I measured and cut roofing paper. I also was busy sorting and packing groceries, ready for storing in the cache. Just after four-thirty, finishing our tea break, we got ready with packboards and rifle and headed down the trail to the river to check whether a bear was on our moose. We'd just gone a short ways when the weather really started closing in. If Gordon did get the bear, it would be a cold, miserable job skinning it in the exposed area by the river so we turned back to the cabin. After the rain slacked off, we were busy for the remainder of the afternoon hanging meat in the shelter Gordon had built yesterday. Hope the birds don't get at it since it's still not covered with meat sacking. Later, after dinner, we turned on the radio – reception was clear and the music was great.

Sunday – Sept. 27th +2C   Cloudy out and very soggy. It rained quite heavily during the night.

Cleared up beautifully by eleven o'clock. Gordon built a doghouse for Celsius and then peeled the upright log legs of the cache while I was busy doing odd jobs in the cabin. After lunch we headed out for the river to check on our moose kill. Right away, glassing from the top of the ridge, we could see the remains had been moved away from the riverbank but nothing was on it, or so it appeared. Ravens and a bald eagle were sitting in the tops of nearby spruce watching the remains. Every once in a while one would fly down and land, then hurriedly take off without feeding. After studying it closely through the binoculars, we could see that part of the remains were covered, the trade-mark of a bear asserting his claim. While we did not see the bear, Gordon was certain it was sleeping in a depression dug behind the moose. The actions of the birds certainly supported this. If the bear wasn't there, they would have remained and fed until stuffed. It's not unusual for scavengers, especially eagles, to gorge themselves to the point where they aren't able to take off and fly. The big problem for us was that if we moved closer, down from the top of the ridge, we wouldn't be able to see the moose remains. If we proceeded down the hill, the next view we'd have would be from a distance of no more than twenty yards. Not a good idea!! Safely approaching the area from any direction was impossible. Willow and other shrubbery enclosed the location on all sides. It would be impossible to sneak up without making noise that would alert the bear.

We remained where we were, waiting and watching until late in the afternoon, hoping the bear would show. By then we were just about frozen. We hadn't planned on sitting and watching and weren't dressed for the cold. We hurried back to the cabin, trying to warm up, but it wasn't until after downing a couple of cups of hot tea that we finally thawed out. We plan on going back to try and get the bear tomorrow morning, weather permitting. Snow pellets and a very strong wind at supper time.

Monday – Sept. 28ᵗʰ +2C   Cloudy this morning and a cool breeze.

After a breakfast of bacon and eggs we headed back down the trail to the river to see if the grizzly was on our moose. Nearing our lookout point, we spotted the grizzly. He'd completely covered the remains of the moose. As we moved closer to our lookout point, he disappeared into the brush behind the moose. It's mostly thick willow with many depressions. While we were watching from our lookout point about four hundred feet above the river and the bear, he seemed to just disappear. We walked further along the ridge towards another spot we'd checked the day before, hoping for a better view. From yesterday's checking, we knew that not too far below was a fairly good location for a shot at the bear. Distance would be between three hundred and fifty and four hundred yards. The direction of the wind and dense bush would make it impossible to get any closer. As we crept along the top of the ridge, we spotted the bear returning to the kill. Gordon snuck down to his shooting location while I stayed on the ridge, watching. The bear was facing towards us when Gordon shot. He seemed to stumble and turned sideways. Gordon shot again but it was impossible to tell if he hit him again. At the second shot, the bear ran a few feet and disappeared in the bush. From where I was on the ridge, I could see the bear for a few seconds before he just disappeared. I believe that was as far as he went. Beyond that point it's fairly open meadow and I think I'd have seen him if he'd kept on going.

We remained on the ridge, glassing the area, trying to spot the bear but no luck. Whether the bear was wounded, was dead or unhurt, was impossible to tell. In that thick brushed, rough area, it would have been foolish trying to follow him. If he was lying in a depression, waiting, you'd be almost on top of him before seeing him. A person would be extremely lucky to get off one shot before he was on you. We decided it would be extremely foolish to take a chance trying to find the grizzly. We finally turned away, returning to the cabin. Hated to leave without checking and making certain whether the bear was dead or wounded but felt we had no choice. We plan on going back to the ridge tomorrow morning, weather permitting, in hopes the bear was unhurt and will be back on the kill. Gordon was totally disgusted that the bear had not been killed outright and blames his poor shooting for that. It was a difficult shot though, since he was shooting downhill and it's hard to estimate bullet drop at that distance.

After lunch we hiked across to the Beaver meadow west of here to pick up traps since we won't be trapping over there this year. Upon reaching the meadow, we were surprised to find a good deal of it was flooded. It appeared beavers had enlarged their dam, backing up more water. We then decided to head for the dam, hoping to get a couple. Just as we started, Gordon spotted two caribou about a mile up the meadow. We watched them for several minutes before they finally entered the timber. When we did reach the dam and, checking the beaver house through binoculars, were surprised to find no recent sign of activity. There wasn't a winter feed bed and no fresh cuttings. It appeared beaver had not used the house since the past winter. Just why they moved or what happened to them is a mystery, although Gordon suspects otter may have been the culprits.

Not finding any beaver, we turned and headed back home. We were glad when we finally reached the cabin and were able to sit and relax. Besides, it was long past tea time!! We'd covered quite a few miles collecting traps, walking in high-topped rubber boots. They are, without a doubt, the most tiring footwear and definitely not suited for hiking long distances. We had decided to wear them today since a lot of the country we had to travel, picking up traps, had been covered with water the previous year.

Tuesday – Sept. 29th -2C   Snowing lightly this morning.

After a pancake breakfast, we headed back up the ridge towards the river and our moose kill. By the time we reached the ridge, it was snowing quite heavily and visibility was poor. From the lookout point, we could see several ravens were feeding on the moose remains – indicating the bear was not there. Gordon thinks the remains had been moved a bit from their location yesterday. We're going to give it one more try tomorrow and hopefully, if he does return, we'll have a good chance to take him. If he's not there, we'll go down and do some checking. We also want to pick up Gordon's small axe that was left there. It's an axe he always has along, wherever he goes.. The following day we'll pack up and head for Rose Lake and our new cabin. Roofing paper has to be installed before it gets too cold. Because we were ten days late arriving and now spending a week on the bear, our schedule is somewhat behind.

By three in the afternoon there was three inches of snow on the ground and still falling heavily. Gordon worked outside for most of the day, cutting wood, closing off most of one side of the porch and sorting traps. I just goofed off and read but did make a pot roast for dinner. It turned out very well – first one from our moose.. By six-thirty, we had five and a half inches of snow on the ground but now, instead of snow, we're getting rain.

Later, Gordon got through on the radio to Larry Schnigg at Tobally Lakes. It seems they've been having bear trouble over there. A grizzly wrecked their main camp at Tobally Lakes. The bear removed the door and three windows from the storage shed and then ate or destroyed about a year's supply of groceries. In the meat house, he just removed one wall, entirely, and then took all their winter meat supply of dried fish and moose. He also did a great deal of damage to other buildings as well as to their main home cabin. Larry has a fishing camp at Tobally with a number of cabins for summer clients in addition to the storage and home cabin. The bear went through them all. Later, checking line cabins on North Tobally and North lakes, he found they also were almost completely demolished.

There's another trapper in Larry's area – Pete Johnson, an old-timer in his eighties. The grizzly visited him and did a lot of damage to his main cabin as well as eating or destroying nearly two years of food supplies. Larry figures he's lucky, in a way, since he and his wife, Maggie, were out cutting trail and had been away from their camp for five days. A helicopter crew working in the area had flown over Larry's main camp and spotted the damage. They then located Larry and flew him and Maggie back to their camp. The grizzly was still there so Larry shot him. It was an old bear with very few teeth left. His ears had been either frozen off or chewed off in a fight at some time. They estimated the bear would weigh about twelve hundred pounds – a really tremendous sized grizzly!!! Larry figures he was very lucky. If he hadn't got back when he did, the bear would probably have completely demolished the entire camp. Also, considering its condition, the bear undoubtedly would not have survived another winter, ultimately starving to death.

Wednesday – Sept. 30th *"0"C*   Clear – sunny – looks gorgeous out. It was quite windy during the night so all the snow blew off the trees. Sure lots on the ground.

After breakfast (omelettes), we hiked back to the moose kill. It was hard walking, especially for me. I wore my high-top rubber boots since my hiking boots are too low for the amount of snow we have. The snow was also very crusted so we made a lot of noise while walking. Not good when trying to sneak up on our moose. When we reached the lookout point, Gordon could see the kill and thought it had been disturbed but couldn't decide what had moved it. We decided to go down the hill, then walk a short distance along the riverbank checking for bear sign. Nothing!! No tracks in the snow along the base of the ridge. We continued on until we reached the small, shallow creek that had to be crossed to reach the site. From where we stood on lower ground along the creek, the moose remains – only thirty to forty yards away but on higher ground, could not be seen. Just as we started crossing the creek, Gordon stopped and whispered, "Lets get out of here – the bugger is still around" !! There, in the fresh snow on the other side of the stream, were fresh grizzly tracks. We turned and headed back up the hill.

It would have been so much simpler had there been another rifle (and another man) for backup. The bear had crossed the creek since the snow, returning to the kill. With the thick, snow-covered brush, it was very unsafe trying to get closer. We returned to the top of the ridge and from there, glassed for quite some time. I'd never been on a grizzly hunt before but have been present at numerous black bear encounters. I've even had black bears on our woodpile and standing on the back step at home but this location, with thick brush, made the situation very tense. Gordon says, exciting, but I say SCARY!!

We decided to return to the cabin for tea and lunch and return later in the afternoon. On our way back, in several places along the trail, noticed fresh moose and caribou tracks. Nice to see they're still around. Also spotted a few marten tracks. It was so nice walking back, sun was shining and it was so warm. After lunch Gordon got busy putting roofing paper on our grocery cache. Oh,

Oh!! He just measured the left-over paper and found we have enough for only half of the cache roof. He measured the paper <u>after</u> removing the two plastic tarps that formerly covered the roof, neatly folded them and had put them away. What a Turkey!! He had to replace the tarps on the cache, then used the left-over roofing paper on the CN Towers (our outdoor plumbing facility), so christened by John Grant.

At four o'clock, it was back to the Ridge with high expectations of seeing the grizzly. We waited and watched until six-thirty and then decided he wasn't going to show up. The sun, going down in the west, had lost its heat and we were half frozen, so decided to head for home.

Thursday – Oct.1st +3C   Rained all night but just lightly this morning. Also very foggy out. Earthquake reported in southern California around Pasadena. That must have been so frightening.

Too wet to do anything much this morning so Gordon is putting up new poles to raise the radio antennae higher, hoping for better reception. He then cut a bunch of firewood. Later, both of us went to reroute a short section of trail. Trail clearing was finally completed but Gordon had a lot of chainsaw problems. After returning to the cabin, he spent a lot of time trying to adjust the carburetor, hoping it would work better. While having tea, he had a brain-wave. He decided the fuel line must be sucking air where the line entered the carburetor. Sure enough, after clamping the hose tight with a piece of snare wire – one pull and the saw started, running smoothly. Sure glad to hear it purr along – a lot easier cutting wood and clearing trail with it than our swede saw.

Later in the afternoon when the weather cleared a bit, we walked back to the river to check on our moose. On the way, spotted fresh wolverine tracks in the snow along the trail. From our lookout point, it appeared the moose remains hadn't been touched since yesterday and, as far as we could tell, the bear had not returned. We're pretty certain he has left as the remains were left uncovered after his last visit. There's really not much left for him to feed on. With the snowfall, he probably figured it was about time to den up for the winter and has headed for higher country.

Friday – Oct.2nd +4C   Stars were shining when I went to bed last night but the sky clouded over later and rained most of the night. Surprise this morning – it's clear, the sun is shining and it looks like it will be a nice day after all.

We plan on going to Rose Lake, finally!! We have lots to do there. We loaded our packboards, fixed packs on the two dogs and got away at eleven-fifteen. It was a gorgeous morning for walking. By the time we reached our chocolate bar tree, an hours walk from Jamie Lake where we usually take a break, I had to take my jacket off and tie it on my pack. It was hot out ! The dogs, running along behind us, really behaved themselves. We saw many marten tracks as well as tracks from moose and caribou and further along, tracks of a grizzly. The tracks were very large, must have been made by an exceptionally large bear. Glad we didn't run into him. Reaching the swampy area, changed from hiking boots to rubber boots. As usual, I got a boot full of water when I slipped off a hummock. Even after changing back to dry hiking boots after passing the swampy sections my feet managed to get sopping wet. It seems I have no trouble locating all the deep puddles along the trail. The hike took us over three hours and was very tiring. The snow on the trail made it difficult walking and further on, walking around the rough, swampy areas was especially tough. It was so good to at last see the river and then, the cabin.

As soon as we removed our packs, Gordon was up to the cache, collecting dry clothing to change into. While he removed packs from the dogs and tied them, I started a fire in the cabin stove. It only took a few minutes for the cabin to start warming up. The heat felt so good!! I had not realized how chilled I'd become in my wet clothing. Brush along the trail was dripping wet from melting snow on branches so both Gordon and I got soaked through.

Once more warm in our dry clothes, while waiting for tea water to boil Gordon took me on a tour of the new cabin. It's located along the riverbank about two hundred yards further downstream. It's quite near the edge of the bank, the east wall being only about ten to twelve feet back from the drop-off to the river With a window installed in the east wall, we'll have early morning light from the rising sun as well as a terrific view. The cabin's much larger than the one we're in now but, so far, has no windows, door or floor installed. It's quite dark inside, especially since the logs haven't been peeled. During the winter when it was built, frozen logs didn't peel very well. We'll get at them tomorrow.

After lunch, while I was getting things organized in the cabin, Gordon took the canoe about three quarters of a mile up river to haul supplies home. This past March when he, Fabian and Robbie Porter had flown out to build the cabin, the plane had got stuck in the deep snow just as soon as it landed. It wasn't possible to taxi the aircraft up river to the cabin location. They had to off-load the plywood, lumber, windows, door and roofing paper up on the river bank. Gordon now has to load it in the canoe and haul it back here. He ended up making two trips in the rain. Quite a change in the weather from when we first arrived. At two-fifteen it was so warm, in fact, our thermometer registered plus twenty-four Celsius. It stayed lovely all afternoon until Gordon was on the river with the canoe. It then started showering and has continued ever since. Must have something against Gordon!!

Saturday – Oct. 3ʳᵈ +2C A little cloudy and quite windy but in the sun, out of the wind, it's quite warm.

It's sure nice here – the scenery is just beautiful. Its great sitting at the table over coffee in the morning, watching through the window as the river in front of us flows by. In the distance the mountains with their snowy crests provide a perfect background. There's really no scenery at our Jamie Lake cabin – just trees and it's only when you're outside that you can view mountains in the distance. After breakfast, Gordon took the canoe back upriver to haul another load of supplies. He figures there'll be at least two more loads to bring back.

While Gordon was busy on the river, I went over to the new cabin and started peeling logs on the inside walls. It brightens things up so much. After Gordon returned with his first load, he started putting rafters and plywood up for the porch roof. The cabin is sixteen feet by fourteen feet and the porch must be an additional fourteen by fourteen feet. We'll have lots of storage space for wood, traps and everything else.

It hadn't warmed up at all by noon because of the cool breeze. A typical fall day. The river is very high this year and has risen another two inches since last night. Guess with the heavy rain over night and it being so warm yesterday, a lot of snow melted on the mountains. We worked on the new cabin all afternoon. I peeled log walls while Gordon finished putting plywood on the roof of the porch. About five o'clock, I decided it was about time to head over to the other cabin and make supper. Just as I started walking away from the new cabin, I spotted something dark across the river, about four hundred yards away, standing in a small patch of willow. Seconds later I noticed something shining – moose horns!! Then I "quietly" yelled at Gordon, "THERE'S A MOOSE"!!!!

Since we'd lost nearly half of our first moose to the grizzly – two front quarters, we'd decided to take another moose if we had the opportunity. We did need additional meat for the winter and I still had a moose tag. As soon as Gordon handed me the rifle, I crept over to a nearby spruce and after laying the rifle barrel over a branch for support, took a quick sight through the scope and fired. Instantly, the moose dropped in the willows, out of sight. I couldn't believe it, everything happened so fast. However, seconds later, the moose was up. Gordon then took over, firing a final shot. We had our moose, rather, My moose!!

It's the first moose I've ever taken. I felt sort of sad for the moose but at the same time, glad we had meat to keep us fed during the winter. If we had not taken him, there's a very good chance he'd be pulled down by wolves later on – a much crueler ending. Next, we collected our axe, knives and plastic tarps, hopped in the canoe and paddled across the river. While I took a couple of pictures, Gordon got busy butchering the animal. He was a large moose, larger than the one Gordon got, but not very fat so may be tough eating. Gordon completed gutting and dressing the animal before we returned to the cabin. We brought back a side of ribs which are now simmering in the soup pot. Tomorrow, we'll quarter the animal, bring the meat back across the river and hang it below the meat cache.

Gordon talked with Larry Schnigg again this evening. Larry reported that, so far, seven of his cabins along the trapline had been wrecked by the grizzly. He still has five more to check out. He'll sure have a lot of work repairing cabins so they'll be ready for the trapping season. There's also a summer fishing camp on the east side of Tobally Lake, now closed for the winter. The grizzly had also paid it a visit, doing a lot of damage.

Sunday – Oct. 4th +2C Snowed during the night and was very windy but now, we have a gorgeous morning with sunshine.

We have, rather had, a sheet of plastic over our porch roof to protect it from last winter's snow. It had a few tears in it and, with the wind, made such a racket that it was hard to sleep. Gordon say's he's tearing it completely off today. It will be nice in our new cabin with the roof covered with asphalt roofing – no plastic. Right after breakfast we canoed across the river to our moose. We finished butchering and hauling it home by noon. While Gordon was doing the butchering, I took the lower leg sections that were now just bone and tendon and propped them against a large tree stump which had washed down and been deposited on the sandbar during high water. After we finished with the butchering, the head and antlers were also dragged over by the stump. We'll be able to watch from the cabin for any bear or wolf that comes for a visit. We hauled the meat across the river and laid it just below the meat cache, atop a pile of green spruce boughs where it'll stay until it crusts a bit. We'll then hang it high, out of the reach of our neighbors.

After lunch I was back peeling logs at the new cabin while Gordon was busy installing roofing. The asphalt roofing comes in ninety pound rolls so hauling it up a steep roof incline is a bit interesting. We used a rope so I was able to help a bit. I'm terrified of heights so stayed on the ground, pulling on the rope which stretched over the roof. One end of the rope, stretched over the roof, was tied around the roll of roofing. When Gordon lifted the roll as high as he could, I, on the other side of the cabin, pulled the rope tight and wrapped it around a tree so it wouldn't slip. He then climbed on the roof and, pulling from above, got it up the rest of the way. Took a little time but it worked. Later, he had to take one more trip up river to get the last two rolls of roofing paper, cans of gas and a few other assorted items. One roll of roofing was quite badly damaged. Gordon, at first, thought it was done by a wolverine but closer inspection showed a bear was responsible. We do have a lot of bear diggings around the cabin and across on other riverbanks. The bears feed a lot on the tender roots of plants and grasses. So far we've had no trouble with them bothering our cabins. Have to keep our fingers crossed!! Gordon finished roofing this afternoon. It took seven rolls to cover the entire roof. He's tacking it down along the roof edges but will have to wait until tomorrow to complete the job. Looks good but it's getting too dark for hammering roofing nails. Hard on the fingers!!

It's not nice out this evening. It's turned colder, clouded over and looks like rain is coming. At least, with roofing on the cabin, we'll be able to work indoors if it does get miserable. Radio reception is really good tonight. Heard many stations calling in. Steve Picconi, a trapper up the Liard River, called to advise us that his wife, Carol, got a big grizzly. Guess it takes a woman to get one!! Good for her!!!

Monday – October 5th -2C   Rained during the night and turned to snow by morning.

We finished breakfast and then went over to work on the new cabin. Gordon, with his chainsaw, cut an opening for one of the cabin windows. Makes it much brighter. In fact, you can now see what it's like inside the cabin. He needed light for installing and leveling floor joists. Later, I took a break from peeling logs and returned to the other cabin to bake a pie and make a huge pot of soup. Then it was back for another stint of log peeling.

After a break for lunch, it was back to work on the cabin. By supper quitting time, Gordon had all the floor joists installed and half the plywood flooring nailed in place while I managed to finish peeling a lot more of the logs. The cabin's really starting to look good. Managed to get through to Watson Lake Flying this evening. It showered on and off all day and continued into the night.

Tuesday – Oct. 6th +1C   Looks like a nice day. The mountains are in view this morning with just a bit of cloud halfway up. They're exceptionally beautiful with a band of cloud wrapped around their mid section while protruding crests shine in the morning sun.

We'd placed a stake through some of the meat scraps and offal we'd dragged down the sandbar, just below where we'd got our moose. When we checked this morning, the stake wasn't there. Some animal must have dragged the remains away. Later today we'll have to investigate. The river has gone down by quite a lot. The other night Gordon was talking to Freddie Hasselburg, another trapper, who mentioned the Liard River had risen a foot and a half overnight. Right now, from our window, we can see a small spruce floating down stream past the cabin.

We'd brought half a dozen of Carol's tomatoes over with us from Jamie Lake. They were just starting to ripen but now are a bright red. I bet the bunch left at Jamie Lake have nearly all ripened. Too bad I don't know of a way to slow the ripening process so we'd still have them in December. We hung our meat this afternoon. Gordon put screening around the meat cache to keep birds away. The floor installation is completed in our new cabin and also, the door opening has been enlarged and framed. Tacking the roofing paper down has also been completed. Progress!!

Late afternoon, we took the canoe and went across river to check our moose kill and find out why the stake was down. Coming upriver and while crossing, we kept watching the brush for signs of the animal responsible for moving it but saw nothing. It wasn't until we were getting out of the canoe that Gordon spotted grizzly tracks and told me to stay back. Sure enough, grizzly tracks all along the bar. With rifle in hand, we slowly followed along the bar to where the kill was. We discovered a partial rib-cage, which was badly bruised from the moose fighting and unusable, was missing. Also, the moose hide we'd carefully placed over a fallen log to dry was gone. Gone too, was the new pair of mukluks that were to be made from it. I told Gordon the bear probably took it into his den for a bed. We dragged the head and horns, also the four legs, down the sandbar a ways to a very large dry tree that was washed up on the bar. Gordon had brought along some light steel cable which we now used to tie the moose head to the tree trunk. Everything is in view from the cabin and also within good shooting range – if the bear decides to come back.

We'd originally planned on going further up river to cut a load of dry firewood. There's a good stand of dead spruce right along the river bank about a mile and a half upriver, handy for cutting and loading in the canoe. We decided against going today. Sound of the chainsaw might scare the bear away. There sure seems to be quite a few bears around this fall. We've never seen grizzly out this late in previous years. Perhaps an indication of a late fall.

Wednesday – Oct. 7th *-10C*   A little nippy out this morning but such a gorgeous day. Not a cloud. There is a rim of ice along the edge of the river, though.

No bear sign this morning. Regarding other animal life – we've been conducting a survey – chocolate versus my bannock. My bannock won!! Five out of the six mice caught preferred bannock. Will definitely have to present a paper to the Government Pest Control people!! After breakfast we went over to our new cabin and got busy peeling logs. Just about finished the job by three-thirty in the afternoon, then we finally quit for the day. One more session should complete the job. Gordon will have to finish most of what's left. There are two ridge poles and one top end section that is too high for me. The next job will be chinking fiber-glass insulation between the wall logs and corners where needed. Strips of insulation were placed between the logs when the walls were being put up so there shouldn't be much chinking required.

After tea, we took the canoe and went up river to Lynx creek in hopes of catching a Dolly Varden for dinner. No luck – never even saw a fish. We then went further up, cut down a big dry tree, cut it into stove-wood lengths and loaded it into the canoe. On the way home we stopped a short distance from the mouth of Lynx Creek and tried a few casts into some of the rippley areas. Gordon finally hooked a Dolly and soon had it wriggling in the canoe. Supper at last!! Further along, we pulled into the bank, cut and loaded more wood as well as the smaller branches for kindling into the canoe and then headed home. After cleaning the trout, Gordon split wood while I made supper. In between, I ran out and gave him a hand stacking wood. The fresh trout was very good. A nice change from moose. Fish taste so good here – must be the cold, fresh running water that does it.

Thursday – October 8th -8C Another beautiful morning, think more so than yesterday. Bits of ice flowing down – river.

We plan on canoeing down-river this morning. We'll go a short ways past Twin Lakes Creek, then pull the canoe up on shore and head towards Ridge Lake, clearing trail along the way. We plan on just cutting a walking trail for now. There'll be a wider skidoo trail cleared later from Ridge Lake to connect with the meadows along the river where we trap. Our dog, Katy, whined during the night keeping us awake until Gordon got up to see what the problem was. Anyway, a drink of water stopped that. She has a horrible habit of stepping on the edge of her water dish and dumping it.

Right after breakfast we hopped in the canoe and headed down river, past Twin Lakes Creek, to the clay banks where we left the canoe. The clay banks along the east side of the river are quite a sight. They rise from the waters edge to a height of over a hundred feet in places. Some sections that have slid away from the main bank sit isolated, almost like pyramids, along the shoreline. It was a gorgeous day for our trip. We followed the blazes that Gordon and the boys had made during the summer when they were cabin building at Ridge Lake. Some sections needed very little clearing while other areas were a mass of obstructing willow, downfalls, etc. We managed to clear a good third of the trail to Ridge Lake before quitting for the day. We cut and cleared trail from eleven this morning until five in the afternoon with only a short break for tea, hamburgers and bannock. It had been so warm working in the sun that Gordon stripped and left his jacket, along with my light vest, beside the trail to be picked up on our way back. We figure it will take at least another couple of days to complete the trail to Ridge Lake.

After caching our tea pail as well as the chainsaw, gas and oil under a big spruce, we turned and headed back for the river. It felt good sitting in the canoe and relaxing while the purring motor pushed us upstream to the cabin. The dogs were especially glad to see us back again. Don't think we'll have any trouble falling asleep tonight.

Friday – Oct. 9th -7C   High overcast. Looks cool out this morning, especially when you look at the river and see large floes of ice drifting downstream.

Last night the dogs acted up several times. At about nine-thirty last evening they started quietly woof, woofing. Gordon went to check and returned reporting there must be a moose or caribou on the sandbar in front of the cabin, towards the creek side. He could hear their hooves crunching on frozen ground. Later, the dogs acted up again. This time we think it was a marten up in the tree beside them. We heard a scream which Gordon says sounded like a marten. Later on, more barking. The dogs were looking towards the river. This morning in daylight, we could see the moose head, cabled to the log, had been shifted. Some animal certainly tried pulling it away. Too bad they didn't come during daylight so we could see whoever it was.

After breakfast, Gordon went back to work on the new cabin while I stayed behind, baking a lemon pie and cinnamon buns. I burnt one batch – Darn it!! Baking kept me busy until after eleven. Then it was back to chinking and peeling more logs in our new home. Gordon finished banking the cabin and installed the stovepipe jack. The place is starting to take shape. Today was another gorgeous day, real sunny and quite warm. By mid-afternoon the river was clear, no more ice flowing downstream.

Saturday – Oct. 10th -7C   Another nice day. More ice flowing down the river.

The dogs really acted up last night but Gordon couldn't see anything in the dark. He checked things out this morning and found fresh caribou tracks in the snow behind the cache. After clearing breakfast things away and making lunches, it was into the canoe for another trip down river to the junction with our Ridge Lake trail. We had to break ice along the shoreline in order to get the canoe into the river. Lots of ice and slush keeping us company on our way down but it was still nice traveling in the sunshine. Upon reaching the clay banks, we pulled the canoe ashore and then headed up the trail to where we'd left off the day before. We worked for another two to three hours cutting trail before taking a break. Everything went well and the trail looks good. The weather had really changed during the past hour. Low clouds had moved in, accompanied by smatterings of rain. Wind had started to blow quite strongly so we decided it might be smart to head back to the canoe and home.

It only took us fifteen minutes to walk back the distance we'd slashed out during the past hours plus another forty-five minutes to reach the canoe. This trail takes us up and out of the valley, into the higher country where we want to trap this year. Gordon says Ridge Lake is only about another twenty minute walk beyond the point we'd reached today. It'll probably take at least another two to three hours of slashing even though the brush isn't as dense as what we were working through today.

By the time we reached the river and our canoe, weather had turned really miserable so we didn't stop to make tea. We shoved the canoe into the river and came right home. On the way back it got very windy and with freezing rain, made for a cold trip. Surprising how cozy our little cabin feels on a day like today. After we finished tea and lunch, Gordon was back to the new cabin, installing the large window in the east wall where it will overlook the river. He wants to finish the installation before we return to Jamie Lake.

Sunday – Oct. 11ᵗʰ +3C   It's cloudy, a little foggy and windy. It rained heavily during the night so the ground is sopping. All the ice along the river's edge has melted and there's no more slush flowing down.

   Not a good morning for me. I could not get to sleep so I'm tired. It's not a nice day to go down river and cut more trail, anyway. Instead, I did laundry while Gordon finished installing the window and also a door in the new cabin. Sure looks good now with two large windows, so bright inside. We plan on installing another small window but it will have to wait until after we build cupboards, bed, etc. to determine the best location for it. While I finished chinking around the windows Gordon installed a small stove to help speed drying the log walls. We hope to move in within a couple of days.

   This afternoon we took a break and headed up river to Lynx Creek, hoping to catch a trout. Tried casting in several pools and riffles but not a strike. The water is so clear that any fish movement is noticeable but nothing showed. Wonder if they've moved to the deeper pools. Will have to check them out another day. No fish so deciding not to come home empty-handed, we went a bit further upstream to cut a canoe load of firewood to bring back. Also on our way back, we checked out the moose head and legs we'd cabled to that dead tree. Tracks indicated a bear had been at it. We'd left the head securely cabled to a log at least twelve inches in diameter and twenty feet long. Signs showed how the bear yanked and pulled, trying to get the head loose from the twenty-five foot log frozen in the ground. Finally, the log broke. Talk about strength!! No sign of the moose head and we weren't inclined towards checking the brush to determine what had become of it.

Monday – Oct. 12th "0"C   Thanksgiving Day. It's cloudy – rained during the night. Snow flurries first thing this morning. No ice on the river, no snow on the ground.

Gordon was busy all morning cutting and splitting small, straight spruce into slats. In the afternoon we nailed them along the grooves between the logs, covering the insulation. What a difference!! Looks so clean and bright. I also finished peeling the bark from the last log. Hurray!! Glad that job's done. Just before supper, Gordon also installed propane lights in the new cabin, running the propane supply lines from the cylinder in the porch to the three overhead lights in the cabin. With lights, we'll be able to work in the evenings at finishing the cabin. We again tried for trout this afternoon but again, no luck. We'll have to settle for mooseburger, made from the brisket section, for supper tonight. After supper we worked until nearly ten o'clock in the cabin and now have just about all the slats nailed on. Then – to bed.

Tuesday – Oct. 13th -10C   Coooool but beautiful and sunny. The mountains are all covered with snow, a change from two days ago.

Katy had a whining session last night – seemed like forever. Finally, Gordon screamed, "Katy – SHUT UP" and she did. He just about sent me up through the roof with his bellow but at least it brought results. Last night, when we were walking back from the new cabin, Gordon suddenly stopped and asked for my flashlight. He had heard something swimming in the river. Turned out to be a muskrat. It's the first one I've seen here. The muskrat wasn't the least bit concerned having the light shining on him. While getting a pail of water from the river this morning, Gordon spotted grayling swimming around and a bit further along, just opposite the cabin, a school of thirty to forty whitefish. He thinks the Dolly's will follow. Hope so, a trout dinner would be nice.

After breakfast, we again headed down river to do more clearing on our Ridge Lake trail. After reaching the end of the cleared section, we continued onwards, cutting and clearing brush for the next three hours. We finally stopped for lunch under a big spruce. An ideal location since it was growing along the bank of a tiny stream. A few swipes with the axe to remove dead branches along the tree trunk and we had a comfortable backrest while we sat on our piles of pine needles at its base. The stream was the first one we'd reached since leaving the river, providing water for our tea.   Nothing is more enjoyable than a lunch break in the woods. It doesn't take long to get a fire going. Small dry twigs and branches for kindling are always found around the trunk of a growing spruce. One match and your kindling's ablaze, then larger sticks are added until the fire is just right. Next the tea pole, about four to five feet long. One end, sharpened to a point, is jabbed into the ground at just the right angle so your kettle of water will be suspended above the fire. While the water's heating, you're busy cutting a couple of "toaster" sticks. Willows provide the best sticks. They have to be green, about the thickness of your thumb, two feet long and most important – be forked at one end, wide enough to support a sandwich. Unless you like the taste of green bark, it's also a good idea to peel the forked end. With experience, you'll find yourself drinking tea and eating a nicely browned sandwich within minutes. It wasn't long before we were sitting, backs against the tree trunk, cup of tea in one hand and a sandwich in the other. With the pleasant aroma of scorching pine needles floating in the air, we were completely at peace with the world. It made us realize just how lucky we were to be here, enjoying a wonderful life, just the two of us out on our trapline.

After finishing lunch, Gordon decided it was time I had a look at the new Ridge Lake cabin. So right after finishing lunch, we left our gear and headed up the trail. It only took a few minutes walking before the lake and then the cabin came into view. The cabin is situated at the south end of Ridge Lake, about two hundred feet from the lakeshore and up on a bench about twenty feet above lake level. Behind the cabin is a small meadow enclosed, as in a bowl, by surrounding ridges. From the dock on the lakeshore to the cabin, there's a natural walkway composed of flat rocks. Just down the lakeshore from the cabin, a short ways westward, is the creek that flows from the lake. On the other side, eastward a couple of hundred feet, there are a number of springs flowing into the lake that supply ice cold water all year round. The cabin is sixteen feet by thirteen and a half feet, inside measurements. I was a little disappointed in the size since Gordon kept telling me it was the largest cabin on our trapline. It's actually narrower than the new one at Rose Lake. Also, even though the door was left partially open for circulation, the logs had not dried and some had even darkened a bit. Until the grey mold is washed off, the interior won't be very bright – something we can easily remedy after we start using the cabin.

The cabin does have an attached porch along the front, which will certainly be handy. There's also an outdoor "biffy" – nearly all enclosed (something we don't have at Rose Lake) as well as a dandy cache. When we return and spend some time here, we'll cut narrow slats to nail between the wall logs to cover the insulation. A bit of work will sure make a difference, brightening everything up. He'd also dug out a small storage area beneath the bed for storing fresh produce. It's a hole in the ground about two and a half feet square, floored and lined with boards. Everything they'd left behind, when building the cabin, looked good. Carrots, potatoes, onions, oranges, grapefruit and cabbage had kept well – still nice and crisp. But, mice had gotten into the apples and ate several and spoiled the rest so we chucked them. Finally, our inspection completed, we closed the cabin door and headed back

While walking back down the trail we decided, if weather permitted, we'd come back one more time to finish clearing the last section to the lake. While we could walk it in about fifteen minutes, it would probably take from two to three hours of brush cutting to make it suitable for the skidoo. The last section runs through an area of thick, heavy buckbrush. The trip back up river to our cabin at Rose Lake wasn't as nice as it was coming down. Sky had clouded over and wind was blowing, quite a change from the beautiful weather we'd enjoyed this morning. After supper it was back to the new cabin to complete tacking slats in place. Next comes the baseboard and hopefully after that, we move in.

Later that evening Gordon filled me in on some of the discoveries he and the men had made when they'd first flown in to Ridge Lake on their cabin building expedition. They'd found three dozen traps hanging in the two big spruce growing on the bench just below where the cabin is located. Someone, many years ago, had a camp there. From the depth of the fire pit and amount of ash, it must have been used quite a lot. Quite possibly a tarp or tent had been stretched between the two trees. The upper spreading branches of the spruce provided a cover and pretty well protected the area below. An ideal location for a trappers camp. The conjecture is that Hugo Brodel, an old-time trapper, left the traps there – probably between forty and fifty years ago. The traps, even after being out in the weather all these years, are stronger than the new ones you buy today. We can't check with Hugo since he left for that big trapline in the sky, many years ago.

Wednesday – Oct.14th -3C   Cloudy out. Some fog. Ice flowing downstream this morning.

Yesterday on our way back from Ridge Lake, after reaching our lunch site where we'd left the chainsaw, Gordon tried starting it. Trouble!! It kept throwing the chain so we brought it back home where we have more tools to work with. This morning he tried fixing it but no luck. It threw three different chains so he's pretty sure a bearing has gone. Our other chainsaw is at Ridge Lake so, after breakfast, he's planning on heading back there to retrieve it. I insisted on going with him.

Right after breakfast, wearing our warm parkas, we shoved off in the canoe. Lots of ice and slush coming down but it was still pretty nice out, even when it started snowing. After reaching and pulling the canoe up on the clay banks, it took another hour and five minutes – really hoofing it, to walk the uphill trail to Ridge Lake. We found the lake about half frozen over, quite a change from yesterday. By the time we reached the lake the weather had really improved and it had turned into a very nice day so we decided there was no mad rush to return. We started a fire in the stove, Gordon went up in the cache for the chainsaw as well as a tea pail, cups and the makings for tea. He also found a package of chocolate truffles. We ended up having a leisurely cup of tea along with cookies – our lunch.

A short while later found us heading back down the trail to the river and our canoe, then home to Rose Lake. No problems except my back started bothering me. It had bothered me in bed last night, especially my right hip, which really hurt. Walking didn't seem to bother it but I could still feel pain. I hadn't told Gordon about it as I knew he'd be really concerned. By the time we got back to Rose Lake cabin I could hardly bend because of the pain. Don't know whether I over did it the last couple of days or got a chill. I have had something like this before but not as painful.

After we had a bowl of hot soup and tea to warm up with, Gordon went back to work on the cabin while I stayed behind and baked a cherry pie, then took a pain-killer and laid down to rest. Later, I went over and watched him put trim around the window and door casings. I'm taking it easy tonight while he's back slaving away putting up more trim – sure looks good. We want to go back to Jamie Lake the day after tomorrow and also want to move into the new cabin before we leave. Signals pretty good this evening so Gordon talked with Don Taylor for awhile.

Tuesday – Oct. 15ᵗʰ -2C   Snowed early this morning. All the trees are covered with white.

My hip is very sore. Wish I knew what caused it. I'm in slow motion this morning so will just lay around and rest. We still hope to leave for Jamie Lake early tomorrow. Gordon worked in the new cabin all morning. Looks super. I just sat and watched him – lazy me !! It's snowing very heavily so think winter has finally arrived. We have a good four to five inches of snow, although the sky started clearing this evening. Hopefully, it will be nice in the morning. Signals good this evening so Don Taylor and Gordon are exchanging news.

Friday – Oct. 16th -3C   Overcast and a little windy. Lots of ice and slush flowing downstream. Ice is starting to build up around the edges and along the sandbars.

My hip is very sore. Was a very painful journey up the path to the little girls room this morning. The only halfway comfortable position for me is to lie on my sore hip. I must have pulled or strained a muscle in my side. Don't know when I've had anything so painful. Even with my back problems in nineteen seventy-five – seventy-six, it wasn't nearly as painful as this is. Gordon is threatening to call in a helicopter to airlift me out.

There are fresh marten tracks all around the meat cache. Gordon said he could see where they stood on their hind legs and sniffed the air for the meat scent. He's going to cut down a couple more trees that are growing near the cache to prevent them from jumping across to it. The trees are far enough away so there's only a slim possibility they could make the jump but – he doesn't want a repeat of two years ago when they ate a good part of our meat. Hope they do stay around till opening of trapping season on November first.

We're definitely not going back to Jamie Lake just yet. It's at least a two and a half hour walk – probably take a lot longer now with the snow, over a rough trail. I just couldn't make it. Hope our fresh stuff is keeping well. Bet our tomatoes are all ripe. Hope they're not spoiling. We're out of fresh veggies here so will be nice to get there and enjoy some. Had I even imagined something like my hip giving up on me, we'd have brought a few fresh vegetables back from Ridge Lake. Gordon cleaned up around the outside of the new cabin, then enclosed one side of the porch. He also cut up all the log end pieces for firewood and stacked them in the porch.

Saturday – Oct. 17th -4C   Real nice and sunny out this morning. Lots of ice on the river. There were three ducks in the water, swimming between the ice floes. They'd best get out soon.

It's sure disgusting just lying around. It's so gorgeous out and I want to go back to Jamie Lake. My hip feels a bit better today but still can't do any walking. I had two very bad sessions yesterday. I got up to go outside but just couldn't walk, the pain was almost unbearable. I could not lift my leg but had to just shuffle it along on the floor. Poor Gordon, he was just so worried – so was I. He's blaming himself for "dragging" me out here, even though it was mostly my idea that we come back. He says this will be a good lesson for both of us – to start taking things a little easier.

Gordon tried fishing today since he saw trout in the river out front of the cabin. No luck, the ice flows kept snagging his line. Too bad!! He then paddled between floes and crossed the river to retrieve the two moose legs for the dogs to work on. By the sounds, they're sure enjoying them. He also cleared an area and put up poles for the radio antennae, alongside the new cabin. It's all ready to hook up when we move in. We should have been in by now but with my hip, he feels we're better off staying where we are for the present. He also reported seeing a lot of marten tracks around the two cabins, the cache and across the river by the moose kill.

Sunday – Oct. 18th -13C Foggy out this morning. Lots of ice buildup but still a lot of open water. The creek is just about frozen over.

My hip is still very sore to walk on and I can just manage to get up for a few minutes at a time. We've decided this morning that if I don't improve by Wednesday, we'll call for a helicopter to take me out and close up for this winter. It's not fair to Gordon having to be my nursemaid !! This afternoon he was busy manufacturing a big table for the new cabin. After that he got more firewood and then started making a good, clear walkway from here to our new home. He chopped and cleared away every little twig along the pathway, leveled every little hump or ridge that I might have to lift my foot over – all ready for the time when I feel able to shuffle to our new home.

I've been trying to persuade him to move me over to the new cabin this afternoon but he refuses. I've started feeling a bit better today, especially lying down, but it's still painful to walk. I don't think, in fact, I know I wouldn't be able to make the step up to go through the door at the other cabin. Late this afternoon, Rhea Stockman and Steve Peconi called via the radio and we had a chat. Gordon was also able to contact Don Taylor.

Monday – Oct. 19th -2C   Foggy out again. Gordon thinks it will clear by lunchtime.

I'm feeling better today – it's not quite as painful and I can walk, raising my foot off the floor a little. I even put on a pot of soup bones to boil. Gordon lifted the pot of water but I did get up and put the seasoning, etc. in. I know my hiking boots would still be too heavy for my leg today. Gordon's promised to move me over tomorrow if I improve a little more. River still not frozen over but lots of ice coming down. At noon, Gordon with his binoculars, spotted a wolverine working on the moose head. I also had a look at him. Later, Gordon cut more wood and then worked in the cabin, cleaning it up. At coffee break he called Don Taylor and they had quite a chat. Signals very good.

About three-thirty, I saw something over by the moose kill. Through the binoculars, I first thought it was a bear but then realized it was a wolverine. It looked so big with the binoculars on him. I called Gordon in but by then the wolverine had run off into the bush carrying the last moose leg. A short while later Gordon came running in to tell me the wolverine was back on the sandbar. We could see in the snow where the wolverine had followed right down Gordon's track to the kill – not the least bit afraid. A wolverine is the curse of the trapper. They'll break into cabins and caches and whatever they can't eat, they urinate on and destroy. They're called "Skunk Bears" by some natives because of this habit. They'll also follow a trapline, destroying any trapped animals, wrecking trap cubbies and carrying off traps. Not a nice animal. Their fur is prized for parka-hood trim because frost will not adhere to the hairs and can be easily brushed off.

Tuesday – Oct. 20th +2C   It's cloudy out with a little wind this morning. It rained quite heavily during the night then turned to snow.

It is one month today, exactly four weeks since we arrived. Time is going by so fast, except for me – it's dragging right now. It's Gordon's sixty-second birthday and here I'm all "lamed up". Hopefully this afternoon I'll be able to make him a cake. If I don't, it'll be the first one I've missed. Also, his parcels are at Jamie Lake. Mid-morning, I finished reading "The Leopard Hunts in Darkness", by Wilbur Smith. Very good. I'm now starting on a different project, knitting a little sweater for myself.

"WOW" – at three-thirty this afternoon, Gordon moved our bed and then me, over to our new cabin. It's so nice and bright and big compared to the old cabin. Of course, there's nothing much in here yet other than for one cupboard and the table. Just a small stove until the other one cools off so we can transfer it over here. It's still quite damp inside the cabin as the logs haven't thoroughly dried yet but with the stove going, that'll soon be changed. The cupboard he built, with a large top area, will be excellent for working on. Jamie had some counter tops, left from the houses he was building, that were damaged in transit. He cut the tops down and gave us two sections. White arborite on top with a raised back ledge and curved front. I'll paint the cupboards white when I'm feeling better. Gordon will gradually bring the supplies in as we need them – whenever he has the time. First thing he's doing is putting up the radio antenna and bringing the radio and transmitter over.

After he walked me over here, Gordon mentioned he'd thought we'd never move into this cabin. He was so sure I'd be airlifted out of here. If I had been, he was going to close the trapline for good. What a Turkey !! Hard to believe we're in our new home. It's so much larger and – so much to do yet. Gordon has started building more cupboards. It doesn't feel like home and probably won't for a few days. It'll take us a couple of days to get settled in.

Wednesday – Oct. 21st -15C   Its such a gorgeous day – not a cloud. The mountains are beautiful all decked out in their white coat of snow, all a-glitter with the sun shining on them. Overnight, ice blocked the main channel of the river next to our shore so now we just have a small lead of open water in front. The far channel is still flowing, full of ice and slush.

It seemed strange, waking up in this cabin. It's just not home yet. It stayed much warmer in here during the night than it did in the other cabin. The ceiling is much higher here so thought it would be cooler. We didn't keep a fire on during the night and even then I didn't have to pull our big, spare blanket over us as I've had to do in the other cabin. Once we get this place completed with cupboards and shelves it will look so good. When Gordon brings the curtains and oil cloth for the table from Jamie Lake, it'll take on a homey atmosphere.

I feel better this morning but was quite stiff and sore when I first got up. My hip has now loosened up and feels good. I can't go very far yet but it's coming along. While Gordon was building a cupboard, I decided I felt strong enough to make a small batch of buns. It seemed to be so much work !! I would have hated having to make a batch of bread. I just couldn't have done it yet. Gordon tended the stove and put the oven on for me. The buns turned out super!! Then, right after lunch, I made a cake. Must be feeling better!!

Just after two this afternoon, Gordon went to check out a new area to see if he could find a shorter and smoother trail to Jamie Lake. I wanted to go so badly but knew I just could not make it. It's such a gorgeous day – would have been great for a good walk. Gordon has finally allowed me to go outdoors with the aid of a walking stick, to the little girl's room. It will be a good week tonight that I've been laid up. Late afternoon he returned from his exploration trip – hunting for a trail through the meadows. He found they weren't frozen hard enough to allow him to safely walk over the boggy sections so returned without finding a new route. Water level in the river rose about six inches this afternoon. Gordon claims the ice must have jammed up someplace below.

Thursday – Oct. 22ⁿᵈ -18C   A beautiful, chilly, but sunny morning. The river has frozen over as far as I can see, except for the narrow channel in front of the cabin. The creek, flowing into the river just above here, is keeping the channel open.

By ten this morning Gordon had decided I was improved sufficiently and could be left alone for awhile. After carrying in lots of firewood and fresh water, he hitched Celsius to the toboggan and left for Jamie Lake to check things out there and bring back a bunch of supplies. Katy and I are not happy but Katy is far more vocal than I. She's not the least bit happy being left behind. Since these dogs were trained for racing, it will be interesting to hear what Gordon has to say about Celsius, pulling the toboggan by herself. It takes me between two and two and a half hours walking, each way, so it should take Gordon between five and five and a half hours to reach Jamie Lake cabin, load up and return. It'll probably take longer with unbroken snow on the trail. Seems like so much walking for the few supplies he can bring back. He's especially concerned about the cache and the supplies there. We also have a lot of meat hanging at the new cache so hopefully nothing was able to get at it. We do have a wolverine here, checking this one out.

We now have enough snow – or nearly enough – to use the skidoo. Our problem is that the skidoo is hanging in the trees across the creek and we can't bring it over here until the creek freezes. It would have been such an easy trip for Gordon with the skidoo. There just aren't enough big trees on this side of the creek to hang the skidoo from. We have to have it out of the reach of animals when we're not here. Heard an aircraft fly over just after eleven-fifteen. Turned the radio on but no calls.

Gordon returned about four-thirty. Celsius was played out. The rough trail was just too much for her. He brought back a box of groceries, mostly fresh stuff and eggs. The tomatoes are frozen. He doesn't know if they froze at the cabin or on the trail. Hope it was on the trail. I hadn't put them in the storage cooler under the floor, an oversight. We hadn't expected to be away from Jamie Lake for so long though.

He mentioned seeing more marten tracks than have been showing in the last few years. About as many as when he and Jamie came out the first time, the winter of nineteen seventy-eight – seventy-nine, so hopefully we'll do well. Nothing touched our meat although tracks showed a lot of activity around the cache.

Friday – Oct. 23rd -10C   Some cloud out this morning but looks like it will break up.

I'm still stiff and sore in the morning, especially my thigh, but hopefully it will loosen up soon. At breakfast we were talking about wolves and not seeing any tracks of them this year. Haven't even heard them howling. Noticed the mountains haven't as much snow on them as they did a few days ago. Must be warm air above melting it. Gordon brought a bunch of groceries down from the cache this morning for me to sort and pack away in our new cupboards. I stayed on my feet all morning – until about twelve forty-five. Really doing good, eh !! A short ways up the trail Gordon cut down a dry tree for firewood. He'd brought Katy with the toboggan for hauling it home. After cutting the tree to stove-wood lengths and loading it on the toboggan, they headed back. It was very hard pulling for Katy so Gordon helped out. We've decided that the racing harness, given to us with the dogs, just isn't suitable for pulling loads so Gordon's modifying them. He's had dog teams in the past and used them a lot in the nineteen-forties when trapping the Yukon's White River country.

Since we don't have much to do today, we're assembling a bunch of trap cubbies. A completed cubby looks somewhat like a three sided, six and a half inch square box with one side missing. The box is from twelve to fourteen inches long. One end of the three-sided box is covered with wire mesh while the other end is left open. The boxes are set on the ground (open side to the ground) usually beneath a spruce where it will be kept clear of snow. Bait is placed inside the box (cubby) near the back. The trap is set to partially block the open end or entrance. When the animal sticks his head in to retrieve the tasty bait, WHAMO, you've got him. The traps we use are the humane Conibear variety that renders the animal unconscious immediately and dead within a few seconds. They're a double jawed, body grip type that closes with terrific force around the animals head and body. Leghold traps are never used and have been outlawed for many years in the Yukon.   This year Gordon's planning on placing his cubbies above ground, nailed to trees. He thinks the scent from the bait will travel further to lure animals in but most important, caught animals will not have their fur destroyed by mice as happens when they're on the ground. Assembling them before-hand will save a lot of time on the trail when the days are shorter and colder. If we do place them in trees we'll have to close the bottom side as well, since that side would be open when they're not sitting on the ground. Gordon went off later with Katy and the toboggan and set out ten cubbies, wired to trees, all ready for opening day November first.

Gordon put a couple more shelves up after supper. Place starting to look lived in !! I even brought in a pair of curtains from the old cabin.

Saturday – Oct. 24ᵗʰ   "0"C   Cloudy with snow flurries. Got quite windy at night.

Our muskrat swims by every day. A narrow channel is still open along the river in front of our cabin but just stretches from the creek to here. Yesterday Gordon noticed that some animal had been working on the moose head. The nose, with the hide chewed off, is a bright red which really shows up across the river but – we can't see it unless we step outside the cabin. The animal that's been working on it must come at night – probably a wolverine.

This afternoon after lunch Gordon took me for a walk. The first time since I hurt myself, other than for walking from cabin to cabin. We were checking for a trail from here that would follow through a series of meadows, hoping to have it come out at the Coal River and be right across from the trail leading from the river to Ridge Lake. It would make one big loop through good trapping country. I probably walked at least two to two and a half miles – really something !! I feel OK, no aches yet but will know tonight or tomorrow morning for sure. We had heavy snow showers for an hour or so and then the sky cleared off. By the time we were ready for bed, Northern Lights were dancing across the sky – very bright. Lying in bed, we can watch their display. Nice !!

Sunday – Oct. 25th -4C A little cloud. Feels warm out this morning.

I'm not as stiff and sore as I thought I'd be after that walk yesterday – really pleased. I was a bit sore when I first got out of bed but not too bad. So far, it's been a lovely fall. Not too cold but lots of snow. Just as I was getting ready to go for a walk Gordon, over by the other cabin, called for me to come over. There, on top of the antenna pole that's attached to the cache, sat a marten !! We've had marten occasionally getting at our meat in the cache but couldn't figure out how they managed to do it. He's pretty certain now that they're even able to climb up the tin wrapped cache legs. They have very sharp claws and must get sufficient leverage, somehow. I took a couple of pictures of the marten atop the pole. Hope they turn out. Also hope he sticks around for another week, especially when we discovered he'd devoured a good portion of the T-bone section of our moose.

This morning we decided that if I could walk the Jamie Lake trail as far as the swampy section and back without problems, I should be OK to walk the full distance to Jamie Lake in another day or two. We took off and hiked all the way to the rough section and back. We were gone for over two and a half hours and must have covered at least four miles, according to Gordon (I think it was further). I was tired but don't seem to have any ill effects. Hard to believe that it was only Wednesday, four days ago, when I wasn't able to stand to wash or even sweep the floor – I was still so weak and shaky.

We saw our wolverine again dining on the moose head across the river. I'm baking cinnamon buns tonight to go with our nine o'clock tea. They turned out just great.

Monday – Oct. 26th -11C   Another nice morning even though it's starting to cloud over. The Northern Lights were so bright last night, especially enjoyable watching them while snuggled up in a warm bed.

After breakfast I went for a walk by myself to the little meadow just east of here and then climbed to the top of the ridge above it. Wanted to see how my hip would feel and am really pleased that it feels good, not sore at all. Gordon went exploring up-river way, through an area with thick brush. No trail there so we decided it would be too rough for me.

This afternoon we crossed the creek and then crossed the river. Gordon went ahead, checking ice every few yards. Still not very thick in several places. When it cracked, with the report sounding right beneath our feet, we jumped and danced across very gingerly. Gordon said it was perfectly safe but it sure didn't look all that thick to me. We wanted to check the moose head. Lots of animal tracks, wolverine, mink and marten but very little of the head remaining. After we returned, Gordon took the skidoo down from where it had hung in the trees and drove it home. He filled the fuel tank and completed whatever maintenance was required. It's now ready for use, just as soon as we get enough snow. Sky did cloud over about three this afternoon and shortly after, it started to snow.

Tuesday – Oct. 27th -5C   Snowed overnight and cloudy this morning, but mild.

Five weeks ago from today, we'd arrived at Jamie Lake. After breakfast we started getting ready to head back to Jamie Lake. Gordon then had second thoughts, deciding it would be wiser to give me another days rest since my hip was a bit sore this morning. He'd also like to bring in more dry wood before we leave so we'll have lots when we get back – especially if it turned really cold with lots of snow. It's quite a job getting wood later on when you're floundering through three feet of snow. He's also going to move most of the meat over from the meat cache and store it in the grocery cache. That cache is higher and more secure from animals. We brought just about all the groceries from the cache to the cabin. At least we know what we have here and what we'll need brought in later.

Later this morning it started snowing lightly but not enough to really help with skidoo travel. Our trails – a good portion of them are so rough that traveling just pounds the machine until there's lots of snow. After coffee, we decided to go for a walk through the bush to Rose Lake. For quite some time, we'd been talking about cutting a trail through the bush to the lake but something else always seemed to have higher priority. We took off , crossing Marten Creek and following a game trail for quite a ways before it faded out. Surprising how a good, well used trail can disappear within a few hundred yards after faint, rarely used paths have split off from it. We finally reached the lake after trying several different routes. The lake isn't that far from our cabin but there is a real tangle of brush for a good part of the way. We'd brought Celsius, hitched to the toboggan, along with us so she could get some exercise. She whines and cry's whenever we leave without her. Walking around the lakeshore on the ice, we discovered quite a number of muskrat "push-ups". Muskrats feed on vegetation growing on lake bottoms and shorelines. When winter arrives and ice covers the lakes, they build igloo-like mounds of vegetation on top of the ice. These igloo-like mounds freeze rock hard and are soon covered with the winter's snow, providing relatively safe feeding huts for them. They keep an entrance, through the ice and into the mound, open all winter. During winter months when it's forty below and there's three feet of snow on the ground, the muskrat's happy inside his domed dining room, munching away on dinner.

By the time we'd completed our walk around the lake, the clouds had cleared away and the sun was shining. It was so warm in the sun that we took our jackets off. Felt more like March weather, warm with wet snow on the ground. After we returned to our cabin and finished lunch, Gordon took the skidoo and went up our one smooth trail behind the cabin, trying to locate more dry trees for firewood. He also hoped to find one large enough to provide a couple of stools for the cabin.

Arriving at Ridge Lake via the Otter aircraft

View from our Ridge Lake cabin – next door to Heaven

Morning sunrise on the trail

I've graduated to my own skidoo - YIPPEE!! No more skimmer

When we'd gone for our walk this morning, Katy was so disappointed being left behind that she cried until we returned. Celsius, on the other hand, was a total pain. She wanted to come with us but was lazy and did not want to pull the toboggan through the brush, especially through the rough areas. Gordon was some mad. The less she wanted to pull, the more determined he was that she'd pull. He dragged her, he used a switch on her but nothing helped. But, on the way home when she must have figured the end of the road was near, she was good. She even pulled Gordon on the toboggan (until he fell off on his butt). Gordon claims Celsius is nothing but a spoiled pet.

Wednesday – Oct. 28th -3C Snowing. Snowed quite heavily during the night. We must have from four to five inches of fresh snow. Our river channel in front of the cabin is still open.

We worked around the cabin all morning finishing up several little jobs. Really looks like winter this afternoon – lots of snow still coming down and very dull out. Gordon decided there was too much snow for me to go to Jamie Lake today, especially since my hip was quite sore last night. He decided to take the skidoo and start packing the trail to Jamie Lake, hoping to at least get as far as the rough, swampy areas. If the weather is OK, we'll head for Jamie Lake tomorrow. My snowshoes are at Jamie Lake. Gordon has a pair here as well as another pair at the other cabin. Right now I'd never be able to manage snowshoes anyway. So, I'm home by myself, sulking and washing clothes. I'll pamper Gordon with a pan of hot cinnamon buns when he returns. Real punishment, eh !!

Gordon finally returned, thoroughly wet – soaked through completely. He'd managed to get as far as the top of Ridge Run hill, close to Jamie Lake, with the skidoo – thoroughly packing the trail. The way it's snowing right now, the trail will soon be covered over again. We plan on going all the way to Jamie Lake in the morning, with the skidoo. I'll be able to ride part of the way since there's enough snow now. After changing into dry clothes and sampling my cinnamon buns and a cup of hot tea, he's back outside building a house for Celsius. He's then planning on cutting more lumber with the chainsaw, enough to finish enclosing the front porch.

Cutting lumber with the chainsaw is quite a job. A straight, green jackpine, about sixteen to eighteen inches in diameter is the best source of lumber. The tree is dropped so it will fall across a couple of logs on the ground, keeping it from falling onto the ground. The section of the tree you're planning on using for lumber is then limbed. Next, you make a straight, lengthwise surface cut all along the top of the log, marking it. Then the work starts. You start at the but end of the log and, following your marking cut, saw the log lengthwise for whatever length of board you require. After that cut, it's back to the but and make another cut parallel to the first at whatever thickness you want the board to be. Anyway, more sawing and then stretching to get the kinks out of your back and you've got your lumber. With practise, pretty even boards can be produced. BUT – it is hard on the back !!

Thursday – Oct. 29ᵗʰ - 6C   Foggy out and really damp.

After breakfast we packed the skimmer, hooked it to the skidoo and with dogs following, headed for Jamie Lake. I road for the first section, as far as the ravine. I walked from there, all the way until we were through the swamps since it was too rough for me to ride. Gordon gave me a ride across the ponds – luckily. The ponds, beneath the snow, were covered with overflow. The weight of the snow causes the ice to press into the water beneath, cracks then appear and water flows over the ice. The overflow water can be anywhere from a couple of inches to over a foot in depth. The snow that covers the water acts as insulation so it takes many days of cold temperatures for it to freeze. If the depth of overflow is not too great and you travel fast enough, you can keep from bogging down. Gordon gave the skidoo full throttle and we literally flew across. I'd certainly have had wet feet if I walked through that section. The dogs just trotted along behind, not bothered at all by the water.

On our way to Jamie Lake, Gordon nailed the trap boxes (cubbies) up in spruce trees, a good six feet above ground. We're not using sets placed on the ground anymore. Mice chew on the fur of animals caught in ground sets and had ruined a lot of good pelts in past years. We hope that having them quite a ways above the ground will solve that problem. After we crossed the ponds and reached the next patch of timber, while Gordon was nailing another trap box in place, I took off up the trail with the dogs following. I walked for more than an hour before he caught up with me. We decided it was time for me to ride again, which I did – all the rest of the way to Jamie Lake. Even so, I must have walked at least two-thirds of the way from Rose Lake to here.

We got a fire going just as soon as we got inside the cabin and after it warmed up a bit, made lunch. A cup of hot tea sure hit the spot, although I hadn't been cold. After lunch was over Gordon went back over the trail and finished putting trap boxes up along the last section. They're all completed along this Run so now all that's left is baiting and setting them on November first. It's good to be back "home" but we both agree that even though this cabin feels homey, we like the new cabin at Rose Lake better. This cabin has one hundred and forty-four square feet of floor space whereas the one at Rose Lake has two hundred and twenty-four square feet. Much roomier ! The new cabin is also so much brighter since the logs were peeled before they darkened whereas the logs inside this cabin were peeled later and are darker. Another point, the view we have from our cabin on the river is so much nicer. There is more snow here than at the river, about twelve inches of heavy, wet snow.

I was tired by the time we reached the cabin and also very, very wet. Gordon was more concerned about my hip than I was. It's fine, a bit tired and tomorrow will tell if I overdid it. Gordon finally received his birthday parcels today – just nine days late. We had been at the river for twenty-seven days. We hadn't planned on being away so long but had no choice with me being "laid up" since the fourteenth of October. We'd hoped to have the cubbies up in trees for all the Jamie Lake Runs by now. Oh well, we still have time ! Lots of marten tracks around the cabin. You could see, by their tracks, where they'd even been look-ing into the cabin through one of the windows. Nosey !! In the porch, and right on the doorstep, they'd left a token of their regard for us – a pile of droppings !!! Really nice neighbors. Oh well, the culprit better keep away since trapping season starts in a couple more days. Our meat, in the new cache, was fine. Nothing had managed to get at it.

Friday – Oct. 30th -18C   Real nice and sunny and a little cooler. At least the snow will be crusted and drier. Last year our cold weather started on the twenty-eight when it was minus twenty. After that, it just kept on getting colder.

My hip feels really good – in fact, I got up and was dressed before I real-ized I had no pain. Hope it keeps up !! This morning, after breakfast, we took a bunch of assembled trap boxes and went up Canyon Run. It was just a wee bit touchy getting around Jamie Lake shoreline since there was a lot of overflow under the snow in places. Turned out to be a gorgeous day with not a cloud in the sky, a great day to be out on the trail. We, I should say Gordon, put up twelve trap boxes – all ready for setting. We followed our trapline trail as far as the ridge overlooking the creek but did not go down. Shortly after we got on our Canyon Run there were fresh moose tracks which, most of the way, followed our trail – right down to the creek. Rather late in the year to see them roaming around here. By now moose are usually up in higher terrain where the snow doesn't get as deep so early. We also found a few fresh marten tracks made since the last snowfall.

After we returned home and had lunch, Gordon took off down the River Run trail, putting up three more trap boxes between the cabin and the first meadow. I stayed home and made a pan of Nanaimo Bars as a "sweet" surprise for him. Also making chicken and noodles for supper.

Saturday – Oct. 31st -6C   Snowing heavily. We must have received between one and two inches overnight. Have approximately thirteen inches on the ground.

If it doesn't quit soon, Gordon will have to start packing trails with snowshoes. It's a dry snow so it's still easy going through it with the skidoo.

We're going up River Run with the skidoo right after breakfast to set out trap boxes. Tomorrow, first day of the trapping season, we'll go around the trails to bait and set as many traps as we can. Hope the weather is nice. Shortly after we left, the sun started to shine – beautiful. Went nearly to the river, rather, I did. There's a meadow not too far from the river where I stayed behind and made tea while Gordon continued on setting out the last few boxes. While he was gone I got busy getting our tea fire going. Even with wet snow over the ground and covering the trees, it's not difficult to start a fire – if you know how.

The first thing Gordon had shown me when we came to the trapline was how to get a fire going in rain or snow conditions. It's very important since you're totally dependent on your own resources when a hundred miles from the nearest help. Anyway, I learned the best and driest kindling in the woods is provided by the small dead lower branches attached to the trunk of a growing green spruce. Upper branches keep moisture from the lower ones and when a match is applied to a pile of the small, lower ones, they generally start burning immediately. Quite often people think that only dead trees provide dry wood. By the time Gordon returned, tea water was boiling and I even had a couple of forked sticks ready for toasting our sandwiches.

It had taken us a bit over three hours to set out trap boxes along this line and a break for tea was especially welcome. By the time we'd finished, around two o'clock, the sky had clouded over and it wasn't near as nice out. Returning didn't take near as long, just a little over an hour. I can now understand why Gordon hadn't wanted me to come along today. It was so rough and with all that snow to break trail through, it was tough going. I had to get off and walk in several places. Coming back on a packed trail was no problem. The trail to the river is very twisty. If we come back next year, we're going to do a lot of straightening or find another route up and across one especially steep hill. Will have to explore further into the heavy timber for a better way around it. After we were back home I got busy and made a fresh pie for tonight's dinner.

Sunday – Nov. 1ˢᵗ -16C   Foggy out and very dull looking but should start clearing up soon.

Trapping starts today so right after breakfast we're off to set traps at the cubbies we have ready. First off, we set traps a short ways on Canyon and River Runs and then headed down Jamie Run to set a few more. Noticed wolf tracks along the way so Gordon put out a wolf snare. There also were caribou tracks along the way so possibly the wolf was following them. There's a little slough part way to the river that was just covered with caribou tracks where they'd been pawing and feeding. Must have been there for quite some time. Carrying on, we skidoo'd down the big hill and crossed the big meadow on our way to the river and our Wolf Run.

Reaching the river, Gordon took his axe and gingerly walked across, testing ice thickness every few yards and also checking for overflow. Ice was good until he reached the far side and ran into overflow. There were ice-jam buildups all along and across the river which looked as though they'd been made just a few days ago. While we were at Rose Lake we'd noticed the water level of the river had risen quite a lot. It must have been caused by ice floes downstream jamming and forming a dam. Water must have been really high here since ice chunks were shoved way up on top of the river banks. Anyway, we finally found a safe way across and set a few more traps out on our Wolf Run. We stopped and had lunch and tea under our big spruce – nice !! On our way back Gordon rerouted, going by our first moose kill, the one the grizzly had taken over. He pawed through the snow, retrieving the axe he'd left there We also noted fresh wolverine tracks around the site so, tomorrow, plan on returning and setting a trap for him. We'll also set out traps across the river on our Wolverine Run if the ice is safe to cross on.

Monday – Nov. 2ⁿᵈ -7C   Very dull and just started snowing. Hope we don't get much more. We already have more snow this year than we had last year by December ninth, the day we returned to Watson Lake.

By lunch time it was very blizzardy out, lots of snow and very windy. Not a nice day to be out in, so we stayed home. In the afternoon I went for a short walk to the meadow on River run while Gordon did odd jobs around the place, wood, water hauling, fixed the stove door damper and other things. Not cold out but real nasty with that wind. Visibility next too nil !!

Tuesday – Nov. 3ʳᵈ -8C   What a change from yesterday – it's gorgeous out!! Not a cloud, the sun is shining, mountains are bathed in a pink glow from the rising sun.

Went down Jamie Run after breakfast, checking traps. We got a marten in our first set and then, a little further on, we had a wolf in our first snare. A good way to start our first day. We reached the river via Jamie Run and found lots of fresh wolverine tracks around the old moose kill so Gordon made three sets for him. We had hoped to cross the river to our Wolverine Run but found lots of overflow and even open water so ended up by putting out a marten set on the riverbank on this side, then returning home. Halfway home, were really surprised to find fresh wolverine tracks on our new skidoo trail. They seem to be all over this year.

Right after lunch, Gordon unhooked the skimmer from the skidoo and took off on Ridge Run to pack trail and set traps along it. The snow is quite heavy so he felt the skidoo wouldn't climb the hill with the skimmer dragging behind. While he was packing trail, he picked up a marten from the set at the base of the hill. Now he's got his work planned for tonight – skinning. Too bad the weather is so mild – it's gorgeous – but the rivers, streams, etc. are not freezing over solidly. Really have to be careful checking ice before crossing. We're planning on going to Rose Lake tomorrow and then, hopefully, we can work that end. We don't think we'll be able to cross the Coal river to go to Ridge Lake. Ice on the river just won't be safe. We have to follow the river and sandbars for about three miles or so before we branch of on our trail to Ridge Lake. Sure too bad if we can't make it. We'd sure like to get all our runs set out. I tried snowshoeing for a while today. Tiring but it was OK – my hip and thigh didn't object at all. Gordon hit a tree with the skidoo the other day, cracking the fiberglass hood over the engine. He's going to try gluing, then riveting plastic material over it to keep it from cracking further.

Gordon's frying steak for supper since he does such a great job of it. I must admit, his moose is much tenderer than the one I got on the river. He's so proud of that fact – but at least, we didn't have to pack mine near as far. We were surprised to have the sky rapidly cloud over late in the afternoon and start snowing. At seven o'clock we were still getting snow – really coming down. But another surprise, by bedtime the sky had cleared and stars were shining brightly.

Wednesday – Nov. 4ᵗʰ -16C   A little colder out, should help the overflow and build ice on creeks and river. It's also quite foggy this morning.

I measured the snow depth and found we have sixteen inches on the ground around the cabin. We're all packed and ready to leave for Rose Lake just as soon as we finish breakfast. The dogs will enjoy the run. It's ironic, we got the two dogs to pull the toboggan since, other years, there never seemed to be enough snow for the skidoo early in the season. This year we have two dogs instead of one and have nearly too much snow!!

It was a beautiful day for our move. I was able to ride the skimmer to the bottom of the big hill, then walked up to the top of the ridge. Going was good along the top so I climbed back on the skimmer for another ride. Checking traps, we discovered our fifth trap was missing. We'd caught a marten but somehow, lost him. We don't know what happened since fresh snow covered everything. The trap was missing from the drag and hunting through the snow produced nothing. Pretty sure an animal, possibly a wolverine, had dragged it off. It was so disappointing!! Anyhow, further along, we did pick up five marten so that was pretty good. I rode on the skimmer until we crossed the pot hole section – a lot of overflow. Gordon kept checking the sloughs and found he couldn't go over our old trail since there was a lot of water beneath the surface. He had to snowshoe a new trail around through the brushy edges. I snowshoed from the potholes and past the real rough area, then rode as far as the ravine. From there to our Rose Lake cabin, following the new trail we cut last year, I snowshoed. That section of the trail is very rough. When we came up the trail to the cabin, we found marten and rabbit tracks all over the place. Looked as though they must have held a conference. They had been all around the cache and cabin and along the shoreline.

It didn't take long for me to get a fire going in the cabin stove while Gordon unloaded the skimmer and brought supplies in. A few minutes later, bringing a pail of water from the river, he mentioned having to chop through six inches of ice. Wish it was that thick all along the river. After lunch we put on snowshoes but were able to go only a short distance up Marten Creek. Lots of overflow so we turned back and headed across to Rose Lake to set traps in the cubbies we'd placed there. Lots of overflow on the lake. There also were quite a few marten tracks around the lake and along the trail – looks good. When we returned, I headed for the cabin while Gordon crossed the river to the sandbar to check on my moose kill site. Sure enough, fresh wolverine tracks. After returning he set three fish lines through the river ice. Hopefully, we'll have fresh trout tomorrow.

By seven this evening, temperature had dropped to minus twenty-one. That's ten degrees colder than it was at supper time. Sky is clear and full of sparkling stars. Radio reception is very clear so we talked with Don Taylor for quite awhile.

Thursday – Nov. 5ᵗʰ -27C Getting colder. Should freeze the overflow and build more ice on river and streams. There is high thin cloud so perhaps it won't stay cold for too long. Sun shining on mountain tops – pretty.

Yesterday there was so much moisture on the logs when the cabin warmed up. The cabin was built with unpeeled logs. They were peeled when we came out this fall but still didn't have time to completely dry before winter arrived. Now, with heat from the stove, they thaw and moisture comes through to the surface where it causes a thin layer of green mold to form. Wiping them down with a cloth removes both moisture and mold. Bit of a chore but worth it, having them bright and clean again. Moisture will keep coming through until they're thoroughly dry so I'll just have to keep wiping them for awhile. The ridge poles and the top "V's" have all dried and look good.

After breakfast this morning we got our mukluks out. Mukluks are basically high-topped moccasins that reach just below the knee. They're usually worn with insoles and three to four pair of heavy wool socks. They're made from native-tanned moose or caribou skins. Besides keeping your feet warm in just about any temperature, they're very comfortable. Dressed in our winter gear, parkas and winter mitts, we stepped outside to strap on snowshoes and with Gordon, axe in hand in the lead, headed up river. Attempting to cross just in front of the cabin to the sandbar on the other side, we ran into overflow. Proceeding further upriver, we finally managed to cross and broke trail along the shoreline until we were just across the river from the mouth of Lynx Creek.

Lynx Creek was covered with overflow – bank to bank, so snowshoed still further upriver until, locating an overflow free section, we crossed the river and entered the timber. We'd only gone a short distance through the bush before we reached a meadow we hadn't known existed. While narrow, it stretched eastward – the direction we wanted to go, for a good mile. We snowshoed the length of it, noticing several sets of marten tracks along the way. Reaching the far end, we entered the timber and only snowshoed a few hundred yards before coming out on the bank of Lynx Creek. We decided the route we'd just followed from the river was a lot better than traveling the creek with it's constant overflow. We then got busy clearing trail from the end of the meadow to the creek. Creek banks were pretty steep so it took a while finding a slope that would be climbable for the skidoo. Crossing the creek and just a short ways further on, we reached the sloughs and small meadows we'd explored last winter. We then figured out where we'll clear trails, not much to clear, and finally headed home.

We had seen many marten tracks through the bush and meadows. Looks really promising. Since there still isn't much ice, we plan on taking a dog and the toboggan tomorrow and cut trail to connect our trail from the river to the first big meadow and then, further on, clear trail from slough to slough. We'll also set a few traps. Hopefully there will be enough ice by tomorrow to travel by skidoo. We're trying to get away from following creeks where we've had so many problems with overflow in the past. With trails through the timber, we can trap the areas without as many problems – just as long as we're able to cross the river and creeks.

Gordon checked his fish lines when we returned and had two Dolly Varden but lost one when it threw the hook. We were still able to have fresh trout and steak, along with the cake I'd just baked, for supper. I'd brought an oilcloth cover from Jamie Lake which looks very nice on the table. This place is starting to look really "homey". Today had turned out being another gorgeous day – so sunny and warm. We really enjoyed our hike on snowshoes. Good exercise !! Clouded over this evening so hope it doesn't snow.

Friday – Nov. 6ᵗʰ -12C   Snowed about four inches overnight. If we get much more it will be very difficult to get around. All that extra snow won't help the overflow situation either.

After breakfast Gordon checked the ice and decided it was Okay to cross the river with the skidoo. Our plan was to follow yesterday's snowshoe trail upriver past Lynx Creek, then leave the skidoo on the sandbar across the river from where we'd entered the timber. The new snow will make it harder to see marten tracks but at least we know they're there, even if tracks are covered.

Later, going upriver past Lynx Creek, we crossed the river three times in order to travel along sandbars before reaching the point where we'd leave the skidoo and proceed on snowshoes. Thankfully, we only ran into a couple of short sections of new flooding on the river. We left the skidoo on the sandbar at the turn-off point, strapped on snowshoes and, with Gordon pulling the toboggan loaded with lunch and trapping gear, followed yesterday's trail across the river and into the timber. We'd decided against bringing one of the dogs to pull the load since we'd probably not take the toboggan past the end of the long meadow. The dog would be very unhappy being left behind while we were clearing the trail between the sloughs on the other side of Lynx Creek. As it turned out, there wasn't much toboggan pulling anyway. After crossing the river and entering the timber we figured out where we could cut a trail for the skidoo from the river to the meadow, with very little axe work. Half an hour later found us heading up the meadow, riding the skidoo. After making a marten set at the far end of the meadow, we followed yesterday's cleared trail through the timber as far as Lynx Creek before stopping to check for overflow. Sure enough, water was about eight inches deep over the ice along our side of the creek but the sandbar on the far side was clear. The next half hour or so found us cutting brush and throwing it onto the creek ice until we had a makeshift bridge over which we finally crossed. From there on, until late afternoon, we cut trail connecting the chain of potholes and sloughs.

Most of the sloughs and potholes were covered with overflow. The weight of the snow causes the ice to crack, then water wells up and floods over it. The snow on top of the ice acts as insulation and keeps the water from freezing. The unwary trapper on his skidoo, seeing a wide open expanse of snow-covered terrain, opens the throttle, speeds ahead, and minutes later is sitting on a motionless machine, stuck in overflow. It takes a lot of hard work packing brush to build a platform to pull the skidoo up on. Next, it's clearing all the half frozen slush from the machine so you can get the track turning. By the time you're finished, you've probably spent a couple of hours, are tired from wrestling that D——ED machine and your feet and hands are sopping wet. Soaked through from standing in water and clearing slush from the machine. Not the best situation to be in when it's minus thirty or lower and you're a couple of hours from the cabin. The worst scenario is when the skidoo, with driver, goes right through the ice. This has happened to a number of Yukoner's.

We set a total of seven traps out during the day before turning and heading home. On our way back we checked a trap we'd set yesterday and were surprised to find a marten. Pretty good !! Returning home along the trail we'd made that morning was great until we reached the section right across the river from our cabin. The trail, where we'd crossed the river this morning, was now covered with several inches of water. It was our last crossing but there was so much new overflow that Gordon thought we'd have to leave the skidoo and snowshoe the last hundred yards to our cabin. He walked and checked several areas up and down river before finally deciding to try returning over the mornings trail. With full throttle, the skidoo literally flew along the packed trail until it reached the slush. The skidoo broke through in several places but got across. I snowshoed and needless to say, got my snowshoes and mukluks covered with slush. We sure need cold weather to freeze that overflow. Checked the traps by the cache and found we had another marten.

Saturday – Nov. 7th -21C Sunny and, thank goodness, it's clear. Some fog over towards the mountains. Still lots of overflow showing in the river.

After finishing a few chores around the cabin, Gordon took off to see if he could locate a better trail from here to the ravine. That section of the trail to Jamie Lake is terribly rough and nearly kills him as well as the skidoo. The last time he tried locating one, through a series of potholes, he had to give up since the ice on the potholes wasn't thick enough to travel on. Of course, an hour after he left, we fogged in. He had hoped to have clear skies and the sun, to help with directions while he hunted for a new route through the maze of sloughs and potholes. My hip was bothering me this morning so I didn't tag along. We've done a lot of snowshoeing the last couple of days so I'm staying home to give it a rest.

Last night Gordon was busy cleaning and cutting up the T-bone section of the moose. After deboning the meat, he cut the bones into smaller pieces. Right now the bones are in a large pot of soup cooking on the stove. It should be ready for his dinner when he gets back. Also made up a large batch of cabbage rolls for supper and will freeze the rest for later.

By the time Gordon got home at one-thirty, we were fogged in solid. He thinks he got about two-thirds of the new trail blazed. Quite a lot of it follows grassy and swampy areas so there won't be a lot of clearing to do. When it started fogging in, he returned since it would have been impossible to keep directions straight through all those sloughs. I haven't seen fog this thick since I don't know when. You can't see anything, really depressing. I'm glad we're not on the trail some place. During the evening Gordon built shelves in a corner of the cabin for storing our spare clothes. I then covered them with Mactac sheeting. Looks pretty good and they'll sure come in handy.

Sunday – Nov. 8th -14C It was clear and minus twenty-three last night at bedtime. Gordon was up during the night and claims he's never seen such a beautiful sky – display of northern lights, bright stars and a full moon. Of course, by morning, it had to cloud over and snowing again.

After breakfast we packed up and headed back up the trail to Ridge Run and Jamie Lake. I walked to the ravine and then rode for a wee bit and then walked again. So much snow – it was sticky and the trail was still so rough through the pothole section. Hope they'll be filled with snow and smooth out for our next trip this way. We picked up another three marten between Rose Lake and the potholes. Rather disappointing since we'd expected a few more, but then, it's only been four days since we were last down the trail. It was a very dull day with continuous light snow falling.

When we reached our cabin at Jamie Lake, we found the radio antenna down. Gordon picked up the lead-in wire just as the dogs ran by. Celsius managed to tangle in the antenna wire and broke it. Hope Gordon can fix it so we have radio reception. After lunch, Gordon replaced the drive belt on the skidoo and drove down River Run as far as the first meadow in order to check it out. Worked fine so we dressed and headed up Jamie and Wolf Run way. We got a marten in our set on the river bank but unfortunately another marten ate most of it so the remains ended in the bait box. We reset the trap and hope to catch the greedy cannibalistic so and so. To date we have caught seventeen marten but have lost two of them, eaten by other marten. Sure wish we could get across to the ponds and meadows to set traps. We only have about seventy-five sets out so far. Checking, we found the river ice, bank to bank, was completely covered with overflow so turned around and headed for home. Later in the evening as we were getting ready for bed, very fine rain began falling. Some weather !!

Monday – Nov. 9th -4C Temperatures great but sure not for freezing overflow. The warm temperatures combined with the overflow are making it impossible to travel over a lot of our trapline. Cloudy this morning with light snow.

We decided to check Canyon Run this morning. Found lots of overflow on Jamie Lake but, by following the shoreline, managed to get around it. We picked up three marten in eleven traps. Not bad I guess but not as good a catch as we'd hoped for. Also found we had a marten, an educated marten, that followed our line and checked out every tree we had a set in. On the way back, Gordon made a couple of marten sets on the ground at the base of trees so hope they'll work and we'll catch him. We walked down the hill at the end of the line to the creek. Didn't see any marten or mink tracks but caribou are all over the area. Number of wolf tracks indicate they're following right along with the caribou. Sort of like following behind a mobile dinner tray.

After lunch Gordon headed out to check a few traps through the meadows along River Run. He found we have another educated marten out there. It also followed along our trail and ran up each tree where we had a set and inspected it. Several times it left it's calling card, a pile of droppings on the top of the box. Not really all that respectful!! Drizzle and snow flurries this afternoon. I stayed home and put on a roast for supper. Also baking a lemon pie. The snow is so wet with temperature warming up to zero.

Gordon only managed to get a short ways up River Run. Tough going for the machine with the warm temperatures. Soggy snow kept plugging up under the tracks so he turned around and came back. He did manage to pick up another marten. Sure wish it would turn cold. Reception again very good this evening. We again talked with Don Taylor and Steve Peconi.

Tuesday – Nov. 10ᵗʰ *"0"* Cloudy, complete overcast and very dull. Another really warm day.

Gordon skinned marten this morning. After lunch we walked, carrying our snowshoes, down Jamie Run to the river. It was just too soft and soggy for the skidoo. By the time we reached the river the weather closed in and then it started snowing. Big, wet snowflakes coming down with almost no visibility. We wanted to check the wolverine sets we'd put out around his old moose kill. As we approached the first set, made under the spreading branches of a very large spruce, Gordon called out, "We got him". Snowshoeing closer, he stopped and muttered, "Oh No". A beautiful big Golden eagle was in the trap. From a distance the brown feathers of the eagle, half hidden under the spruce branches, had looked like the brown fur of a wolverine. It appeared the eagle had been in the trap for only a short time and appeared unhurt. Gordon finally managed to wrap his jacket around the bird and released him from the trap. The trap jaws on the large Conibear body type traps, don't close against each other so the eagle, caught by the neck, seemed OK. When we released him he tried flying but didn't seem able to. We finally left him sitting on a log. Hopefully, tomorrow when we return to check – he'll be gone. We feel so badly. Such a majestic bird.

After leaving the eagle, we continued a short distance down river to check the trap where last time the marten in it had been eaten. Sure enough, we had another marten. This one wasn't damaged. It's very likely that he was responsible for eating the previous one. We tried crossing the river to our Wolverine Run but just couldn't make it. Lots of overflow and, halfway across, the ice wasn't strong enough to support us. We checked a couple more sets and returned home.

The afternoon had really turned miserable, raining and snowing all the time while we were out. We got so wet and the traveling was really tough, snowshoeing in the soggy, sticky snow. It kept sticking to your snowshoes so every few steps we had to stop and knock it off. Told Gordon I was glad we couldn't get to Wolverine Run as I'd have been totally exhausted. After lunch and tea, Gordon started skinning marten. I decided to hike a short distance down our River Run and check the first three sets. At the last set I got a marten, must have been caught just minutes earlier – a beautiful black male. Really surprised Gordon when I showed it to him. We've decided that if we return next year we're getting another skidoo – for me. Still snowing tonight at bedtime.

Wednesday – Nov. 11th   *-2C*   Foggy, sky a solid gray mass. Looks like we have a dull day.

When Gordon was out at ten this morning, temperature had dropped to minus four. Hope it is cooling off and he didn't misread the thermometer. The snow is still very wet, heavy and mushy – making for tough going. Irregardless, Gordon finally decided to take the skidoo and head up River Run to check that line. Yesterday we found the soggy snow so wet that the rawhide webbing in our snowshoes had become soaked and stretched. We figured we'd wreck them if we continued using them in the warm temperatures. They're now in the cabin, drying so the webbing will shrink and tighten in the frames. Our trapping is certainly hampered by the warm weather which makes it tough traveling by foot or machine.

I baked bran muffins, also a chocolate cake – should say two cakes. I was sure everything was mixed in properly but the batter seemed so thin. Then I realized I'd put in double the amount of boiling water. Nothing to do but add more ingredients. Anyway, both cakes turned out OK but now we're low in sugar at this cabin. Next trip from Rose, we'll have to bring back a supply.

Gordon finally got back late in the afternoon. He said the going was pretty tough. He only picked up two marten on the entire run. There were lots of tracks going right up to the trees the sets were on but for some reason they weren't going up. Hard to figure out. Maybe the bait is not attractive enough, dampness would restrict air movement so scent wouldn't carry far. We'll have to wait and see the reaction when temperatures cool down.

Thursday – Nov. 12th -4C   Cloudy – at least it didn't snow overnight.

Yesterday Gordon did a bit of damage to his snowshoes so this morning, after breakfast, was busy replacing the rawhide lacing in the toe sections. After that job was finished, we took the skidoo and went down Jamie Run – hoping to be able to check our Wolf Run. When we reached the river, it didn't look good. Gordon started snowshoeing across the river, checking ice, but kept breaking through to overflow. Lot's of it, all the way across the river. We decided to leave the skidoo. We then gingerly snowshoed across to the other side. By moving quickly, we managed to cross on the thin ice crust without breaking through and getting wet. Gordon's idea was to check only one or two traps since we had lots of snow to break trail through. Anyhow, in our first trap across the river that we'd set by the mouth of the creek, there was a marten. Further along, the next two traps each produced a marten. Three out of three was great and so we kept on going, breaking trail to the other five traps. We caught three more marten. Six marten out of eight traps was Fantastic !! Too bad we weren't able to set more traps further on but just as well we didn't. I was really tired by the time we snowshoed back to the skidoo. Also, my snowshoes now need repairing. Out of the six marten, three are small but nicely furred. Three are really big and one is especially gorgeous. On our way back we checked to see what had become of the eagle we'd released from the wolverine trap yesterday. Gordon followed his tracks a short distance and saw where he'd hopped up on the trunk of a fallen tree, probably to rest. Then, slight indentations in the snow from his wing tips indicated he'd jumped off and flown away. Sure glad to see he was free again.

After we got back to the cabin and finished lunch, Gordon got busy skinning the marten that weren't frozen while I fleshed the skins. The way we've been going this year, we probably would have caught quite a few more marten if the ice on the streams and the river had frozen so we could have crossed earlier. Oh well, that's trapping!! You can't second-guess nature. There seems to be so many tracks around but we can't cross a number of the streams or even follow upriver to Kettle Creek to check them out. After he was finished skinning, Gordon took the skidoo and packed the trail up Ridge Run. We plan on leaving for Rose Lake in the morning.

Friday – Nov. 13th -6C   Bit cooler and cloudy out.

First thing after breakfast Gordon skinned the two marten he couldn't do yesterday when they were frozen. By the time he finished, the sky had cleared, sun was shining and it had turned into a beautiful day. We packed up in a hurry, let the dogs loose, started the skidoo and headed down our Ridge Run trail for Rose Lake. Travel was good since most of the dips and hollows were now filled with packed snow. Was even good through the normally rough area around the swamps and sloughs. In fact, trail was good enough for me to ride on the skidoo behind Gordon. We were very surprised at not finding a single marten in our sets. Lots of tracks all over but it seemed they just weren't interested in checking out the sets. Gordon's beginning to think that perhaps ground sets are better than tree sets but, at least, we've not gotten any marten that were chewed by mice. We did, finally, pick up a marten from the set nearest the cabin as well as a second one from the set we'd placed under the cache.

After lunch we hitched Katy to the toboggan, strapped on snowshoes and broke trail over to Rose Lake to check traps there. Overflow on the lake was something else !! Poor Katy broke through three times in the area where small streams entered the lake. Oh, that water must have been cold !! She was out as fast as she went in and, after a good shake, was just about dry again. We found the lake criss-crossed with tracks. We found we had two marten in our sets.

Gordon set another couple of traps along the eastern lakeshore before we turned and headed for home. Still lots of overflow on the river. We'll be checking it tomorrow. By the time we were ready for bed the temperature had really started dropping and was already down to minus eighteen. Hope it stays there for a few days or, better yet, goes even lower.

Saturday – Nov. 14th -10C   Fogged in now but should clear. So much for colder weather !! It clouded over and snowed, according to the amount on the skidoo seat, another four inches. All our trails are again covered and it certainly won't help with the overflow.

There are so many marten around this year – at least from the sign we've seen. It's so disappointing not being able to go after them. We're beginning to think we won't be able to get up to the Ridge Lake high country since we need cold temperatures to freeze the swampy, wet sections of the trail. We just have to get to Ridge Lake eventually. Hope our fresh stuff, stored in the pit under the floor, hasn't frozen yet. We have so much stuff stored there and it would be a shame to lose it. Wonder if we'll even get up to Kettle Creek cabin. Travel on the river ice this winter has been impossible.

After breakfast, we took the skidoo across the river (no problem crossing) and followed our old trail past Lynx creek to the big meadow that we'd discovered last time. We left the skidoo at the far end of the meadow and snowshoed the rest of the way to the creek and then, across the sloughs. So much snow but only a little overflow on the sloughs, thank goodness!! It would have been pretty tough going for the skidoo since it sinks a lot lower on the trail than we do with our snowshoes. So much new snow has fallen since we first broke trail If we could use the machine, it would be such an easy run to check. We did pick up another three marten from our seven sets but, Darn It, one was eaten with just the head remaining. Sure disappointing. We snowshoed on further and put out a few more sets. Some were for mink since there seemed to be a lot of mink sign around.

We would have liked to explore further but since it had started snowing heavily and with visibility almost nil, thought it was time to turn around and head back. If we had kept on trying to locate a trail, with our very limited visibility, it would have been hard seeing just where to go to connect one small slough with another. We're hoping that tomorrow's weather will be sunny so we can return and find a trail to the section we're trying to reach. Looks so easy on the map but — not so easy when you're on foot in the bush.

Sunday – Nov. 15th -15C   We're all fogged in and if the fog doesn't lift, we stay home today.

We took our time over breakfast, hoping visibility would improve but no luck. We'd planned on exploring new country today but that will have to wait for another time. We need the sun to keep us on track when we're traveling over relatively flat, featureless terrain. We can't use the river or streams as the ice just isn't thick enough to be safe. Besides, most of them are covered with overflow. Trees are covered with so much snow – reminds you of winter scenes on Christmas cards. Following along our trails is like going under archways since the weight of the snow bends willows and smaller trees inwards. At least Gordon, in the lead, gets the dislodged snow down his neck instead of it going down mine.

I ended up doing laundry this morning while Gordon was up the creek a short distance cutting firewood. He was having chainsaw problems and found the thin rubber fuel line had broken. Three hours later, after a lot of innovating and by using a section of the plastic hose from our spare skidoo supplies, he got it working. He was sure glad to hear the sound of the chainsaw as it came back to life. If it was beyond repair, he really wasn't looking forward with much anticipation to cutting wood with the swede saw for the rest of the trapping season.

Monday – Nov. 16th -26C   Colder and foggy.

After breakfast, we snowshoed over to Rose Lake to check traps. We didn't catch any marten but we did set out a couple more traps. Still remained foggy until just after lunch, then it finally started to break. Gordon cut and split firewood during the afternoon. I went on a short hike back over the trail to Jamie Lake to relocate a trap. Also put out one more set along the way before I returned. By the time I got back I was ready for our afternoon tea break. Later in the afternoon the fog had pretty well cleared away and, for a few short minutes, the sun shone before it dipped below the hills in the west. Temperature started dropping and, by bedtime, was down to minus thirty-one.

Tuesday – Nov. 17th -32C   Cold – but beautiful out. Fairly clear and sunny. The sky looks so nice – red towards the sun with just a bit of high cloud in the background.

Over breakfast we decided to do more exploring up Lynx Creek way. Maybe we'll yet get up our trail to Ridge Lake and the cabin but not today. The river is still unsafe in and around the overflow. It just won't freeze when it's covered with a deep insulating layer of snow. We have a lot of fresh fruit and vegetables, stored at Ridge Lake, that are probably frozen by now. We dressed warmly, started up the skidoo, crossed the river following our old trail and headed back upriver past Lynx Creek to the area we'd been exploring two days previously. We saw lots of fresh sign of marten along the way but, up to the creek, hadn't caught any. We put on snowshoes and hiked the last section through the pot holes and finally, in our last trap, had a marten. Gordon had actually set the trap for mink but we weren't complaining. When we first spotted the marten in the trap, with mink tracks all around, we were sure it would be damaged and were very surprised at finding it untouched by the mink.

From there on, it was snowshoeing through new country, trying to locate the best route for a new trail to higher country and over to Ridge Lake. We snowshoed for several hours before coming out on a small creek and, would you believe it, found blazes on a few trees. It was the headwaters of Twin Lakes

Creek where Gordon and Jamie, following the creek from the river, had trapped years before. At least we then knew exactly where we were. But, it was where we did not want to be – too far to the south. Now we'll have to try again, another day. Lots of marten sign but we didn't set any traps.

By the time we finished exploring, the sky had clouded over and it was hard to see far ahead. The tree growth was just so thick, very picturesque with branches loaded with snow, but visibility was really reduced in the semi twi-light. On the way home, just as we reached the creek and the skidoo, Gordon yelled, "We got another one". Sure enough, we had another marten. It was great !! We got home just after four o'clock and noted the temperature had warmed to minus eighteen. A few minutes later, snow started to fall. Just can't seem to miss a day without it. While Gordon split wood before supper, I made a big batch of bannock.

Wednesday – Nov. 18th -27C   Clear out except for a bit of cloud over the mountains upriver to the north.

After breakfast, we headed back up the trail for Jamie Lake. I started on ahead, on foot, while Gordon finished loading the skidoo and harnessed the dogs. I hadn't gone far before he caught up to me and from there on, rode most of the way back. There were very few animal tracks made since the last snow. We only caught one marten on our way back. It was caught in a set just before Jamie Lake. When we reached the cabin, we found our antenna down again and a marten in the trap we'd set under the meat cache. Must have just been caught since it wasn't frozen.

I really enjoyed today's trip from Rose Lake, even though we didn't get much in the way of fur. It was such a beautiful, very sunny day, the clear sky a deep blue. Gordon feels we should have taken the day off for exploring, taking pictures and simply enjoying the gorgeous day. It was one of the nicest days we've had. Later on at bedtime, the star- filled sky was alive with waving ban-ners of Northern Lights. A beautiful sight !!

Thursday – Nov. 19th -14C Warmed up – cloudy – looks so dull after yesterday. We can't seem to have two sunny days in a row.

Plan on going up Canyon Run after breakfast. Last year we had closed Meadow Run on the nineteenth and Canyon on the twenty-first of November. Our trip up Canyon was good. Jamie Lake still hadn't enough ice for us to safely cross on so we again followed around the shoreline, except for the bay which we did cut across, since it made the distance a lot shorter. We picked up three marten and also found our elusive marten is still around, busily checking our tree sets. Gordon had first thought of closing this line but, after seeing quite a lot of sign, decided not to. We'll check it one more time this season.

There was so much snow on the trees that several large ones had broken off and fallen across our trail. Luckily, Gordon had brought the Swede saw along so we were able to cut sections from the trees so we could drive the skidoo through and continue on. Further along, where the trail ran through a stand of smaller spruce, we found two dozen or more arched over the trail, bent down under their snow load. Took a while to clear them away and open that section of trail. When we were first here last year and found all the downed and broken-off trees, we though the wind was responsible. Now we know it's the weight of their snow load that caused the destruction. We know there'll be many more down when we come to check our trails next year. By the time we returned home and were eating lunch, snow had started falling again.

Friday – Nov. 20th -6C Sure warmed up. We received a good inch of snow overnight. Very dull today so breakfast by candlelight this morning!!

Gordon took off this morning to check our River Run while I stayed home. I did get my morning exercise by walking to the meadow, checking and re-baiting the three traps along the way. Returning, I got busy baking pies and a pan of buns before stretching out and reading "Last of the Breed" by Louis L'Amour. Enjoyed it.

Gordon got back from the River run late in the afternoon. The return trip took him well over four hours of steady going. Reaching the river, he'd noticed it was pretty well covered with overflow but still decided to cross on snowshoes and continue to where we'd had our Wolf Two run set out last year. Not too many tracks so he only set one trap along the way. Actually, I had expected him to close the line today but he decided to give it one more run. He only picked up one marten in all that distance.

Saturday – Nov. 21st -8C   Cloudy again but not near as dull as yesterday morning.

After breakfast, we skidoo'd down Jamie/Wolf Run to the river. Going was good and just a trace of overflow over our trail along the river. We followed along the trail off the river and up Wolf run, expecting at each set to find a marten. Right to the end, where we'd turned around last time, traps were empty. A real downer!! Instead of heading home right then, we decided to snowshoe onwards, hoping to find marten tracks that would show they were still in the area. We couldn't follow on the creek ice since it had patches of overflow, thin ice and even open water in some sections. A while later, reaching the beaver house we'd located last season, we were surprised to find the beaver dam above the house was totally destroyed. It was probably washed out by high water rushing down in the spring time. The creek bed was very low. Gordon was sure surprised to learn just how deep the creek and pond had been when the dam was there. We then decided to turn around and head back to the skidoo. We must have snowshoed at least two miles and in all that distance hadn't seen a single fresh marten track. Pretty discouraging.

On the way home we detoured to check the trap across the river from Wolverine Run and were surprised to find a marten in it. The two previous times we've checked it, we've had a marten. We plan on returning tomorrow and crossing the river – if ice is safe – and set traps on Wolverine Run. Then, turning the skidoo, we headed back home to our cabin at Jamie Lake.

We've come to the conclusion that after the fifteenth or twentieth of November, marten must move to higher terrain where it's warmer. This has been the pattern over the last three years when we've been here. Tracks all over the country until mid November and from then on, nothing. They just seem to disappear. We're sure hoping to find a trail from Rose Lake to Twin Lakes Creek, then up to higher country, where it'll finally connect with the area around our Ridge Lake cabin. Country up there is several hundred feet higher in elevation and always warmer so it would be interesting to see if our theory does make sense. One theory, bandied about by trappers, was that marten migrate from one location to another. Mice, their main food source, become scarce so they move to an area where mice are more plentiful. Gordon doesn't think much of that idea. He feels there would always be a few staying behind, hunting their old familiar haunts even if their prey wasn't as plentiful. The last years all the marten disappeared over just a very few days. We'll just have to try and find out what the answer is. Anyway, it sure has us as well as other trappers on our radio circuit baffled. Checking before going to bed, we discovered it was snowing again. Wonder when it'll decide we've had enough??

Sunday – Nov. 22nd -10C   Still cloudy and very dull out.

I shocked Gordon this morning! I got up first, got the fire going to warm up the cabin, then made coffee. Second time in two months is pretty good, I'd say !! Although the early morning was cloudy and dull, by the time we finished breakfast it had turned into a pretty nice day. We started the skidoo and took off down Jamie Run to the river, hoping to cross over and set traps on Wolverine Run. Because of relatively thin ice, it took Gordon, on snowshoes, a lot of checking on the half mile crossing before he located a safe passage. I drove the skidoo across and then headed up our old route along the back eddy. Surprisingly, there was fur sign. An occasional marten track, one fox track as well as a couple of lynx tracks. We made a few sets for marten as well as one for lynx. There's a draw coming down from the high ridge above that lynx have followed down to this back eddy every year since we've been here. We want to climb and see what it's like on top but so far haven't checked it out. With all the deep snow, we didn't feel like climbing it today.

On the way back, we noticed a fresh set of marten tracks along the bank of the creek just before it enters the river. They headed upriver so we followed. Tracks went all the way up and then branched off to our Wolf Run. Sure enough, at the first set, he'd circled around the baited cubby for a couple of times before curiosity got the better of him. He is a beautiful black marten. Sort of brightened up the day!!

After we returned home I prepared lunch while Gordon loaded meat from the cache into the skimmer. After lunch he hauled the load to the top of the hill on Ridge Run, ready for relaying to Rose Lake when we head there tomorrow. He wants to start hauling supplies now since we'll probably be closing the traps in this area on our next trip. Later in the afternoon,he skidooed over to the second lake to dig up a number of trap boxes we had stashed there.

Monday – Nov. 23rd -10C   Foggy out this morning and impossible to tell if it's cloudy or clear.

We headed for Rose Lake right after breakfast. Trail was well packed so I was able to ride to the base of the hill on Ridge Run. After reaching the top of the hill with the skidoo, Gordon loaded the two hind quarters of moose, he'd cached yesterday, into the skimmer. The trail was in pretty good shape so even with the heavy load in the skimmer, I was able to ride on the skidoo, behind Gordon, as far as the rough sections. While he was crossing the first bumpy area, the rubber hitch to the toboggan broke so I left him repairing it while I walked on ahead. I walked at least two-fifths of the way from Jamie to Rose Lake. We didn't find any fur in our traps today and only noticed an occasional track

After reaching the cabin, I made lunch while Gordon snowshoed over to check traps on Rose Lake. Nothing in the traps and only a few scattered tracks around. So, we've been "skunked" today. Later, he went across the river to check out the moose head and, finding that a marten had been nosing about, set a trap for him. A measurement of the river ice in front of the cabin showed it to be a good nine inches thick – with no overflow. Maybe we'll be able to travel the river after all. He set a fishline through the hole he'd chopped when measuring the ice, determined to catch a trout. Checking before bed, discovered white flakes fluttering down – must be snow !!

Tuesday – Nov. 24th -9C   We're again in fog, also, the sky is clouded over. Snowed about two inches last night and it's still coming down.

We just got word by radio that the Yukon Game Branch will be doing a trapline check in the near future. They plan on taking trappers on a flight over their lines so they can figure out where trails should be cut in order to give them access to the best trapping. Good idea !! They plan on starting with lines closest to Watson Lake, gradually expanding to cover lines further out. If they do follow through with this plan it'll sure be a boost to the trapper. We can certainly use the aircraft's assistance in finding that trail off Lynx run to Ridge Lake. After finishing breakfast, we put on our mukluks and parkas, started the skidoo and headed out to check Lynx Run. Most of the way, the going was good so we were able to take the skidoo right up to our last trap. We picked up three marten along the way and also noticed quite a bit of marten sign. Really quite good compared to some of the lines we've checked in the last few days.

After resetting the last trap, we strapped on snowshoes and broke trail upwards towards higher country and the Twin Lakes/Ridge Lake area. Gordon found that, even when wearing his six foot long snowshoes, plowing through the deep snow was harder than expected. The snow hadn't packed even with the warm days we'd had last week. Without snowshoes, you sank right up to the top of your hips. Wearing them, the trail you broke was still knee deep. During the next several hours, except for a short lunch break, we snowshoed through swamps, meadows and across ponds but mainly through timber, trying to locate the best route for a trail. The sun finally peaked out to help keep us on the right track. We kept thinking how much easier it would be if we had flown over and checked the area from the air. Snowshoeing was hard with so much snow and by late afternoon we were ready to turn around and head back to the skidoo. It was a real treat to remove my snowshoes and actually <u>ride</u> all the way back to the cabin!!

By the time we reached home it was after four o'clock. After shutting down the skidoo, the first thing Gordon did was check his fish line and, "WOW", he had a trout. So for supper, we're having trout and cabbage rolls. Nice ending to a beautiful, relatively sunny day. But again, by suppertime, the sky had clouded over and started snowing.

Wednesday – Nov. 25th -17C   Cooled off – clear out. Looks beautiful. We even have mountains in view this morning – first time in many, many days. A bit of a wind came up last night so a lot of snow fell off the trees. The spruce across the river, without their mantles of snow, now look black.   After breakfast we loaded up and skidoo'd down river towards Twin Lakes Creek and our trail to Ridge Lake. Snow was so deep on the river, well over two feet, but much deeper along the sandbars. A cloud of snow blew over the hood whenever we crossed them. At times it was hard to see through the snow that enveloped us. Really surprised that the skidoo just purred right through it. We left the skidoo on the river at the junction of our trail to Ridge Lake. Strapping on snowshoes, we headed out – breaking trail along the path we'd cleared in the fall. Gordon had, at first, figured the going would really be tough and it would take us at least three days of hard trail breaking to reach the cabin at Ridge Lake. To our surprise, going was not as tough as expected and we managed to cover at least three-quarters or more of the distance to the cabin. We packed a real wide trail for the skidoo and even cleared a few small trees and willows out of the way. Next time we come, we'll be driving the skidoo up our packed trail and then snowshoe the rest of the way to the cabin. We were surprised to find it had only taken us a little over two hours to come as far as we had.

Coming back, I had a real thrill when I either stepped on the tail of my snowshoe or it hooked on a snag. Anyway, I went head-first into deep snow. Just as I was starting to get myself sorted out, I got a "charley-horse" in the back of my thigh. Oh, that hurt!! Try as I might, tangled in my snowshoes, I just couldn't get loose. When I hollered for help, Gordon came to my rescue, unstrapped my snowshoes and finally I was free. Sure scared Gordon. Being up ahead, he hadn't seen my dive into the snow and when I called, thought I'd hurt myself. After a five minute break, we continued onwards. We were surprised to note that it only took us an hour and a quarter to get back to the river. Upon reaching the skidoo, Gordon started the machine but it quit almost immediately. Guess this morning, going through deep snow, we must have got moisture in the carburetor which caused the throttle control to freeze in the open position. Try as he might, Gordon couldn't get the machine started. Finally we left and walked the three miles to Rose Lake. We'll return tomorrow, take the carburetor apart and thaw it out and then, hopefully, the engine will start.

Quite a letdown to our beautiful day!! Walking back, we carried our snow-shoes. The trail we'd made that morning had firmed up so we could walk on it without breaking through the crust. There were a few small areas where over-flow had seeped over the trail but they'd already frozen so it made for easy going. We'd seen quite a few tracks today all along the trail up to Ridge Lake and are planning on returning tomorrow. We'll finish packing trail and on the return, put out a few marten sets. Now it looks as if we'll be spending a good part of the day just getting the skidoo home. One thing for sure, it will be checked over thoroughly before going any distance from the cabin.

By the time we reached the cabin, just after four o'clock, temperature was down to minus twenty and still dropping. It reached minus twenty-three by seven in the evening but later, by nine when a breeze sprang up, it rose several degrees. Getting in bed tonight, I felt really tired and realized my back was sore. Must have been the snowshoeing or could it have been my head-plant ??

Thursday – Nov. 26ᵗʰ -10C Foggy this morning. We've also received a trace of fresh snow overnight.

We were pleased to have warmer weather for our return down-river to the skidoo. We have a skidoo manual here so last evening Gordon was busy studying it, trying to figure out what the problem is with our machine. He's pretty sure he knows what the problem was and yesterday, if he'd known how simple the remedy was, we'd have ridden home. It was getting late and darker and colder yesterday when we had the problem so it wasn't the best time to work on it. Anyway, we returned this morning, armed for battle. We hitched Katy to the toboggan, loaded with firewood (just in case we had to build a fire for warmth) plus, a pail, more tools, the skidoo manual and then headed down the trail. Real easy going since the skidoo trail had frozen hard. After reaching the skidoo and checking it, what Gordon had predicted was correct. Yesterday, while running through flying snow, minute snow particles had melted in the carburetor. When we left and went to pack trail, the water vapor had frozen the throttle needle in the open position. After warming the carburetor a couple of minutes and then tapping it, the needle released and a minute later, with the first pull of the starter cord, we were on our way. We were delighted!! Gordon mentioned he's learned a lot from this episode with the carburetor. From now on, when coming to a stop, he'll run the engine for a couple of minutes before shutting it down – especially if we've been breaking trail through deep snow..

After returning to the cabin, Gordon declared a "Day Off". So we just puttered around with Gordon splitting a bit of wood, then setting out a few more hooks for trout. I snowshoed over and checked traps on our Rose Lake line and after returning, baked a pie. The rest of the day, we just lazed around in the cabin, drinking tea and playing cards. Sort of a nice break!! By four o'clock it was snowing again. Radio signals were good so we booked our return flight for December tenth. That's just two weeks from today! Hard to believe it's nearly time to close up – especially when we've not been able to check a lot of the country we were looking forward to seeing. A lot of trappers have reported problems with overflow and the extra heavy snowfalls so guess we're not alone.

I'm ready to go home and yet I'd like to stay. It's rather sad thinking of closing up. Anyway, we decided to live it up with steak and mushrooms, potatoes and vegetables, followed by raisin pie and tea for our dinner this evening. But, before dinner, we opened our carefully hoarded "Bishop of Riesling" wine (our only bottle, unfortunately) to accompany cheese that had also been saved for a special occasion. I wonder if this would be considered typical trapper's fare?? We did have a terrible problem at first. No corkscrew to uncork the bottle with!! Our anticipation crashed to the floor until – amongst a mixture of nails Jamie had given us – we located a couple of aluminum roofing screws. With shaking hands and the aid of pliers, a piece of wire was attached to the screw and seconds later, the cork popped out. Life was again worth living!! While I poured, Gordon switched on the radio. Minutes later we were sipping wine, relaxing as music filled the cabin. Think this trappers life does have it's good points!!!

Friday – Nov. 27th -6C   Almost clear – just a bit of cloud or fog over the mountains. A bit of a breeze but should be a sunny day once the sun comes up.

First thing after breakfast this morning, we headed down river hoping to reach Ridge Lake today. Reaching the junction, we turned and followed the trail we'd packed two days before. Going was good except for the two short, steep hills and the hummocky sections where I had to get off while Gordon drove the machine over them. We were able to travel with skidoo to the end of section we'd previously packed, then snowshoed the rest of the way to the cabin. Snowshoeing was totally enjoyable ! Our morning breeze had calmed down, everything was so peaceful and still. The spruce, covered with cloaks of snow, shone and sparkled in the early morning sun. The only sound intruding was the "swish, swish" of our snowshoes as we strode along. A short while later, passing through the last stand of timber, we reached the creek flowing from Ridge

Lake and then, a few strides further on, the lake. A picture postcard scene. Spread before us was the white, snow-covered lake surrounded by stands of skyward-reaching, snow-capped spruce. From the eastern shoreline, ascending ridges rose to become the mountains overlooking all. A lovely scene that made me feel a bit guilty for intruding.

Snowshoeing the last few hundred yards, we reached the cabin. Snow had really piled up on the roof and was a third of the way up to the eaves along the outside walls. It took several minutes to clear snow from the doorway before we were able to open the door and peer in. The walls were completely covered with hoar frost, from the floor to ceiling. We'd expected to find frost on the walls but not near as much as there was. The cabin had been built from green logs that never had a chance to dry before freezing temperatures arrived. The moisture in them had come to the surface and frozen. It will take a long time with heat from the stove to dry them completely – something we won't be able to do this season. Upon checking our root cellar, we found most of our eggs were not frozen. Hard to believe, with the cold temperatures we've had!! Mice had gotten into the cellar and it appeared they really loved vegetables. They'd eaten the entire inside from the cabbage and demolished a package of carrots. The onions were like frozen rocks. The oranges seemed to be half and half – tasted good so we ate a couple of the frozen ones. Told Gordon we'll eat them like orange popsickles!! Most of the potatoes seemed Okay – we'll know better tomorrow whether they were frozen or not.

After completing a check of the cabin, we built a fire outside beneath the nearest spruce. Ground beneath it was completely bare of snow. It wasn't long before we were eating toasted sandwiches and drinking hot tea. Finally, we decided it was time to head back so loaded the vegetables in our packs and headed down the trail. We'd first planned on setting traps today, especially after seeing a lot of fur sign, but then decided that since we only have a short time left it wouldn't be practical. We feel the priority should be exploring the far end of our Lynx run so that the top end will eventually connect to Ridge Lake.

When we reached home, Gordon was sorry we hadn't set out traps today. If we have time, we'll go back in a day or two and try our luck. While checking his fishlines, he found he'd caught a Burbot, commonly named "ling cod". They are sure an ugly looking fish. I fried it for supper tonight and found it wasn't at all bad but still prefer our Dolly Varden trout!! After supper, Gordon was busy repairing one of my snowshoes. Webbing in the toe section broke today so he's soaking strips of moose hide and restringing it. It should dry overnight and be tight and useable for tomorrow. Surprised today at finding the creek flowing from Ridge Lake was not frozen – just a bit of ice along the banks.

Saturday – Nov. 28th -5C   Snowing heavily – we must have received at least two inches of new snow overnight. Visibility is Nil!!

About ten-thirty, weather started to clear up so we dressed and decided to go back and set traps along the trail to Ridge Lake. We'll be going as far as the junction of the trail from Ridge Lake, anyway. We plan on hauling the canoe and motor and caching them just off the river alongside the trail. They'll be at a handy location for us when we fly to Ridge Lake next fall. With the outboard motor in the skimmer and the canoe tied firmly behind it, we started down the trail. We were surprised how easily the canoe slid – almost floated along over the snow. No resistance whatsoever, so it was a quick trip to our turn-off point. After caching the canoe, with motor and paddles beneath it, under a big spruce, we continued up the trail to Ridge Lake. Travel was much easier today along the well packed trail. In fact, I rode all the way except for four short but steep hills. On our way up to Ridge Lake, we set fourteen marten cubbies. The day had turned warm after the snow stopped falling and the sky had cleared. Really turned into a gorgeous day. We again left the skidoo a short distance from the lake and cabin and continued on with snowshoes. As we approached the creek, Gordon spotted an otter on the edge of the ice, eating a fish. Nice to see but being behind, I only caught a glimpse of it. While Gordon was setting a couple of marten traps near the cabin, I built a fire under the porch overhang and made tea. Just as we were finishing tea, the sound of the Cessna one eighty-five aircraft flying over the river was heard. We could hear it circle a few times before it finally headed southward towards Watson Lake.

Traveling along the river on our way home, the setting sun provided us with another beautiful picture as it slowly sank behind the mountains in the west. A lovely ending to a very enjoyable day. By the time we reached home, just after five, it was already quite dark. You sure notice the daylight hours getting shorter at this time of year. After we'd finished supper, Gordon got on the radio and called Don Taylor. We were curious about the aircraft that had flown over this way earlier in the day. We were informed that it was a flight chartered by the Game Branch. They had planned on landing at Rose Lake but not seeing activity at the cabin, returned home. Sure too bad – it would have been great having visitors and perhaps having a chance to check some of our country from the air. Apparently the Game Branch is discontinuing familiarization flights with trappers until after we get colder weather. Ice conditions are terrible around the country with overflow on almost all lakes and rivers. Just before going to bed this evening, we took a last peek at the temperature. It was only minus three. The moon is shining brightly over mountains and valleys – a very lovely scene.

Sunday – Nov. 29th -13C   A little cooler and just a bit of cloud.

Should be drier out today. Yesterday the snow was wet and,by the time we returned home, we were soaked. Still drying our mukluks and wool pants. I've noticed we have a "Peeping Tom" over by the "Little Girls Room" (my name for the outdoor biffy) . There's a rabbit that, lately, has been sitting right by it every morning. Doesn't run away when we visit it. Kind of nice to see. We went up river to check our Lynx Run this morning. Rather surprised at finding we only had one marten when we had counted on two or three. Noticed more sign along the far end of the Run where it heads into higher country. We snowshoed for most of the day and finally, we're sure, found a way to the creek and the meadow that will lead us to the Ridge Lake area. If it's nice tomorrow, we'll return and either blaze or ribbon the route. We have to mark it since it will look so different next fall without all this snow. There are so many more potholes, etc. than those shown on our large scale map. We saw lots of fur sign and were just wishing that we had more time to put out more sets.

Monday – Nov. 30th -18C   Clear out. Mountains really stand out, silhouetted against the pale blue sky – lovely.

Peter rabbit winked at me this morning!! He was in a fringe of trees next to the outhouse, only about five feet away. When he squatted down in the snow, only his ears could be seen. He sure blended into the background. Gordon thinks I've gone Bonkers!! Anyway, after breakfast we're off to Jamie Lake to close the traplines over there. Today is clear and sunny and should be a nice day for the trip. We decided it would be better to do it now since we could get more snow and miserable weather later on. The trip to Jamie Lake was very good, even with the hard pulling for the skidoo caused by the deep snow that had accumulated since we were last over the trail.

We found everything was fine at Jamie Lake except for the radio antenna. It was down again. A fire in the stove warmed the cabin and a short time later we were sitting, drinking a hot cup of coffee. Later, while Gordon was resurrecting the antenna and doing some chores outside, I started taking inventory of the supplies in the cabin. I then packed a couple of boxes for the cache. With Gordon's help, we next took inventory of the supplies remaining in the cache. We certainly won't need to store many supplies here since we're planning on flying direct to Ridge Lake next fall rather than back to Jamie Lake.

Tomorrow we'll start closing down our trap Runs. So nice out during the night. A three-quarter moon seemed so bright.

Tuesday – Dec. 1st -12C   Clear out. Will be a gorgeous day for our trip up Jamie/Wolf and Wolverine Runs.

We hurried through breakfast, put on our warm clothing, started the skidoo and headed down the trail. After reaching the river on our Wolf Run, we were treated to the most spectacular sunrise. It was just so beautiful, watching as the sun slowly rose above the hills in the east. Spruce and pine lining the hilltops were etched in black against the light behind while, through gaps in their ranks, flashing rays from the rising sun shone through. As the sun slowly rose, the rays flashing through the trees were constantly changing, as if alive. Such beauty!! When we crossed the river and turned eastward into the meadow along Wolf Creek, the sunlight was so brilliant that it was hard looking ahead. White snow over the big meadow seemed to reflect every sunbeam. Only wish I'd brought my camera along today.

We checked and closed all our traps on Wolf Run. We did pick up two marten and also noticed a few sets of fresh tracks. Maybe it's the warmer temperatures that have started them moving again. We turned around and headed back to the river, then followed it down to the junction with Wolverine Run. After checking the ice – it was good – we crossed and started checking traps. We ran into a bit of overflow just past the first trap so Gordon ended up snowshoeing ahead, checking trail, while I drove the skidoo. We found a couple of places with deep overflow so had to re-route around them. There were also a couple of areas where the ice had worn thin and all that was left was a thin shell. It was lucky he decided to go ahead and check. Usually we just sail over these sections. We picked up one more marten on the Run, a bit disappointed as we'd been expecting two or three more. Oh well – next year??

The trip back home was quite enjoyable. The trail was in great shape. The heavy snows had filled all the holes so there were no more rough, bumpy sections. All in all, we had a real good day. Wish it would stay sunny for awhile though. Cloud had cleared off earlier today but it started moving over again this afternoon. Baking a lemon pie for supper to go with our spaghetti and meat sauce.

Wednesday – Dec. 2nd -7C   Broken conditions today but looks nice.

During breakfast, we decided to check and close River run today. Because of the rough trail, Gordon went by himself. He only picked up one marten. It was in the last set, just before he reached the river. Not so great!! He mentioned the going was tough, especially with many trees down across the trail. Heavy snow loads have toppled a lot of spruce and pine this winter. He brought back all the traps and trap boxes from that line. Claims he's never going to use that run again. We caught very few marten along it and with very rough terrain, it's just not worth it.

After lunch, we went to close up Canyon run. A short ways along the trail, just after leaving the lake, we found the trail blocked by a huge spruce that had fallen right across it. The tree was too large to chainsaw through so we put on snowshoes, planning on packing a new trail around it. Good idea but in heavy timber, where trees were close together, it was quite a challenge figuring out where we could turn the skidoo. Sure enough – going down the slope to get around one large tree, Gordon ran smack into another one. No damage but we had a heck of a time pulling the skidoo backwards so he could turn it. We finally got turned around and back on track but, only a short distance further on, had to repeat the performance. Sure a lot of trees down since our last snowfall, more than we've ever seen before. With delays caused by fallen trees and the amount of new snow on the trail, checking the line took a lot longer than it usually does. We were both surprised at the amount of new snow on the trail since our last trip over it. The skidoo really had a workout today. We only had marten in one trap – not so great. We caught him in a set we'd placed at the base of a tree. We had another cubby, set higher in the branches above. Wonder if he's the elusive marten that had been going from set to set, checking them but not reaching for the bait.

We have definitely decided that, next year, we'll set out the Runs from Jamie Lake right at the first of the season and close them by the tenth to fifteenth of November. Possibly check them two to three times and then close them up. From the records I've kept since coming out to the trapline, it appears that marten must start moving higher after the middle of November. There are very few tracks around here after that. Also, when we were trying to lengthen our Lynx Run and were snowshoeing into higher country looking for a trail, there were so many more tracks than at lower elevations. We have also noticed a lot of marten tracks, after we left the river and reached higher country, on the trail up to Ridge Lake. Next fall, we're flying in to Ridge Lake and will clear trails and work outwards from there. Finished taking inventory this evening and did some more packing.

Thursday – Dec. 3rd -9C   Very foggy out, visibility zero!!

Gordon's skinning out the two marten we got yesterday while I finish packing up the last of the gear in the cabin, ready for storing in the cache. We're saying "Good-bye" to Jamie Lake for this season and heading back to Rose Lake. Sort of sad to leave but we'll be back again next season.

It took us just two hours to reach Rose Lake. The trail was super, just a trace of snow had fallen since we were last over it. I walked most of the way over. Really enjoy walking, especially on a well packed trail. The two dogs romped along behind me, happy to be free. The fog had cleared up and with the sunshine, it was a great day for our move back to Rose Lake. Along the way, Gordon closed the traps and hung them in trees – ready for next season. We didn't catch anything but did see a few new tracks. When we got home to Rose Lake, we discovered a raven had made himself at home in our porch. We'd overlooked putting the bag of dog pellets in the cabin when we left. The raven had torn the bag apart and scattered pellets all over. Not a nice neighbor!!

Gordon checked his fish line but didn't find any trout. When he was cutting the hooks from the line, he dropped his new pocket knife into the river. Now he's out there, reaching through the hole in the ice, trying to fish his knife out. He finally got it!! He had tacked a rectangular, open-ended gallon can on a long, skinny pole and finally managed to snag the knife. Smart cookie!!. We snowshoed over and closed our Rose Lake line, picking up one marten. Also noticed a few tracks. By five this evening, temperature had dropped to minus twenty. Checking later, found the temperature had dropped a few more degrees. Will be a cold night. Sky is clear and a deep blue. With snow covered mountains in the distance, makes a very beautiful picture. .

Friday – Dec. 4th -19C   Foggy and very dark out.

Think Gordon must have mistakenly got up in the middle of the night – it's so dark. Actually, the time was seven-thirty but it seemed more like night-time. Looking through our east facing window, we can't even see the trees across the river or any faint glow from the rising sun. Daylight hours are certainly getting shorter!! I was just exhausted this morning and didn't even wake when he got up to put wood in the fire and make coffee. Think all that walking and snowshoeing yesterday was a bit more than I thought.

After breakfast, went down river and up the trail to Ridge Lake, checking traps. We again left the skidoo about a mile from the cabin. The last section still requires some clearing so we just snowshoed it. We picked up three marten, our first for that Run. Not bad for the length of time the traps have been out. Too bad we didn't get an opportunity earlier to work this line and another, out from Ridge Lake. We feel we'd have done really well in the higher country. Oh well, they'll be there for next year. It was a real good trip even though foggy for most of the way. When we first started down river, you could hardly see the shoreline. While we were at Ridge Lake cabin, I insisted that I was going to carry one of the padded, chrome chairs back to the skidoo. Gordon then decided he'd better pack one back as well. So we started out, each with a chair under an arm. I also brought along a small pot while Gordon had his axe and a marten in his other hand. It was close to a mile back and I don't think Gordon was too impressed with my suggestion. There always seemed to be trees that, brushed by a chair leg, dislodged snow over his head. I was OK since he did a great job clearing the trail for me.

It wasn't until after returning to Rose Lake, sitting on real chairs, eating lunch in the warm cabin that Gordon admitted my idea was a good one. After using wooden blocks to sit on during the past months, it was a real treat to sit in a chair that had a back. You can actually lean back!! He's really very pleased with our addition. Next fall we'll fly two more chairs out to Ridge Lake to replace the ones we swiped from there.. After lunch, Gordon headed for Jamie Lake with a small box of supplies that we'd need there when we came out next fall. It would save having to backpack them over next fall. He also wanted to return to pick up a load of traps and trap boxes and bring them back here. It was getting quite dark by the time he returned and I'd started worrying. He actually made the trip in real good time over the packed trail. Said the skidoo just purred along.

Saturday – Dec. 5th -35C   Clear and cold.

I got up at six-thirty this morning. I just couldn't sleep any longer. Got up and started the fire to warm the cabin and then put coffee on. We hadn't built the fire up last night before going to bed but, even without it, the cabin was still nice and warm. We've found it's really easy keeping this place warm. It turned out to be a beautiful morning with not a cloud – just so bright. It was gorgeous last night, sky had cleared and we had a full moon. This morning we decided that we'd like to stay here forever!! It's so peaceful – the scenery spectacular. We're both already regretting that the ninth or tenth, when we're picked up, is so near and we'll be leaving all this. Our return next year seems so very far away!! We still have Lynx run to close. We'd planned on closing it today but now we're not going – it's just too cold to take the skidoo out.

While I was puttering around inside the warm cabin, Gordon was out – checking the thickness of the river ice. Results from several locations showed the ice depth was between nine and eleven inches, ample for the Beaver aircraft. He also snowshoed across the creek to a stand of big spruce where, in past years, we've hung the skidoo out of reach of animals. Since there were a number of trees that were loaded with snow and leaning every which way, he decided it wouldn't be smart to leave the skidoo there. Instead, it's going to be stored on the roof of the "Black Hole". The amount of snow he shoveled off the roof was sufficient to build a sloping ramp to the roof. Now all he's got to do is drive it up and onto the roof . Hopefully, covered with a tarp, it won't look appealing to a bear or wolverine.

At lunchtime, we decided that since the temperature had warmed two degrees and with beautiful sunshine, we could have an enjoyable afternoon outdoors. So we strapped on snowshoes and headed out to try and finish locating a trail around the rough, pothole section of the trail to Jamie Lake. Several hours later, after a lot of snowshoeing, we finally did locate a better route which will make it so much easier for the skidoo. By following through a number of grassy meadows, we won't have much clearing to do. We were also very pleased to notice quite a lot of marten sign – real fresh. Pleased with the results of our afternoon jaunt, we turned and headed back to the cabin. It was surprising how fast the temperature dropped when the sun starting sinking in the west. It was already down to minus thirty-seven by the time we got back.

Sunday – Dec. 6th -14C   Much warmer. Clouded over during the night and snowing lightly. About two more inches of fresh snow already.

After breakfast we headed out to check and close our Lynx run and then flag the route we'd located beyond our traps. We got one marten and one mink in our traps. It was actually very sad today, knowing it was the last time we'd be traveling the trail for this year. Leaving the skidoo at the end of the packed run, we continued on snowshoes, following the track we'd made previously. We marked the route from one slough to the next with blazes or orange ribbons, as far as the big meadow. Next year it will be so easy to follow the route to higher country now that we've located a connecting trail. When we come next fall, we'll clear the sections where it's necessary. Be a lot easier clearing trail when you're not floundering around in three feet of snow!! It had been disappointing this year, not finding a trail into higher country any sooner. Oh well, at least we know where to go next season. Surprised to find the small sloughs and creeks still had overflow on them.

After returning home and finishing lunch, Gordon started packing a runway on the river with the skidoo. As I watched from the window, it looked as if a snow-blower was coming down river. There is so much snow that it just billowed out in front of the machine. Sure beats packing with snowshoes though!! Gordon can't get over how the skidoo performs in heavy, deep snow. He first started packing runway along the river right in front of the cabin but ran into deep overflow so now he's upriver a short distance, packing along the sandbars.

After he finished runway packing, during our afternoon tea break, we started talking about the past season. It's hard to believe that trapping's over for another year and all our runs are closed. We tallied our fur count. It consists of : one wolf, one wolverine, one mink and sixty-two marten (including one that was lost and two that were eaten by other marten). Actually we only have fifty-nine good marten pelts. We figure we have fifty percent more fur this year than last year. Several marten were badly damaged by mice last year but none were damaged this year. Just hope fur prices stay up as high as predicted!! We both agree we'd be out here regardless of fur catch or the prices. It's just such a wonderful life. The actual trapping and the anticipation attached to it is just the icing on the cake.

Monday Dec. 7th -11C   Foggy out with a skiff of fresh snow overnight.

At breakfast time we heard on the radio that trapper Pete Johnson from over by Tobally Lakes, who'd been hurt in an accident with his all-terrain vehicle in September, was sent out to a hospital in Vancouver. The doctors then discovered he has terminal cancer. Such a shock. He's one of the real old-timers and has trapped his line for many, many years. Such a shame it has to end this way.

After breakfast we both went outdoors – Gordon to shovel snow off the porch roof while I took the skidoo and re-packed the runway. Worked on it for about two and a half hours while Gordon, after finishing the shoveling job, cut and placed small spruce along the runway edges for markers. They're also a big help to the pilot in determining height above the white snow surface – especially when snow is still falling. Later on, we talked to Stan and Jim at the Flying Service, reconfirming our flight for the tenth.

Tuesday Dec. 8th -25C   Cooled off again. It was so clear during the night but scattered cloud this morning. The cooler temperature should freeze our runway – especially the two stretches of overflow on it.

This morning we snowshoed up to the top of the hill, along the route we plan on following next year to connect with our old trail to Jamie Lake. We wanted to finish blazing and flagging sections between the sloughs. They won't require much clearing next fall and will save us from traveling the rough sections we've been using. We think the new route will save us nearly an hour of rough walking or three-quarters of an hour when using the skidoo. After completing that project, we snowshoed back to the big meadow that's located about a mile west of our cabin. From there, we tried finding a trail that would connect it and a series of grassy meadows to the big bend of the Coal River. We had hoped to come out on the west bank of the river, just across from where our trail heads up to Ridge Lake. Surprise – we came out where we'd hoped to!! We're really pleased!! .The advantage of using this route when traveling to Ridge Lake rather than following the river was obvious. When traveling the river, we often had problems with overflow and at times just couldn't get down river. Secondly, there was a lot more sign of marten through the sloughs and patches of timber than we'd found along the riverbanks. We're both happy with our afternoon scouting trip and are already looking forward to clearing that trail next fall.

Started snowing again late in the afternoon and by the time we returned to the cabin, visibility was just about zero. After supper we did more packing, getting ready for our departure.

Wednesday – Dec. 9th -11C   Fogged in this morning.

We took our time over breakfast and then started packing and storing gear in the cache. By eleven, fog started lifting and the mountains came into view – nice. Heard that Watson Lake was also fogged in this morning. Gordon wanted to take a picture of us girls (me and the two dogs) but Celsius, who's always at my back when we're skidooing, would have nothing to do with me today. On the other hand, Katy – the big baby – loves attention and I just couldn't get her away from me. So now I still don't have a picture of the three of us together.

It was so gorgeous at twelve-thirty, temperature only minus eight. Clear, bright and warm in the sunshine – wishing we had some area that needed checking instead of being here packing, in preparation for closing up our home place. Sad!! By three-thirty, all our work was done with just odds and ends left to pack and haul the few feet to the river – when we hear the plane coming. By suppertime, temperature was down to minus fifteen and still dropping.

Thursday – Dec. 10th -20C   Broken cloud conditions – no fog today.

Hopefully, the plane will make it out here this morning. We're all ready except for the last few items that are being put away. At nine this morning we heard that Don MacIntosh had passed away last night – apparently from a heart attack. He's a trapper from out in the Hyland River area and was just sixty-five years old. He'll be missed . We also got word our trip is delayed. Weather was bad in Watson Lake yesterday so they are behind in their flying. Maybe have a flight late this afternoon – if not – then tomorrow. Gordon's been under the weather for about three days – either a touch of flu (where would he pick the germs up from, out here ?) or it's something he's eaten.

Friday – Dec. 11ᵗʰ -14C   Overcast and fog. Gordon says it's rather question-able whether we'll get home to Watson Lake today.

After breakfast with everything packed up, we just sat around playing cards. Finally, around noon, we said "Let's have lunch" I dug through three boxes, located the fixings and made lunch.

Just after we finished and were stretched out on the bed reading, there was the sound of an aircraft. Signals were out so we'd had no prior warning that the Beaver was on its way. Minutes later, Stan Bridcut – the pilot, landed and taxi'd in. The plane was loaded with lumber, barrels of gas and next years groceries for Rose Lake. Stan wasn't able to help with the unloading. He still has to take things easy because of an earlier operation. Gordon and I off-loaded and re-loaded the plane but it did take time.

We got the cabin cleared of all the gear we're taking out with us and just after three, took off. Stan said it was getting very late and if it got too dark, we'd have to stop at Stewart Lake for the night. As it turned out, we reached Watson Lake airport just after four. Minutes later, it was quite dark. It was a good flight but a bit rough. My worst two hours of the trapping season always is the hour flight in and the hour flight out. It was good to be home but know we're going to miss the trapline.

1988

I'M EXCITED – WE'RE OFF
TO EXPLORE NEW COUNTRY

$W_{ednesday}$ – Sept. 14th

After an exhausting and frustrating summer and fall at Watson Lake, it was actually a relief to find myself on board the Otter floatplane heading back to our trapline. For a gal who normally doesn't have much trust in airplanes and flying, this was quite a turnaround. Probably just a sense of relief at finally getting away from it all. It's really hard to believe, after all the planning and anticipation, that in about an hour we'll actually be landing at Ridge Lake.

Our summer and early fall had been extremely cold and wet with rain just about every second day. Because of all the moisture, the hay crop had been exceptionally good. Some areas had grown to heights of seven and eight feet but since the heavy rains had knocked a lot of it down, cutting was a real challenge. We didn't have any good haying weather until mid-August and as a result haying wasn't completed until the twenty-fourth of the month. Quite a lot later than normal. It was a real relief to finally see the last bale stacked in the hay barn. Most years we start haying early in July and are finished by the end of the month.

My garden also took a lot of time. It's my pride and joy and essentially my project although I do allow Gordon to help with some of the work – weeding, hilling potatoes and the other fun chores associated with gardening! The garden

– 241 –

is located at the south end of the hay field and covers about an acre. I grow all the different types of root vegetables with colorful clusters of flowers interspersed throughout the rows. The flowers were lovely and sure brightened up the garden. I also had more than twenty-seven hundred hills of potatoes as well as a lot of cabbage in addition to the vegetables. We finally finished harvesting potatoes on the ninth of September and took the cabbages and carrots out on the tenth. Fresh garden produce is always in short supply in the Yukon so all the surplus was sold just as soon as it was removed from the ground. After we finished with the garden, it was a rush to get the farm machinery stored away and our home winterized. Next, we had to assemble and pack groceries and the gear we'd need for the coming winter months on the trapline. Last evening just before dark, we finally trucked the last load of supplies to the Flying Service float dock – all ready for our morning flight.

We were scheduled to take off at eight-thirty this morning but when we contacted Watson Lake Flying at seven, were advised the chances were slight for a morning flight. We were advised that our flight had to be delayed and wouldn't be leaving until the afternoon. Anyway, they called a short while later at seven forty-five and said "Let's go". What a rush. We got away at ten. We had four truck loads of groceries, skidoo, dogs etc. to load into the two aircraft. Robbie Porter and Bob Watson, hired to help cut trail, were also coming with us. Gordon, Robbie and I, plus one dog, the skidoo and lots of groceries were loaded into the Otter. The Yukon Game Branch was sending the Beaver aircraft out to Ridge Lake to fly the area with Gordon so we were able to make use of the empty space on it. Bob Watson, one dog, a bottle of propane plus the stove and other gear were loaded into the Beaver. John Russell, our local Game Warden and Conservation Officer, had planned on coming out on the Beaver but at the last moment was unable to get away. To assist trappers on remote traplines, the Yukon Game Branch arranges for an aircraft to fly trappers over their lines. These overflights certainly help in locating the best possible routes for trapline trails. It sure saves the trapper a lot of time and is really appreciated. It's a service they provide trappers every few years and is certainly welcome and very helpful.

The flight to Ridge Lake was excellent, smooth and sunny most of the way. When the lake finally appeared with its wind rippled surface reflecting the sunshine, it looked lovely – almost as if it was smiling a welcome to us. Our cabin, nestled on the edge of the small meadow about a hundred yards from the south end of the lake looked, as we flew over, to be in good condition. No signs of a visit by a grizzly. Within a few minutes, after circling to land from the north, the Otter was settling on the water and taxiing to our makeshift dock.

We'd just finished tying down the Otter in preparation for unloading our gear when the Beaver flew over and, minutes later, landed. Anyway, it didn't take long to unload the Otter since we had lots of help manhandling the skidoo and the rest of the stuff. The pilot was anxious to get back to Watson Lake for his next flight and really appreciated the quick off-loading job. Within a few minutes, as we began unloading the Beaver, the Otter roared down the lake on its take-off run, heading back to Watson Lake. A short while later the Beaver, with Gordon and Robbie on board, took off for an aerial survey of our trapline. Hopefully, they'll be able to locate the best and easiest routes for trails through the new country we plan on opening up this year. It should be a lot easier than trying to figure out trails during winter months on snowshoes – as we've done for the past three years. Sure should save a lot of trail cutting, we hope!! Anyway, while they were away sightseeing Bob and I were busy hauling groceries up to the cabin and getting tea ready for their return. Sure enough, about an hour later, the sound of the Beaver was heard and within a few minutes they were landing. Gordon and Robbie hopped from the aircraft but the pilot had decided he'd better get back for his next trip so waved good-bye, turned the plane and took off. Minutes later all was quiet except for the faint throb of the engine noise receding in the distance.

After a quick cup of tea and biscuits, the boys hauled the last of the groceries from the dock to the cabin while Gordon and I were getting things sorted out in the cabin. Sheets of plywood, a bundle of insulation and other assorted building material had been left inside. While Gordon was carrying out the plywood, I decided to take out a large roll of insulation. Boy, what a surprise!! I couldn't lift it. It was soaked through with water. It took both Gordon and Robbie to pack it out. At first we couldn't figure out how it got full of water. The cabin roof is solid and doesn't leak so the conclusion we eventually arrived at was that water in the meadow must have really risen and flooded the cabin during spring breakup. Anyway, it was only a short while before willow clumps around the cache were extra colorful, adorned with blankets of dripping pink insulation.

After they finished hauling all the groceries and gear up from the dock, the boys next started fixing up their campsite. About thirty feet from the cabin were two large spruce, standing about twelve feet apart. A pole was tied between the two trees, about eight feet above the ground. A large tarpaulin was tied to the pole and stretched about twelve feet to the rear where it was anchored to the ground. Beneath the sloping tarp a thick layer of spruce boughs were placed for a mattress. They provided had a comfortable bed in the back area. In front, there was still plenty of room to sit and smoke or drink tea beside the small fire that was usually smoldering. The overhangs from the tarp along the front and sides could be tied down or up, depending on wind and weather. It wasn't long before they had a very comfortable camp.

Robbie next took off for a quick look for moose. Just before we'd landed, he'd spotted a bull moose in a little lake just to the south of Ridge Lake. Anyway, he was back within a short time to report the moose was no longer there. We'll have to take another look this evening since that's when they're usually out feeding. With warm temperatures, as we're having today, moose spend a lot of time feeding in ponds where it's cooler and the flies can't bother them as much.

Gordon next started building an outdoor cupboard while I unpacked groceries. Robbie was busy digging a garbage pit while Bob was fixing up a place for the two dogs beneath a couple of big spruce. I spotted some cranberries which I just had to pick. They'll make a nice sauce to go with tonight's stewed chicken dinner. Our son Ronnie had sent us chickens from Hythe, Alberta so I'd brought one out with us. Donnie, another son, had sent a thirty dozen case of fresh eggs from Grande Prairie. With all the fresh vegetables I've brought from home, we're set for winter.

After supper Robbie and Bob went to look for moose – each went to check a different area. Shortly after they'd left it started to rain. By the time the men got back, an hour later, they were soaked. They hadn't seen any moose – maybe tomorrow. Moose tracks all along the trails. Lots of sign. We'd even found fresh tracks around the cabin when we arrived, right up to the window, so they can't be far away. Just after the men returned, the rain turned to snow. Hope it doesn't last too long since we'd really appreciate good weather for trail cutting.

It wasn't long before we all headed for bed, the men to their lean-to and bedrolls while Gordon and I stretched out on the bed he'd constructed in the cabin when it was first built. With a foam mattress it was quite comfortable. My first night in our Ridge Lake home. Later, while lying in the darkness, thinking of our flight this morning and my first sight of the lake and the cabin, I realized how my life had changed since I'd started coming out to the trapline with Gordon. I'd come to enjoy life in the bush and was really looking forward to another fall and winter on the trapline.

Thursday – Sept. 15ᵗʰ "0"C   A little cloudy this morning but looks like it may be nice later. A few breaks to blue sky are showing. Snowed some overnight so everything is just so wet. Hope we have good weather for trail cutting.

Gordon made a pancake breakfast for us. Afterwards, while Bob and Robbie were constructing an outhouse at the far end of our little meadow, Gordon was busy re-locating the stove inside the cabin. Up to now it had been sitting under a tarp, outside the cabin. He planned on installing it along the wall adjacent to the window that faces the lake. I vetoed that since the stove would have been too near our table, which will sit (when it's built) just beneath the window, and would have made it uncomfortably warm for anyone sitting there. If we moved the table further along the wall, we'd have lost our view. Anyway, we decided to install the stove across the room and into the corner next to the door. Next, after climbing up on the roof and cutting a hole through the roof for the pipe jack, the stovepipe was connected. As soon as that was done, a fire was lit in the stove. Minutes later, we stood outside and watched smoke curl upwards from the first fire in our new home.

After a lunch of home-made chicken noodle soup and bannock, the two men left to start blazing a trail around the lake while Gordon stayed behind to install a larger window in the cabin wall facing the lake. The smaller window was then installed in the end wall. The cabin sure looks brighter now. While we were working inside, our dog "Rebel" started to bark. I figured an animal was in the little meadow behind the cabin and reached for Gordon's rifle. Just then Gordon called out, "Oh, it's Don Wilkinson". Don and his assistant guide, together with four horses, were coming down the trail. They figured that Fabian Porter, who was going to be guiding with Don, would be here. Apparently the original plan was for Fabian to be here but when plans were changed, Don wasn't advised. The men had tea with us and I made them bannock. Just as they were getting ready to leave, it started to snow. Real wet stuff so they'll be just soaked by the time they reach their camp, a good three hour ride away.

About five o'clock Gordon and I headed to a little lake, that's only about a ten minute walk from here, to see if there were any moose. No moose but lots of sign. Many ducks were swimming and feeding in the lake. We also saw a beaver swimming along with a large piece of willow that he'll likely add to his winter feed pile. We got back to the cabin about six-thirty. Bob and Robbie were back from trail blazing. They hadn't seen any moose either.

After returning, I made supper. Hamburger balls in a mushroom/onion sauce together with rice and fresh cauliflower. Right after supper the men decided to head out and check the small lake again. Never know when a moose might show up!! While they were away Gordon put up a couple of shelves above the bed. Tomorrow, he plans on building cupboards and installing the propane stove. It will be such a help to get some supplies up on shelves instead of having them all in boxes. Right now we have boxes all over. The stove we have in here is not the greatest. It was made from a hundred pound propane bottle, same as our other stoves, but the door on this one was bought from a supplier in Ontario. The draft/damper is at the top of the door and doesn't draw very well so, most of the time, I end up leaving the door open a bit in order to get a draft so the fire will burn. It's the pits for cooking on, this way. Gordon plans on revamping it by installing another draft at the bottom of the door. With stuff piled all over, the cabin sure isn't all that homey but will change in a couple of days.

Men just got back. No moose. It's getting cold out and will sure freeze tonight.

Friday – Sept. 16ᵗʰ -2C   We were fogged in this morning but by about nine o'clock it had pretty well cleared up. Looks like it's going to be a clear, sunny, beautiful day. I didn't sleep much last night. Just couldn't go to sleep so am a bit bushed this morning.

We had bacon and eggs with toast for breakfast. I made up a lunch for Robbie and Bob and they went off to finish blazing trail. Will be gone all day. Gordon went to check out the moose situation – none, while I cleaned up the cabin. As soon as Gordon returned, he started installing the baseboard along the walls before building cupboards. I kept busy outside cleaning up the mess from last fall's cabin building. Later in the morning, we spotted the Otter flying over on it's way to Don Wilkinson's camp at Twin Lakes. A short while after that, about eleven, we heard a helicopter fly over. Sure a busy place!! Gordon and I next went searching for a number of small, straight spruce. They had to be about three inches in diameter. After they're cut down, they're trimmed and then cut lengthwise with the chainsaw. The halves are then tacked, curved side inwards, to cover the insulation that's between the logs. Besides covering the chinking, they sure improve the appearance of the walls.

We had applied for a lease, on a bit of land along this lake, for a base camp for our trapping operations. The Yukon Territorial Lands office (Forestry) have to check it out – all our structures, distance from the lake, etc. Sure enough, at twelve noon, we again heard the helicopter. Kevin Risteau, one of the Forestry personnel, had come in to do the required inspection. He flew in with the Jet Ranger helicopter. We were fogged in when they'd flown over at eleven so they'd landed on a sandbar at the river and waited for the fog to lift. Trappers have no protection for their cabins if they're not registered in their name. Anyone can come to an unregistered cabin and take up residency in it and there's nothing you can do about it. With your main base cabin area registered, all other cabins on your trapline are protected as well. Naturally, we have to pay an annual lease and taxes on it but it's worth it. Anyway, it didn't take long for all the paperwork to be finished and soon the chopper was heading back to Watson Lake.

All the fog had cleared by noon and it had turned into a gorgeous day, sunny, warm and no wind. Looking up the lake northwards, we have a view of the Logan Mountains stretching northeastward towards Twin Lakes. They're all covered with snow, looking beautiful but cool – glistening in the sun.

The men got back to camp late this afternoon. They finished blazing a trail so will have to head out that way pretty soon and check it. Gordon finished building me a cupboard this afternoon. I immediately covered it with MacTac. Sure helps to brighten up the place. After supper the three men went checking for moose again. No moose but they did see six beaver.

Saturday – Sept. 17th -6C   Gorgeous day but cool even with the sun shining from the clear sky. Last night was so lovely. Nice clear sky with the stars shining and Northern Lights dancing.

After breakfast the three men left for trail cutting. I stayed home sorting out groceries left from last year, checking to see exactly what we have when combined with the supplies we brought in this year. I packed twenty boxes of groceries, all ready for storing in the cache. I pretty well filled the cupboards in the cabin and also stashed several boxes under the bed. Things are starting to take shape.

At one-thirty, I took time out for lunch – eight grain bread with pepper salami. WOW – is it hot!! To go along with it, I had a bottle of vegetable cocktail juice. Quite the combination. I'm waiting for a cherry pie to bake. Just can't seem to get enough heat in the stove for baking. I don't like making a big fire when I'm alone. It's so nice out, warm like it should be. Nicest day we've had this fall, I think. And I'm wishing I was out on the trail with Gordon

At four o'clock I started supper and, while preparing it, kept watching out the window hoping to see Gordon return early. Sure enough, not too long after I started watching, I saw movement in the brush across the lake and spotted a big caribou bull. He had a very good rack. He came to the lake edge and stood there drinking. I put on my boots, thinking I'd rush down the trail and get closer to him but by then he'd decided to swim across. In no time at all he was on our side of the lake. The brush was so thick that I just couldn't see him when he reached the shore. I took Gordon's .270 rifle and tried following for a ways but finally decided I'd never catch up to him. Too bad the men weren't home. The dogs didn't even spot him. We sure could have used the meat

Gordon returned just before six-thirty. He'd been cutting trail for four hours and looked so tired. He said Robbie deserves a lot of credit. The trail is so straight and will be great for skidoo's. When they left this morning and were about a couple of miles down the trail, they reached a place where the only way across a creek was by walking along a log. Robbie had lost his footing and fell in. Br-r-r that would be cold!!

Sunday – Sept. 18th -6C   Sunny this morning – will be a great day for hunting. Not a ripple on the lake.

After breakfast, we're going hunting in two different areas. Robbie and Bob plan on heading up to the higher mountain slopes and look for caribou. Gordon and I will be heading southwards, hoping to reach a small lake we'd spotted when we flew in. From the air the lake, with waterlily pads covering much of its surface, appeared to be an ideal location for moose.

A short while later, breakfast dishes washed, Gordon and I strapped packboards on our backs and headed southwards. It was all new country to both of us. We had been to Ridge Lake before but only in the winter time, always when snow covered the ground. We'd never been south of Ridge Lake. Gordon hoped to find a game trail that headed southwards. During the next hour we climbed to higher ridges, then back down to swampy sloughs, looking for that elusive trail. Some of the walking was very tough, especially one section where we had to feel our way across a swampy meadow. Finally, after reaching the crest of a rise, we found our game trail.

From there on, we were on solid ground which made for easy walking through nice open country. About half a mile further on, we came over a rise and there, a few hundred yards ahead, was our lake. A really beautiful pond nestled in the mountains. A sandy shoreline stretched around the north and eastern sides of it. The rest of the shoreline appeared to be boggy. A lone white swan was swimming, feeding in the lake. A lovely picture. Minutes later, after removing our packs and stretching out on the ground relaxing, I commented "Lets stay here all day and watch. There just has to be a moose around". Only a few seconds passed before Gordon spotted a bull moose coming out of the trees about a half mile away. We watched it for a few minutes and then, while I remained where I was, Gordon started creeping through the grass and low bushes towards a small spruce that stood about three hundred and fifty yards from the moose. It seemed to take forever for him to crawl the distance, especially the last fifty yards, then crouch behind the spruce. I watched as he slowly raised his rifle and took aim. Seconds later, there was the sound of a shot and the moose dropped.

I ran over to Gordon as he carefully approached the animal. He prodded it with a stick but there was no movement. It was dead. It was a very large bull with a pretty good sized set of horns. Best of all, it looked to be in good condition. It should provide good eating for this winter. A real relief knowing that we now have our winter's meat supply. Next, the work began in dressing out the animal. Quite a job, opening it up and removing the entrails, being careful not to puncture the stomach or other parts that might leak into the body cavity and spoil the meat. The moose was quite fat and in good shape. Finally, about an hour later, we finished dressing it out. We washed our knives and hands in the lake and then got ready to make tea.

We walked about thirty yards further along the lakeshore to where several huge spruce were growing. An ideal spot for lunch. While we were drinking tea, we could sit on piles of spruce needles with our backs resting against the tree trunks. It was while we were digging in the piles of spruce needles under these trees that we discovered someone had been there before us. The remains of several beaver stretchers were embedded in the spruce needles near one of the trees. The stretchers had to be at least forty years old and possibly a good deal more. It would have taken many, many years for the spruce needles to build up over the stretchers to the depth they'd reached.. It made us wonder just who the trapper or trappers were and how they'd managed to reach this lake. Very likely they were here long before flying into traplines was possible.

We built a small fire and soon had our tea water boiling. Minutes later we were stretched out, backs resting against the spruce, munching on sandwiches and drinking tea. We felt very pleased and thankful for our good fortune in getting a moose. We relaxed and stretched out for a short rest but all too soon it was time to get ready for our hike back to camp. In addition to our lunch gear and axe, we packed the backstraps, tenderloin and a side of moose ribs onto our packboards. Lastly, Gordon swung his rifle over his shoulder and we headed for home. This time we took a different route along a game trail and found it good going except for one section, about a third of a mile of swamp, which we just couldn't avoid. It was boggy and wet with a creek we had to wade across. Real fun, especially with a heavy load on our backs. Finally got back home about four o'clock. We'd just finished hanging up the moose meat when Robbie and Bob showed up, packing a caribou. They'd had a longer walk than we did but had good going. They'd seen a lot of caribou up on the ridge just behind camp. One thing's for sure. We have loads of meat for this winter. Some of it will be going back with the boys to Watson Lake – after we're finish trail cutting.

We all enjoyed a dinner of moose tenderloin – really excellent flavor and tender enough to cut with your fork. Right after the meal, the boys stretched out under their leanto. Gordon put up a spice shelf for me. Then I sorted spice containers after I'd finished the dishes. Right after that it was time for bed. I don't think we'll have any trouble sleeping tonight.

Monday – Sept. 19th -10C   Beautiful, clear night again. The stars were so bright. Sure cool out this morning but sunny. Not a ripple on the lake. Should be a great day.

The three men left at nine-thirty, heading for the lake where we got our moose. They'll finish cutting up the carcass and start packing the rest of the meat home. They took Rebel and Smokey, the two dogs we got from Steve and Carol Pecconi last winter. Big, strong dogs so they should be able to help with the packing. I stayed at home and plan on making a big pot of vegetable soup for lunch. After that was started, I re-sorted, stored and put things away in the cabin – giving us lots more room. I even widened our bed by about six inches (by adding an extra board). I also enlarged the root cellar by removing another three pails of soil. The cellar is located under the floor (beneath our bed). It's where our vegetables will be stored for the winter. It had been much too small.

We obtain our wash water from the lake, right at the dock. Our drinking and cooking water comes from further down the lake, east of the cabin. It's down a short rocky slope. Trail is good but you have to watch your step so as not to slip on the rocks. Several small springs are there. They flow into a pool before flowing into the lake. The water is much nicer, colder too than lake water – ideal drinking water. The spring stays open all winter (at least it was open last winter) so it will be much handier getting water there than chopping a hole through the ice after the lake freezes.

Gordon and the two dogs were the first to return to camp. He had a heavy load on his packboard. The dogs also had pretty good loads and were just about played out. It was really too rough a trail for them. They had to cross the creek a couple of times and, of course, their packs got wet which made them a lot heavier. Robbie and Bob showed up a few minutes after Gordon. Bob packed a whole hind quarter. It was heavy. Robbie also had a really big load. Gordon mentioned that problems with the dogs made it extra difficult for him. With his loaded packboard on his back, he found it difficult continually bending over helping the dogs and adjusting their packs. They were fine while traveling on the solid game trail but once they reached the boggy section through the swamp, problems arose. The men hung the meat up on a pole tied between two trees, had a quick lunch followed by a short rest, and then they were off to get the remainder of the meat. This time the dogs stayed home.

Before Gordon left, I had him cut out a larger section of the cabin floor so I'd be able to dig a larger root cellar. I pretty well completed digging it this afternoon. I'll have to get busy making up another bannock mixture as well as get things ready for supper. The boys will be starving by the time they get back with their second load.

It was just after six-thirty when the dogs started barking and minutes later the three men appeared on the trail to our meadow. After they'd off loaded their packs, they strung another pole between two of the trees and hung the meat from it. After that, a tarp was suspended above everything to keep off any mois-ture. Looks like it just might rain. Really clouded up this afternoon. The tarp is suspended well above the meat so air can circulate around it. If the tarp was laid right on top of the meat, it would keep the rain off but the meat would likely spoil since air wouldn't be circulating on all sides. Yesterday when Gordon dressed out the moose, we saved some of the fat for Bob and Robbie. The chunks of fat were laid on poles under the spruce where we'd had tea. We'd covered them with spruce boughs to keep off the "Whiskey Jacks"{actually Canada Jays but they've been renamed in the north}. Anyway, when the men got there today the fat was all gone. Looked like a wolverine or marten had taken it.

Tuesday – Sept. 20th +2C   A pleasant change from last evening. Cloudy but it looks like it'll be a nice day. A lot of blue sky showing. It rained some during the night.

After breakfast, Robbie and Bob built a meat cache and hung the meat in it. The cache is a good twenty feet above the ground so the meat should be safe from most animals. Building it was another big but necessary job that had to be done. Gordon enlarged the cold storage area under the bed and framed it up. It's now all nicely lined with plywood. All the vegetables, plus the eggs, were then put in it.

After lunch Gordon built our table. After it was completed, I covered it with red and white checkered oil cloth. Looks good with the red drapes I'd hung on the larger window on Saturday. The small window has blue flowered curtains. This place is really starting to look quite homey. It's not nice out this afternoon. A real fall day, cloudy, with a bit of wind. It's snowing up in the mountains – upper ridges are obscured. The Beaver and Otter aircraft flew over, heading further north but the dogs didn't sing for us this time. They usually did at Watson Lake whenever an aircraft flew by. Gordon talked via radio with Bill Seeley, pilot of the Otter.

I decided to burn one of the piles of branches that were left over from last year's cabin building. Gordon and I both figured it would burn slowly but, in no time, we had a huge bonfire. Poor Smokey, the fire was fairly close to his big tree. He went as far back as he could on his chain but think it still got a little warm for him. Gordon enclosed more of the porch with slabs to keep the wind and snow out. We'll be using the porch for storing wood and for the supplies that aren't put up in the cache.

After a dinner of pot roast, gravy and veggies, Gordon, Bob and I went and cleared trail from the cabin to the creek – along the trail that heads down to the Coal River. The men cleared trail while I threw the debris on a pile for burning. Gordon said we'd burn it all so Robbie came over and helped. We ended up by also cleaning up a bunch of last years cuttings. Sure looks a lot better now and it certainly made a real bonfire. Theres still lots more to clean up though. All the tops and branches from the spruce that were used for cabin building will be piled and eventually burned.

Wednesday – Sept. 21st +2C Cloudy out this morning. Looks like it might rain or snow.

We had hoped the two men could go up Twin Lakes way to cut trail but weather looks unsettled. Since it's a long walk there and back, Gordon wants them to camp out rather than hiking back here every day. Radio signals are very poor. Haven't been able to reach Watson Lake Flying or Don Taylor – our radio contacts. Sure glad we had Kevin in here the other day and also that Gordon was also able to talk to the pilot yesterday. Everyone will now know we're OK.

After a pancake breakfast, Gordon took the chainsaw and went clearing trail across the creek enroute to the Coal River. Bob and Robbie were busy putting up a brace between two big trees. It'll be used to hang the skidoo from so it'll be out of the reach of animals when we leave at the end of the season. I cleaned up the cabin and am doing laundry. The fun things!!

Bob Watson is a Watson Lake native and will be sixty-five years old in December. He's the son of Frank Watson, a man who came from California to the Yukon, married a native woman and settled at Watson Lake. Bob lives at Windit Lake which is about two miles north of Watson Lake. Watson Lake was named after his Dad, Frank Watson. His mother, Grandma Watson died a year ago. No one seems to know how old she was but she had to be in the nineties or even over a hundred. Bob thinks she was one hundred and six. He has a fantastic memory and tells us tales of the early war years, all the aircraft that went missing or crashed and where they're located (near Watson Lake) and the exact years they occurred. In the 1940's, military aircraft were being ferried from the United States to Alaska then onwards to Russia. Quite a few were lost enroute. He also had many tales of what he'd done during the earlier years of his life, not bragging, just factual information. He moved to the Ontario/Quebec area when he was in his mid fifties and returned to Watson Lake two years ago.

Bob is a very hard worker. He moves slowly but gets so much done without having to be told. For example – yesterday he vanished at four o'clock and by five Gordon was getting concerned. He decided he'd better go look for him in case something had happened. He found him. Bob was out with his machete clearing trails. After supper he was back doing the same. Something you don't see in too many men. He can see what has to be done and suggests ways to do it that makes it easier or handier for others.

Later in the morning the three men built a bridge across the creek that flows from the lake. The creek doesn't freeze in winter so the bridge will sure make it a lot easier for crossing, either by foot or with the skidoo. Jumping from rock to rock as we'd been doing had been a real challenge – often ending with wet feet. After lunch Bob and Robbie brought in a load of dry firewood. While Robbie cut it up in lengths and split it, I stacked it in the porch. Bob was busy building a ladder for the cache. Gordon was inside the cabin building another cupboard with a work surface on the top. Will sure make it handier for me.

Light rain this evening. We burnt more brush piles before having evening coffee.

Thursday – Sept. 22nd +2C   Overcast with a bit of rain and the odd snowflake. Not nice out.

Robbie and Bob were all packed last night and had planned on going up the lake towards Twin Lakes creek this morning. They'd camp out there for a couple of days while cutting trail. Because of the way the weather's looking, their departures been postponed. Instead, the three men worked around camp. Robbie built a sawhorse and kept busy cutting, splitting and stacking wood while Bob hauled in more dry trees for the winter woodpile. Gordon kept out of their way, installed two propane lights in the cabin and then connected up the propane stove. Should be a great improvement to the cabin lighting. The gasoline lamp was not the greatest for reading or doing any close-up work by. I'm anxious to try the propane stove so will bake a cake this afternoon. It's just a small stove that we were lucky enough to obtain from a recreation vehicle. We have a twenty-four inch, full size propane stove coming in on the next flight. When it arrives the larger stove will be installed here and the smaller one will be taken to Rose Lake cabin.

After lunch Gordon and Bob cut trail until tea time. Robbie was busy cutting and splitting more wood while I tried baking a cake in the new oven. Not the greatest success. My pans were a bit too small for the amount of batter but the cake was eaten at tea time anyway. After tea I stacked all the split wood in the porch while the three men went back to cut trail until suppertime. By then it was snowing lightly. Still no radio signals. Wish the weather would change so we could contact the outside world.

Friday – Sept. 23rd +2C   Snowed overnight – a white blanket over everything this morning.

After breakfast, Gordon started sawing more planking. It's needed to finish the walls of the porch. Bob and Robbie kept busy getting more firewood. Just too wet to go trail cutting today. The porch is starting to look good, just about all enclosed. Later in the afternoon Gordon installed a window in the west porch wall but still has to build and then hang the door. There is so much wood stacked inside the porch, half has been split but the rest will be done this winter. You can never have too much wood on hand for a Yukon winter!

We all had a lazy afternoon. Not much that could be done outside without getting soaked. Bob and Robbie spent most of the afternoon stretched out in front of their fire under their lean-to, smoking, reading and drinking coffee. Gordon and I puttered around in the cabin, sorting and putting gear away. The lake is so calm. No wind and not a ripple over the entire surface. The snow hasn't melted off the trees. Their reflection in the lake is just beautiful. Radio reception is great, we have our choice of a dozen stations to listen to.

Saturday – Sept. 24th -3C   A little cooler this morning. We're fogged in but there's a bit of a breeze so hopefully it will blow away.

After breakfast Robbie and Bob packed their gear and headed up the trail towards Twin Lakes creek. They'll camp out for a couple of nights and start cutting a trail to meet the one Gordon and I cut from Lynx Run last winter. Still have very light snow falling but think it's just from the fog. It is a cold, raw morning. Still no radio signals from Watson Lake Flying.

It gets pretty hot in our cabin since the stove's going most of the time while I'm preparing meals. Gordon decided it would be a good idea to cut a small window opening for ventilation in the gable end of the east wall. After that was done he hinged the window so it can be opened any desired amount by using a drawstring. Besides cooling the cabin, the extra window also makes it much brighter in here. I kept busy, after doing up the breakfast dishes, by insulating the outside of the walls – jamming fibre insulation between the logs. Finally finished just before noon. By lunch time the fog had lifted and it was lovely out. The men should have a good day for cutting trail.

After lunch Gordon and I hiked a short ways down the trail that leads to the river and our Rose Lake cabin. We did more trail clearing on a section that hadn't been finished last winter. It's a section, about a mile or so from Ridge Lake, that had really thick brush along it and required a lot of axe and chainsaw work. Now that we've finished clearing it, walking and skidooing through there will be no problem.

Sunday – Sept. 25ᵗʰ "0"C   Overcast this morning but feels so warm. It was beautiful last evening and overnight. The sky had cleared completely and with a full moon everything was so bright and lovely. This morning I woke up to the sounds made by a flock of cranes flying over.

After breakfast, decided to try my hand at baking. "Can she bake a Cherry Pie – Gordy Boy" ??

Yeah!! And it looks GREAT!! First pie baked in the propane oven. Sure beats the other stove for baking. Gordon did chores outside this morning while I was trying my hand at baking. He gathered up the remains of our insulation, which had been draped over the buckbrush for drying, stuffed it in a bag and hung it under the cache. Next, we cleaned out and sorted all the stuff in the porch. Surprise, surprise!! We now seem to have all kinds of room in there. Later, we walked to the top of a knoll that's about a couple of hundred yards west of our meadow. You get a beautiful view of the lake and mountains from there. That's where the cabin should have been built. Of course it would be more of a chore to haul water, wood and supplies up there. Maybe the location for a guest cabin in the future.

After lunch Gordon, rifle slung over his shoulder and carrying the chain-saw, and I – carrying the saw gas and oil, headed up the trail past Ridge Lake to a smaller lake that's about two miles further away. Once we got there we did some trail clearing, planning on connecting to the section of trail that Gordon had cleared on Saturday. We cleared trail for the next few hours but did not connect up before deciding it was time to head for home. On our way back we were in a snow shower for most of the way. It sure cooled off the air!!.

Moose tenderloin for supper tonight. It's certainly good eating!! So tender and flavorful. Some moose are quite strong and tough to chew but the one we got couldn't be better. And of course, my pie for dessert. We both admit it turned out really super but do agree the crust didn't turn out quite as flaky as those baked in the wood stove. Possibly I didn't have the propane turned up high enough. Will try it a little hotter next time. Sure gets dark fast out here. At seven the sun is still shining but by seven-thirty it's getting dusky. By eight o'clock it's pitch black. Of course we're in a valley surrounded by hills and mountains and big trees.

Monday – Sept. 26ᵗʰ -5C   Cloudy but lots of breaks in the overcast. Looks like it will be a nice day.

We still haven't been able to call out on the radio.. Signals have been non-existent but this morning we can hear some traffic from Atlin, B.C. way. Hopefully signals will pick up so we can report back to Watson Lake Flying and get any messages they may have for us. This is a constant worry when signals are out for so long. We keep worrying that our radio is not working. Believe it or not, at nine-fifty we did finally get word to Watson Lake Flying. We'd been hearing them but until now they couldn't read us. Now we know our transmitter works. We booked the Beaver aircraft for October fifth. They'll bring in the rest of our supplies – gas, snowshoes, dog food, two chairs, etc. and fly Bob and Robbie back to Watson Lake. We are so relieved to know everything is fine.

Gordon split and stacked more wood, clearing up what remained by the cabin. It's turned into another gorgeous day. The lake is like a mirror with the mountains perfectly reflected in it. Hope it shows in the pictures I took. We went for a walk to the small lake south of here. We've named it "Beaver Pond" because of the number of beaver there. There's a game trail leading from the meadow where our cabin's located, all the way to Beaver Pond. As we followed along the trail we noticed that just where it entered the spruce, fresh moose tracks appeared on it. Tracks came in from the side and were very fresh. Must have been made only minutes before. We snuck along the trail trying not to make any noise, certain we'd spot the moose around the next bend. No such luck!! We reached the pond just in time to see the ripples he'd left while wading across a small bay. That was all – no moose!! One end of the pond had ice on it. Ducks were swimming and feeding across the pond in a small opening left between the ice and shore. They'll likely leave today since the open area will probably freeze over tonight.

While waiting for lunch, Gordon took his fishing rod down to the dock and tried catching our dinner. Not much luck. He only caught one small greyling. Unfortunately, he doesn't have many small hooks. After lunch we took the chain-saw plus gas and oil and headed down the trail to the river – our Ridge Lake Run. We planned on clearing the last section of trail which still needed to be brushed out. We worked for several hours and only had about another twenty feet left to clear when we ran out of gas. Such disappointment!! The trail we cleared sure looked good though, nice and wide.

Robbie and Bob returned about five o'clock, just a few minutes after we got back. They reported they'd been able to connect the trails up as hoped and that we should be able to use the skidoo on it this winter. They had pretty tough going through part of the area because of rough ground and thick patches of small spruce. The spruce aren't hard cutting but when they're close together, it takes a lot of sawing to clear a trail wide enough for the skidoo. We're glad they're back and everything worked out OK.

Tuesday – Sept. 27ᵗʰ -2C Snowing lightly this morning but sky is clearing to the north.   The dogs acted up three different times during the night. The first time this has happened since we arrived here. Gordon kept getting up but could see nothing and the dogs didn't seem to be overly concerned. This morning when Bob and Robbie came in, they told us that during the night they'd seen a large antlered caribou right behind their lean-to. Robbie said he'd had a really good look at the caribou through the scope on his rifle while Bob shone the light from the flashlight on the animal. So that's the reason for the dogs barking. Gordon was concerned about our meat but knew it couldn't be a bear since the dogs weren't too excited.

After breakfast we finished a few chores around camp then hoisted the skidoo up between two trees by means of a pulley and the block and tackle. It's now high enough so nothing, especially bears, can get at it. A section of the tree trunks, about six feet above the ground, were wrapped with tin for about four feet. The tin will keep animals from climbing the trees.

We had an early lunch, tied gear on our packboards and with the dogs following, headed for the river via our Ridge Lake trail, on our way to Rose Lake. Walking was good on the cleared trail with only the occasional tree, fallen over winter, to clear away. It took us a couple of hours to reach the river. It was a nice day for the move, sun shining from a clear sky. Bob was especially happy to reach the river. He was still quite tired from the trail cutting they'd done during the previous days. We were sure relieved to find the canoe and outboard motor intact. No sign of a visit by wolverine or bears. The canoe was quickly shoved into the water, the motor refueled and Surprise!! The motor started on the first pull. The men placed their gear in the canoe, climbed in and, with Gordon handling the motor, headed across the river to a sandbar on the other side. Bob and Robbie climbed out on the sandbar with their gear while Gordon returned for me. Because of shallow water at our launching point we'd had to relay our load. We crossed the river and proceeded upstream to the next sandbar where the men were waiting for us. From there on to Rose Lake cabin, they'd be able to ride. During spring, summer and early fall, the Coal River has a good volume of water with depths of three feet and more over much of its length. Early spring, the river runs full, bank to bank and often floods away back into the timber. During these times the river will often have a depth of eight to ten feet. At this time of year though – late fall, smaller streams that feed it are starting to freeze up and its depth can drop drastically within a few days.

The two dogs howled when we first left them but, after we called a few times, decided to follow along the riverbank. When we had to follow the river where it was deepest, close to the further opposite shore, the dogs jumped in the water and swam across. That water must have been cold. Rebel was Okay in his crossings but a couple of times we figured Smokey would drown. He'd swim across and try getting up the bank and, of course, he'd try at the steepest part.

We had to give him a hand a couple of times but eventually he smartened up. Poor dogs, we all felt sorry for them swimming in that cold water. If they'd been real smart, they'd have followed along on one side of the river. We were continually crossing back and forth, following the deepest channel.

All in all, it was a good trip up river. We experienced a feeling of real satisfaction when, rounding the last bend, the cabins finally came into view. We kept studying them as we crept closer, hoping we'd not find a broken window or a door hanging ajar that would indicate a bear had paid them a visit. A real relief minutes later, when the canoe slid up on the sandy bank, to find the cabins were just as we'd left them. The smaller cabin, located on a lower section of ground, did show signs that it had been involved in a flood. The wood stove was still full of water.

While Robbie and Bob were busy moving their gear and settling into the smaller cabin, Gordon brought our gear and groceries up to the main cabin. I was busy getting the stove going and coffee water heating. We were all in agreement that a hot cup of coffee would really hit the spot. Even with the sun shining and very little wind, we were still chilled from traveling on the river. Must be the cold water flowing by. Anyway, shortly after coffee, it was time to get busy with supper. After supper Gordon and I checked the boxes of groceries that had been brought in on the flight that had picked us up in December. Jamie had sent the groceries in but wasn't just sure what all had been sent. Everything was fine and all the supplies we'd requested were there. Only one small oversight. Instead of two large, three pound cans of jam, we found two – eight ounce jars of jam. Will just have to take it easy on jam this season.

Wednesday – Sept. 28th "0" C   Snowing out this morning. Can't see the mountains, just a fringe of trees showing across the river. What a change from yesterday!!

After breakfast, Gordon and Robbie are going up the Ridge Run trail towards Jamie Lake to cut out a new section of trail that we'd blazed last winter.

The new section will run along the edge of several large swamps and will make it a lot easier skidooing and walking during the winter. The old trail was through sections of very rough, hummocky ground that just hammered the skidoo. Bob will be staying behind since he's not feeling too well. He has a sore hip and his back hurts. Whether it's from an old car accident injury that's acting up or a chill, we don't know. I gave him a four-seventy aspirin. Hope that will give him some relief.

This cabin is so nice, so bright. The logs we scraped last winter stayed really clean and now have a golden hue. They did not change color or darken. Even though this cabin is only about six inches wider than the one at Ridge Lake, it looks so much larger. When we return to Ridge Lake we're taking the wood chisel and will start rescraping the logs in the cabin there. The bark has already been removed but there's a fine layer of "skin" remaining on the logs which has turned dark. Will be able to scrape the layer off with the chisel.

After lunch Bob tried fishing and caught a Dolley Varden trout. A nice fish in the two to three pound range. It will go great with the moose ribs that were left over from the soup I'd made for lunch. It's not been a nice day, just wet and soggy. By the time Robbie and Gordon returned from trail cutting, around mid afternoon, they were soaked through. A good fire and hot tea warmed them up a bit. After supper the men did chores outside. Boiled traps, built a stand for the gas barrel and burnt brush. I painted cupboards and put MacTac on the shelves. Sure brightens up the place.

Thursday – Sept. 29ᵗʰ +2C   Snowed and rained most of the night. Windy this morning but quite warm. Really soggy outside but warm in the cabin.

After breakfast, Bob was outside building a fire for boiling up the rest of the traps. Traps are boiled each fall before the start of the trapping season. You have a large container, often a ten gallon drum with one end cut out, that is suspended over the fire. It's filled with water which is brought to a boil. A good quantity of short spruce bough tips are then placed in the water and boiled for half an hour or so. Next, the traps are placed in the boiling water with them. Traps are boiled for about fifteen minutes and then slowly taken out of the water and placed on a pile of spruce boughs to dry. The boiling performs two functions. It removes all human scent from the traps and, from boiling with spruce boughs, covers them with a light waxy coat that keeps them from rusting.

While Bob was looking after the traps, Gordon and Robbie went and put up the walls of our "Biffy". The new outdoor toilet just won't be near the same as the one it's replacing. When using the old one you were quite cosy sitting beneath a wall and a roof of orange tarp while the other three walls were enclosed by spruce trees. I can hardly believe it though. A closed in "Biffy" after three whole years!! What more could one ask for!! Gordon just came in, remarking that the wind is really raw. While the men were working outside, I'd painted the inside of the door and the frame around the big window. Surprising what paint does to brighten up a place.

After lunch the men framed up the cache, put a roof and walls on it and then covered the roof with roofing paper. It looks just like a little cabin perched atop four upright poles. Previously the cache consisted of a platform atop four poles. Supplies were stacked, stored on the platform and covered by a tarp. The new cache will be a lot handier. Now all you'll have to do is open the door and reach in for your supplies. Before, you first had to untie the rope that kept the tarp in place over the supplies. After you retrieved what you were after, everything had to be tied down again. A real Pain!! While the men were working outside, I put a second coat of paint on the door and the two window frames. Looks good. Pretty soon will really hate to leave this place.

The dogs are not happy at the moment. The three men took the canoe and have gone upriver about two miles to where Lynx Creek flows into the Coal River. They plan on cutting a trail from the mouth of Lynx Creek to a large meadow that's about a mile further upstream. The trail we cleared and used last winter came in off the river to the meadow and was just so rough. We also had to climb a pretty high river bank which often gave us trouble. Anyway, later on last winter we scouted out a new route from Lynx Creek to the meadow. The men will be clearing it this afternoon. The new trail from Lynx Creek gradually climbs out of the creek valley and then runs through an open stand of spruce all the way to the meadow. Should be pretty easy trail clearing.

There's a very cold wind blowing, sky is clouded over and it's damp and chilly. Temperature is only plus 5 Celsius. Not a nice afternoon. I'm busy making a stew out of the meat and vegetables that we have left. Have lots of canned and dried goods here. Oh, oh, by four-thirty it started raining heavily. The men will be soaked. Because of all the fresh snow and rain we've had over the past couple of days, the river has risen a lot. The river sure has changed its course this past year. In front of the cabin, the sandbar is not near as long as it used to be. Also the main channel across the river, which had been very narrow, is now quite wide and the channel on this side is now the narrow one.

The men just got home, soaked through. On the way back they tried fishing at the mouth of Lynx Creek where there's always trout but were "skunked". Not even a strike. They said the water was very muddy after all the rain and snow so that's likely the reason for not catching anything.

Friday – Sept. 30th +2C   Showered overnight but cleared up and was sunny by morning. There's still some cloud around. The river has also risen a bit more.

After breakfast we closed up camp in preparation for our departure down river to Twin Lakes creek and a hike back up to Ridge Lake. Gordon, with the canoe, took Bob and Robbie across to the sandbar on the other side of the river. They'll be able to hike a good ways down river. He then came back for me and took me down to the second sandbar where I got off and started walking downstream with the dogs. Then it was across the river with the canoe to pick up Robbie and Bob and relay them further downstream. Anyway, I ended up walking the length of three sandbars while the men did two. Walking was excellent on the hard-packed bars. I must have covered close to two miles, at the very least. The dogs also enjoyed the run, especially with someone accompanying them. From all the run-in over the past three days the river is very muddy, making it impossible to tell where the deeper channels are. Hence our decision to have only light loads in the canoe so there'd be less chance of it's getting hung up or damage to the motor on boulders in the river. It took us quite a lot longer today to reach the mouth of Twin Lakes creek but at least there was no damage done to the canoe or motor.

We cached the canoe, motor and paddles, as well as the toboggan and skimmer we'd brought from Rose Lake, under a couple of large spruce – well back from the creek and above it's high water marks. The rest of the gear was strapped onto our packboards and then we hit the trail. Hiking up the trail was pretty good except for a couple of spots where freshly fallen trees blocked it. The men, with their axes, soon had the fallen trees chopped into lengths and thrown off to the sides. There was one stretch of trail where a number of trees, intertwined, had fallen. The trail was rerouted around them since it was easier doing than clearing that jungle of limbs. It took us between two and a half to three hours to get back to Ridge Lake. It had been an enjoyable trip, both the canoeing and walking. The weather was great, sunny and warm but the ground was still very wet from all the rain and snow we'd had over the past days. We all ended up with wet feet. It wasn't much fun for Bob though. Walking had been quite tiring and hard on him with his sore hip. It's still bothering him a lot.

We were really pleased to find that neither birds nor animals had bothered our meat. We'd been a bit concerned about it. After a welcome pot of tea and lunch we all had a short rest. Then a few small chores were finished off, such as nailing tin around the legs of the meat cache. Bob, despite his sore hip, insisted on piling and burning more of the limbs left from cabin building. We dug in our packs for the chisel we'd brought from Rose Lake. I then started to scrape the cabin logs the same as we'd done on the cabin there. What a difference it makes when that thin layer is scraped away!! It's going to be a big chore but will be worth it. Also, our new propane lights here are such an improvement. We plan on putting new ones in the other cabins next year. (If we come back)

Saturday – Oct. 1ˢᵗ -2C   Fog this morning. Signals still not good.

After breakfast Gordon and Robbie headed down the trail to the lake where we got our moose, hoping to get a bear. They figured there was a good chance a grizzly would be feeding on the remains. Also, they plan on going further down the valley southwards to see if they can find a route for a trail to connect with our old "Wolf Run" from Jamie Lake. Gordon asked Bob to stay behind since his hip is still sore. There will undoubtedly be rough walking in some areas. Bob was very disappointed at not going but realized he would have been a drag on Robbie and Gordon. Told him he could go tomorrow when they start clearing trail. Bob walks very slowly with his sore hip and would have really held them up. Instead, he's now outside cleaning up around the cabin and will undoubtedly be burning brush later on.

I did a batch of laundry, baked a lemon pie and made up a batch of "lazy" cabbage rolls. Decided they would have taken too much of my cabbage if I made them the regular way. After that I took the chisel and scraped more logs. After washing the dishes I decided to try my hand at fishing. I caught two greyling. Was hoping for four but my hands got so cold that I quit.

Gordon and Robbie got back about five-thirty, pleased with their scouting. They found a trail and cleared about a third of it along the far end. They plan on going and finishing it off tomorrow. No bear sign at the moose though!! After supper we had a gorgeous evening. Not a cloud in the sky. It will surely get very cold tonight. We also saw what we believe was a satellite. Gordon says it was traveling too fast to be a plane.

Sunday – Oct. 2ⁿᵈ -9C   Got nippy out last night. It was a beautiful clear night with stars so bright. Now we have a beautiful morning with not a cloud – just bright sunshine.

We still can't get radio signals and don't know if it's because of poor signals or if it's because of our being located down in a sort of dip. It is a great concern even though we're sure our radio is okay since we periodically hear transmissions from other radios. We got through to Watson Lake only once in the past three weeks. We'd like to take the radio to Rose Lake and test it. Gordon is planning on putting up higher antennae poles and locating the antennae in a different direction – hoping that will make a difference. We do have an aircraft booked for the fifth so will find out if signals are poor or if it's our radio that's the problem.

This morning after breakfast Gordon and the two men headed down the trail southwards to finish clearing the trail they'd blazed yesterday. Bob insisted on going. Yesterday his hip was so sore that I gave him one of my Feldenes. Said he felt better today. Not sure if the pill helped him or whether he was determined not to be left behind. Neither the dogs nor I are very happy at being left behind. I'd have liked to go as well but Gordon said it was pretty rough going over the last section of trail. It's something I've missed out on this fall, checking out new trails with Gordon. Had the two men not been here I'd have been with him. I made up three hamburgers and three bannocks for each of them for their lunch. Hamburger and bannock go so well together on the trail. Robbie and Bob had never had it before. Think I should start a MacDonald's outlet at Ridge Lake!!

While they were away I wrote a few letters, ready for the plane on the fifth. While I was writing I heard a thump inside the cabin. A little bird had flown in through the partially open door and was trying to get out through the window. His poor little head must have hurt when he hit the glass. I opened the window and he was gone!! A little later, got through to Watson Lake Flying. Not the greatest signal strength but clear enough to receive a message advising that Gordon's meeting will be in Whitehorse on the twenty-fourth, possibly for a week's duration. He will not be pleased since it was originally slated to be held during the first week of October. We had arranged for either Robbie or Bob to stay here with me but now I don't know what we'll do. The meeting is being set up by The Yukon's Department of Renewable Resources. Gordon was appointed as a member of one of the Boards.

The men got back about six-thirty. Think they were all very tired. The trail is all finished except for a short stretch across from Beaver Pond and another short stretch on the far end which Gordon and I will finish up at a later date. After supper I did more log scraping. Starting to look brighter already. Robbie also pitched in and scraped some while visiting us this evening.

Monday – Oct. 3rd -6C   Another beautiful day – sunny.

During breakfast, we were talking about fish, especially Burbot (Ling-Cod) and what ugly things they were. During the conversation, I ran down to the dock to check on a fish line I'd left in the water overnight. When I saw what was on the line, I let out a yell or three for Gordon. The three men all came running down to see what I was so excited about. I had a big Ling-Cod on the line!! I couldn't believe it – nor could the guys. On Saturday when I'd caught two Greyling, one – a female, was full of eggs so when I cleaned the fish I'd thrown the eggs in the water about four feet from the dock. Last evening I discovered the roe was gone. Yesterday afternoon I'd taken a very crooked stick with about eight to ten feet of fish line attached, stuck a piece of greyling tail to the double hook that was tied to the line and put it in the water. It was probably four feet from shore but just where the bottom shelves off to very deep water. Then (to Gordon's amazement) I tied the pole to the dock by a piece of yellow plastic ribbon. This morning when I got there, I found the ribbon was broken and the pole was just barely on the dock. I pulled at it gingerly, thinking I'd lost the hook as the fish line was slack. Lo and behold – this ugly thing came up from under the dock. I think it was then that I yelled. I was sure I'd lose it but Gordon finally got his hands around the burbot and pulled it up on shore. The men are all shaking their heads over my fishing expertise. Bob will show us how to clean this beast. I put the line out again but this time I tied the pole with heavy twine.

Later I worked with the chisel scraping more logs. What a difference it makes!! The men relocated the radio antennae and raised it higher. Incoming signals are good but the Flying Service has difficulty reading us. Very annoying and discouraging. After that they cut and stacked more wood. You can never have too much for the long winters in the Yukon. Gordon and I left the men working on the woodpile and hiked over to Beaver Pond, hoping to collect a beaver or two. We saw four come out of a house. Where they were swimming, there were too many willows between us for Gordon to get a clear shot. While we were at the Beaver Pond there were sounds which I first thought were made by an owl. Then Gordon says "listen to the Beaver". The beaver were having a conversation in their house. It sounded so weird listening to them. After they finished talking they came out. Would be interesting to know what they were saying!!

Tuesday – Oct. 4ᵗʰ -4C   Another nice day – just a few clouds.

Got through to Watson Lake Flying this morning. Jim, at the Flying Service, said signals have actually been very good and thinks it's possible our antennae is at fault. Stan, one of the pilots, is cutting a new antennae and will bring it out to us when he flies in tomorrow morning. Hope the weather co-operates. Should have had a movie camera here this morning. I'd just come out of the cabin when Robbie hollered – "Rose – get that marten!!" A marten was trying to get at the meat that we'd hung in the high cache. The cache platform is supported by three legs (trees with the tops cut off) which had the bark peeled from them and then were wrapped with tin. The marten would race up one of the cache legs until he hit the tin wrapped section. As soon as his two front feet reached the tin and lost their grip he'd spin out and fall headfirst to the ground. He tried and tried climbing up to get at the meat. We began to feel sorry for the poor thing. All that effort!! It was a very large marten and appeared to be in excellent condition. We stood outside for the longest time laughing at his antics. He finally gave up and scampered off into the bush. He'll undoubtedly stick around, hoping for better luck next time.

Later the men took off to clear a short section of trail from Beaver Pond to connect with the game trail leading to the lake where we got our moose. I'm making a big pot of soup for lunch and, just as soon as it starts simmering, I'm going to start work on another log. Robbie scraped some of the logs last night. Sure does brighten up the cabin when that dark skin is removed. Outside, the front porch is nearly all enclosed. Also, a number of shelves have been built along the walls. The door and a window have been installed so it's just about finished.

Gordon revamped our wood stove last night. The stove was manufactured in Watson Lake to our specifications. It's made from a hundred pound propane bottle. We bought the door for it from a Company in Toronto that manufactures them especially for propane bottle stoves. The door was well made but the draft in it just doesn't work worth a darn. The opening for the draft is located near the top of the door and is connected to a flue that runs down the inside of the door, all the way to the bottom of it. Looked real good. No sparks from inside could fly out when the draft in the door is open. Their theory was that the colder air outside the stove would flow into the open draft at the top then flow down the flue to the fire and really get it burning. The big problem we found was that the top draft didn't draw air in at all. That outfit in Toronto should have realized that hot air inside the stove would rise up the flue and prevent any colder outside air from entering the stove. We had to keep the stove door open a crack in order to keep a fire burning. Anyway, Gordon cut a square hole in the bottom of the door. It took him three hours as the door is made of heavy gauge metal and he didn't have the proper tools here. The new draft he installed works beautifully. That's a smart "Cookie" I have for a partner!!

At twelve-thirty the temperature was about twelve Celsius. It had turned into such a beautiful warm day that I decided to go out and lie on the dock in the sun and read. I didn't feel like staying in the cabin. Temperature went up to plus fourteen. I finished reading "The Other Side of Midnight", by Sidney Sheldon. I've read better books written by him!! Just after finishing my reading, the men returned from their trail cutting – all soaked with sweat. They finished the trail but all agreed it was just too warm a day for anything strenuous. Maybe try something really tough after lunch – like fishing.

After a snack, Bob and Robbie headed down the lakeshore a ways to try their luck at fishing while Gordon and I again headed over to Beaver Pond to see if we could get a beaver. We spotted two of them. Gordon had a shot at one but missed. Seems to be a lot of muskrats around the beaver houses. Will have to try for them later on.

Wednesday Oct. 5ᵗʰ +1C Sunny – will be another gorgeous day.

After breakfast we waited for the Beaver to fly in with our supplies and fly the two men back to Watson Lake. While waiting, Robbie and Bob cut more wood while Gordon did brush clearing around the cabin. A good part of the little meadow our cabin is located in is covered with clumps of buckbrush. It's not very thick and only about five feet in height but a nuisance to walk through. Having some of it removed is a real improvement.

The Beaver flew in about one o'clock and brought in another radio and antennae for us to try out. We immediately hooked up the new antennae and found, to our great relief, that our radio then worked great, even better than the radio they'd sent in for us to try. We took down our old antennae and gave it to the pilot, Roger. He'll take it back and have it checked. It will sure be good to finally get our transmissions out. Don Taylor over at Stewart Lake was having small seizures from the sixteenth of September onwards, trying to reach us with a message for Gordon regarding a meeting in Whitehorse on the twenty-fourth. It's the Trappers Compensation and Review Board hearing that Gordon has to be present for. The Yukon Government will send a helicopter in to pick him up and, after the meetings, fly him back out here. We've arranged for Bob Watson to fly in with the chopper to help look after the place and keep me company while Gordon's away. I do not want to fly out even though it would be a great time to do Christmas shopping. I don't care for flying so I'll stay here and try not to be lonely.

After the radio was checked out and the freight unloaded, we said our " Goodbye's " to Bob and Robbie. Minutes later, with the men aboard, we watched as the Beaver became airborne and headed back to Watson Lake. With the two of them gone, the place seemed awfully quiet all of a sudden. The sky had clouded over while the plane was here, a bit of a wind had picked up and the air was cooling off somewhat. Hope it clears again. It would be great having good weather for awhile. So many things we want to do and so much country we want to explore before winter sets in. We had two chairs come in on the flight. What a joy to sit back in them. A big improvement over the wooden blocks we've been using. After catching up on the mail that came in, Gordon started re-doing our bed. I had found that lying on a three inch thick foam mattress wasn't the most comfortable. He's putting a thick layer of small spruce boughs down under the foamy. Should be like a "water bed" tonight. Gordon tried the radio again. Got through to Rhea Stockman in Watson Lake who reported temperature was plus two over there.

Thursday – Oct. 6th +1C Another nice, sunny day. This makes it a whole week that we've had beautiful clear weather.

It was rather nice getting up and being alone again. It's so much more relaxing being by ourselves. In fact, we stayed in bed until nine instead of getting up at seven. We even played cards for awhile. After we were up, I went down to the dock to check my fishline. Sure enough, I caught a little Ling-cod. Oh, they're UGLY!!! Anyway, we let it go. It was too small. After breakfast we did up a few odd jobs. Gordon cut more lumber with his chainsaw and made a door for the outhouse. I piled branches and afterwards started fires and burnt them up. Later, I scraped more logs. Walls are starting to really look brighter but oh, the fibreglass insulation between the logs is itchy if you rub against it. I got it on my arms and all over my clothes. Once the scraping is finished, Gordon will tack small split saplings in the grooves between the logs. They'll cover the insulation that was placed between the logs when the cabin was built.

After tea break we hiked over to Beaver Pond. Spotted a couple of beaver but Gordon couldn't get at them. He did get a muskrat which he'll skin tonight. It clouded over this afternoon so wasn't very nice.

Friday – Oct. 7th +2C   Cleared up nicely overnight so it's started out being another bright, sunny day.

This morning while I scraped logs, Gordon worked on the cache legs, trying to make them more bear-proof. He took large four and five inch nails and drove them, about a third of their length, into the cache legs. Nails were driven in all around each leg just below the tin and spaced about two to three inches apart. About twenty nails were used for each leg. Next, the heads were removed from the nails. The protruding ends were then filed to sharp points. Hopefully animals, especially bears, will have second thoughts about climbing after our meat.

At two forty-five we packed up and headed down the trail to the river – on our way to Rose Lake cabin. Gordon took the chainsaw, rifle and a piece of meat on his packboard. I packed a larger section of meat, the radio, bacon and eggs, cheese plus an assortment other little things. The dogs each carried about fifteen pounds of fresh vegetables in their packs. We stopped on the way so Gordon could work on a section of trail. He rerouted it to avoid a really rough, hummocky section so it took us longer than usual to reach the river. With the sun, shining from a clear sky, it was a nice day to be out on the trail.

Once we reached the river we shoved the canoe, with motor attached, into the water and then, with all our gear on board, climbed in and backed off from the riverbank. With the second pull of the starter cord the motor fired and we were away, headed up river while the dogs ran along on the riverbank beside us.

They loped along for about a mile before deciding to swim across to the sandbar on the other side. They prefer being with us on the same side of the river. Unfortunately, because of the way the deeper river channels flowed, we had to switch sides at about every bend in order to keep in deep water. After the dogs crossed the first time, they ran along on the sandbar on that side for about a mile but when we had to switch sides again, dove in and started swimming up- river behind the canoe. That river water was cold. They swam quite a ways and then, I guess, decided they'd had enough and climbed up on shore and ran along. We felt sorry for them. When we were past the shallow stretches we pulled up to the shore and talked them into climbing into the canoe. They seemed to be happy, riding the rest of the way.

Upon reaching Rose Lake cabin, we found everything was fine. Unchanged from the way it was left a week ago. It's sure nice here. Scenery is great with a view overlooking the river, mountains in the background. And our nice sandy beach along the river in front of the cabin makes it even more appealing. The sky had started clouding over during the last part of our trip up river and it now looks as though a weather system is moving in.

Saturday – Oct. 8ᵗʰ "0"C   It's raining out this morning. We also had a little snow overnight. Can't see the mountains for the clouds.

I think my husband has gone over the brink!! Think he's taking me for granted. He now wants four wheeled ATV's out here. They would be a real asset when working out of Ridge Lake since much of the area consists of open and thinly wooded areas. I'm anxious to get out and see that country. I missed out on our trail scouting this year with Bob and Robbie here. Rose cabin was built in April 1987 when there was about four feet of snow on the ground. When we came out in October of that year we had to finish off the interior – moving in on October twentieth. We just didn't have any time to fix up the back porch, I should say front porch, since it's the only entryway to the cabin. We also didn't have time to properly clean up around the yard outside, burn slashing, tree branches, etc. so it's a job we plan on doing this fall.

This morning in the rain, Gordon was out in the "forest" with his chainsaw, cutting down a big spruce from which he'll manufacture boards. Once the tree is down and the branches trimmed from it he makes a cut down the center of the log to the length of the required board. From there on, he makes parallel cuts to the thickness of the lumber he wants. It is amazing how he can cut them so straight and only about one inch thick. The boards will be about fourteen inches wide by one inch thick and eight feet long. Its hard work, bent over sawing lumber, but Gordon says it gives him a real sense of satisfaction to see the finished product. He'll use the boards to enclose the porch. Its fourteen feet wide by fifteen feet long so he'll need a good many boards. Last winter he enclosed the porch, very roughly, with plywood we had left over – just to keep the snow from blowing in. To fly lumber in to Rose Lake would be very costly. Aircraft can only come in during the winter months, on skis. The river is too shallow for float operations during the summer. It would be really good if they were able to come in on floats but it's just not possible. If they could, we'd likely alternate flights every other year, one year to Rose Lake and the next to Ridge Lake. That way we'd be able to get each cabin better stocked and not have to backpack so much.

The porch is starting to look so much nicer with the new boards replacing the plywood. All our firewood for the cabin stove is stacked in the porch out of the weather. Gordon also plans on building a closed in cupboard for me in the porch where I can store the extra's – bread, baking or leftover's. The cupboard will protect the stored items from birds, smaller animals and also the dogs if they happened to get loose. It's almost impossible to make things mouse-proof. We have a lot of mice out here. On our last trip, we had a few onions left over which I put into our storage cellar under the floor. When I checked on them yesterday right after we arrived, I found the little so and so's had got in there and decided they liked Spanish onions. They'd eaten about a third of a large one. So, it's back to mouse-trapping time.

A beautiful rainbow over the river this afternoon. Sky is clearing up nicely. Gordon had gone to try his hand at fishing, no bites. The sun is now shining on the mountains. They looked so gorgeous that I had to take a picture. After our tea break we went upriver with the canoe. Tried fishing for a few minutes but no luck so went upstream a little further to where a big dry tree stood on the riverbank. Gordon had brought his chainsaw along, just in case the fish weren't biting. He cut the tree down and into lengths that would fit in the canoe. We then headed for home with our load of firewood.

When we reached home with our load of wood, Gordon decided to pull up to the river bank just below the cabin – a location we hadn't used before. The sand or mud along that section of shore always looked so wet and soft, similar to quicksand, so we'd stayed clear of it. Anyway, as soon as the nose of the canoe slid up on the shore, I jumped out with the tie rope in hand and instantly began to sink – both feet. Of course I yelled at Gordon that I was sinking. At first he actually thought it was quite funny but quickly jumped out, cut a bunch of spruce (small ones) and threw them on the mud so he'd have something to stand on while he tried getting me loose. By the time he got me out I'd sunk quite a ways down in the mud. When we first got here the other day, I'd tried to walk over this section on my way to the river for water. With my first steps, the mud had started sliding so I got out in a hurry. Gordon tried the same spot later with the same results (not really believing me) and decided it was just too dangerous. From then on we got our water further up river towards the creek where the shoreline is sandy. A lot of the river bank is composed of clay and with water added, it's like quicksand. You step on it and at first it feels firm but within a few seconds the top layer disintegrates and you start sinking – fast. The majority of the shoreline along the Coal River is sandy and has many lovely, sandy beaches – some of them over a mile long. Anyway, a while later Gordon moved the canoe further down the shore and unloaded it.

Sunday – Oct. 9th "0"C   Clouded up overnight but is sunny this morning.
Gordon saw a robin out along the riverbank this morning. Either it's going
to be a late fall or that bird's time schedule is a little out of whack. The other
three years that I've been here, we've had ice-flows during some mornings earlier than this. After breakfast Gordon was busy cutting more planks which he
needs to complete the walls of the porch. Starting to look good !! I gathered up
more brush and branches, threw them into piles and burnt them. Later, we canoed across the river and got another "dry tree" for firewood. Only thing was, it
was really "grungy" inside (to use Gordon's description). He said it was like
cardboard and for splitting, was the pits. It didn't split cleanly. He had to pull it
apart. Really poor firewood!!

Monday – Oct. 10th -3C   High overcast this morning. Thanksgiving Day and no
turkey!! Maybe Gordon will catch us a fish.
The dogs carried on barking and whining for quite awhile last night. Gordon
couldn't see anything when he checked but thinks a visiting marten was probably responsible for the commotion. So far, we've had the nicest October –
ever!! Usually we have ice flows by now but there's been none coming down
river so far this year. Gordon just advised me it was a marten sorting through
our garbage pit last night that set the dogs off. He's busy sawing more planks
for the porch but noticed marten sign when he passed by our garbage pit. Sky is
starting to clear up nicely with most of the high overcast moving off to the east.
Don't know why but the stove here at Rose cabin fries bannock to near perfec-
tion. I can't do them near as well on the stove at Ridge Lake. It seems to burn
faster there if I'm not really careful. Here it usually turns a nice golden hue and
is real crisp on the outside. Delicious!!
Gordon manufactured and then nailed up more siding on the porch while I
stacked wood for a couple of hours. Then we took a break for an early lunch.
After lunch, Gordon loaded the canoe with five and a half sheets of plywood

plus twelve, two by eight planks and other assorted gear. We shoved the canoe out into the river and were on our way up to Kettle Creek cabin. It's our most northerly cabin on the trapline. Gordon built the cabin in 1985 and he and I were back there in 1986 for about a week to install the floor and also to build a porch out front from the lumber that he produced with the chainsaw. We didn't go back there last year. The cabin still needs a lot of work on it to make it cosy. At present it only has a slab roof that's covered with a thick layer of moss and over it all, a plastic tarp. The walls also need some work done on them. They'll have to be scraped to get rid of the outer, dark layer and then slats will have to be cut to cover the insulation between the logs. It shouldn't take that terribly long to finish it off, probably a week or so.

It took us a little over two hours of steady going to reach Kettle Creek. Traveling the river was great. Cloud had pretty well cleared off and with sunshine, everything was so vivid. You could see right to the river bottom almost all the way. The water was so clear. Really surprising how fast it clears after a heavy rainstorm. By the time the cabin came into view, even with the sunshine, we were getting pretty chilly. It was a relief to finally pull up on the sandbar in front of the cabin, climb out and walk around. First thing we did was build a fire in the stove and make tea. I'd put some tea bags and sugar in my pocket before we left Rose Lake, hoping we'd take a tea break before starting back downstream. We had our tea and cookies and then spent about an hour checking things over, figuring out what needed to be done with the cabin. The sun was just disappearing behind the mountains in the west when we climbed in the canoe, turned it downstream and started on our way back to Rose Lake.

A little over an hour later, Rose Lake cabin came into view. Pretty fast going but conditions were perfect. River was crystal clear so we could see the bottom and easily judge water depth. We were going with the current and with the motor at about three-quarter throttle, really moved along. Temperature had sure cooled down by the time we got home. The sun had set just after we'd left Kettle so it was quite dusky traveling the last couple of miles. The dogs certainly hadn't thought much of being left behind and were glad to see us back. We'd heard their howling almost all the way to Kettle. Not sure how far it is, the river is so twisty. If my count is right, we traveled past eighteen sandbars that were anywhere from a mile to two miles long. If a person could walk straight across country from here it would be so much shorter.

We had supper and afterwards, at around nine in the evening, Gordon went outside behind the cabin and began cutting down some of the small spruce and willows growing there. The trees aren't all that large. Most of them are only about twelve or so feet tall but are so thick that they form an almost solid wall, blocking most of the light from the south. He's built a fire with them and now has a huge bonfire going. Looks like Fourth of July fireworks when he throws more spruce boughs on and the sparks fly.

While we were on the river returning from Kettle, we saw a muskrat feeding along the shore. He wasn't the least bit concerned when we went past him with the canoe. There were many beaver cuttings along the river banks showing where they've been feeding so must be a lot of beaver in the area. We saw two sections where water was running down from the top of the river bank. Gordon thinks the beaver must have a dam up above someplace and we were seeing the overflow. When we pulled up in front of the cabin at Kettle Creek, we found the shoreline had really been eroded from the high water that had undercut it this past spring. One large spruce, which had been growing in front of the cabin, had fallen into the river and took a good part of the shoreline with it. The edge of the riverbank used to be about thirty feet from the front of the cabin but now the distance has been reduced to about fifteen feet.

Tuesday – Oct. 11th -6C   Sunny but a layer of cloud is moving in.

It's unreal how fast the weather can change. Early this morning it was beautiful out and so sunny but then a layer of cloud moved in and by nine-thirty it had started raining, heavily. We hope it's only a shower. Sure enough, a short while later, the rain stopped and the sky started to clear. Gordon finished nailing planking on the last two sides of the porch while I neatly stacked away all the wood he'd cut earlier. We now have a good supply of wood at both camps, actually at all the cabins. Think Don Wilkinson must have had hunters at Kettle. Saw fresh signs of a campfire on the sandbar when we were there yesterday.

Wednesday – Oct. 12th +4C   It rained for awhile during the night. This morning there's fog in the valley but otherwise it's clear so should be another gorgeous day. The ground is still not frozen.

After breakfast we closed up camp, loaded our packs and the dogs in the canoe, jumped in and headed down river to the mouth of Twin Lakes Creek – on our way back to Ridge Lake. It was a beautiful day for our move. I'd really enjoyed the all to short time it took us to reach the mouth of Twin Lakes creek. After reaching the creek, we pulled into shore, unloaded the canoe and then removed the motor. We carried the canoe to higher ground, well above spring run-off levels, and stashed it under a large spruce. The outboard motor and paddles were then placed beneath the canoe. Next, we tied dog packs on Smokey and Rebel. They each had eighteen traps to carry from the river to Ridge Lake – pretty good loads!! We then strapped on our loaded packboards. Gordon had his snowshoes on his packboard plus a gallon of oil, two large beaver traps, dog harness, skidoo cover plus his rifle. In my pack was the axe as well as a variety of small items, plus Gordon's muckluks, my heavy woolen pants and a piece of indoor/outdoor carpet (about forty-five by thirty inches) to be used as a rug when we bathed – MY LUXURY ITEM!! I also carried, by hand, a gallon of white paint which I intend to use on our cupboards as well as on the door and window frames. If anyone had seen me in the middle of the forest with a gallon of white paint in one hand and a rug on my back, they'd think I had flipped – totally. Finally "snapped my twig"!! It would have been so much easier for Gordon to fly the paint in, when he returned from Whitehorse with the helicopter around the end of October, but I wanted to do the painting while he's away. We then took off and headed up the trail.

It was a beautiful day for our trip back to Ridge Lake. It was so warm with the sun beating down. About halfway, we stopped for a short break, a chocolate bar and rest in the shade of a big spruce. Our loads were pretty heavy. It felt good to take our packboards off, even though it was only for a short time. The dogs also appreciated the break. They were a real asset, carrying the traps. We were about two hours on the trail before reaching our cabin at Ridge Lake. Everything looked fine, nothing had disturbed the cabin.

While unloading my pack, I discovered that when I'd leaned my head against the spruce where we'd taken our break I'd picked up a big wad of spruce gum and now it was stuck in my hair. Does wonders for your hair!! Gordon said he'd try to remove it for me with hand cleaner. A bit later after lunch, he tried the radio and got through to another trapper, Glen Stockman, based at Pine Lake. When we checked our meat at the cache, we found the plastic tarp over it was off of one end. Must have been the wind. When we discovered a piece of meat laying on the ground we began to wonder but, after checking the rope the boys had hung it with, we found why it broke. It had been rubbing against a piece of tin on the cache leg. The meat was OK and was rehung. Gordon tied a heavier plastic tarp over the whole meat cache to shelter it from rain and snow.

Thursday – Oct. 13th -3C   Was clear when we went to bed at eight-thirty last night but later must have clouded over as it sure rained and got windy. This morning everything is just so wet. Cloudy sky.

Gordon did up odd jobs during the morning while I made homemade soup, a cherry pie, a batch of bannock mixture and even scraped a bit more of the wall. After lunch we were still getting showers so Gordon worked on the ridge beam (middle beam supporting the cabin roof) scraping off the darkened layer of skin. About three-thirty it started clearing so we headed up to the ridge above the west shore of the lake to see if we could find a better trail to the head of Twin Lakes Creek. We did eventually locate a better route. It's going to be so much better traveling along it, both by foot or by skidoo when we finish clearing a few sections. The trail Robbie and Bob had cut parallels the west shore of Ridge Lake but is over very rough and wet ground. During winter with the wind, the trail would continually drift over with snow. Also, along the route we picked, there are far better places to set traps. Gordon is really pleased with our scouting. The men had agreed their trail was a rough way but think they may have decided it was the best way because there'd be little brush cutting required along the shoreline.

After we returned and had supper, Gordon worked for a while on the logs. Starting to look good but still lots to do.

Friday – Oct. 14th -3C   Snow showers this morning and a skim of ice around the lakeshore so it must have been quite a lot colder during the night. Temperature was down to minus six when we went to bed.

About ten o'clock, Gordon and I hiked back to the ridge where we'd blazed trail yesterday and cleared trail for the next two hours. Then it was home for lunch and back again to clear trail for another couple of hours. In all, we slashed trail for about five hours today. Coming home along the cleared section only took twenty minutes. We now have just a short section left to clear on the first ridge. We'll probably finish it tomorrow morning. When it's completed we'll have a really good trail, wide and relatively smooth. After we're through with this section tomorrow morning, there's another ridge we want to explore. Very likely we'll clear a trail along it as well.

Gordon talked with Darrel Nelson tonight. He's another trapper, located not far from Toobally Lakes. We haven't been able to raise Don Taylor or Watson Lake Flying on the radio since our return from Rose Lake.

Saturday – October 15th -4C   Sunny out. Will be nice for trail cutting along that ridge west of the lake.

Gordon talked with Watson Lake Flying this morning. Stan reported a Cold Front was moving in so guess our weather will be changing. Be nice to have the ground freeze as well as all the potholes but we'll sure miss the nice weather we've been having. The dogs did a lot of howling during the night. The most likely reason for their carrying on was the sound from wolves howling in the distance.

After breakfast we were back up to our ridge. Finished cutting that trail and are very pleased with it. It took us twenty-five minutes to walk the first ridge. It's so easy compared to the trail the men cut around the lake. After we'd finished clearing, we hiked over to the second ridge and started blazing a trail along it. We hadn't gone very far before intersecting a game trail that headed exactly where we wanted to go. We followed it, Gordon blazing the occasional tree along the way. It took us just about two hours to blaze that trail. Very good, considering we didn't know exactly where we or the trail was going. Turned out it ended up right where we hoped it was heading to, a meadow where our trail joined the one that the boys had cleared around the lake. Took us twenty-five minutes to walk back to the first ridge. We're coming back tomorrow, weather and time permitting, to clear the trail we blazed today along the second ridge. It'll be much easier to clear since there's no where near as much buckbrush along it as was along the first ridge. Gordon is really pleased with it. We were going to have lunch in the meadow but Gordon couldn't get any water for tea. The ice along the edge of the pond in the meadow wasn't safe to walk out on and Ridge Lake was too far away. No tea – no lunch so we decided to head home. Got back at three-thirty, a bit tired and hungry.

At five o'clock, we decided to go to the Beaver Pond to see if we could get a beaver. We blazed a trail – just the occasional tree, since we were heading through new country to the far end of the pond. When we reached the pond, we found it almost all frozen over except for a narrow open channel starting in front of the beaver house and extending right up to the dam. We waited patiently for about an hour. It was so still with not a breath of wind. The only sound came from the tinkling of shell ice cracking along the creek edges and the occasional muted splash as a muskrat, feeding along the edge of the ice, dove in for a last tasty morsel before winter closed his lunchroom down. We had the feeling that everything was just waiting for winter.

Just as we decided it was about time to leave, ripples and the telltale "V" of a swimming beaver were noticed down near the dam. We didn't move when the beaver turned and started swimming towards us. Gordon waited until he was across from us in the stream. He slowly raised his rifle. Seconds later there was the sound of a shot and we had our beaver. That section of the stream bed and all along the shore where we'd been waiting was comprised of large boulders. They made it very difficult for Gordon to retrieve the beaver. He cut a long pole and tried getting as close to the beaver as possible by jumping from boulder to boulder. A tricky and dangerous business, especially stepping on boulders just below the surface of the water. If you slipped you could be lucky and end up in six feet of water. If you weren't lucky you'd likely end up in the creek with a broken leg. After several unsuccessful attempts with the pole, we finally decided it would be best to wait until the beaver floated down to the dam.

Gordon eventually retrieved the beaver near the dam. It was only then that we realized what a large animal it was. We estimated the beaver, a male, had to weigh between sixty and seventy pounds. All the time Gordon was trying to retrieve the beaver, about an hour, and although the water was at times near the top of his rubber boots, he'd managed to keep his feet dry. Just after we got the beaver on shore – you guessed it – Gordon stepped in a deep hole hidden by leaves and filled his boots with ice cold water. By this time, it was getting pretty dark. We hadn't brought a packboard so we each grasped a hind leg of the beaver and tried dragging it along. The going was tough since buckbrush made it almost impossible for us to walk side by side. Gordon finally tied a rope to its feet and dragged it by himself. It was fortunate that we'd blazed a trail earlier since it was now quite dark. If we hadn't the blazes to guide us, they looked whitish on the trees, we'd have been stumbling along as we tried to find a way back. It was a real relief when we eventually reached our cleared trail and a few minutes later reached home.

After supper, Gordon was busy out in the porch skinning the beaver while I did up the dishes and then worked on logs. By the time he finished, I was stretched out on the bed reading, trying to keep from falling asleep. When he checked outside just before going to bed, he found the ground all white, covered by the snow pellets we'd heard falling shortly after we'd returned to the cabin.

Sunday – Oct. 16th -2C   Not a nice day. We had a bit of snow overnight and it's now cloudy and real windy. If we didn't have the wind it wouldn't be too bad.

After breakfast, Gordon fleshed and washed the beaver skin, then hung it out to dry. He wants it to dry a bit, especially the fur side, before nailing it on a stretcher. I baked cinnamon buns. Much to my disappointment, again they did not rise. Flavor was good but they're tough. I thought perhaps I'd done something wrong the other day with the last batch but have now decided my yeast is at fault. I have more yeast here so I'll try again before Gordon flies out on the twenty-second. He may have to buy me a new can of yeast when he gets to Whitehorse.

Gordon built a fire down by the lake to heat the tub of water for trap boiling. The tub is made from half of a forty-five gallon drum. New traps have a thin layer of grease on them to prevent them from rusting. This has to be boiled off the traps. After Gordon completed his trap boiling he started another project. He cut down a number of small, straight spruce, removed the branches and then cut them lengthwise with his chainsaw. This evening we'll start tacking the split sections in place so they cover the insulation that's between the logs. While he was busy outside, I scraped more skin off the logs, about a three foot section, and then put two coats of white paint around the frames of our windows. Looks good!!

We've had snow showers off and on all day. It's cold out!! Not at all pleasant. When we left home to come out here this fall, Gordon had decided that we wouldn't need our beaver pattern for stretching pelts since he wasn't going for beaver. Beaver pelts aren't worth a great deal and are so much work. Anyway, he called Glen and Rhea Stockman at Jackpine Lake for measurements. They didn't have any but another trapper, Lawrence Leigh, called back. He's around the Dendale Lake area, away over in the eastern part of the Yukon. Anyway, he was good enough to give us the measurements. A beaver has to be stretched a certain way, sort of an egg shape, so we drew the pattern on plywood. The pelt was then stretched, held in place by nails tacked about an inch and a half apart all around.

Monday – Oct. 17th -7C   A skiff of snow overnight but cleared up and is sunny this morning.

We left at ten-thirty and headed out to finish cutting trail along the second ridge – a short section we hadn't completed on Saturday. Everything went really well and we were surprised at just how quickly we finished it. After we reached the end of the ridge, we decided to make tea and have our lunch. We checked the area, trying to find a stream for water. We couldn't find any water nearby that appealed to us so it was decided that I'd build a fire while Gordon went further down the meadow looking for a stream. Sure enough, only a few yards further on, he found good water. A short time later it was really nice. We were stretched out under a big spruce completely relaxed. The fire going, the sun shining – just a little breezy. We toasted our sandwiches and were just starting to munch on them when Gordon poured a cup of tea for me and then one for himself. My tea tasted fine but the reaction from Gordon, after his first swallow, was decidedly negative. He sloshed his tea out, exclaiming "YUK" and a few other words, while spitting a mouthful of tea on the ground. SALT, he yells. I'd taken a small plastic bag, filled with what I thought was sugar, along with our tea things. The bag had been in the tea pail along with tea bags that had been left over from the men's trail cutting trip. I never dreamed it wasn't sugar but was salt. Poor Gordon!! He loves sugar in his tea, especially when we're out like this. Don't think he was too pleased with me. I felt so badly but it was funny. He had to drink his tea without sugar. Poor Baby!!

After we got home, about four-fifteen, we started to scrape more of the cabin logs. Gordon is really pleased with the appearance of the wall after he'd tacked the slats on last night. He's determined to finish off another wall. He did complete about half of the back wall before calling it a day and crawling into bed.

Tuesday – Oct. 18th -8C   Fog in the valley but should burn off. There's a skim of ice over three quarters of the lake this morning so it must have got cold during the night. Temperature was down to minus ten when we went to bed.

After breakfast we packed enough pre-cut boards on our packboards to make eight trap cubbies. All told, thirty-two pieces. You need two pieces, six and a half inches by fifteen inches long, for the sides plus another two pieces, eight inches by fifteen inches, for the top and bottom of each cubby. With packs loaded, we left for the lake where we'd got our moose. On the way we dropped boards for cubbies at five different places while the rest were left at the lake. We saw many signs from marten, tracks all over. There were also fresh tracks in the snow made by moose and caribou that showed they're still moving about in the lower country. When we first reached the lake I waited while Gordon walked across to check the moose remains. SURPRISE!! He ran across fresh grizzly tracks going and coming from it. Since the surrounding area was quite heavily covered with buckbrush, he couldn't see whether the bear was still there or not. He couldn't even see the moose remains. He'd have had to get within a few feet of it before he could see it clearly. He returned to where I waited, deciding it would be stupid to take a chance on going closer and perhaps being mauled or worse by the bear. We sat and watched the area for quite awhile but didn't see anything so returned home. We saw several grouse on our way back but didn't have the twenty-two with us. Gordon tried snaring one with a boot lace tied to a long skinny pole. No luck!!

Gordon is really pleased with the marten sign. He figures just about every marten in the Yukon must be around the moose remains since there were so many tracks there. We've also noticed quite a number of tracks around our cabin. Gordon can't wait for November first, the start of trapping season. He's pretty disgusted that he has to fly out on Saturday to Whitehorse for that meeting. We'd hoped to have all the trap boxes and traps distributed along the trails before the end of October. It would have made it a lot easier for us when we started setting traps on November first.

Gordon tried calling Mabel Robson in Watson Lake. She's an elderly lady and former trapper. Signals were poor so he wasn't able to get through to her. He did get through to Rhea, her daughter, who relayed our message onwards wishing Mabel a Happy Birthday. Also got word that Bob Watson will be coming out with the chopper on Saturday, as planned. Rhea mentioned that her dog Snowball got mixed up with a porcupine and, since she wasn't able to get all the quills out of his face, it's swelling. She has an aircraft coming in tomorrow to take the dog out to the vet. Will sure be an unexpected expense for Glen and Rhea. They're about twenty minutes flying time further out in the bush than we are. Flying is so expensive. They also mentioned that they hadn't got their meat yet. That's also very unfortunate since trappers use a lot of meat during the months they're out on the trapline. Apparently they saw a moose a couple of weeks ago (ten days) but let it go since temperatures were still quite warm and they were afraid the meat wouldn't keep. You can smoke it and it will keep but that means a lot of extra work. Usually another moose would have shown up. Too bad!! We feel pretty fortunate! Our meat is certainly keeping well. It has a thick crust on the outside.

Made spaghetti sauce. It turned out really good, enough for three meals. Oh yes, when we were at our moose lake earlier today, we saw that solitary, lonely Swan again. Very likely the same one that was there earlier. The lake had all frozen over except for a narrow, short channel at one end of the lake. The swan kept calling and calling. It must have lost its mate, possibly to a marten or fox and just doesn't want to leave. I feel so sorry for it.

Wednesday – Oct. 19ᵗʰ -10C   Not a nice day. It's cloudy with a light snow falling, combined with a nasty little wind. Not a day to go walking, especially in the open valleys, although it wouldn't be so bad in the bush.

We decided to work on the inside of the cabin and finished scraping quite a few more logs. Gordon then cut and nailed more slats in place. Another couple of sessions like today and we'll have it finished. The logs are dry and hard peeling. It also takes quite a bit of time fitting and nailing the slats between them but is sure worth the effort. We also tapped styrofoam insulation in and around the window casings so they'd not frost up. We also put a temporary layer over the window, just for tonight. We'll be removing the styrofoam and tacking a plastic covering over the windows tomorrow. The plastic, stretched tight across a window, acts as a storm window and keeps them from frosting up.

Thursday – Oct. 20ᵗʰ -10C   A little light snow early this morning but not really enough to add to the one inch we've already got on the ground.

It's darker in here with styrofoam over the windows. Makes the windows look as though they're coated with frost but it did keep frost from forming on them overnight. Will replace it with plastic later on today. Then the cabin will brighten up again. Gordon's even shaving by candlelight this morning. I was first up this morning and made the fire. First time this trip. It's Gordon's sixty-third birthday and that's his special treat – being able to stay in bed while I warmed up the cabin and put the coffee on.

By the time we'd finished breakfast there was still no change in the weather. It was not a nice day for going out on the trail. Instead, Gordon and I got busy and built houses for the dogs. Rebel is using his house but Smokey isn't. Oh well, give him time. I worked on more logs inside the cabin and also, between doing dishes, etc., made two pans of Nanaimo Bars to substitute for Gordon's cake. He loves them!! Made him oyster stew for lunch – one of his favorites. For supper, we had baked ham, au gratin potatoes and a big salad. Also opened up a bottle of his favorite wine. We had a little birthday celebration, just the two of us. After dinner, I gave him a big box of chocolates. There was also a parcel and birthday cards from Jamie and Patti as well as a bottle of Bols Apricot Brandy and a book. He was surprised again and so pleased. I also had fifty dollars worth of Western Scratch tickets for him. That will really flip him – he likes those silly scratch ones.

Gordon talked with Rhea this evening. Their dog, the one that tried chewing up that porcupine, is much better now since the vet removed the quills. They have between four and six inches of snow on the ground over there. They were able to use their skidoo today. We only have about an inch and a half. Also managed to tack plastic over the windows this evening. Looks good. Hope it works and the windows don't frost up. Later, Gordon tried his tickets and got twenty-four dollars worth of winnings on his fifty tickets. Won't get rich at that rate.

Friday – Oct. 21ˢᵗ -14C   It's really nasty this morning. Snowing and very windy. A real blizzard with visibility only about half a mile. It's so cold out with that wind.

By the time we finished breakfast, conditions seemed to be getting even worse. Gordon sure won't be able to fly out tomorrow if the weather doesn't smarten up. It will really be too bad if he can't get to the hearings in Whitehorse, especially since there are only three persons on the Board. There's another fellow on the Board, an accountant representing the Government, who has no knowledge of trapping and is very much against agriculture in the Yukon. One of the Board members is a Yukon native trapper. He will be very displeased if he feels native lines are in jeopardy. Can't blame him!! I feel Gordon is the only one on the Board who is a trapper, farmer, former big-game outfitters and also, being a former Justice of the Peace, would have knowledge in all the areas the

Board is expected to cover. Probably that's why he was chosen. But then, I may be a bit prejudiced!!

It's four-thirty and still miserable. We now have about four inches of snow on the ground. Rhea reported they have a foot of snow at Jackpine Lake. This weather is very general, apparently really nasty in Watson Lake. I baked cinnamon buns again today. They rose OK but I burnt them instead. This oven is so small and the element is right under the pan. Gordon is going to rig a piece of tin underneath to deflect some of the heat. We also stretched the beaver – finally. I even helped a little. Gordon is outside getting more firewood. Temperature has remained steady at minus fourteen since this morning. Just finished reading "Not a Penny More – Not a Penny Less" by Jeffrey Archer. Enjoyed it but not as much as "Kane and Abel", also by Archer, which I'd started reading when we were at Rose Lake.

Saturday – Oct. 22nd -28C   Cleared up nicely overnight but the temperature certainly dropped. Hard to believe the change in the weather. Sure hope the helicopter comes in. Gordon wants me to go out with him but I'm so nervous of flying that I'll just stay here and pout!!

At ten Gordon called out, "I hear the chopper" and a few minutes later it landed in the little meadow behind the cabin. I'm very disappointed, hard to say why. I want Gordon to go out for the meetings but at the same time was hoping it would fog in or snow so he couldn't get away. I had coffee on but the pilot, Claude, said there was a cloud bank moving in and was in a hurry to return. So, after bringing in our new and bigger cookstove and having a very quick cup of coffee, he and Gordon took off for Watson Lake. It's only been a few minutes since they left but I'm already so lonesome. It's going to be a long nine days until he returns.

Bob Watson came in to stay at camp and help look after the place. After we had lunch Bob cut a section of our meat up into smaller portions. It was frozen solid but he managed OK with the swede saw. He's now out after wood. I know he'll do a lot of chores around here. He's always so helpful. I was teasing him when he arrived and asked him if he was afraid I wouldn't feed him. He brought in six loaves of bread. It cost him nearly fifteen dollars. Prices are unreal. One loaf was three dollars and fifty-nine cents while a .small loaf of rye bread was three dollars and ninety-nine cents. He also brought two dozen eggs, a pound of bacon, two pounds of margarine, two rolls of paper towels, four rolls of toilet paper, a large jar of coffee whitener, jam, shortening, bottle of syrup and ten pounds of potatoes. He wasn't supposed to bring any groceries in but that's Bob, always considerate.

When we took a break for a cup of tea this afternoon, Bob was telling me all about his relatives and their doings. Quite a family. Gordon has known them since he first came to the Yukon in nineteen forty-three. Hard to believe so many years have gone by. Temperature warmed up this afternoon and was just minus twelve at three o'clock. During the past two days Gordon and I had been hunting everywhere for our axe file. Just couldn't find it. Gordon decided it must have been chucked outside with all the shavings, etc. from the log peeling and he'd have to bring a new one in on his return trip. This afternoon while I was stoking the fire and shoving the ashes around, I found the file – in the stove!! I know I must have put it in the stove when I was burning some of the shavings. It's probably ruined by now with the hot fires.

By four-thirty the weather had changed and we were getting snow again so it's fortunate the chopper came in early. Bob and I each cleaned a bit of log and then it was time for bed.

Sunday – October 23rd -13C   Cloudy out with light snow.

By ten o'clock the weather had cleared up nicely and the sun was shining. I had Bob take Smokey and go to the river to bring back the toboggan and traps we'd stashed there. Rebel sure isn't happy being left behind. I'm busy making a pot of soup and doing a big batch of laundry. I also taped plastic window coverings over the two outside porch windows.

Bob got back from the river just after one. It was a good three hour trip. Footing was slippery with the snow and his boots, with worn soles, didn't provide much traction. We had lunch and afterwards put up the new radio antenna. Actually, it's our old one that hadn't worked so well before and had been sent out to be repaired. It was returned to us via the helicopter. I was a little concerned about putting it up. I'd never done it before and was afraid of breaking a wire. Anyway, it's up and it works really well. I had a good chat with Don Taylor over at Stewart Lake. He'd just returned to his lake today after a trip to Watson Lake. Bob came in a short while later and reported seeing wolverine tracks near our meat cache and also down by the creek. We'll surely have to watch that it doesn't get at our meat. Warmed up to just minus five by bedtime.

Monday – Oct. 24th -7C   Sure lonely without Gordon. It's quite nice out this morning but overcast.   After breakfast and with the dishes done, I tried my hand at carpentry. I built ten cubbies, houses for traps, this morning. Quite pleased with my efforts. The cubbies are actually just a four sided box with sides about twelve to fourteen inches long. One end of the box is covered with wire mesh. Bait, fish scraps usually, is put inside the box – all the way to the mesh covered back of the box. A trap is placed at the open end and is sprung by any animal entering the box to get at the bait. The boxes are usually placed up in spruce trees for marten. On the ground, near streams, they're also very effective for mink and weasel. We only use quick kill Conibear traps. These traps have been tested in most countries in the world and are classed as humane traps. Most animals don't even move after they're caught.

We noticed fresh marten tracks around the cabin this morning. They'd also gone over to inspect the spruce where we have a small section of meat hanging. By eleven we were fogged in, just solid. Shortly after, Bob reported seeing two marten at our meat cache, a large brown one and a jet black one. Also, in the snow, we spotted more wolverine tracks. Guess he's keeping a close watch on our meat, probably hoping we'll forget to take the ladder down one day.

In the afternoon after lunch, Bob and I went up the new Run that Gordon and I had cut along the ridge to the west of the lake. We put out ten trap boxes, also left a trap hanging by each box. Saw a few marten tracks and lots of rabbit tracks.

Tuesday – Oct. 25th -7C   Full moon last night. It was so clear and bright for the first while. Later it clouded over and this morning is not the nicest – windy with snow flurries.

After breakfast, Bob was busy hauling in more wood while I brushed a second coat of paint on the cupboards and door frame. Starting to look pretty nice. After lunch Bob took his axe and went to scout and blaze a short trail through the stand of timber behind the cabin that extends all the way upwards to treeline. It could be used as a short spur line for trapping or possibly, depending on the steepness, a route for the skidoo to follow up to the lower slopes of the mountain. Talked to Rhea. She reported it was nasty out there with a lot more snow than we have and also a strong wind. She mentioned that Watson Lake reported miserable weather too. We're the lucky ones I guess with just a light wind and light snow falling.

Bob got back by late afternoon to report he'd not had much success. From down here, the mountain looks as though it rises in gentle slopes all the way up to and above treeline. His scouting today showed it to be quite different. The base of the mountain actually rises in a series of slopes that are quite steep. They're covered with an open canopy of tall spruce but there's a thick growth of smaller trees growing amongst them. Looks like a bit of a job, more than we'd anticipated, finding and then clearing a trail up to the open country above. Anyway, after Bob realized he'd need assistance in locating a trail up the mountain, he turned back and blazed a short trapline run where we can set a few marten traps.

Just after we'd finished supper, I heard a dog let out a little "Woof". Bob took the flashlight and went out to check. He was back in a minute reporting, "I see something". I ran out with him and found a medium-sized brown marten at the meat we'd hung in a tree near the cabin. There were a couple of pieces that we'd brought down from the cache so they'd be handier. I tried taking a picture while Bob shone the light on the marten but couldn't get close enough. When Bob went to get the meat and bring it into the porch he lifted the plastic sheet covering it and was face to face with the snarling, hissing animal. It wasn't very happy losing its dinner.

Wednesday – Oct. 26th -11C   Cloudy last night but not too heavy since we could faintly see the moon through the clouds. Was a full moon but with the cloud we didn't get the beautiful nightime display we'd expected.

By ten o'clock this morning the sky had cleared up nicely and the sun was shining. I tacked three trap cubbies together. Bob then took and set them out between here and Beaver Pond. On his return he reported seeing two sets of wolf tracks in the snow on the pond. There were also tracks of a wolverine along the trail as well as a number of marten tracks. Looks good!! I finished the rest of the painting this morning – a last coat of paint on the grocery cupboards. Also placed a layer of styrofoam behind the cupboards to see if it would prevent condensation forming on the cans. Everything looks so nice and clean. Last night I even painted the table. I'm going to run out of work pretty soon!!

After lunch Bob set another four marten trap boxes out in the timber just beyond the meadow where the helicopter landed. He also put a mink set in place down by the creek – all ready for Gordon when he gets back. Bob said he noticed many tracks today, never had seen so much sign. Just hope it's not the same marten making tracks all over. I scraped more logs. Only have one more bottom log and one and a half ridge poles left to do. Later on when Rhea called, she reported they have over two feet of snow. Evidently many stations are re-porting lots of heavy, wet snow. They're busy breaking trail while here at Ridge Lake we only have between six and seven inches of it. She reported that Glen had cut a finger badly, on the skidoo. Cut it from the tip all the way to the knuckle, right to the bone. Ouch!! Hope it heals up without getting infected. They're a long ways from help. A bit further than we'd have to go. Later in the evening, we received a radio call through the Trappers Association in Whitehorse. Gordon sent a message that everything was going along well up there. Good to hear from him.

Thursday – Oct. 27ᵗʰ -14C   Very foggy. Can't even see as far as the lake this morning.

I expected it would get really cold during the night. All afternoon the temperature remained around minus five but by six o'clock it had started to drop and by seven was down to minus twenty. When I checked at nine, temperature had risen to minus sixteen and by bedtime was up to minus ten. Too bad, we were hoping for colder temperatures to freeze up the sloughs and lake.

What a gorgeous afternoon. The fog has finally lifted from the entire area. Not a cloud – clear blue skies. You can see the snow-covered mountains to the north, just beautiful. This morning I made up a double mixture of bannock to have on hand and also mixed a large batch of pie dough while Bob was getting in wood. The temperature has remained at minus fourteen all day. Would have been such a nice day to be out on the trail if Gordon had been here. Bob went down the trail towards the river to put up a few more trap boxes. Think he'd rather go by himself than have me tag along. While he was gone I baked a raisin pie for supper tonight and made up three pie shells to have handy. Once we start setting out traps I won't have much time to do anything special. More likely won't have the energy after being out all day. The dogs have really been carrying on – watching the lake, but I couldn't see anything.

Bob was back early. He was only able to put up two trap boxes since he'd forgotten the nails needed for tacking the boxes to the trees. What a waste of the afternoon. Think he felt a little sheepish since he kept busy for the next while, hauling in firewood.

Friday – Oct. 28th -10C   Very dull out. Can't decide whether it's fog or low cloud.

After breakfast Bob went back out to the River Run to finish up what he'd started yesterday. He wanted to get away real early but with one thing and another, didn't leave until about ten. He is a bit slow getting organized and leaving but it's usually a good habit. It's usually when you're rushing that you forget things. While Bob was away the dogs started barking. I took Gordon's binoculars but couldn't see anything. When Bob returned, he mentioned seeing a cow and a calf caribou on the trail just across from the creek. That's probably why the dogs had been acting up!!

After lunch Bob took more traps and headed for the lake where we got our moose, setting out traps and trap boxes along the way. He also wants to check if a bear has been at the moose remains. After he left, I got busy and made two pumpkin pies as well as a bunch of plain buns. All turned out well. The fog finally started lifting, revealing a clear sky above. Nice!! Don Taylor called on the radio to report he'd phoned Whitehorse to the Trappers Association to find out why I hadn't been hearing from Gordon. Turned out it was because Northwestel had not connected up the radio in the Trappers office. What an outfit!! He advised that Gordon plans on returning to Watson Lake tonight and hopes, if the weather's good, to fly out here tomorrow.

Bob returned late in the afternoon from his jaunt to the lake. He reported he'd put out another four cubbies along the way. Reported seeing lots of marten tracks. He had baited the trap boxes when he put them out on his way to the lake and found, on his return, that the bait had already been taken from a couple of them. So he rebaited them. He checked the site where we'd got our moose but found only the hide was left. It had been pulled out on the lake ice. The moose head still remained but was pretty well cleaned up. Everything else was gone. There were lots of marten and wolf tracks at the site. He spotted a black marten scampering away as he approached. Bob just can't get over the number of tracks around. He'd sure like to stay and do more exploring.

Saturday – Oct. 29ᵗʰ -12C   High overcast and foggy, light wind.

Talked to Don Taylor at eight forty-five and gave him a weather check. Not good out here at the moment but fog is breaking up. Light snow reported at Watson and Stewart Lakes. Sure hope Gordon gets in. At nine-fifteen talked to Frontier Helicopters at Watson Lake. They reported two miles in snow so are holding off on the flight. Also talked to Gordon for a few minutes. Snow flurries out here during the following hour but the sun is trying to get through. Just have to wait and see.

Bob and I took down the antennae that Watson Lake Flying had loaned us. It's all ready for the chopper pilot, Claude, to return it to them. It's good to have our own antennae, especially now that it has an extra long lead-in that reaches inside the cabin and all the way to the shelf where the radio's located. The Watson Lake antennae was shorter and only reached to the porch. When we wanted to use the radio with their antennae we had to take it out to the porch to connect it. Now I keep the radio on nearly all day. It's real handy.

One-thirty and just heard Claude and Don talking. Watson Lake has bad weather and it's also "iffy" out here so no flight today. Don will call me in the morning. I'm just so disappointed but I just knew this was going to happen. Bob walked up to the first ridge behind camp to see what was bothering the dogs. He though wolves might have made a kill up there but instead found lots of caribou tracks. He also spotted three of the caribou and could have easily shot one. Looked like the caribou had been following our trail.

Sunday – Oct. 30ᵗʰ -10C   Overcast, light snow early morning.

Snow stopped about seven (eight our time). There was a time change last night but we don't change time out here since it seems that you actually lose daylight with the change. Shortly after seven Yellowknife called to request a radio check so I answered them. Think it was the same fellow we talked to four years ago when we were having so much trouble getting hold of Watson Lake Flying. Just afterwards, heard Claude and Don Taylor talking so called and gave them a weather report for here. Claude advised weather is improving in Watson Lake but there's still light snow at Stewart Lake but that conditions seemed to be improving. Sure hope they do. Light snow out here again. At ten-fifteen heard from Claude, requesting a weather check and advising that he planned on taking off in about half an hour. Stewart Lake weather is good but we are in and out of light fog. Blue skies one minute but next minute they're gone. I think it will burn off – I hope!!

Gordon arrived back here at about ten forty-five. Sure was good to have him come home. Ron Franks came along for the ride. Was good to see him also. Gordon had stayed with the Franks while he was in Watson Lake. He reported the meeting in Whitehorse had gone quite well and was a good starter. Gordon brought back an assortment of fresh fruit, a chicken and also ice cream. Be a real treat. Sheila sent out a pumpkin for Halloween and a fresh pineapple. So very thoughtful of her. There's also a pile of mail that Gordon brought in. Ron and the pilot, Claude, stayed just long enough to have coffee. We then thanked Bob for all he'd done for us, loaded his gear in the chopper and minutes later, with Bob and Ron aboard, Claude took off for Watson Lake.

After lunch Gordon and I went for a stroll up our trail to the lake where we got our moose. When Gordon was flying out to Watson Lake, he and the pilot had spotted an old cabin with it's roof caved in, down by that lake.. We went to explore the area, hoping to find it. It would be interesting to know who built it and when it was built. We weren't able to locate it. We'll go next fall and check around further before the snow comes. It appeared from our checking today that there could be a trail along there. The trail we've cleared is on the other side of the lake.

Monday – Oct. 31ˢᵗ -18C   Clear and a little nippy.

After breakfast we made up another ten trap boxes and went back up the trail to our Moose-kill Lake – hereafter renamed "Swan Lake" in memory of the lonely swan that kept calling for it's lost mate. We set out trap boxes along the trail, beyond the ones Bob had put up. It was such a gorgeous day. Gordon had tied the boxes on our small toboggan and decided to pull it by hand rather than hitching up the dogs. He thought we'd have trouble crossing the swampy, rough meadows and thick patches of willow with the dogs, so left them behind. As it turned out, we could have used the dogs. The swamp, we'd thought would be just about impassible, was fairly well frozen. By hopping from hummock to hummock, we managed to cross with no difficulty.. The meadow was a bit more touchy. It was not near as frozen under its cover of grasses but by stepping gingerly from one frozen section to another, wearing snowshoes, we managed to get to the other side with dry feet.

Gordon had decided it wouldn't take us very long today and so we wouldn't need to bother bringing lunch. It turned out being a lot longer day than expected. We returned at four-thirty, hungry and thirsty. Never Again he says, but really – I've heard that several times in the past three years!! We've now decided to take our skidoo tomorrow. There's just about enough snow so if we take it easy we'll be Okay. Tomorrow, we'll go back up today's trail and open up twenty-two sets. There were so many marten tracks. Gordon said he has never seen as many in all his years of trapping. We're certain we'll even pick up a few on our return trip tomorrow. Also saw wolf tracks on Swan Lake and around the remains of our moose so we also planning on setting out wolf snares tomorrow.

Tuesday – Nov. 1ˢᵗ - 6C Broken conditions this morning. We had a little fresh snow overnight.

Trapping starts today so, right after breakfast, we're going out on our Swan Lake Run with the skidoo. By eight we were on the trail and shortly after were setting the first trap for this season. We finished setting up the Swan Run during the morning and returned home just before lunchtime. After lunch we headed up the trails we'd cut along the ridges west of Ridge Lake. We're now calling that one our Ridge Run. We used the skidoo this afternoon. Could use more snow but it wasn't too bad. Since we had a skiff of snow overnight, didn't see too many real fresh tracks but there were lots that had been made before the last fall. We broke through some shell ice around the lake edge on our way out so on the way back had to make a bit of a detour. I'd been riding on the toboggan when it broke through the slush so ended up with me and the toboggan both getting wet. Further on it was good going on Lake Run so we managed to set out a few more traps. All told we set a total of seventeen traps this afternoon. A good start!! We're so far behind with setting up trap boxes in trees because of Gordon's being away but will manage to do Okay, we hope!!

By the time we got home the weather started to get nasty. Snow just lightly falling but along with it a miserable cold wind had sprung up. Think we're in for a bit of bad weather similar to what they've been having at some of the other locations. I was pretty wet before we got home so was quite chilly but soon with the warm cabin and a change of clothing was fine. Making a big pot of spaghetti sauce. Gordon bought me a large stainless steel stock pot (twelve quart) while he was in Whitehorse so I just had to try it out. It's going to be great for soup. We're also having pumpkin pie with fresh whipped cream for dessert tonight. Later just before going to bed, we had cantaloupe and ice cream. We're sure suffering so much, being out here!!!

Wednesday – Nov. 2nd -11C   Cleared during the night, the stars were shining but this morning we're again fogged in.

After breakfast Gordon took the skidoo and went down to the Coal River to bring back the skimmer we'd left there last fall. We need it here since the toboggan is just not good enough. The toboggan is not large enough to haul gear on and doesn't ride or follow behind the skidoo properly. The skimmer has a rigid hitch that prevents it from sliding sideways like the toboggan does.

The fog finally lifted and it's turned into such a beautiful day. Not a cloud in the sky and a lot of heat from the sun. Temperature is about minus twelve right now but feels much warmer. I'm making a big pot of chicken noodle soup and bannock for lunch. Also nailing a bunch of trap boxes together, ready to take up towards Twin Lakes Creek this afternoon for setting out. Looks so nice northwards with the mountains in view – all snow covered, glistening in the sun. Just lovely.

While waiting for Gordon to return from the river, I went for a walk to Beaver Pond. It was just too nice to stay indoors. Gordon returned and reported the trail was very rough. The next time we go there we'll be using snowshoes unless we get a lot more snow. He picked up a marten in our set by the creek. When I went for my walk to Beaver Pond, I picked up two marten. I was just so excited. Our first fur for this year.

After lunch we started the skidoo and headed out to check our Lake Run. We picked up another marten. We went further up the trail towards Twin Lakes and put out a few more sets. It's new country to both Gordon and I. Most of it was fairly good going. In order to go much further down that trail we'll have to go for a full day. When we reached Twin Lakes Creek and the place where Gordon and the men had dropped several logs across the creek for a temporary bridge, Gordon thought it might be a good idea to place a few more small spruce atop the logs to make it safer. The creek was frozen above the makeshift log bridge but was wide open below. The open water showed that it's a very deep creek, not a good place for a swim!! This is the only big creek we'll have to cross before connecting to our Lynx and Rose Lake Runs. After we'd crossed the creek, we went another mile further before deciding it was time to turn around and head for home.

After we got home Gordon checked the ice on our lake and reported it was about two inches thick Not very safe yet!! Also, a lot of the ice is covered with overflow. Had another treat tonight – ice cream with bananas. Gordon brought a big tub of ice cream (so very sweet and thoughtful of him) but temperature here just isn't cold enough to freeze it hard so we have very soft ice cream. Still good!!

Thursday – Nov. 3rd -10C   We had a very strong wind for awhile last night but the sky was clear, filled with shining stars and dancing Northern Lights. Quite a display!! Later, it must have clouded over since we found fresh snow on the ground this morning and more still coming down.

Gordon's making hotcakes for breakfast. We'll have them with the chokecherry syrup Ruth Wilkinson (a friend of ours in Watson Lake) sent back with Gordon. Also have fresh grapefruit. Wonder how the other trappers fare?? After breakfast we were busy nailing trap boxes together. When we ran out of the boards we'd precut in Watson Lake, Gordon cut more from scraps of plywood that were left over from cabin building. He did the sawing while I nailed them into trap boxes. During the morning it got quite nasty out with blowing snow. We're still determined to head up to Swan Lake this afternoon, regardless of weather.

After lunch, about one o'clock, we hooked the loaded skimmer to the skidoo and took off down the trail. The trail was mostly through fairly heavy timber so there wasn't much wind. It was actually quite nice out. We picked up six marten on our way. That was super great!! It was hard to see marten tracks since we'd had quite a bit of fresh snow. At our last set we left the skidoo, strapped on snowshoes and headed out to find a trail to connect with the one that Gordon and the boys had partially cleared earlier in the fall. We snowshoed through a section of open timber where the going was really good, then down a slope to a swampy area which had a creek running through it. We crossed the creek on the ice. Ice couldn't have been very thick since you could plainly hear water rumbling beneath it. We then followed along the edge of the swampy area, where the going was good, and not too far ahead connected up to the trail the boys had cut this fall. Overall, it was pretty good going. On the way back Gordon cleared a few patches of brush out of the way. While traveling along the edge of the swamp, he broke through the ice crust a few times but managed to get out before getting wet feet. With the grassy vegetation in the swamps and the snow cover they received before any real cold temperatures, swamps still aren't frozen. We didn't carry any trap boxes or traps with us (they were left in the skim-mer) since we didn't know if we'd be able to snowshoe through the swamp. Going was actually great so plan on coming back tomorrow and set out traps.

On the way home, in the set closest to the cabin, we found a marten. It must have walked into the trap just minutes before we reached it. A real pleasant surprise. After we reached the cabin and parked the skidoo, we hiked up to the meat cache for a section of moose meat. I didn't have any left in our storage cupboard in the porch and we needed meat for tonight's supper. Gordon will have to saw the hind quarter into meal sized pieces. He uses a Swede saw for cutting the frozen meat. It does a super job with very little waste. He keeps a special blade, hanging in the porch, just for meat cutting. While he was looking after the meat, I walked over to check the trap we'd set along the creek at the lake outlet but found nothing. While I was gone, Gordon took off to check the four sets Bob had put out beyond the meadow back of the cabin. Lo and Be-hold, we had another marten – making a total of eight for today. Gordon sure has his work planned for this evening. He'll only be able to skin two of them since the others are too frozen.

Our supper tonight, without meat since it's still frozen, was pork and beans with lots of fried bacon and bannock . Dessert was rhubarb sauce and strawber-ries with Nanaimo squares (G's birthday cake) so we're really not suffering. Oh yes, also had pickles. Radio signals have been fairly good lately. Heard Rhea and her Mom talking. Rhea sounds so depressed. Nothing going right for them. Too much snow and the ice on the lake is not freezing very well under its deep snow cover. Also, the finger that Glen cut has become infected. His asthma is also so bad that if he was in Watson Lake he'd be hospitalized. And to top it all, no meat yet. Not even a track to show a moose or caribou in their area. Can't think of anything else that could possibly go wrong. We feel badly for them.

Thursday – Nov. 4th -8C   Snow showers and overcast. Seems the sun is trying to come out as occasionally you can make out a glimmer through the clouds.

After breakfast we packed up the skimmer and skidoo and headed back down the trail we'd been over yesterday. Hopefully we'll get to where we were yesterday and a good ways further. About eleven o'clock, we passed Swan Lake. We traveled through heavy snow showers most of the time. Periodically the sun would break through for a few minutes and shine but mostly it was cloudy, snowing and warm. We followed along yesterday's snowshoe trail with the skidoo and broke through into slush a few times. Nothing major, even though some overflow was pretty deep. Anyway, we managed to put out ten more sets along the cleared trail – where the going was good. We left the skidoo once we reached the far meadow and snowshoed onwards, looking for a route that we could follow with the skidoo. The meadow, generally a half mile to a mile wide, meandered southward for several miles. We snowshoed along the eastern edge of it, between open stands of spruce for most of the distance. Occasionally it was necessary to cross the creek to the west side of the meadow when we ran into rough going on the east side. After snowshoeing for a couple of hours, we felt we'd gone far enough for the day. We're pretty pleased with the extension to our trail, especially after seeing so many marten tracks criss-crossing the area. Next time we return on this Run, we'll continue onwards, hoping to meet up with the Wolf Run that we'd set from Jamie Lake last year. It can't be much further but it will require cutting trail through two short sections before we're connected to it. When it's connected, we'll have a nice long run from Ridge Lake to the river and across to Jamie Lake. Gordon had mentioned, when he picked the skimmer up on Monday, that the river was frozen so we should be able to cross and get to Jamie Lake OK.

On the way back home we found a marten in our second trap. He'd just been caught so we didn't come home empty handed today. We weren't expecting anything today since those traps had been checked yesterday. All in all, it was a very interesting day. I'm tired though. Don't know if I'm just out of shape or it's still the after affects of a fall I had this spring, when I hurt my back. It seems to tire out much quicker this year.

Saturday – Nov. 5th *-10C*   Very foggy out. Can't even see the lake shore.

By the time we finished breakfast and packed up, the fog was starting to break. We went up Lake Run towards Twin Lakes creek and off towards Lynx Run, hoping to locate the trail Bob and Robbie had cut for us this fall. This new trail should join up with the one we used from Rose Lake last season, our Lynx Creek Run. When connected, we'll have a continuous trail from Ridge Lake to Rose Lake. Since Gordon was not along with Bob and Robbie when they cut the trail, he's not exactly sure where the trail goes. We rode the skidoo as far as we'd gone with the machine last time then strapped on snowshoes and started exploring the general area, looking for the trail the men had blazed in the fall. After going only a short distance we found blazes the men had left. They followed a game trail that meandered through a series of small meadows connected by patches of open jackpine. Lots of marten tracks and even a fresh moose track. We followed quite a ways along the trail after it left the meadows and entered the timber. Gordon was very pleased with the trail clearing the men had done and hopes it's like that for the rest of the way.

I was wishing I'd brought my camera along. The fog had lifted earlier and we were enjoying a gorgeous day. In the little meadow where we stood, the elevation was about forty-two hundred feet. We could look across the valley to the west and see the mountains, covered with cloaks of pure white snow, shining in the sun or you could turn a hundred and eighty degrees to the east and behold another, much closer, panorama of peaks. Just beautiful!! We built a fire beneath the high spreading branches of a large spruce that grew along the edge of the meadow and had hot tea with our lunch. After lunch and a short rest, we got busy and set out a few more traps. We were really pleased to have located the trail and now know where it goes. The trail into this area opens up so much country for us, so many meadows and valleys that are now easily accessible. Just hope we have enough time to explore and trap all the areas. We already know that we don't have enough traps.

On the way back and just before we reached our second ridge I, riding in the skimmer, screamed at Gordon to stop the skidoo. (I'm going to have to figure out a way of getting his attention easier). He finally stopped and I pointed and ordered "Get them". There were five grouse sitting on spruce trees next to our trail, four on one little spruce and one on another. He could have just about grabbed them, they were so close. They were not the least bit concerned. Gordon reached for his twenty-two rifle and then into his pocket for shells and then, "Oh No, I changed my pants before we left home and didn't take any shells". I was so disappointed. Grouse would have tasted so good – a change from our moose. Can you honestly believe that a person would pack his rifle and not take shells?? My TURKEY does!! Oh well, we did pick up two marten when we checked our traps this morning.

After we got home Gordon went to change the spark plug in the skidoo and nearly had heart failure. He couldn't remove it!! He tried and tried and even bent the spark plug wrench before he got it out. He was really worried that it had seized up or something. The sparkplug, the original, had been screwed in so tightly at the dealers. He was really relieved when it finally broke loose and could be removed. Skidoo problems out here are something we sure don't want. After supper we listened to music from our radio while nailing more trap boxes together. Then it was off to bed.

Sunday – Nov. 6th -9C   Broken sky condition this morning. The clouds in the eastern part of the sky were so beautiful. With the sun shining on them they displayed every possible pink and orange shade. Lovely!!

After a breakfast of hotcakes and coffee, we started the skidoo and headed down the trail towards Swan Lake. After reaching Swan Lake we'd planned on doing some exploring, hoping to find a trail through the pass in the mountains that headed eastwards to Crisco Lake in the Northwest Territories. From Swan Lake there is a valley with a small stream and a series of meadows that heads eastwards. We figured it would take us between three and four hours to check the valley. After leaving Swan Lake we had to climb about three hundred feet in order to reach a jackpine ridge that extends along the east side of the lake. Getting to the top of the ridge was a bit of a problem since we had to find a way through a section of huge boulders. After checking out several possible routes we finally located a way that was passable even though it is pretty rough.

When we reached the top of the ridge, we ran across fresh wolf tracks. Checking, we found a section of the boulder field where they'd been bedded down while chewing on the front quarter of a moose. We're pretty sure it was from our moose. We'd cached some of our moose at Swan Lake. The meat had been hung from a cross pole suspended between two trees, about twelve feet – maybe more, above the ground. Anyway, a grizzly had come down to feed on the moose entrails and the scraps left from the carcass and, while there, had also managed to pull down our meat. It appeared that after he'd left, the wolves had come in for their share. The shoulder blade and a piece of moosehide was all that was left from a hundred and twenty pound front quarter of moose. Under a large spruce a few feet away were several wolf beds, nice and dry and really cozy.

The first mile or so was really easy going through an area of open jackpine growth but when the ridge ran out and we once more dropped down to the valley below, our progress slowed. We had to leave the skidoo and snowshoe up the valley, figuring out the best way for the trail. Then it was back to get the skidoo and bring it up. We had a few problems with unfrozen creeks that ran in from side valleys. It was then necessary to chop trees down and build makeshift bridges to cross over on. We also ran into several sections where the creeks had overflowed over their original ice. If water atop the ice was only a few inches deep, we could travel through it with the skidoo but when it got deeper we had to get off the ice – quick. Getting off the creek was easy but when you turned into the snow along the shoreline there was usually a real problem.

Most times the lower section of snow would be a soggy, wet mass and jam up the skidoo track. Next thing you knew, you're sitting on a bogged down machine that's in a foot of soaking wet, soggy snow. The only thing you can do (other than utter a few unflattering comments about the idiot that was driving the machine) is grab your axe, jump off and race for higher ground, hoping your mukluks won't be soaked through before you reach it. Then it's brush cutting time – throwing brush in front of the skidoo so it'll have something to climb up onto, out of the slush. Once the platform of brush is in place, you restart the skidoo and with one hand controlling the throttle, shove and rock the machine till you're ready to drop, trying to break it free from the mush it's sitting in. If you're lucky and the slush isn't too deep, the skidoo will begin to grudgingly inch forward, then all of a sudden, it jumps ahead. You're out, thank goodness. Next, you wipe the snow and slush off the front of your pants and parka. Actually, you usually don't get too wet falling forward when the machine makes its leap. Fortunately, this time we were lucky. The snow along the bank of the creek wasn't saturated so we kept moving until we were well clear of the creek and overflow.

Usually we take time for a break around noon but it was later today. We finally stopped and built a fire and had tea and our lunch under four large spruce. Really well sheltered! Lunch was especially enjoyed since it was past three o'clock when we took our break. After lunch, we snowshoed for another mile or more, marking out a trail, then turned around and returned to the skidoo, started it and headed for home. We did set out a few traps today but, even after six and a half hours of breaking trail, we still hadn't reached Crisco Lake. We must have been within a half mile of the lake. Oh well, we'll get there next time. On the way home, while traveling along the shore of Beaver Pond, we could see by the tracks where a bull caribou had started to cross the pond on the ice but, seeing our skidoo trail, had turned and headed the other way – on the run. A few minutes later we crossed through the last stand of spruce and our cabin came into view. It's been a long day and its sure great to be home. I'm going to stretch out and relax for a few minutes before starting supper.

Monday – Nov. 7th -11C   Fog again this morning – solid.

We had a <u>very</u> interesting, maddening, you name it – kind of day. It ended up well despite all our problems. We should have stayed in bed!!

After breakfast, we decided to go down the trail to the Coal River to check the few traps we had set there. Since it's a very rough trail, Gordon decided we'd hitch the two dogs to the toboggan rather than take the skidoo. We'd walk, without snowshoes, since the dogs and toboggan would pack the trail ahead of us. It normally takes only about an hour and a half to reach the river since it's only about six miles away. Gordon placed the bait, extra traps and my vest in the box that's strapped on the toboggan. I didn't dress as warmly as I do when we're using the skidoo, just a light wool shirt and jeans, etc. Walking keeps me warm so I wouldn't need heavy clothes. Anyway, this would be the first time the two dogs were hitched together. We sort of expected they might try a bit of chewing on each other but, once in harness, behaved themselves. Gordon started leading the way down the trail with the dogs following behind him but soon they were trying to get around and ahead of him. Guess they though the Master usually rides the toboggan or runs along behind it. Not walk in front!!

I was trotting along behind everyone. To my thinking, they were all nearly running because I couldn't keep up. Minutes later we got to the creek that has our little, narrow bridge across it and Gordon says "Take the rope that's tied to the back of the toboggan so you can help guide it across the bridge". Seconds later, with Gordon leading, the dogs were across the bridge – but – the toboggan slipped a little sideways and tipped over into the creek. Everything was dumped out. Gordon ran back and pulled the toboggan out, still hitched to the dogs while I was busy retrieving my vest and the traps from the creek. The next thing we knew, when Gordon came back to help me, the dogs took off at a fast trot up the hill, following the trail we'd made with the skidoo a couple of days earlier. We grabbed the traps, bait, etc. we'd retrieved from the creek and started after them, thinking they'd stop shortly and also hoping, when they came to the junction with Lake Run, they'd take the River Run. When we reached the junction where the trail divides – of course, they'd headed up Lake Run. Anyway, we figured they were getting further ahead all the time and the only thing to do was get the skidoo and go after them. Gordon trotted back for the skidoo while I kept on following the dogs, hoping they'd get tangled up or seeing a marten up a tree, stop and start barking.

No such Luck!! I must have walked over a mile before Gordon caught up to me. Also, shortly before he reached me, one of the skis on the skidoo had hit a small root in the trail. Just hard enough to throw the nose of the skidoo sideways but enough to allow the bumper to ram into a big spruce. The bumper now has quite a bend in it but fortunately, no other damage was done. The funny thing is that where it happened was in an open area with only a few trees. The trail goes between two of those trees and naturally that's where the root was. Oh well!! I got on the skimmer and we took off at quite a fast pace down our first ridge then across the meadow to the second ridge. No dogs yet but we did notice that we had marten in two of our traps. We'll pick them up on the way back. Then it was down the second ridge and across another meadow and on to our Twin Lakes Run. Another marten but no dogs. We kept hoping they'd stop. A bit further on, where the trail climbed into the hills, we started running into fog. When we reached the top, it was very foggy. Along the top, there are also a lot of willows, buckbrush, etc. where we thought the dogs would stop or get hung up, for sure. But, No Way!! They'd kept right on going.

A short while later we reached the area that we'd explored with snowshoes on Saturday. The dogs were still heading onwards. They were now even beyond the furthest point we'd explored. The game trail they were following headed through a swampy, hummocky section, real rough and so, a few minutes later, Gordon got the skidoo hung up on a root. He got off and wrestled with the skidoo, trying to free it but with no luck until he decided to really "put the gas" to it. It worked. With motor roaring, the skidoo started moving up and out of the root-bound hole it was in. But about then, one of Gordon's feet got too close to the moving track and rollers. The moving track grabbed his boot with his foot still in it. He was stuck tight!! Said he didn't think he'd hurt his toes. He shut the machine off. I undid the boot laces and a few minutes later, after considerable twisting and turning, he managed to get his foot out of his boot but – his socks and boot still remained wrapped around the roller. He started the machine, gently pressed on the throttle, the track and rollers turned and his boot was free. Sure was lucky!! Could have broken his ankle so easily.

Still no dogs!! We rested for a few minutes then decided to walk ahead through the rough section to see whether we should take the skidoo any further. We only went a short ways, came around a bend and believe it or not, about a hundred yards ahead were the dogs – lying down on the trail. They'd finally got stuck. The toboggan was jammed between two hummocks. We left the dogs where they were, walked back to the skidoo and wrestled with the machine, trying to get it turned around in the very rough area. Just finished getting it turned, looked up, and there were the dogs coming towards us. They couldn't go forward but were able to turn and come back. Don't know who was happier, the dogs to see us or us seeing them. They had to have traveled a good five miles or more, most of it on the run or a fast trot. They're trained to follow a trail and thought they were doing what they were trained to do. They were so tired. I'm sure they'd run all the way to where we caught up to them.

We gave the dogs a few minutes more to rest, then started for home. We stopped just a short ways back to set a trap and then didn't stop again until we reached the traps that held marten. Just as we finished resetting the traps, the dogs showed up. We continued on, collecting the other two marten and resetting the traps. Only had to wait a couple of minutes there before the two dogs again trotted up with the toboggan. Tongues were hanging out quite a ways so we gave them a few minutes to rest before continuing onwards. The dogs were pretty warm, trying to keep up with the skidoo, but not me. By the time we reached home I was so cold and wet. I'd been splashed this morning when the toboggan went into the creek and also when I was fishing out traps. Riding behind the skidoo in the skimmer is chilly but with damp clothes, it was just plain cold!! It felt so good being back in our warm cabin. After changing to dry clothes I made a hot lunch for us. Hot soup and tea were really appreciated!!

After lunch Gordon tried to straighten out the skidoo bumper but not with much luck so right now he's splitting wood. Taking out his frustrations on the woodpile while I'm making a pot of stew. Actually, perhaps it's best that we did go up that run today. We did pick up three marten. There's always tomorrow to do the River Run (with the dogs). Sky had cleared up nicely by the time we got home. Sun shining from a clear sky except towards the pass that leads to Twin Lakes – it's foggy.

When we were getting ready for bed, Gordon checked his toes. He has one black toe and another that's scraped. He was very lucky!! At ten-thirty tonight, temperature was down to minus twenty-four. The Northern Lights are beautiful, just a-dancing across the sky.

Tuesday – Nov. 8th -22C   Didn't get as cold as I thought it would. It's nice out. Clear.

After breakfast we again hitched the two dogs to the toboggan but today Gordon tied a rope onto our lead dog, Smokey, before we started down the trail to the river. Gordon decided we didn't need snowshoes. We crossed the creek and didn't dump anything. Hurray!! Quite a change from yesterday!! Gordon said that if the dogs were too energetic he'd have me ride in the toboggan. Anyway, they were really good today. We'd hoped for a couple of marten on this run but only got one – in the last set at the river. It had turned into a gorgeous morning and had really warmed up with the sun. Actually too warm for us in our parkas.

While we were at the river, we tied the dogs to a good sized tree. We're not taking any chances of them taking off on their own today!! We removed the marten from the trap, rebaited and reset the trap. Seemed like a lot of marten tracks around the area, also tracks made by a mink so Gordon placed another set on the ground at the base of a nearby spruce. Afterwards we walked out to the river, checking on the overflow that's been flooding over the ice. Good, not too deep and it's started to freeze. Ice will build faster that way, with overflow. Last fall we'd left the canoe and motor fairly high up the river bank under a spruce but Gordon thought it might be a good idea to move it even higher in case the river really floods next spring. It was easy dragging the canoe through the snow to a higher location where we then tied it to a big spruce. Should be safe up there, ready for us when we return next fall. Hopefully, nothing will bother it. After that, in a clump of spruce further along the river bank, we set out two more traps.

As soon as we finished trap setting, we untied the dogs and headed back up the trail for home. Most of the way, from the river to Ridge Lake, is a gradual climb. It sure bothered my back. By the time we reached the lake I was totally beat. Don't know how much further I could have gone without a long rest. I'm totally disgusted that I seem to play out so easily this winter!! But it was a beautiful day for a walk. Temperature had warmed up to minus seven by the time we returned but just as soon as the sun started sinking in the west, temperature started dipping again.

Just as we were finishing supper we heard, via the gossip channel on the radio, that Glen Stockman had sunk his Yamaha skidoo while packing runway on their lake and that it's now sitting in about eight feet of water. He's lucky he was able to get out. They claim they have about seven inches of ice covering their lake. We can't figure out how he could have broken through that much ice. Wonder if the machine went through an overflow hole. Their Yamaha is a new machine they bought just this past spring. Anyway, they managed to anchor the machine to a tree that they'd laid on the ice. Hopefully they'll be able to get it out tomorrow. Everything seems to be against them this year. Gordon finds it hard to believe they have seven inches of ice. They've had so much snow!! It would keep ice from forming very rapidly. We have just a fraction of the snow they have but the ice on our lake is only two to three inches thick. But then they had quite a few days with colder temperatures, earlier than we did.

View from the door of our Kettle Creek cabin

BRRR - It's cold outside!!!!

Inspecting furs in preparation for shipment

Santa did visit us at Ridge Lake

Wednesday – Nov. 9th -11C   Snowed a bit overnight but is now clear with just a bit of fog over the lake.

This morning after breakfast, we packed traps, trap boxes, a pail of bait and our lunch in the skimmer. Gordon then started the skidoo, I climbed into the skimmer and a minute later we were off – headed for our Swan Lake and Wolf Runs!! The trail was good. We'd only received a couple of inches of fresh snow over the past days which helped to smooth out quite a few bumps in the trail. Noticed quite a few marten tracks when we were passing the area where we got our moose this fall. Nice to see they're still around. Nothing in the traps along Swan Run. A bit of a disappointment. We did find three marten in our traps along Wolf Run. One was caught in our mink set. It was almost noon by the time we reached the end of the trail that we'd blazed the last time. By then all the patches of fog had cleared off and it was just beautiful. Still lots of heat from the sun.

We left the skidoo, put on snowshoes and headed southwards, trying to locate a trail that would be suitable for the skidoo. The trail would have to connect up with the Wolf Run we'd explored and trapped during the two winters we'd been at Jamie Lake. We hadn't gone very far before we came across wolf tracks that followed along a game trail. They were heading in the direction we wanted to go so we followed, knowing that animals usually pick the easiest way through the bush. Going was pretty easy with only an occasional patch of willow and buckbrush along the trail that needed to be cleared out of the way. Gordon did the chopping and I threw the brush off the trail. We made good time. It was only a bit over an hour later, as we passed through a stand of spruce, that we reached an open meadow that looked familiar. Sure enough, when we crossed to the far side we spotted axe marks that we'd made a couple of years before. Our trail from Ridge Lake via Swan Lake was now connected to our old Wolf Run from Jamie Lake. From now on we could make a complete circuit, Ridge Lake to Jamie Lake to Rose Lake and then back to Ridge Lake. No doubling back on the trail. HURRAY!! Actually though, there are still a couple of sections of the old trail, where we'd only used snowshoes, that will have to be rerouted before we can use the skidoo on them. Also, there's a small creek to be crossed and that means a bit of bridge building. But it'll be done.

By then it was well past the time when we usually stopped for our lunch break. We were tempted to keep going and snowshoe back to the skidoo, eating cold sandwiches along the way. Pretty dry eating without tea. Anyway, reason prevailed. Minutes later a fire was blazing and in no time our tea water was boiling. Toasted sandwiches and hot tea sure did hit the spot. However, it wasn't long before we again strapped on our snowshoes and headed back down the trail to the skidoo. Along the way we rerouted a couple of short sections of trail and cleared a few more trees from it. As soon as we reached the skidoo Gordon started it then turned and drove back down our newly cleared section of trail. He wanted to put out several marten sets before we headed for home. We'd noticed quite a few tracks all along the way. Looks really promising!!

A short while later when Gordon returned, I climbed in the skimmer and we were off for home. It got quite cold on our way back. A wind had come up and it really cooled things down. Was sure thankful that last evening Gordon, with my help, had installed a nylon canopy over the skimmer. I'd sewn a two-way zipper into the nylon before bringing it out to the trapline this fall. Over the summer we'd figured out how to construct a canopy over the skimmer and made certain we brought along the necessary gear when we came out this fall. Anyway, installing the canopy was pretty simple. Gordon riveted four hoops over the skimmer – arched over the top from one side to the other. The nylon canopy was stretched over them and attached along the sides of the skimmer. When you opened the zipper along the top, everything in the skimmer was at hand. Sure is handier. No more snow piling in and burying everything. And best of all, when I ride in it, I don't get covered with snow. Even so, by the time we got back, I was getting pretty chilled. It really felt super after we reached home and were back inside, soaking up the warmth of the cabin. It's been a long day.

Talked to Rhea and Glen after supper. They still haven't managed to get their skidoo out but are making progress. Sure a heck of a job, especially when you don't have the equipment you'd like. Just hope temperature drops down and makes more ice so it'll be safer for them.

Thursday – Nov. 10th -14C Not a nice day!! Snowing and a bit of wind. Good excuse for a day off from the trails. Actually it is nasty out. We are somewhat protected here but it would be real miserable out in the open.

This morning Gordon disconnected and moved the little propane stove out of the cabin. I scraped the section of logs that'd been behind it just as soon as it was out of the way. Gordon's going to install the big propane stove later today. When the cabin was first built the only propane stove we could locate in Watson Lake was a small one from a damaged motorhome. The stove was OK but cooking was pretty restricted because of the small surface and baking was questionable. Anyway, we finally obtained a full-sized propane cookstove and brought it out here. It'll be so much handier, especially the large oven. Actually, the wood stove is tops for cooking and frying but not so great for baking. That's where the propane stove is really appreciated. While I was working on logs Gordon worked on a hind quarter of moose. Cutting it into meal sized sections, roasts, steak, pieces for hamburger, etc.

After lunch he tried to get the stove set up. We got the top burners to work just great. Also, the pilot light goes on in the oven, BUT – the oven would not light!! Very maddening as that is what we mainly wanted, a stove with a large oven. Called Don Taylor via radio and he called the serviceman in Watson Lake but haven't heard back from him. While waiting, Gordon nailed up a few slats between the logs. Also built a shelf by the stove for drying boots, mitts, etc. I kept busy, grinding up enough meat for five or six meals. Just heard that Glen and Rhea got their skidoo out of the lake but now don't have proper wrenches to work on it with.

Friday – Nov. 11th -26C Got a little cool overnight but should help freeze up everything. Shocked Gordon!! I got up and started the fire. Third time so far!! We still don't keep the fire on at night – gets too hot in the cabin.

After breakfast, just as we were getting ready to leave for our Crisco Run, Don Taylor called to let us know that today is a holiday. Anyway, he called Dahl Young, the propane serviceman (also our neighbor in Watson Lake) regarding our problem with the stove. Dahl was at home and Don was able to patch his telephone in with our radio so it enabled us to speak directly with Dahl. He told us what the problem with our stove likely was. Gordon had to adjust the air volume and also, it appeared there was not enough air pressure on the regulator. Gordon was told how to adjust things. Anyway, it seems to work now. Tonight I'll try the oven out by baking a cake.

After we finished with the stove, we were off to our Swan Run. Picked up one marten in a trap we'd set in a clump of spruce just across from the Beaver Pond. Along the way Gordon, removed six traps from Swan Run so we'd have more for Crisco Run. There sure was a lot of fresh sign this morning. Tracks every which way. We also found tracks showing that a wolverine had followed our trail right up to the end of it, to the spot where we'd turned around last time. When we first saw the tracks Gordon was afraid that if we had marten in any of the sets the wolverine would have taken them. When we reached the spot where we'd got our moose, wolverine tracks were all over the place but stayed clear of the trap sets. Gordon put out a blind set on the ground for the wolverine, just in case! We then traveled into the meadow a short ways. Gordon then left the skidoo, put on snowshoes and started up the ridge. He hoped he could locate a better way to the top that we'd be able to follow on the way to Crisco Lake. While he was gone I went on foot to check two other sets that were further along the trail. Was really pleased when I found a marten, a really big one, in the second set. I set a new trap in the cubby, all ready for the next customer. By the time I got back to the skidoo, Gordon had returned. We took off up the new route he'd picked out to the top of the ridge then followed our old trail towards

Crisco. There were only four traps set along the way but picked up a marten in the last one.

We left the skidoo at the furthest point we'd reached last time, put on snow-shoes and started up the valley looking for a route that would be suitable for the skidoo. Crisco Lake is located several miles further up the valley along the Northwest Territories – Yukon border. After a lot of snowshoeing, backtracking, etc. we finally found a passable way along the northern side of the valley. It was very rough going so crossed the creek and found a better way along the southern side of it. We put a few marten sets out along the way, right up to the shore of a small lake. Next time, we plan on taking the skidoo and setting traps along both sides of this lake. After setting the last trap we had with us, we turned and followed our snowshoe trail back to the skidoo.

All in all it was a good day. We got home at five o'clock and **NO LUNCH**. We'd skipped it today. Gordon is doing the cooking tonight – steak and mush-rooms with fried potatoes, while I lean back and relax – reliving our day. After we'd left the skidoo and took off on snowshoes this morning, we'd followed up the valley for several miles – following the creek which ran through it. Along the way we'd come to several other creeks that flowed into it from side valleys. The valley we followed varied from an open grassy meadow, where the going was easy, to flooded, rough, swampy sections that still weren't frozen solid and had patches of almost impenetrable willow growth. Quite a variety – from easy going to real tough slogging.

The most interesting of all were the areas that had been flooded by the beaver dams. Some sections of the valley bottom were flooded for more than a mile by the water backed up from the dams. The ice, under a light covering of snow, appeared to be solid and safe under – ideal to travel on. We were really surprised though, when we checked the ice with the axe. Most times, with just a light tap, the axe went right through. There was just a skim of ice, with a dusting of snow over it. Really treacherous!! We had samples of it all today. Once we had to cross the creek to reach the opposite side of the valley where it looked as though it would be easier going. First though, Gordon snowshoed out to the creek to check the ice and found, after a few swings of his axe, that it was good and solid. He snowshoed out and further along it for a few yards then decided that it might be a good idea to check a second time. Surprise – the axe went right through. There was hardly any ice and below, the water was almost six feet deep. Not a nice place for a bath. Quite a day. Surprised myself though!! Even with all the snowshoeing and fighting through willow swamps, I actually enjoyed it.

Tried the oven later. It worked really well. Made a large chocolate cake. Also baked half of a pumpkin for pie. Thanks Sheila!! (She'd sent the pumpkin out with Gordon when he returned on the thirtieth)

Saturday – Nov. 12th m -13C A skiff of snow overnight. It was also very windy. Overcast this morning and just a little wind. Not really nice. Actually quite nasty!!

After breakfast we skidooed up our Lake Run. Just as we neared the end of the Run we caught, surprisingly, a mink in a marten set that was located a good four feet off the ground. It was quite unusual since mink don't usually climb trees. We again found a wolverine had been following our trail. You could see by the tracks where he went up to check each of our sets. Further along, just after we crossed Twin Lakes creek, in a set we'd put out for mink, we found a marten. He must have reached in for the bait just as the trap went off since his mouth was full of fish scraps. Guess the marten and mink got even with each other. You get caught in my trap and I'll get caught in yours!! Conditions turned really miserable. As the trail climbed higher, the wind picked up and snow started to fall. A few minutes later, reaching the highest point on the trail, we found a marten in a trap we'd set at the base of the only spruce around. The terrain up here mostly consists of open alpine meadows interspersed with sections of thick buckbrush. Spruce and pine seemed to prefer growing in areas a bit lower. Once we reached the top and were pretty well in the open it was really cold with the wind. We only had to travel in the open for a short distance before the trail headed lower, back down into the timber where it would be warmer, out of the wind. We were skidooing down the trail when I started hollering at Gordon to stop. I had a "Charlie-horse" in my thigh. Oh that HURT!! By the time Gordon stopped I was practically lying on top of the canopy with my leg stretched straight out to the back. It really shocked him seeing me like that. He couldn't figure out what had happened. Of course he assumed the worst, that I was badly hurt. Anyway I got out and started walking, trying to work it out. Where we'd stopped was only about fifty feet from our last trap so I told Gordon I'd walk and meet him there. When I got to the trap there was a nice big marten in it. I was surprised and really pleased since I hadn't expected to find anything in the trap.

After resetting the trap, we continued onwards down the trail past the spot where the dogs had got hung up with the toboggan. Some of the sections of trail were very rough, big hummocks with holes between them. Gordon was not thrilled. We put four more trap sets out along the way. It seemed that the further we went, the worse the trail got. We wanted to reach the meadow that connected with our Lynx Run from Jamie Lake. Because of the very rough terrain, we left the machine and snowshoed the rest of the way down to the meadow. We then followed along it for quite a ways. Gordon is not happy with the trail the men cut through this section. Figured he could probably take the machine down through it, with a great deal of difficulty, but there was no way he'd be able to bring it back up. We'll have to locate a better route over this last half mile. We were very pleased with the fur sign though. Tracks wandering all over the place. After checking a bit further up the meadow, we decided it was time to turn around and head back to the skidoo. On the way back home I walked through a couple of the rougher sections but rode the rest of the way. The wind had picked up even more, making travel very unpleasant. We were both chilled by the time we reached home.

Next time we're at Rose Lake we'll go up our Lynx Run and set traps along the way, right up to where we were today. Gordon will be taking the chainsaw along. He thinks he can cut a pretty good trail through the timber, by-passing that miserable, twisty section the men had marked out. Should only take about an hours chainsaw work. Then, when that's done, we'll have a good trail from Rose Lake right up to Ridge Lake. The men had just followed the creek with all its sharp twists and steep banks. Not suitable for a skidoo.

Sunday – Nov. 13th -15C   It was clear overnight – stars were shining. By morning the sky had clouded over and started to snow but – no wind.

We decided during breakfast that if we rushed we could go down River Run to the Coal River and on to Rose Lake. Gordon got the bait, traps and the skidoo ready – all the outdoor work while I packed a box of groceries – bacon, eggs, meat, fresh veggies, homemade soups, spaghetti sauce, bread, cheeses and assorted other items PLUS the radio transmitter. By eleven-thirty we were ready to go.

After the last episode with the dogs, Gordon said he'd take the skidoo across the bridge and then come back and lead the dogs across. Anyway, he found a marten in the set by the creek. A good start for today!! After crossing the bridge with the dogs, Gordon headed up the trail with the skidoo while I and the dog team followed behind. He waited for me at the junction to our Lake Run just in case the dogs got the bright idea of heading up that Run again. Everything went fine though. As soon as Gordon took off down the trail again, the dogs followed. I rode on the toboggan most of the way except for sections where the trail was really rough. We picked up a marten in a set, about half way to the river. It had just been caught. We noticed a lot of marten sign all along River Run today. Also there were fresh wolverine tracks going down the trail ahead of us so they're still hanging around. By the time we reached the river, only took us a bit under an hour, the weather had cleared up and it was really nice out. When we checked the last two traps that we'd set last time, each set under a really big spruce and only about sixty feet apart, we found a marten in each one.

Lots of very fresh marten tracks so they're sure around here. Also noticed the wolverine had checked the sets, tracks right up to them but, lucky for us, hadn't touched the marten.

At the river Gordon took his trusty hand axe and started checking the ice. A lot of overflow under the snow but eventually we found a solid section where it was safe to cross to the sandbar on the far side. We left the skidoo and dogs behind then snowshoed to the far end of the bar and tried to find a safe crossing over the next river channel to the far shore. No luck, just no safe way across and lots of deep overflow. We then returned to the skidoo, backtracked a short distance down river to where a back eddy entered. We followed along it for about half a mile until it eventually swung back to a sandbar along the river. We thought that from there we'd find a way across to Rose Lake by connecting with the meadow trail we'd blazed last winter. Only thing was, we had to get off the river since we didn't want to travel and fool around with overflow. Our trail, the one we wanted to connect to, was still about half a mile further down river. We left the skidoo, tied the dogs and snowshoed through the brush trying to find a way to connect to the old trail. We snowshoed and snowshoed and finally found our blazes. Hard to believe the number of meadows we crossed. Anyway, we backtracked to the skidoo and dogs. We found that Rebel must have been having a good time while we were away. He'd chewed one of his traces almost in half!! Gordon started out with the skidoo, packing the trail ahead, while I followed with the dogs. It was extremely rough going!! He had a heck of a job with the skidoo so I snowshoed. We'll have to go and cut a proper trail through there one day. After a great deal of effort, we eventually reached our big meadow by Rose Lake.

When we reached the cabin we found everything was fine. We had been seeing fur sign, especially marten tracks, all along the way but nothing compared to the number of tracks around the cabin. There were even tracks on the roof of the cabin. After we had the fire going and finished a hot lunch Gordon snowshoed across the river, checking ice. He snowshoed all the way up to Lynx

Creek, crossing the river at three places. When he got back he reported that there is no way we can go to Lynx Creek tomorrow. Just too much overflow. Hopefully in a day or two it'll freeze along the trail he packed. He mentioned that he'd never seen so many tracks along the river bank.

Upon checking our root cellar, located beneath the floor under the bed, we were shocked to find the fresh vegetables and fruit we'd left behind had frozen. Thank goodness there wasn't all that much. I'll still use them in their frozen state. Will keep them outside for now. Can't figure out why they froze. Could be because we have very little snow on the ground around the cabin so the ground would freeze harder and deeper this year. There still is very little snow on the ground, only about ten and a half inches here. Snow showers started about four o'clock but later the sky cleared and tonight the stars are shining.

Monday – Nov. 14ᵗʰ -16C We're fogged in this morning but looks brighter to the south so we're hoping for a nice, sunny day

Gordon didn't feel like wrestling the skidoo or cutting brush along the trail to Jamie Lake today. Instead, we put on our snowshoes and headed up the creek a ways, then turned off to Rose Lake. It's just a little lake located a mile or so back from the river. We put ten marten trap sets out around the lake. There was so much fur sign around the lake, all along the creek and riverbank. Gordon had a surprise while we were at the lake. There was a mound, a muskrat "pushup", along one shore. The area around it was just covered with marten and mink tracks. He snowshoed over and tapped the snow-covered mound with his axe. There was a splash. A muskrat had been feeding inside. We also discovered a lot of the lake was covered with overflow.

Later, after we returned home and finished lunch, Gordon strapped on his snowshoes and headed up along our old Ridge Run to retrieve some of the traps we'd left there last year. We don't plan on using that Run again as it's just too rough. This fall he rerouted another trail to take its place. He took Rebel along to pull the toboggan. Smokey was not pleased at being left behind. When he returned he reported that, a short ways from the far end of the old Run, there were two areas where the side of the hill had slid away, taking out sections of the trail. The hillsides had been pretty gentle inclines but were all clay. Guess, with all the rain we've had this summer, they just slid away.

When he returned he told me to put on my parka and come outside and listen. Sure enough, we could hear wolves howling down river. They couldn't have been very far away from the volume of sound they were making. Rebel and Smokey didn't seem to be very happy, crouching away back in their houses. Wolves usually make a meal of any dog they catch and our two weren't taking chances. We listened to the wolf chorus for several minutes then Gordon tried a few wolf howls. Sure enough, they answered back. This went on for several more minutes. We kept hoping they'd come up river so we could see them. They never did show up. They'd have been safe anyway. Our large calibre rifle, a Winchester .270, is back at Ridge Lake. After we got back inside, Gordon mentioned seeing fresh marten tracks no more than fifty feet from the cabin door. The tracks had been made while he was away this afternoon. He also saw fresh moose tracks. Moose had been feeding on willows around the edge of the meadow before leaving and following our trail to the top of the ridge. Nice to know they're around.

While Gordon was away this afternoon, I installed clear plastic sheeting over the two cabin windows. It acts as a storm window and keeps frost from forming on the glass. Sure makes a difference having clear glass panes during winter months. Without the plastic covering, windows are soon covered with a solid layer of ice and frost which really cuts down the amount of light coming through and really darkens the inside of the cabin. Also received word from the Yukon Trappers Association in Whitehorse, via radio, that everything was fine with our son Jamie. Sure good to get the news. Jamie is also out on his trapline.

Tuesday – Nov. 15th -15C   This morning we're again in fog, just solid.

After breakfast we headed up river with the skidoo to our Lynx Run. There was overflow on the river but along the trail Gordon had packed yesterday it was partially frozen. Lucky for us since we had to cross the river in three places. After we climbed off the river ice at the mouth of Lynx Creek and got on our trail through the bush to our long meadow, travel was a lot more relaxing. A pretty bumpy trail but at least no worries about getting stuck in overflow. We followed the meadow to the far end where the trail entered the timber. We left the skidoo there and snowshoed to the creek – only a short distance ahead. We wanted to check the creek ice out before bringing up the skidoo. There isn't a good place anywhere along the creek bank to where we could turn the machine if we weren't able to cross it. The creek was fine though. Good solid ice so Gordon went back for the skidoo. On the way, while I waited at the creek, he cleared out a couple of trees that had fallen across the trail. The fog had lifted and the sun was shining. It was so nice. A few minutes later when Gordon showed up with the skidoo, I climbed aboard the skimmer and we were off. For the next couple of hours we were busy putting out marten sets. I did some snowshoeing. Many of the little sloughs had overflow under the snow so I went ahead to check the depth of the slush before Gordon tried crossing with the machine. We had no trouble with the sloughs but a couple of the small lakes did have pretty deep overflow so we followed around the shoreline. Anyway, we managed to get through and set out a total of sixteen traps. Lots of fur sign. Marten tracks all over the place.

We finally got to the point we'd reached last year. From there onwards, Gordon had to use his chainsaw to clear a couple of areas before we could go further. Didn't take too long since only short sections of timber separated the meadows. Before calling it a day, we'd traveled quite a ways beyond where we'd managed to go last year. We figure there's only one more short section of trail to clear before we're connected up to the meadows that take us to Twin Lakes Run. That would be great! We had quite a surprise today. When we first started looking for the red flagging we'd tied on bushes last winter to mark our trail, we couldn't find them. We finally spotted them high in the bushes, way above our heads. We knew the snow was deep last year when we'd done the flagging but it's hard to believe there was that depth of snow. There's only about a foot of snow on the ground right now. Quite a difference!!

We got home shortly after five. It was already quite dusky. We really notice our short winter days now. While Gordon refueled and covered the skidoo, I snowshoed a short distance up the trail to Jamie Lake to check a set he'd put there yesterday. Surprise, we already had a marten in it. When I got back and showed my catch, Gordon was as surprised as I'd been. Anyway, he's making supper tonight while I stretch out and read. After missing lunch today together with the hot rum toddy we had right after finishing chores, we've got voracious appetites.

Wednesday – Nov. 16ᵗʰ -9C   Fog again but mild. Can't see the sky so don't know if it's cloudy or not.

After breakfast we headed back over the trail we'd made on Monday when we'd come from Ridge Lake. We wanted to clear and reroute a number of sections of the trail, if possible, through the meadows rather than continue plowing through the rough, swampy areas we'd followed on our way over. Just a short distance down the trail, we passed the trap where I'd picked up the marten last evening. Believe it or not, there was another marten in it. A good start for the day. From there on to the first meadow, it was pretty simple going. We followed a real good moose trail right to the first meadow. Only a few fallen trees had to be removed. We crossed to the south side of the meadow and entered the bush. Quite a patch of willow along the edge but fairly open beyond that, just small scattered jackpine. Pretty rough and hummocky but a passable trail was produced by means of the chainsaw. Gordon did the cutting while I threw the cut up brush off the trail. Once through the bush, we came out to another narrow, winding meadow which we followed for quite a ways. Then it was back into the bush and more trail clearing with the saw. We crossed through four sections of scrubby timber before reaching a really large meadow. Since we weren't sure just where to enter the timber on the far side of the meadow with the skidoo, we decided it would be best to leave the machine, strap on snowshoes and do a bit of exploring. We snowshoed, it seemed like miles, before we crossed the meadow but did find, on the far side, a good way through the timber to another small meadow. From there on, we followed a series of small sloughs and meadows which took us within a half mile of the river. It was then back for the skidoo and chainsaw. Anyway, it was only after we'd completed another two hours of trail clearing that we reached the river.

Sure glad to finally come out in the open and see the river stretching before us. Using this new trail means we'll only have to cross the river once when traveling from Ridge Lake to Rose Lake. The old trail up along the river involved crossing the river several times, worrying about ice conditions and over-flow. From where we stood, it was only a mile to a mile and a half to the junction of our trail from Ridge Lake and the river. We decided to pack a trail across to the junction and check the marten sets on the riverbank over there. We ran into some shallow overflow when crossing but not enough to give us trouble. Glad we checked the traps. We picked up another marten. Anyway, it was starting to get late and we hadn't brought lunch with us so turned around and headed back along our newly cleared trail, setting six marten traps along the way.

The valley we're in, the Coal River valley, was completely overcast all day. The low clouds must have just been in the valley since you could see, far off in the distance, mountain tops shining in the sun. It was such a dark cloud. Almost felt like it was going to rain, especially since the temperature was very mild. We did get some snow showers, just very fine stuff. Actually it had been a really nice day despite the low clouds. After we returned home and had lunch – at four o'clock, we skidooed up to check our traps at Rose Lake. We picked up two more marten, making a total of four today. We only used the skidoo for about two thirds of the way to Rose Lake and then snowshoed the rest of the way around the lake since there was so much overflow. By then it was starting to get dark and Gordon didn't want to take a chance on getting the machine stuck.

We again had a late dinner – spaghetti and meat sauce that I'd brought over from Ridge Lake. A person sure has an appetite out here with all the fresh air and exercise, usually five to seven hours a day or longer – walking or snowshoeing. Really a very healthy lifestyle. All that clean, fresh air. Very exhilarating, especially at minus twenty-five. Nasty out tonight, blowing and snowing. Gordon says we're in for a real blizzard!!

Thursday – Nov. 17th *-20C* A day off today. It is just so nasty out. Cloudy, light snow and very windy. Just not a nice day to be out in. Gordon figures the wind chill would be at least minus thirty-five.

Gordon replaced our stovepipe this morning. When Lloyd manufactured our stove from a hundred pound propane bottle, he welded the wrong sized pipe sleeve on it. The stovepipe fitted over the outside of the sleeve rather than on the inside of it. With slow fires, there's always a certain amount of creosote formed inside the stovepipe which runs down the inside of the pipe and drips into the fire where it's burned. With the pipe on the outside of the sleeve, creosote ran down the pipe and out on the top of the stove. Not a very pleasant odor plus it made a mess on the stove. Anyway, when Gordon was out in October he had a reduction flange made by a tinsmith in Whitehorse. He installed it this morning so the pipe now fits inside. It will be so much pleasanter without that creosote smell. Just to try the stove out, I'm going to bake a chocolate cake right after I finish with my apple pie.

By noon the weather had started to improve. We can see quite a lot of blue sky and the sun's trying to shine but there's still a strong wind. Heard from Watson Lake Flying this morning that Jamie is doing very well commuting to his trapline, all the way from Whitehorse. Lots of driving but he's catching quite a lot of fur. After lunch Gordon went out and cut a couple of boards to use for shelves. Great, what you can do with a chainsaw – cut lumber, firewood, trail clearing and a lot more. The wind eased off a short while later so we took the skidoo and headed towards Jamie Lake via the new rerouted trail. The new trail follows through a series of small sloughs that have short patches of timber separating them. It wasn't until we got to the first section we'd planned on clearing that Gordon realized he'd forgotten to bring his swedesaw along. He'd planned on using it today rather than the chainsaw since the bushy sections had trees that were quite small, mostly willow. But, no saw!! He ended up swinging his axe – a lot harder work. Even so, we pretty well got all the sections cleared between the sloughs except for one patch of timber. It's only a short area but has several big trees leaning across the opening we plan on traveling through. Along the way we did set out three marten traps, a start for this side of the river.

Its five o'clock and Gordon's out on the river chopping holes through the ice. He plans on putting out a couple of set lines in hopes he'll catch a couple of fish. Fresh fish would be a nice change from our diet of moose meat. After supper he nailed up a couple of shelves along the wall above the bed. The shelf that had been there was just too small.

Friday – Nov. 18th -31C Now, that's starting to get a little cool!! High cloud in the sky. Hopefully the cloud will keep the temperature from dropping any further. Of course, it's only about minus twenty-two Fahrenheit and that doesn't sound so bad. The mountains look so nice – all white, the sun shining on them.

After breakfast we skidoo'd up Lynx Run to check traps and then, hopefully, extend our trail to connect with the Twin Lakes Run. It started out as a beautiful day. Clear blue sky with the sun shining but just for the first while. Not long afterwards when the sky began to cloud over, we were certain the temperature would start warming up. We caught our first marten in the set we'd placed at the base of a big spruce on the shore of Lynx Creek. The next one was caught in a ground set located under a tiny spruce on the edge of a grassy slough. Looked like a good place for a mink but the marten got there first. Unfortunately, mice had done a lot of chewing on the marten, badly damaging it. The next two marten were caught in traps we'd set in timbered sections connecting the meadows along our trail. After we finished checking the traps right up to the end of the trail we'd blazed on Tuesday, we left the skidoo and snowshoed onwards, hunting for a way to connect Lynx Run with the Twin Lakes Run.

After clearing a short section of trail through the bush and snowshoing into a narrow, winding meadow, we were really surprised at finding blaze marks on trees along the far edge of it. Sure enough, they were the blazes Bob and Robbie had made this past fall. Finally we'd connected up to the trail from Ridge Lake. We'll now be able to make a complete loop – Ridge Lake to Rose Lake and back again via Lynx Run to Ridge Lake when checking traps. No more doubling back on our trails. HURRAY!! For the next while, we followed the blazes made by the men last fall, choosing the best way for the skidoo. Most of it was pretty good going but a bit of chainsaw work would have to be done before the skidoo could make it through a couple of short stretches. It wasn't long before we reached the trail from Ridge Lake that we'd snowshoed out on Saturday. This morning we'd planned that on our way back we'd complete any chainsaw work that was required on the trail but found we were running out of time. Anyway, next time around, we'll start at Ridge Lake then connect to the Twin Lakes Run and follow it right to here. We'll bring the chainsaw along and finish up the bit of clearing that's needed. Shouldn't take more than an hour.

We snowshoed back to the skidoo and headed for home. On the way back when we reached Lynx Creek, Gordon decided to follow down the creek to the river. While Gordon snowshoed ahead checking ice, I followed with the skidoo. We'd left a few traps hanging in trees, above the sets we'd used two years before, and wanted to retrieve them. Would be nice if we had the time to pick up all the traps that have been left hanging in trees along various creeks. That will have to wait for another day but we could sure use them this year.

Saturday – Nov. 19th -40C   It is **COLD !!!** But it's just beautiful out. The sun is shining on the highest mountain peaks to the north. Will be at least another half hour before its high enough in the sky to shine into our valley here.

It'll be a good day to stays indoors and play cards or read. I'm sort of wishing we were at Ridge Lake where I could use the entire day just for cooking and baking extras. By eleven it was such a gorgeous day with the sun shining that I just had to take a picture of MY mountain at forty below. Sky is so clear and so blue. Gordon just had to see if the skidoo would start in these temperatures. Sure enough, with the third pull of the starter cord, it roared into life. A real surprise for both of us. By one-thirty, temperature had warmed up a few degrees so we decided to pack up and head back over the trail to Ridge Lake. The dogs in harness, followed right behind. Just to be certain, I had a rope attached to the collar of the lead dog. No more heading off on side trails this time!! I was surprised to find it was quite warm in the sun but then there wasn't even a breath of wind. After we'd crossed the river and were on the trail to Ridge Lake I got off and walked a good part of the way, probably halfway to the lake. The trail is still very rough in some sections. We need more snow. Gordon kept the skidoo running at all times, just not taking any chance on it not starting in the cold. I, on the other hand, was just about cooked by the time we reached the cabin. I was dressed too warmly for walking. We picked up another two marten on our river run and also saw a lot of fresh tracks. Hard to believe there are so many around this year! Also noticed wolf tracks following our trail from the river to within a short distance of the cabin. Gordon set a wolf snare about half way up the trail just in case they follow it again.

We found so many marten tracks around the cabin. Hard to believe!! Tracks showed where they'd even climbed up and tried looking through the window. Surprised to see they'd also been right up to the dog houses. Sure nosey. Next, I checked the two meat caches and found everything was fine. They hadn't managed to climb past the tin we'd wrapped around the supporting posts. Since I got back before Gordon, I lit the stove and while the cabin was warming, walked down the trail toward Beaver Pond. From the three traps we'd set along there, I picked up another marten. Tracks showed wolves had also been down the trail. Gordon still hadn't shown up by the time I got back to the cabin so I went and checked the sets we had in the meadow behind the cabin but found nothing. Just as I returned to the cabin, Gordon showed up with the skidoo and dog team. All told, it took us about two and a half hours to come from Rose Lake. Pretty good for a cold day. Later when we checked our fresh stuff in the cellar beneath the bed, we found everything was fine. Nothing was frozen but was sure cold. By five-thirty this evening temperature was sitting at minus thirty.

Sunday – Nov. 20th -18C   A pleasant surprise after yesterday's minus forty. Temperature had remained at minus thirty-two all evening but the sky clouded over during the night and warmed us up. Sky is completely overcast this morning.

We headed down our Swan Run right after breakfast. Ran into a heavy snow shower just after we'd left but it only lasted a short while. Soon patches of blue sky were showing and before much longer it turned into a nice day. We collected two marten along Swan Run and then, down our Wolf Run, found another five marten and a mink waiting for us. Eight animals altogether. It was a great catch!! When we'd reached our last set, a ground set for mink, we found the trap was outside the box we'd set it in. Gordon thinks there's a good possibility that a marten, poking around the set, had caused the trap to fall out. We left the skidoo at the last set, strapped on snowshoes and headed towards the creek, looking for the best way to cross it with the machine. We snowshoed further on, setting four more traps along the way. The traps we set were the ones we'd left two years earlier when we closed down the line. We found that in order to continue along the old Wolf Run with our skidoo, we'll have to cut a short trail across to the next meadow instead of traveling on the creek ice. Seems that most times we just can't travel on the ice because it's either flooded or isn't thick enough to support us.

We'd originally planned on having tea and then finish clearing trail across to the next meadow before we headed back. I suggested that it might be a better idea to return to the skidoo and head for home right away. It would take us at least two hours of snowshoeing before we were back to the skidoo and at least another hour and a half of skidoo travel before we reached the cabin. Also, the weather didn't look so great. A few minutes later it started to snow – heavy snow. Seemed so odd!! A few minutes earlier it was sunny and then all of a sudden the sky turned black with a solid wall of cloud. Looks as though we're in for more snow. By the time we reached the skidoo, we were in a real blizzard with the wind whipping the falling snow every which way. It was a relief to take off our snowshoes, turn the machine around, climb on and head for home. Thankfully, the skidoo started with the first pull of the starter cord. Sure wouldn't want to snowshoe all the way home today. It seemed to take forever, traveling through the storm, to reach Ridge Lake. It was a real relief to see the cabin come into view, smoke still curling from the stovepipe.

While Gordon was refueling and then covering the skidoo with the tarp, I was in the cabin looking after the fire and, most important, getting the ingredients ready for our hot rum toddy. A short while later we were sitting around the stove soaking up heat, both internally and externally. All in all, we'd had a good day. We saw more moose tracks and again, wolf tracks along our trails. Also discovered one of our marten had a porcupine quill in its neck. I felt so bad at one point today. While I was snowshoeing along, intently watching an animal track alongside the trail but not watching my snowshoes, I accidentally stepped on the heel of one of Gordon's. He went headfirst into the snow!! He looked so funny – but I did feel badly?? He wasn't too impressed.

Monday – Nov. 21ˢᵗ -7C Election Day. May the best man win!! Hard to believe the change in our temperature – nice – sky is overcast. We received about an inch of snow overnight.

After breakfast we went down Swan Run on our way to Crisco Lake. Temperature was so mild, great skidooing. At our moose kill site, Gordon set out a trap and a couple of snares for wolves. Tracks showed they'd been digging and prowling around the area. Just past there on our way to Crisco, we noticed where a wolverine had come onto our trail and followed right up to the end of it.

Gordon set out a couple of snares in case it returns. Along the way we picked up three marten from our sets. Not bad for just ten sets. There's a small lake, the furthest point we reached last time,that we've decided to call "Fluffo Lake". Since Crisco Lake is right on the border of the Northwest Territories, we won't be going up the valley that far. Along the way to Fluffo Lake we set out a number of marten traps. Lots of sign all along the way. Finally, after reaching the lake, we ran out of traps but wished we had more along to set around the shoreline. The mountains above Crisco looked so lovely with the sun shining on them. Gordon doesn't think Fluffo Lake ever gets any sun during the winter since it's located in a valley right in the center of mountains and high hills. We traveled all around Fluffo with the skidoo. Gordon walked ahead, frequently checking the ice with his axe, while I followed with the machine. Ice was good and only a couple of places had a bit of overflow.

Tonight after supper, I baked two pies. Afterwards I washed ten marten pelts and put them on stretchers while Gordon skinned out several more.

Tuesday – Nov. 22nd -20C   We had a beautiful night. Clear sky with a full moon – so bright.

We went up the Lake/Twin Lakes way this morning. It was such a nice day for the trip. Gordon mentioned that he though it was one of the nicest days we've had for a long time. Blue skies and the sun felt so warm. We skidoo'd down our Twin Lakes Run as far as the point we'd reached last time. Picked up two marten on Lake Run section and three more on Twin Run. We left the skidoo and snowshoed down the last short section that needed clearing. On the way we picked up another three marten. Pretty good catch today – eight marten in all. When the last section of trail is cleared, Twin Lakes Run will be connected to Lynx Creek Run. We've sure done a lot of snowshoeing, trying to join the two runs but it'll be worth it. We'll be able to travel by skidoo from Ridge Lake via Twin Lakes Run to Lynx Creek and onwards to Rose Lake and then back to Ridge Lake via the Coal River and Ridge Lake Run – one big loop. Will save a lot of time. No more doubling back on our trails. For the next hour or so, Gordon and I worked on the trail. It went through a rather rough section where quite a number of trees had to be cleared out of the way. Thankfully, we'd brought the chainsaw along. Finally, the last bit of brush was thrown out of the way and the trail was finished – all connected. We're already looking forward to our next trip down this way when we'll go all the way to Rose Lake. There were an unbelievable number of marten tracks all along the way, just everywhere.

After setting a few traps, we turned and headed back to Ridge Lake for tea and lunch. Right afterwards Gordon got busy skinning marten. We'd gotten a little behind with the skinning and stretching. After supper I washed and placed another nine pelts on stretchers. The skins are first placed on stretcher boards with the fur facing inwards. After the leather side is fairly dry they're removed from the stretchers. The pelt is then turned so that the fur side faces outwards. They're then put back on the stretcher where they remain for several days until thoroughly dry. After they're removed from the stretcher, they're lightly brushed and then hung in a cool, dry storage location. We should have started skinning and stretching marten sooner. They've really piled up on us. We'll do a bunch tomorrow but I won't wash any more for a day or two until we have stretchers available.

Wednesday – Nov. 23rd   -9C   Snowing lightly this morning and a slight wind. What a change from yesterday and especially from the night!! I got up during the night and honestly think the full moon made it the brightest night I've seen. You could have taken a picture without a flash or read a book. It was just so beautiful out.

We had planned on taking yesterday off. We're lucky we didn't since it's not nice out today. Visibility is poor so we wouldn't be able to see any fresh sign anyway. We're taking today off and relaxing a bit. Just do the odd little chore. I'll work on furs. Gordon has been working too hard. I got up and made the fire this morning and then put the coffee on just so he could sleep in for a change.

It snowed off and on all day. A day off – what a laugh!! I worked on furs from about ten-thirty this morning until ten this evening. My poor aching back!! We've revamped our fur handling a bit. Gordon skins a number of marten and then we wash the pelts with shampoo, both inside and out. Then I rinse them twice in warm water and next, blot some of the water from the fur before placing them on stretchers They're then hung in the cabin overnight, fur side out, and by morning are just dried enough for brushing. Next, they're removed from the stretchers, turned inside out with the fur to the inside and then replaced on stretchers to dry for the next one to two hours. Then they're again removed from the stretchers, turned so the fur is to the outside and replaced on stretchers. I use from forty to forty-five thumb tacks for each marten. It takes me from seven to ten minutes to stretch and tack each pelt. By the time I have eight or ten done, the first ones are ready to be turned. The last stage of stretching and pinning takes about twelve to fifteen minutes per marten. I completed the final work on seventeen marten tonight. It will now be several days before they're dry enough to be removed from the stretchers, brushed and stored. I also washed another eight skins tonight. They'll be put on stretchers tomorrow. It's a lot of work!! I use Silkience shampoo in the wash water but for the second rinse, add a little bit of Downey softener. Makes them smell so nice!!

In past years, we'd just freeze the raw skins and then take them to Watson Lake with us at the end of the season. We could then use the electric washing machine and dryer at home, making the job a lot easier and faster. Since we don't know when we'll be going home this year, I decided I'd better get at them. If we do stay for a long spell, the Yukon Game Branch will have an aircraft fly in and collect our furs around mid-December. They'll then ship them to the fur sale of our choice, usually the Hudson's Bay sale on February 17 – 23rd. The furs have to be in Edmonton by January 7th to be in time for the sale.

I didn't have much of a relaxing day off. Actually, it's much easier on the trail. Gordon did up odd chores, hauled wood, boiled up traps, cleaned up the porch and then skinned out six marten. I helped flesh out two of them. So we're both tired tonight. Oh well, they have to be done and now we'll have more time to relax when we return home. This evening I had a long chat with Mabel Robson, via radio.

Thursday – Nov. 24th -15C   Light snow coming down when we looked out this morning. We're again taking a day off from the trail.

Gordon did hitch up Rebel to the small toboggan and went to Swan Lake. He's going to put out a couple of wolverine sets over there. There have been so many signs of wolverine around this year and since they can be so destructive, Gordon hopes to catch a couple. They've been following our trails and un-doubtedly will begin taking our catches before long. They could be very hard on our marten. Smokey is not happy at being left behind. I'm doing up the eight marten I washed yesterday. It's certainly very time consuming, the way we do our pelts, but it sure pays off. We have averaged anywhere from fifteen to thirty dollars more per pelt than most trappers. Gordon also takes extra pains in skin-ning. When skinning, most trappers cut the feet of the pelt off. Gordon skins them out right to the pads so we lose no fur at all. Very few trappers wash their furs – just skin them and then put them on stretchers, skin side out to partially dry before reversing them to finish drying. Sure easier and a lot less work but ours sure smell nice with all the dirt washed out. Gives us a lot of pride in our work and because of the extra care, the finished product looks beautiful.

Gordon got back at two o'clock. He set out three traps for wolverine. He found three marten in our traps on the section of Swan Run between here and the lake. Really terrific!! He also got us four chickens – grouse. They'll be such a nice change from moose meat. We had pizza for supper tonight, sure good.

Friday – Nov. 25th -16C   Overcast this morning. We plan on going to Rose Lake today and work the lines across the river. We still haven't opened Ridge, Wolf and Canyon Runs. Told Gordon I didn't want many days off – we work harder then than during other days.

After breakfast and a later coffee break, we left for Rose Lake. Everything went well. We had the skimmer full of supplies and groceries. The dogs were even behaving themselves. Rebel always seems to want to be up front so today, even though Smokey is the lead dog, I had Gordon put Rebel in the lead. That lasted for about ten feet. Smokey would not follow behind – he wanted the lead position so Gordon had to switch them again. We picked up one marten on the old River Run (from Ridge L. to the river) but also found one trap was set off and the bait stolen. From the droppings, it was evident that mice must have been in the box, stole the bait and sprung the trap. Also discovered that bait was missing in two other sets. By the time we reached the river, the sky had pretty well cleared up and it had turned into a gorgeous day. After crossing the river, we followed along our trail through the sloughs and meadows to Rose Lake, picking up two more marten on the way.

When we reached Rose Lake cabin, we found everything was fine – just the way we'd left it. We unpacked the skimmer and then had lunch. Afterwards, we skidooed to Rose Lake to check traps over there. We ran into quite a bit of overflow so Gordon had to drive the skidoo along the grassy banks around the lake for most of the way. We picked up three more marten. Also found one trap had been set off. Gordon figures a bird may have set it of since it was a ground set. We had expected to find a couple more marten today but guess we can't complain about our total of six. Gordon has his sights set on seventy-five marten by the end of the month. I think we'll do it since we now have seventy-one marten and two mink, a total of seventy-three furs. Lots of tracks around this year. We still haven't decided when we'll close down our line for this season.

After supper was over I washed eight marten pelts and put them on stretchers. Will finish them up tomorrow. Gordon has the night off from skinning since the marten we picked up today are still frozen. It's getting cold this evening. By nine-thirty the temperature was already down to minus thirty. Sky is clear. Its beautiful out with a full moon, lots of stars and the northern lights dancing across the sky.

Saturday – Nov. 26th -25C   A nice night at the start but later the sky started clouding over and the temperature warmed up a bit. We were hoping for a clear, sunny day but no such luck.

This morning after breakfast we headed up our old Ridge Run trail that goes to Jamie Lake. We planned on finishing clearing the trail through the last two stretches of timber connecting the meadows. On our last trip we'd set out four traps on the section of trail we'd cleared. The first trap held nothing. When the second trap came into view it was evident that we'd caught something. When we reached the set, we were dismayed to find that only about a third of a large mink remained. From the tracks in the snow around the set, it was evident that a marten had enjoyed a free meal. We reset the trap, placing the remains of the mink in the cubby for bait. The marten will very likely be back and next time, hopefully, we'll find him there. We did catch another marten in one of the last sets we had out so actually did quite well.

After checking the last trap, we continued on cutting trail through the neck of timber that connected two small ponds. When that was completed, we went onwards to the next stretch of timber and started clearing trail through it. There was a shallow, swampy creek wandering through this section. It was snow covered. Gordon figured the ice beneath the snow would be quite thick, plenty safe to walk on or run the skidoo over. Within minutes he discovered he'd made a slight miscalculation. First, his left foot broke through the thin ice. He jumped out of that only to put his right foot into another weak spot and ended up standing in water up to his knees. He was in and out so fast. At minus twenty-five, the water froze almost immediately and didn't have a chance to penetrate very far. His feet were still dry so we finished clearing our trail through that patch of timber. We then skidoo'd onwards through a series of small ponds that connected up with our old trail. Gordon made one trap set at the junction before continuing onwards – for about two hundred yards. We'd just started to cross another smaller pond when Gordon pointed to the left towards a small open meadow, saying "I think we're missing the boat by not going that way since it would cut off some of our rough area". Then – "Oh My Gawd, We're in Overflow". We were in about a foot of watery slush, topped with about a foot of snow. We were **STUCK**!!

We unhooked the skimmer but still couldn't move. The undercarriage and track of the skidoo were packed tight with slush. Anyway, we spent the next hour chopping down small spruce trees and laying them in the slush, then lifting the thousand pound skidoo onto them. (It normally weighs three hundred and sixty pounds but with all that ice, water and wet snow it was sure a lot more). After we got the skidoo up on the brush, it had to be tipped on it's side so we could knock and rake all the half frozen ice from around the track before we could try to get it running again. Slush freezes almost instantly in the open air at minus twenty-five so speed was essential. We finally got the skidoo running, turned it around and with wet mukluks and mitts, headed for home.

After hot soup and tea, everything looked pretty rosy but it just showed us again that it's not smart to take anything for granted in the bush. If our episode with the overflow had happened ten miles from the cabin or out on a large lake, it certainly would have been more serious. Gordon nearly always goes ahead of the skidoo on rivers and lakes checking the ice but the pothole we got stuck in today was such a small pond, no more than seventy-five feet across. After this, even these will be checked. When we'd looked back on our way home, it was funny to see the tracks we'd left with our sodden, frozen mukluks. Since they were covered with frozen snow and ice, the tracks we left were immense. Made you think this had to be the home of "Bigfoot".

Later after supper – about seven, we were sitting back relaxed, watching the moon rising across the river to the northeast. It was spectacular, watching as it slowly climbed above the snow covered spruce. First just a sliver of yellow/ orange appeared, then a bit more until, within ten minutes, the full round moon was in view – flooding the valley with light – shadows on the snow and a million frozen, sparkling diamonds reflecting its beams. Truly beautiful. Later tonight Gordon was busy skinning marten while I put the ones I'd washed yesterday on stretchers.

Sunday – Nov. 27th -23C   Overcast this morning. Temperature was down to minus thirty-seven at bedtime. It was gorgeous during the early night, clear and so bright out. From this cabin, the way it's situated – the big window looks out onto the river. From our bed we can look through the window and watch the northern lights dancing across the sky. They outdid themselves last night.

We had planned on going across and up the river to Lynx/Twin Runs but the ice across from the cabin looks black – indicating overflow. Gordon is out checking it now. His knee has been very sore since yesterday so he wants to take things a bit easier today. Bit of arthritis, possibly. Gordon just returned and reported that the ice is OK where we cross the river. Anyway, we changed our minds and decided to go back over yesterdays trail and hopefully hook up to the old Ridge trail from Jamie Lake. I walked all the way to the sloughs and potholes. Gordon dragged a small green spruce, with lots of branches, behind the skidoo and skimmer, grooming the rough sections of the trail. The spruce drag does a really good job of pulling snow into dips and hollows in the trail while also slicing off the high points. We went past all the sloughs and then onwards to the pothole where we'd got stuck in overflow yesterday. That area was completely frozen over!! Gordon walked around the little slough checking it and said that if we'd gone around the edge of it yesterday we wouldn't have had any problems. But how did we know?? Anyway, he picked up a trap that had been left from previous years and reset it at the base of a spruce near the beginning of the slough. We then snowshoed the route he'd pointed out yesterday. With very little effort we managed to clear a good trail that avoids most of the other sloughs. When we reached the old trail, I snowshoed ahead and broke trail while Gordon followed behind with the skidoo and set traps.

The snow was quite deep and so it was tough going for the skidoo over the unbroken trail. We followed our old trail along the Ridge until we reached our

"Chocolate Bar" tree. It's a good sized pine with spreading branches that's right on top a ridge overlooking a small lake. Because of its spreading branches, the layer of pine needles around its base is always clear of snow. The perfect spot for lunch. We built a fire and while I was getting tea ready, Gordon broke trail a short ways further. I had bannock sandwiches in my pack from awhile back. They'd always been kept outside, frozen. Gordon said they'd be fine even though they'd been made a couple of weeks earlier. Anyhow, as I was placing them in the sandwich toaster that I always carry, I noticed mold spots on them. Darn It!! There went our lunch!! I threw them out for the birds to feed on. It was so disappointing and I was hungry!! We couldn't believe it!! I guess that during the several times I'd carried them on my back, they'd thawed and spoiled. We won't do that again. Today was also the first time we'd stopped for tea in a long time. We had to settle for tea, cookies and a chocolate bar. It was still nice though, taking a break and relaxing.

After lunch I was back snowshoeing up the trail while Gordon followed behind with the skidoo – putting out trap sets. We found that quite a few trees had fallen across the trail. Since we'd only expected to find the occasional one, the chainsaw had been left at home. It took a bit longer and a lot more effort for Gordon to clear them away with his axe. We followed the trail until we reached the point where it drops down a steep hill for a couple of hundred yards. We left the skidoo at the top. While Gordon set traps I snowshoed up and down the hill, packing it so it would be OK for the skidoo when we came back on our next trip. I snowshoed it three times and Gordon did it once (he was busy trap setting) so it's pretty well packed and shouldn't give us any trouble once the snow sets. The hill is only about a mile and a half from Jamie Lake. It would have been nice to break a trail all the way to the cabin but it'll have to wait for another day. It was getting late and we were both getting tired.

We noticed a lot of fresh animal sign that had to have been made within the last day or two. Fresh tracks just about everywhere so should catch a few marten on this line. The marten are still running around out here. Some trappers have reported that they've stopped moving on their traplines. Gordon managed to put out fifteen sets today. It'll be interesting checking this line in a few days time to see if the marten actually are still moving around out here. Finally, we turned the skidoo, I climbed in the skimmer and we headed for home. I was just about beat and ready to call it a day.

After supper Gordon skinned and placed another five marten on stretchers while I fleshed four for him. They are a lot of work. After that it was time for bed.

Monday – Nov. 28ᵗʰ -20C   Nearly clear out. Just a bit of scattered cloud.

After breakfast we skidooed up to our Lynx Run, crossing the river three times without running into overflow. After we left the river at Lynx creek, we followed our trail through timber, meadows, sloughs and ponds for several miles. Gordon walked ahead of the skidoo, checking for overflow whenever we came to a slough or pond. Sure don't want a repeat performance of the fun we had two days before. There was a bit of seepage over the ice in a couple of sloughs but not enough to bother the skidoo until we came down a hill and through the timber to the last pond. Sure enough, right where our packed trail crossed the pond there was a big open hole with lots of overflow spreading into the surrounding snow. Time for snowshoes again, breaking a new trail around the pond. It was a pretty open area so it wasn't long before we were back on track and heading down the trail. Up to this point we'd picked up six marten. A nice catch!!

When we were crossing through the last section of timber leading to the creek, Gordon somehow missed the trail we'd cleared the other day. It was the first time we'd used that section of trail since we'd cleared it and it wasn't well blazed. Anyway, we managed to get the skidoo turned around and back on the trail to the meadows that lead to Twin Lakes. Everything was great. Lots of new snow on the trail but not enough to bother the skidoo. We traveled to the end of the meadow, Gordon setting out four more traps along the way. We left the skidoo there and snowshoed further along, Gordon with the chainsaw clearing the occasional patch of brush along the way. It only took us half an hour to complete the clearing of the last section of trail. At last the trail from Ridge to Twin to Rose was officially, completely finished!! No more short brushy sections to plow through along this trail. It will be wonderful!!

A few minutes later after eating a chocolate bar – our lunch, Gordon started the skidoo and with me in the skimmer, headed back for our cabin at Rose Lake. We'd been out checking traps and clearing trail along this line for a good six hours. Gordon's tired so we're planning on taking a day off tomorrow. He wants to do something different for a change. But knowing him, he'll probably work harder than he would on the trail.

Tuesday – Nov. 29ᵗʰ -18C   We had expected it to be cold this morning and were pleasantly surprised to find it had warmed up. Also, very fine snow is falling.

We slept in, something different, then I got up and looked after the fire. The fire usually burns slowly all night and by morning isn't putting out much heat so the cabin cools down. I soon had a rip-roaring fire warming the cabin, coffee was on and wash water was heating for the "Lord and Master". How to spoil the Senior Partner!! It's a day off for him so I thought I'd do it up right.

By eleven the temperature had warmed to minus sixteen and much heavier snow was falling. Gordon climbed up in the cache and brought down an assortment of groceries I needed. I especially wanted the canned mushrooms that we'd ordered last winter. Turned out they'd sent mushroom soup instead. I'm making a big pot of clam chowder for Gordon. Figured he deserved it on his day off. Right now he's out on the river, about a mile or two away, checking the ice condition. He's planning on packing a runway just in case the Game Department flies in. It'll also be ready for us when we decide to return to Watson Lake. We need a landing/take-off strip that's at least two thousand feet in length and also has a turn-around area for the aircraft. We'll also need to pack about a twelve hundred foot taxi strip from the runway to just below the cabin. From there, our supplies will be relayed by toboggan to the cache where they'll be stored. Also, a forty-five gallon barrel of gas is coming in on the aircraft. It'll have to be rolled up and stored near the cabin. The runway is located about a half mile from the cabin along a straight stretch of the river.

About two-thirty, after we'd had lunch and relaxed for awhile, Gordon decided to take the skidoo and start packing runway. While he was doing that, I hitched Smokey to the toboggan and headed out to check our line on Rose Lake. It had been four days since we'd last checked it. Rebel was not happy at being left behind and voiced his displeasure with continuous howling. When I left, it was snowing heavily.

I found a marten in the first trap we'd set on the lake but left it and went on to check the rest of the sets. I'll reset that trap on my way back. Smokey was very good, really obedient. At the second to last set, I picked up another marten but found that half of it had been eaten by another marten. Marten are very cannibalistic!! So very disappointing. Wished we'd never caught him to begin with. That marten must have had about a hundred dollar meal!! I reset the trap and started back but had only gone a few feet before I broke through the top layer of ice on the lake and was into overflow. Thankfully it wasn't too deep. I ran out of it and didn't get too wet. We then crossed to the other side of the lake to check the last trap. First though, I tied Smokey to a small spruce but forgot to first shake the snow from the tree. Naturally, when I bent down to tie the dog, I jiggled the tree I was tying him to and the load of snow on the spruce tumbled down my neck. Oh well!! Next, while I was getting a trap and bait ready before I checked the last trap, I suddenly realized that when I'd reset the trap, where the marten was eaten, I'd forgotten to wire the trap to the drag. I started back to fix that oversight and then realized I had all that overflow to run through again. So instead, I plowed through the deep snow around the lakeshore – through snow that was over my knees. I should have gone back to the toboggan and got my snowshoes. Anyway, I managed and got everything squared away before I returned to the set where I'd found the first marten. I was just resetting that trap when Gordon appeared on the scene. He took over and finished setting the trap for me.

Just before he arrived, I'd been thinking that a person in an unmarked area like this could easily get confused. It had been snowing heavily and the visibility was just about zero while I was checking traps. Gordon had been worried about me. Said it took me so long. It had only been about an hour and a half but seemed much longer. Guess he cares!! He said he'd only made five passes on the river. The snow was so heavy. He couldn't see much and then, because of the depth of the snow, snow began getting into the engine so it started missing. Anyway, he decided to shut runway packing down for today and came looking for me.

Had a call from Don Taylor tonight to let us know that our son Jamie wants to talk with us. He's arranged to patch us in to Jamie's phone call, sometime tomorrow morning. Sure has me wondering what's up?? Still snowing heavily at bedtime. Will be a lot of snow by morning. We'll have to break out a lot of trail again.

Wednesday – Nov. 30th +1C   What a change in weather!! We've received more than eight inches of snow since yesterday – heavy, wet stuff. This morning it's raining lightly. We have two feet of snow on the ground but with the warm temperature and rain, should settle down somewhat.

It's not a day for the skidoo, snow's so wet and heavy. Just a bit of a breeze. It would be very wet out on the trail, especially in the bush with the trees just a-dripping. We'd be soaked in minutes. So a day off is imposed on us. No trapline checking today!! Just noticed a big patch of overflow on the river out front. We did decide, about eleven-thirty, to try packing the section of trail to Ridge Lake that goes through the meadows and then to the river. We especially wanted to pack the section that crosses the river, just in case there was overflow. We found it tough snowshoeing in the heavy snow. Gordon broke trail all the way, about three miles. There was no overflow on the river for which we were really thankful. We were pretty pleased when we finally reached the river and had that section of trail broken out for the skidoo. If it's not too warm tomorrow, the snow shouldn't be so sticky and we'll likely head back to Ridge Lake.

We snowshoed for just about three hours and had about a six mile jaunt. My poor back was so tired and sore by the time we returned to the cabin. The snow really stuck to Gordon's snowshoes while he was breaking trail. He was forever stopping and knocking the snow off them. The webbing in my snowshoes got really wet and then stretched. We brought them in the cabin so the webbing would dry and shrink back into place. After they dry, a bit of repair work will have to be done on them. Guess Gordon didn't have enough exercise. After we returned he snowshoed a trail up river, about a mile. He's now using the new trail, hauling firewood with the skidoo. The trail follows along a sandbar for about half the distance while the rest is along the river. We have a skidder affair, made from the skis of an old snow machine, to haul logs on. Works really well, easy to pull.

I'm making a pot of stew for supper. My carrots and potatoes that we'd stored here had frozen awhile ago so I'm using them in the stew. I've never used frozen vegetables like these but know people who have and found them to be quite Okay. Right now at five o'clock, it's already getting dark. The temperature is plus one, it's quite windy and freezing rain is falling. Not Nice!!

Thursday – Dec. 1ˢᵗ -12C   What a change in weather!! Another beautiful morning, the sky is clear and the sun is shining. The mountains are spectacular, all white against the blue sky. Makes a person want to put on ski's and go up there.

By eleven forty-five we were packed up and ready to leave for Ridge Lake. The trail we'd broken out with snowshoes the day before had partially drifted over. The fresh snow, whipped up by the wind, had filled in quite a bit of the trail, especially through the open meadow sections. It was pretty tough going. Gordon ran off the trail a few times. It was quite a job getting the machine back up on the packed trail again. Even so, I was able to ride on the skimmer for most of the way to the river. While on the trail, crossing through a series of small meadows, we came to one meadow – only about fifty yards across, that had overflow around one side of it. The overflow looked to be frozen and our trail through the center of the meadow looked solid so Gordon opened the throttle on the skidoo and charged ahead. Sure enough, about two thirds of the way across, the skidoo broke through into a foot of overflow. He had to unhook the skimmer and then manhandle the skidoo onto a snowbank so he could clear the track of slush. Once it was going again, he snowshoed back and pulled the loaded skimmer across bodily, hand over hand. When we looked down through the hole in the ice, it appeared to be hollow underneath but lower down there was real deep water. We were lucky that both the skidoo and the skimmer hadn't completely broken through. It would have been a real tough job getting them out of there. The rest of the way to the river was fine. Also, the trail across the river was only a bit drifted. A real surprise!!

Once we crossed the river, we were back on unbroken trail. I snowshoed, breaking trail a good half of the way up to Ridge Lake. Gordon had a bit of a job coming along with the skidoo. Part of the trail is along the sloping side of a hill. Naturally, the skidoo and skimmer insisted on sliding off to the lower side – into deep snow. But we made it even though it did take us a lot longer than usual, about double the time it usually takes. Thankfully, it was a beautiful, sunny day.

After reaching our Ridge Lake cabin we got the fire going and had lunch. Afterwards, Gordon took his axe and snowshoed down the length of the lake. He wanted to find out how thick the ice was. After chopping holes in several locations, he found the lake has about an eight inch layer of ice over most of it. On top of that there's a sixteen inch blanket of snow. If he has time, he'll start packing a runway on it tomorrow. Jamie would like to fly out here. Evidently he has some papers he'd like his father's advice on. Gordon may not be able to complete the runway tomorrow. It will take several hours with the skidoo to pack it properly.

I did some baking after lunch. Made a delicious lemon pie to go with cabbage rolls for our supper tonight. Also baked an apple pie to have ready for our next trip to Rose Lake. This evening we finished work on a few more furs. Took seven marten off the stretchers and brushed them out, all ready to be stored away. The finished furs look so beautiful. I had thirty-three marten on stretchers but only seven were totally dry. Will have to wait a few more days before taking the others off.

Friday – Dec. 2ⁿᵈ -17C   Looks like a gorgeous day – clear skies.

Gordon spent all morning, actually up to two o'clock, packing a runway on the lake. There was a bit of overflow around the holes he'd chopped yesterday when he was measuring the ice thickness.. It was a nice sunny day. Just great for skidooing back and forth, packing runway. Tomorrow, he'll place small spruce markers along the edges of the strip. A good job done. Weather permitting, Jamie will be flying in soon. While Gordon was out on the lake, I did up a big batch of laundry. Also prepared a large pot of soup. Will freeze a good part of it for use at later dates.

After a late lunch we skidooed up our Swan Run. When we got to the Beaver Pond, Gordon got off the skidoo and walked ahead. Of course there was overflow so he had to put on snowshoes and pack a trail around it. We had no problems with the heavy snow on the trail, a real surprise. When we reached Swan Lake he wasn't taking chances and walked the trail ahead of the skidoo, just in case there was overflow. Sure enough, more overflow. He had to reroute the trail around it also. While he was ahead on snowshoes packing the new trail, I was supposed to follow with the skidoo. Of course I had problems!! I'm not that used to running the skidoo (I'd rather not run them, if I had a choice) and maneuvering it in that depth of heavy snow. It was a real challenge!! I finally got the hang of it and managed to balance the machine on the new trail Gordon was breaking out ahead of me. Further on we did pick up two marten in sets at Swan Lake. We then snowshoed a short ways up the Crisco Run. Just after we leave Swan Lake, there's a pretty steep ridge that has to be climbed to reach the plateau above. Gordon decided that trail should be broken out with snowshoes before trying it with the skidoo. We snowshoed up to the plateau and a short ways further onwards before turning back to the skidoo. The trail up the ridge should set up and freeze overnight so it'll be climbable with the skidoo when we come back in a day or so.

On the way back home Gordon spotted a bunch of grouse. He stopped and started shooting at them with his twenty-two rifle. It was getting dusky and the birds were sitting in a big spruce, hard to see. He actually only saw one at first but when he shot, the tree seemed to explode with flying grouse. Birds were flying all over It was rather comical. One minute everything was quiet but the next, beating wings filled the air. We started looking for them without first putting on our snowshoes. The snow was way above our knees so we didn't go far. Even so, we did manage to get two grouse before giving up. They'll be a nice change from moose.

After dinner we worked on furs. Gordon skinned another two marten while I washed and placed eleven pelts on stretchers to dry, fur side out. After that we removed four marten from stretchers, brushed and then stored them away. Nice.

Saturday – Dec. 3rd -22C   Clear out. We're just waiting to hear from Watson Lake Flying to find out if Jamie is coming out today. Signals are very poor and by nine-thirty were non-existent.

We had breakfast and finished up a few chores around the cabin, undecided about going out on the trail today. We decided not to go. A good choice since the Cessna aircraft flew in with Jamie, just after twelve. We'd begun to wonder if they were coming since the weather had started to move in again. It was good to see Jamie. It had been late August when we'd last seen him. He brought out quite a few supplies for us. Included was a gallon of ice cream, really welcome!! Guess we'll have to stay another month or two in order to use all the fresh stuff he brought in – four dozen fresh eggs, three pounds of bacon plus a big chicken. All kinds of chocolate bars plus two dozen soft drinks, milk, oranges, apples bananas, cantaloupe, tomatoes, celery, carrots, cauliflower, cabbage, lettuce, onions, green peppers, sausages and more. We're going to be busy – just eating!!

He and Gordon discussed Jamie's business questions during the next hour. Weather had worsened by then. The pilot, Stan, thought they'd better start back especially since the forecast had mentioned the possibility of freezing rain in the Watson Lake area. A few minutes later the Cessna was airborne on its way back to Watson Lake.

By the time the plane left at three o'clock, the sky was completely overcast and temperature was minus fourteen. It was too late for us to go out on the trail so Gordon checked and closed down the three traps we'd set in the meadow behind the cabin. He brought in one marten, caught in the last set. While he was out, I worked on furs. I'd just finished turning eleven pelts, leather side out for drying, when he returned. Shortly, I'll be doing the final turning. They're then replaced on stretchers to finish drying, fur side out. Then about a week later, when they're completely dry, they're brushed and stored. While Stan was here, he'd mentioned that our runway was great. He'd suggested to Gordon that it would be even better if about half a dozen of the tallest spruce, growing on the approach path to the runway, were removed. So right now Gordon's at the far end of the lake cutting them down. Stan mentioned that if they were removed it would increase his landing approach by at least half a mile – especially beneficial when visibility was not so good.

Jamie had never been to Ridge Lake before. He sure though it was beautiful here. Just couldn't get over it. Bet he wishes he could stay. After he'd gone, I felt really homesick for a short while.

Sunday – Dec. 4th -6C   Snowed very lightly overnight but the sky is clear this morning and a warm wind is blowing.

After breakfast Gordon brought several boxes of groceries down from the cache and put them in the porch. After our furs are completely dry and brushed, we need a safe, dry place to store them in. The cache is ideal so the groceries were moved down and the furs were moved up. After that was done we skidooed up Swan Run and onwards to our Wolf Run. There was so much snow!! Really tough going. Gordon, riding the skidoo, was sinking a foot or more down into the soft snow. The bumper and hood of the skidoo were pushing snow like a caterpillar tractor. I did a lot of snowshoeing, breaking trail in some areas and just following the skidoo where conditions were a bit better.

Thankfully, it was a beautiful, sunny day. We did pick up nine marten on Wolf Run. One marten had been damaged by mice. The damaged marten was hanging down from the trap box where it normally would have been safe from mice. But there was the stub of a branch sticking out just far enough to touch the animal. The mice must have climbed up the tree and then out on the stub and dined on the marten. Looked like they'd also chewed patches of fur from the animal to take home and keep warm in. Little Devils!! It was very disappointing finding the animal damaged, especially since it was a large, dark marten. Further on, we noticed otter tracks where the animals had followed and slid along the creek. Just a short ways further was our last marten trap. It had been sprung and the bait was gone. Weasel tracks were all around so Gordon thinks a weasel was responsible.

After checking and re-baiting the last trap we made a big loop through the deep snow in order to turn the skidoo. Finally, I was able to take my snowshoes off and climb into the skimmer for the ride home. The trip back was quite enjoyable. Because of all the new snow freshly packed on our trail, the bumps along it had been smoothed out.

In the evening after supper was finished and the dishes put away, I washed and placed eighteen more marten on stretchers. Gordon skinned another three and then brushed out seven pelts, all ready for hanging in the cache.

Monday – Dec. 5ᵗʰ -13C   When Gordon first got up this morning he reported the sky was clear but by nine-thirty had started clouding over. Also there's a bit of a breeze blowing now.

Right after breakfast we took off up Swan Run, heading for our trail to Crisco Lake. The trail to Swan was excellent since we'd been over it the day before. We were a bit concerned about Crisco, especially the section of trail we hadn't been over for several days. The skidoo climbed the Crisco trail to the top of the ridge without any problem for which we were thankful. The rest of the trail was, surprisingly, very good.. I rode nearly all the way to the creek that flowed through the valley. It appeared that a lot less snow had fallen up this valley than had dropped on Ridge and Wolf Runs.

The sky cleared up nicely so we had another beautiful, sunny day even though there was quite a cold wind blowing. Our trails had been completely covered over by the last snowfalls and in the valley, were also completely drifted over in the open areas. About a mile down the valley, as I was peacefully riding along in the skimmer, I got quite a surprise when Gordon suddenly exclaimed, "I forgot the bloody tarp". At first I couldn't figure out what he was talking about. I though he'd forgotten the skidoo cover which we usually carry. Then I realized what he was talking about!! Just a few yards ahead, we had a wolf in one of our snares!! He hadn't been caught very long before we arrived since he wasn't completely frozen. Looked as if, following along our trail, he'd walked right into the snare and then made one lunge and collapsed. The only snares that are allowed in the Yukon are the ones equipped with a locking device. When they're pulled tight, they don't release. The animal blanks out within a very short time from lack of oxygen. A very humane snare compared to those used in the past. We were sure pleased with our catch, me especially. Gordon wasn't that exuberant since he's the one that has to skin it. Normally, hauling a wolf back to your cabin is pretty simple. Gordon would simply wrap a tarp around the animal then tie it to the skimmer and skid it home. We temporarily left the wolf and continued up the trail.

A short ways further on we noticed fresh moose tracks, just made this morning. The moose now have one less wolf to worry about. They sure must have a hard time moving around in this snow since it reaches more than half-way up their shoulders. When we reached the creek, we found the water had dropped and consequently the ice had also dropped and our packed trail with it. So, on with the snowshoes and more trail breaking, packing a new trail to meet with the old one further downstream. After joining up with the old trail, Gordon went back and brought up the skidoo. While he was away retrieving the machine, I continued snowshoeing – trying to find signs of our old trail. We didn't have this area blazed. The old trail had been completely obliterated by the new snow. However, I did manage to snowshoe out a trail all the way to Fluffo Lake. After Gordon and the skidoo caught up to me, I rode on the skimmer all the way to the far end of the lake to check our last trap. Travel on the lake wasn't bad since the snow had drifted quite a lot and was packed. After checking the last set, we'd planned on crossing the lake and then following down the far shoreline. Thankfully, Gordon thought he'd check the ice first. Sure enough – he found the top layer of ice was only about an inch and a half thick. Underneath it was at least ten inches of water covering the original solid ice. No place for a skidoo!!

We left the skidoo took our snowshoes and hiked across the lake checking ice along the way. Noticed where an otter had been playing, going in and out of holes he'd poked through the top ice and further on, where he'd been sliding over snowdrifts. Trails all over. Looked as though he'd really had fun!! Overflow was everywhere so we finally turned around and headed back to the skidoo. We turned it around and headed back. When we reached the wolf, we had a bit of a problem trying to figure out how we'd tie him on the skimmer. His frozen legs jutted out and had to be positioned so they wouldn't bump into trees and get broken. Eventually we got it figured out and headed back down the trail for home. On the way back, Gordon reset some of the snares that had been covered by the last snowfall. We did not catch a single marten today. Gordon thinks they're probably up along the higher ridges. We'll have to find a trail up to the high country if we want to find out whether he's right. Some of the areas that look promising are really high. Getting a trail to them will be a real challenge. All in all, we did have a good day.

Tuesday – Dec. 6th -32C   Cold out but clear. We sure notice the shorter daylight hours.

After this morning's breakfast of omelets with bacon and toast, we decided to work some of it off by breaking trail up towards the Lake/Twin Runs. We'll go as far as we comfortably can, making sure we'll be back before dark. We started out at ten-thirty. It was pretty tough going for the skidoo since it had to break trail through more than a foot of snow while I was riding behind on the skimmer. Anyway, after getting bogged down a couple of times, I ended up snowshoeing a lot of the way. Even though snowshoeing through the deep snow was pretty tough, I was enjoying it. Everything, from the largest, tallest spruce with tops high above to the clumps of buckbrush and willow huddled below, was covered with a thick blanket of pure, white snow – all glistening in the sunshine. It seemed the further we went, the more beautiful the scenery became. The sun was shining and the mountains looked gorgeous. Words can't begin to describe the beauty!!

Along the first ridge we picked up a marten. When we started up the second ridge, where Gordon had made a set for wolverine, we picked up another one. Further along at the end of that ridge, we found another marten in that trap. Our original intention had been to just break out the trail as far as Twin Lakes creek. But after we'd caught our fourth marten in a trap set just before the creek, we agreed to continue onwards. The going was now a bit easier. There didn't seem to be as much fresh snow on the trail out here as there was back at Ridge Lake.

It was a bit cool with a light breeze but was still so very nice out. Scenery was getting more spectacular all the time as the trail climbed higher. Before we knew it, we were on top of the plateau. We crossed all the open meadows, lots and lots of snow – most of it freshly fallen but more had drifted in. We then started down the trail on the other side, reaching the campsite Robbie and Bob had used last fall when clearing trail.

We left the skidoo there and continued down the trail on snowshoes. I broke a lot of the trail, my decision, while Gordon set traps. On the last section where the trail went down the slope and through the trees, we should have had more traps to set out. There were so many fresh marten tracks, just everywhere!! We were still very pleased with today's catch of nine marten. After yesterday when we hadn't found any in our sets down in the valley leading to Fluffo/Crisco Lakes, today was a pleasant surprise. After finding nine marten in the trap sets that were at higher elevations, Gordon is more convinced than ever that marten move higher when temperatures drop and the snow gets deeper.

It had been a great day, sunny and no problems with the skidoo. We got back to the cabin just before four. It was already getting dusky. Days are sure getting shorter!! Hot tea was really welcomed. Tonight, we're celebrating!! Earlier, we had decided that when we reached the hundredth marten, we'd have a bottle of wine. So tonight it's spaghetti, garlic toast and wine. We now have a hundred and four marten!!

Later, stretched out on the bunk totally relaxed, events of the day drifted through my mind. I remembered the large patch of grouse feathers I'd spotted alongside the trail. Mother Nature's notepaper, in the form of unbroken snow, revealed that an owl – hunting for dinner was responsible for the grouse's untimely end. We also saw fresh moose tracks towards the end of the trail. It's sure nice to find you have neighbors. The moose have a tough time with deep snow at this time of year. Usually they're up in higher country where there's less snow and it's easier getting around. It never ceases to surprise me, finding how bountiful Nature can be. Ridges and valleys that appear devoid of life are often teeming with wildlife as shown by the different tracks in the snow. Also, if you stop and listen, the sound of birds can be heard – a woodpecker pecking on a dead snag as he hunts for his lunch or perhaps the scolding of a Canada Jay. It's certainly not the empty land it appears to be to most people.

We had a pleasant surprise this evening. Don Taylor called with a message from our daughter, Debbie Rose. Later in the evening when she again called, Don patched us into the phone line so Gordon could talk to her directly. She wanted to let us know that she's located a house that'll be available for the ski holiday we're taking in February and March. Sounds great. The house is at Canmore, Alberta. It's wonderful, this modern technology!! Hard to believe. The two of us sitting out here with only a single side-band radio – two mountain ranges away from Watson Lake, being connected to a phone line so we could talk directly to our daughter, a couple of thousand miles away at Kananaskis (Banff), Alberta. It was so good, hearing her voice.

Wednesday – Dec. 7ᵗʰ -38C   Pretty nippy out!! Clear skies and no wind.

We'd planned on taking two days off after we finished checking all our lines from Ridge Lake but didn't think we'd have them done so soon. We thought it would take us two days to check each line because of the heavy snowfall we'd received since we'd last been over them. As it turned out, we did each of them, Twin and Wolf Runs, in a day. Thank Goodness we'd been able to get them both checked. It would be pretty tough doing them in this temperature. You'd keep warm enough while snowshoeing but riding along on the skidoo or skimmer would be a different story. It's also pretty hard on the skidoo when it's this cold – metal gets quite brittle. Usually we don't use the skidoo when the temperature drops below minus thirty-five. The two dogs, Smokey and Rebel, are curled up in their houses with noses buried beneath tails. Only their eyes were visible when we checked them. They looked quite content.

Seems there are always odd jobs that need to be done, even on a day off. Gordon has the wolf to skin while I'll be busy with extra cooking. And when

I'm finished with cooking, I can always wash a few more marten. We're short of thumb tacks so will have to wait for the marten that are on stretchers to finish drying before we can use those tacks. It looks so nice outside. Clear sky – sun just coming up. Cold, but it is so cozy inside the cabin. Nice!!

I made up a batch of cinnamon buns and again they did not turn out right. Up to now, at Ridge Lake, I've not made a single pan of buns that turned out the way they should. They are heavy. Just would not rise. Must have something to do with the altitude. I'll try baking a batch at Rose Lake next time we're there to see what happens at that lower altitude. Made up a double batch of bannock mixture plus a huge pot of soup stock. Will make soup tomorrow. After that I worked on furs. Gordon skinned out three marten and then skinned the wolf. It's a large, black one but has pretty coarse fur. Not really a good wolf. Skinning was pretty tough going as the wolf was still partially frozen but, after struggling with it for over an hour, the job was finally completed.

Thursday – Dec. 8ᵗʰ -18C It was minus thirty-eight at bedtime so we kept the fire going in the stove. At five, when I got up to put more wood in the stove, the temperature was still showing minus thirty and the stars were shining. By morning the temperature had warmed to minus eighteen and light snow was coming down. Also, there's a nasty little wind blowing so we're glad to take another day off.

At noon the falling snow was still being whipped around by the wind. Temperature was still at minus eighteen. Really miserable out. We sure don't need any more snow. Can't say that we won't have a white Christmas. We've decided to spend Christmas out here. Jamie had brought out a bunch of very green bananas for us when he came out on Saturday. They've now ripened so we had one at lunchtime. Gosh they taste good!! A person sure does miss those little extras at times.

Friday – Dec. 9ᵗʰ -16C   Overcast this morning. We had more snow during the night. Plan on going to our Rose Lake cabin today.

By eleven-thirty we had the supplies we needed for Rose Lake loaded in the skimmer and the cabin closed up. When leaving for any length of time, we have to make certain all freezables are packed away in the storage compartment beneath the bunk and water pails are emptied. The clouds were clearing off and the sun had just started peaking through when we left for the river. The trip down the trail to the river went well despite the surprising amount of new snow we found covering it. It was evident that a lot more snow had fallen in the valley than we'd received in the higher country. Also, by the time we reached the river, the sun had disappeared behind a cloud bank.

The river was a white expanse of snow. You couldn't see anything to indicate where our trail crossed it. Gordon found it impossible to stay on the old trail hidden beneath the snow. Every time he ran off the trail, the machine buried itself in the deeper snow on the sides. He then had to wrestle the skidoo back up onto the old packed trail, hidden beneath the snow. You could only tell where the trail had been by walking or snowshoeing ahead, feeling the different snow depth. While he was fighting with the skidoo, I snowshoed ahead, across the river. Because of the snow depth, my freshly broken snowshoe trail wasn't much help. Gordon tried following it but the skidoo continually bogged down. He finally left the machine and slowly walked across the river, feeling out the packed trail beneath his mukluks as he slowly shuffled along. Anyway, we eventually reached the far shore. It was with a feeling of real relief, about half an hour later,that we saw the machine finally ride up the riverbank and onto the trail through the trees.

I'd begun to wonder if we were ever going to get across the river with the skidoo. Talk about deep snow!! From there on, everything went quite well. We did have a bit of a problem while crossing one of the sloughs. We ran into overflow, quite deep, but Gordon opened the throttle – wide and we got through. I'd been prepared to roll off the skimmer to lighten the load but would have gotten sopped, rolling into the water-soaked snow. Just as we reached solid, dry snow, the machine quit. Tracks and undercarriage were plugged solid with slush. We quickly cleared them and for the rest of the way to Rose Lake, had no more problems. We actually had a good trip, considering the trail conditions. We didn't find any marten in our sets. Quite a surprise!!

Gordon decided today that we definitely need a small machine for me. If I had my own skidoo, I wouldn't be riding in the skimmer. It would be a lot easier for his skidoo, especially when plowing through deep snow and overflow. We do have two long track Tundra skidoo's out here. Great machines but they're too much of a machine for me. I can't wrestle them. He'd like to get me an Elan. After we got a fire going in the cabin, the skimmer unloaded and the dogs chained up, it was time for lunch. Hot tea, soup and sandwiches never tasted better. By the time we finished lunch, the cabin was comfortably warm so we just sat back, relaxed, soaking up heat from the stove for the next while. After that, it was off to check our traps around Rose Lake. We picked up two marten. We skidooed about two-thirds of the distance, only. The rest of the way was snowshoed. We didn't want to take any chance on getting stuck in overflow on the lake. After we got back to the cabin, Gordon snowshoed down to the river and packed the two trails we'll follow across it on the way to Lynx Run. No overflow on the river, thank goodness. If the weather is good tomorrow, we'll check our Lynx Run. Otherwise we'll go and check the Run along the ridge heading to Jamie Lake.

Saturday – Dec. 10th -11C Overcast. Gordon says the clouds look very soggy. It sure is dark out this morning. Gordon even had to put the propane light on. Up to now we've pretty well managed with a candle in the mornings.

With the weather looking so uncertain, we decided to check traps along the trail heading to Jamie Lake since it was the shorter Run. After we started out, we found it hard to even see the trail because of all the new snow that covered it. The snow had been blown about by winds and completely obscured a lot of the trail. I did a lot of snowshoeing for the first part, then Gordon broke trail while I followed with the skidoo. I even managed to not slide off the trail. We couldn't believe the amount of new snow that was on the trail. If you slid off the trail, you were up to your hips in snow. The Tundra was pushing snow right over the hood for most of the way, even where the trail was broken out with snowshoes. We had to break trail almost all the way, otherwise the skidoo just couldn't have made it.

About and hour after we'd started out this morning, the cloud had cleared off and we had another sunny day. We enjoyed being out, even with the tough going, breaking trail. We'd originally planned on going all the way down to our cabin at Jamie Lake but decided against it. There was just too much snow to break a trail through. We won't be visiting the cabin at Jamie Lake or opening the trails to Canyon and Wolf creek this year. We did pick up ten marten today from our traps along the ridge. Very good for the number of traps we had set out. A good fifty percent average on this line today. When we were checking the sets, we found that two of the trap boxes had the back screening pulled off. The majority of the traps boxes are nailed up in trees, anywhere from four to six feet above the ground. The back of the plywood box is open except for the wire mesh tacked over it. Looks like we have a very smart marten along this ridge. He must have climbed the tree, tore the screening off the back of the box and then fed on the bait. First one tasted good so sampled the second one. Further down the trail, Gordon had placed another box that had the screening missing from the back. He'd stuffed the back with spruce boughs and branches. Sure enough, they'd been pulled out and the bait was taken. Gordon said he can just picture a marten up that tree, pulling out the stuffing and grinning. Annoying but pretty comical. Some marten are pretty smart!! When we finished checking the last trap, we turned the skidoo and headed for home. I rode all the way back. A real relief after all the snowshoeing.

Sunday – Dec. 11ᵗʰ -10C   A skiff of snow overnight and overcast this morning.

Hopefully, the sky will clear. We're going up Lynx Run today and Gordon would sure like sunshine so he can see the trail. This is the last Run we have left to break open since the last heavy snowfall.

By ten-thirty we were in dense fog but got ready anyway and skidoo'd across and down the river on our way to Lynx Run. We had a hard time seeing the trail because of poor visibility in the fog along the river. We found the first river crossing was OK. No overflow. When we reached the second crossing, there still wasn't any overflow. For the next half mile or so, travel was good along the trail Gordon had packed the other day. Our luck ran out when we reached the third and last crossing. We ran into overflow. Just a trace at first but Gordon thought he'd better put on his snowshoes, follow the trail across the river and check it out before barging ahead with the skidoo. Sure enough, half-way across he broke through the top layer of ice and into a foot of water. He got out even faster than he'd gone in, racing back to the skidoo. He figured there was still a good chance he could get across with the skidoo since there was a thin layer of ice atop the overflow. Anyway, he got on the skidoo and with throttle open wide, tore down the trail and across the river. I strapped on my snowshoes and crossed at a bit slower pace.

From there on, travel was fairly good but slow. Crossing meadows, where our trail was pretty well filled in, the skidoo had to push a lot of snow. After crossing the first meadow, we snowshoed the short distance through the timber to the creek. We wanted to make sure we could continue on our trail across the creek before we brought the skidoo up since turn-around space was limited. Thankfully, the creek wasn't covered with overflow. While I snowshoed on-wards, Gordon turned back to get the skidoo. I picked up a marten in the set we'd put out across the creek. When Gordon caught up to me, I took off my snowshoes and rode in the skimmer for awhile. The going was fairly good. It appeared this area had not received near the amount of snow that the country from Ridge Lake to Jamie Lake had. A short ways further ahead, the trail passed through some pretty rough sections so I got off and walked. Later when we reached the series of sloughs, Gordon walked ahead checking ice on them while I followed with the skidoo. We did run into small amounts of overflow but nothing major. We picked up another two marten in the slough areas. After we had passed the last slough, Gordon ran the skidoo while I rode. A short time later after crossing the creek, we emerged from the timber and entered the meadow that leads to Twin Lakes. Just before we left the timber, we picked up a mink in one of our marten sets. The mink had climbed the tree to get at the bait. This was the second mink we'd taken in tree sets this year. A short ways further on, we found a marten in a trap we'd set out along the edge of the meadow.

During the morning the fog had cleared away giving us another beautiful, sunny, warm day. It was just so enjoyable being out on the trail. Sound seemed to carry really well today. While we were away up the trail, almost at the far end, the sound of our dogs howling back at Rose Lake could be plainly heard. They were conducting their usual canine chorus as sleigh dogs do. Gordon and I had a bet going. I'd told him that we'd have at least six marten in our traps today. He said, "No" – we'd only have four. By the time we reached the far end of the meadow, we had five marten. He only wanted to go a short ways further, to the next set before heading back. This time I said, "NO – We'll check the next three sets before turning back". Sure enough, the last trap held a marten. I won!! Now he has to do the dishes for the next two days!! By then it was getting late. We had a lot of trail to cover before we'd be back in our warm cabin at Rose Lake.

Gordon turned the skidoo, I climbed in the skimmer and we were off. The return trip was easy, traveling along the trail we'd packed this morning. I rode all the way back to the river. When we reached the riverbank, I got out and snowshoed over to the other side while Gordon drove the machine across. There was a lot more overflow over the trail but he managed to make it. The other two river crossings were also showing overflow but not enough to bother us. I was able to ride in the skimmer right up to the cabin. We also noticed that a lot of the packed runway was covered with overflow. We sure hope we'll get colder temperatures so it will freeze. Gordon's planning on doing more packing tomorrow.

We noticed the temperature was minus seven when we got home. Shortly afterwards, a wind came up and the temperature warmed to minus four. Tonight at nine it was only minus five. Snow is starting to get a little sticky.

Monday – Dec. 12th -23C   Cooled off overnight. The forecast was for mild temperatures but we're sure pleased that it has turned colder. Will really help freeze the overflow so we can finish packing our runway on the river. It's beautiful out, clear skies. The mountains look gorgeous, sun shining on their white peaks, outlined against a background of blue sky. We should be out on the trail today since it's so nice.

Gordon worked on marten this morning while I did a bit of baking. After lunch he put on his snowshoes and checked the river for overflow. He was hoping it would be OK so he could start packing runway. No luck!! There was just too much overflow. A few minutes later he came in and said "Let's go for a trip to Rose Lake". We loaded all the marten carcasses on the skimmer, then hauled them out to the shore of the lake where they were left for animals to feed on. By then dense fog had moved in and reduced visibility to a few hundred feet.

In the evening Don Taylor called to advise us that the Game Branch was planning on flying out to Ridge Lake on Thursday. Hopefully, the runway there is still in good shape with no overflow.

Tuesday – Dec. 13th -18C   Very foggy out this morning.

Fog had cleared up pretty nicely by the time we finished breakfast. We're heading back to Ridge Lake as soon as the dishes are washed and the skimmer is packed. About half an hour later we closed the cabin door, hitched the dogs to their toboggan, started the skidoo and were off. Besides the skimmer with me aboard, the skidoo was also pulling a fairly heavy sled. The sled had been manufactured from the skis of old skidoos. Gordon had it specially built to haul the logs on when they built Rose Lake cabin. The sled slid along behind the skimmer like a dream, all the way to the river. No problem whatsoever. We left it on the riverbank, stashed under a large spruce. Gordon will pick it up one day when the skimmer's not so loaded (i.e., without me in it). It was really good traveling back along the trail we'd packed the other day. We picked up one marten on River Run. I felt it was a bonus since we hadn't expected any. Marten sign is getting scarcer in the lower areas.

We snowshoed across the river checking for overflow. None. A real pleasant surprise!! From there on, we took turns breaking trail up to Ridge Lake. Quite a depth of new snow had built up on the trail during the last few days. We had to break out the steeper sections for the skidoo but when the trail leveled off I was able to ride in the skimmer. The dogs, hitched to the toboggan, followed along behind. Patchy cloud had been drifting across the sky all morning but by the time we reached Ridge Lake, we were in sunshine.

We'd been noticing, especially during the last few days, that marten sign was getting much scarcer. On the way up from the river today we'd only seen fresh tracks in a couple of places and found nothing in our traps. If we find little marten sign on our next round of trap checking, we'll very likely close the trapline down for this year. Gordon already has regrets about possibly closing down by the end of the month. He loves being out in the bush, especially here at Ridge Lake. When we were coming along the last few hundred yards of trail leading to the cabin, we had to stop and admire the view. The sun was shining on the snow covered tree tops, outlining them against a background of hills and mountains. It was just lovely. It looked so warm, even though the thermometer showed a minus twenty reading.

While Gordon was unloading the skimmer and refueling the skidoo, I was busy in the cabin lighting a fire in the stove. It's surprising how quickly the cabin warms once the fire's burning properly. It wasn't long before we were sitting at the table drinking hot tea and eating lunch. After lunch Gordon went down to the lake, chopped a hole through the ice and tried fishing. No luck!

After that he was off with the skidoo – packing runway on the lake. He checked the ice in a couple of places and found a good twelve inches of blue ice, plenty thick enough to land the Beaver on. After he finished packing runway, he extended the turn-around area for the aircraft – right up to the dock. Will make it handier for loading and unloading the plane. Hard to believe we'll be going back to Watson Lake in few more weeks. Time has sure flown. Gordon's already looking forward to coming back here in April. We've decided to add another room onto the cabin. April is a good time to cut and haul the building logs for the addition.

Wednesday – Dec. 14th -16C   Its overcast this morning. The sky to the east is crimson, a prelude to the sunrise that'll be with us in about an hour.

By the time we'd finished breakfast, the sky had really clouded over. We'd decided during breakfast that we'd head out and check the traps along Wolf Run today. A short while later we were on our way. Sure wasn't as nice going today as it had been yesterday when the sun was shining. There was also a nasty wind blowing. Even though the temperature was only minus sixteen, it felt cold. The trail was really good. There hadn't been any new snow since the last time we were over it. There were a few short sections where it had drifted in, mainly around Swan Lake, but no real problems. It was a little disappointing but not surprising to find, when we reached the end of the run a couple of hours later, that we'd only picked up one marten and one mink. The mink and marten were caught in sets that I'd checked so Gordon said I should have checked all the traps on this line. By the time we turned around and started for home, the sky had really darkened with low clouds. We were certain that we'd soon be in a snowstorm but were lucky, only a few flakes drifted down. The wind had gotten stronger though, making our return trip pretty cold and miserable, especially through the open areas.

By the time we reached home, the sky had started to clear but the wind had really picked up. Sure glad to get in the warm cabin. By the time Gordon had finished refueling the skidoo and covered it with the tarp, stars were shining from a clear sky. Sure changeable weather. Later, received a message from Don Taylor advising that a Game Branch representative expects to fly in sometime tomorrow morning. So we won't be going on the trail tomorrow!! After supper I washed another bunch of marten pelts so will be busy most of tomorrow putting them on stretchers. Will be good to get caught up. It takes so long for them to dry thoroughly. If we didn't have to close the cabin within a few days and go back to Rose Lake, it would help. We do need to go back there and check traps. We don't want to leave them unchecked for more than four days, if possible.

Thursday – Dec. 15ᵗʰ -5C   Clear this morning but windy – very gusty. The Northern Lights were just so spectacular last night. There was an arch of light right over the cabin, stretching as far as you could see. It was dancing across the sky accompanied by several shorter bands along the sides. They were so brilliant, so beautiful. Sure don't see them in the cities.

We waited until one o'clock in the afternoon for the plane to arrive with the official from the Game Branch. The aircraft from Watson Lake first flew to Quartz Lake, then on to Toobally Lakes where a survey was completed with Larry Schnigg. They picked up furs he had ready for the Fur Auction and then flew over to here. They spent a good hour and had lunch with us. Roger (pilot) brought us a case of oranges plus another larger box (think it was from Sheila) that was filled with lettuce, tomatoes, Xmas candy and nuts. Very thoughtful of her. She also sent our mail. Will never have time to look through all the newspapers and magazines that were sent up. Anyway, we had a good visit.

After they left, Gordon loaded the small propane stove that they'd brought in onto the skimmer and then hauled it down to the river and cached it under a spruce. On the next trip to Rose Lake, we'll pick it up and haul it the rest of the way to the cabin. At the river, he hitched the log skidder that we'd left there the other day behind the skimmer and brought it home to Ridge Lake. While he was gone, I finished putting the furs that I'd washed last evening onto stretchers. After he returned and we'd finished supper, we talked about closing down our trapline. Finally, the decision was made to close the trapline down over the next couple of weeks and fly back to Watson Lake around the fifth of January. It was really hard making up our minds to leave. We've enjoyed being out here so much.

Friday – Dec. 16th -6C   Cloudy and still windy but we're going to Crisco today, regardless.

After breakfast we skidooed up the trail to Swan Lake and onwards to Crisco. It was mild out but still a bit nippy with the wind. We traveled as far as Fluffo Lake with the skidoo, left it there and continued on with snowshoes – checking our trap sets around the lake. We picked up two marten. Crisco Lake valley is the windiest place. Trees are nearly all bare of snow, blown clear by the wind. Next year Gordon wants to explore the ridges that extend from Swan Lake to Crisco. He feels that trapping along them would be great and traveling up there would get us away from the valley floor with all its creeks, beaver dams and rough, swampy areas. From the valley bottom, the ridges look great. Might be a real surprise when we scout them out though!! On our way back, it was beautiful with the sun shining on the mountains. I felt rather sad thinking of closing down our trapline within the next two weeks and preparing for our return to Watson Lake. I've even tried talking Gordon into staying until the end of February, the end of the trapping season. We've really enjoyed being out here. It's been hard work but we'll miss it so very much.

Saturday – Dec. 17th -5C   Broken conditions so hopefully it will be nice and sunny when we go up Twin Run. It's so mild out for this time of year. Hard to believe!! Nice if it would stay like this or even a little colder for the rest of the time we're here. Water was dripping off the roof all night.

After breakfast we took off with the skidoo for Lake Run. It was really nice and warm out. We picked up two marten from the traps along the ridges. Where we had our wolverine set, we found a rabbit. The dogs will have a treat tonight. We traveled up Twin Run and then all the way down from the plateau to the meadows below. No snowshoeing for me today. Felt real good about that. The trail was excellent so we had no problems. We picked up another two marten on Twin Run.

We had tea and lunch under a big spruce tree that grew all by itself on the plateau. Afterwards we snowshoed up a long ridge, noticing quite a number of marten tracks along the way. We also discovered another large meadow on the other side of the ridge. It has wide open spaces which will make it a cinch for putting a trail through next year. With very little clearing, we'd be able to go a long ways further and form a loop that'll give us a much longer Run. Gordon was very pleased with all the sign and at the same time felt so bad (me too) that it's only two and a half weeks before we leave. We'll only be able to travel the Runs once or twice more before we leave. It's just been so enjoyable out here. The scenery is so beautiful. We're really going to miss it so. Also noticed quite a number of moose tracks around. They're moving down to lower country again.

After we returned home at four-thirty, we had tea and then, except for a break for dinner, worked on furs until ten-thirty. We had a really enjoyable time on the trapline today, also very informative. There's quite a controversy amongst trappers and fur biologists regarding the movement of marten at this time of year. According to the signs we've noticed, it appears marten definitely move up to higher terrain. Some trappers feel they go into hibernation. We've seen a lot of fresh sign up in the higher country and very little in the low areas.

Sunday – Dec. 18th -25C Cooled down a lot overnight. The sky is clear and the stars are still shining at eight o'clock in the morning. We're taking a day off from running the lines. In fact, I got up, warmed the cabin and made coffee this morning. Gives Gordon a chance to stay in bed a little longer.

After breakfast we finished up more of the furs. I washed eight more marten and will place them on stretchers this evening. While I worked on them,

Gordon skinned the four marten we'd caught yesterday. After I was finished with my marten, I baked butter tarts and a pumpkin pie. Hopefully our whipped cream is still good since we plan on using it with the pie. We have so many groceries here. Will never use up the perishables and goodies before we leave.

It was a beautiful afternoon, clear sky and with the sunshine, hard to believe it's December eighteenth. Gordon just left to go snowshoeing up the mountain behind the cabin. He wants to see what it's like in the hills and mountains back there. He also wants to check for fur sign as well as a possible route for a trail up that way. Bob Watson said there was no way a trail could go up there but we're sure it can be done. It's beautiful up on the mountain plateaus in the fall. Lots of caribou feeding in the open mountain pastures. Quite a sight!! By three o'clock I just had to go for a walk (with wet hair) but only out onto the lake. The mountains looked so beautiful with the afternoon sun shining on them. I just had to take more pictures. Surprised to find when I returned to the cabin that the temperature was still minus twenty-three.

Monday – Dec. 19ᵗʰ -30C Cold out but nice and clear. Will be sunny again but we'll miss seeing our mountain view today. We're going down to our cabin at Rose Lake for a few days just soon as we have breakfast.

We got away shortly after eleven. Travel along the packed trail was really good, especially when compared to the trail and the snow we had to plow our way through last time. Today the trail was packed hard so travel, either by skidoo or on foot, was really easy. Sure a nice change. On the way to the river we spotted fresh wolverine tracks as well as a number of new marten tracks. Glad to see they're still around even though we didn't find any in our traps. Surprised to find that our trail on the river had completely drifted over. Only a faint impression left to show us the way across. We slid off the trail a number of times while crossing the river but once we were in the timber, away from the open river, the trail was super – all the way to the cabin

When we reached Rose Lake we found the valley completely covered in fog. Such a change from Ridge Lake. Temperature was just minus twenty-seven though. We unloaded the skimmer, tied the dogs up and had lunch. After lunch we skidooed to Rose Lake where we found a marten in one of our traps. For such a small lake and valley it has certainly been good to us. We also spotted many new tracks along one side of the lake. Last time we were here, we'd left a number of animal carcasses on the far shore and also in the ravines over there. Looks like marten have been feeding on them. Snow in the area, all around, had been packed by their activity. Gordon put out three sets in the immediate area so hope we'll catch a couple more over there. Also noticed moose tracks around the lakeshore where the moose had been feeding on willows. After checking and setting the new traps, we returned to the cabin. While I sorted and put away the supplies we'd brought over with us today, Gordon went up river to do a bit more packing on the runway. We'll be flying out from Ridge Lake but want the load of supplies that's coming in to be off-loaded here. Temperature has warmed up to minus twenty-four. Hope it will be even milder for trap checking tomorrow.

When Gordon returned from his scouting trip up the mountain behind Ridge Lake cabin yesterday, he reported that he'd had an enjoyable and very informative afternoon. He'd headed up the slope that begins just east of the cabin. It climbs to a height of forty-six hundred feet over a distance of three miles. The first pleasant surprise was finding, part way up, that the snow was quite packed so his snowshoes only sank about two to three inches. Snowshoeing was great!! It was even easier snowshoeing than walking had been in summer since all the low shrubs and bushes were now buried beneath three feet of snow. Just after he'd started climbing he spotted a marten track. Turned out it was the only track he saw on his four mile hike. Up above and out of sight below, he found a high plateau that extended about six miles to the north. Most of the climbing was quite gradual and enjoyable since it was done over pretty open terrain. Huge spruce were scattered along the lower slopes, then the balsam at mid levels were followed, higher up, by a few stunted pines. The plateau, all along the top, was completely clear of trees. There was only about six inches of rock-hard drifted snow covering the ground. The view was fantastic, especially with the late afternoon sun highlighting mountains in all directions. It was also possible to see a good part of our trapline – most of the area we'd been over this winter. It was too bad he hadn't brought his camera along. The only disappointment was the lack of fur sign on the higher slopes. At the same time, it did let us know that we're now at the higher limits of the marten range, at least for this time of year. When he was describing his jaunt, it made me wish I'd gone with him. But, there's always a next time!!

Tuesday – Dec. 20th -34C   Cold out but nice and clear.

After breakfast we dressed warmly, started the skidoo and headed up our Run along the ridge we follow to Jamie Lake. The trail was good, hard packed from our last trip over it. The sun was shining and the mountains looked beautiful. We found four marten in our sets. Noticed very many marten tracks, really fresh, in the meadows but none on the ridge. They must have been down in the meadows hunting mice. It didn't take us very long to check the entire line. No trail to break out today. We were back at our cabin just before noon.

After lunch Gordon took the skidoo and checked the traps he'd set at Rose Lake yesterday. No Luck, no fresh tracks. After returning, he headed down the trail to the river to pick up the propane stove that had been left there a few days earlier. We won't be hooking the stove up until our return next year. Don Taylor called in the evening with word that Jamie was enquiring about our plans for returning to Watson Lake.

Wednesday – Dec. 21st -36C   Another gorgeous but cold day. The mountaintops in the distance glisten white under their covers of snow. Lower down the slopes, patches of windswept spruce and pine, still hidden from the rays of the sun, appear black in their nighttime attire. The slowly rising sun makes the ever-changing coloring of our mountains pretty fantastic.

At twelve o'clock the temperature was still minus thirty-five. We decided it was just too cold for the machine (and us) to go up our Lynx Run. Instead, I resorted and repacked groceries and made an inventory of what will be left here for next season. While I was taking inventory Gordon was outside placing spruce tree markers along the edges of his runway. The markers will make it a lot easier for the Beaver pilot to locate our runway when he comes in with our supplies.

After lunch, clam chowder for Gordon, we walked up the trail to the far end of Rose Lake. The trail was packed hard so we didn't have to use snowshoes. A nice change!! At the far end of the lake we did put on our snowshoes and then proceeded to check out the area between the lake and the river. We followed a number of small potholes, where snowshoeing was very easy, all the way to a back channel of the river. We were lucky and came out to the river exactly where we'd wanted to. Next year, after a bit of clearing, we'll run a short line through there. All we'll have to do after that is cross the river to the far side where there's a series of interconnected sloughs and meadows. We're hoping they'll extend far enough up river to provide us with an easy, accessible trail to our cabin at Kettle Creek. The section of trail we scouted out today from the end of Rose Lake to the river will save three and a half to four miles of river travel where, it seems, we're always fighting overflow when traveling by skidoo.. While snowshoeing through the sloughs and potholes, we also came across another open area that stretched out in another direction, seemingly for miles. Will sure be interesting checking it out next winter. Saw quite a lot of fur sign all along the way. Marten tracks criss-crossed the sloughs and meadows where they'd been mouse hunting.

Radio signals have sure been good lately. Talked to Don Taylor this evening and also listened in on conversations from other people out on traplines. Some trappers are certainly having problems!! One trapper, John Anderson, who has a trapline about a hundred miles east of us, got burned out. His cabin totally destroyed. Another family, where the wife and two children had been flown out to Ft. Nelson, has a problem. She now wants to fly back to the trapline but the Flying Service won't take her back unless they get paid first. So now she's stuck in Ft. Nelson with two kiddies and no money while he's out on the line with one child, running low on groceries. Also, her husband only has thirty-five gallons of gas left. He'll have to save some of it for traveling out with. They're having an airdrop of supplies tomorrow, weather permitting. Makes one wish we were closer together so we could help them out.

Thursday – Dec. 22nd -36C   Another clear but cold morning. When I got up during the night, the sky was covered with high cloud and the temperature was only minus twenty-five. It was quite a surprise this morning to find the cloud had cleared off and the temperature had dropped. Anyway, it's too cold to go up Lynx Run.

After breakfast Gordon called Don Taylor for the forecast. He advised us the weather is not due to change before Christmas and perhaps even longer. After hearing that bit of news, we decided to return to Ridge Lake anyway. It's only a couple of hours away via our short river trail. Almost all of our supplies are a Ridge Lake. Definitely all the fresh stuff. It didn't take long to close the fire down, empty the water pails, put groceries away and pack a few things in the skimmer. Gordon had the skidoo running, warming up, while we finished up in the cabin. A few minutes later we were heading down the trail. I, bundled up in my parka with the hood covering my face, rode in the skimmer while the dogs, in harness, trotted along behind. The trail was rock hard, easy going for the skidoo so we made good time and arrived at Ridge Lake in a little less than two hours. I was glad to get out of the skimmer and move around. I was getting pretty chilled from sitting that long. Anyway, it only took a few minutes to get the fire in the cabin stove roaring, warming the cabin. NICE!! The dogs also seem to prefer it here. After we unharnessed them, they trotted over to their houses – inspected them and then promptly laid down and curled up in the snow. Guess they figure a REAL HUSKY doesn't need a house!!

After lunch we snowshoed up along the ridge on the east side of the lake. Our Lake Run is on the west side. It was easy snowshoeing. Hardly sank in the snow at all and in the sunshine, snowshoeing was really enjoyable. We snowshoed the full length of the ridge along the east side of the lake, all the way to the far end of the lake without seeing any sign of animals. Just the occasional tracks of rabbits showed. We'd considered clearing a trail down the east side so we wouldn't be traveling along the west side all the time. After checking it out today, we've decided against it. As soon as we snowshoed down to the end of the lake and headed back to the cabin, following the western shoreline, we noticed rabbit tracks all over the place. There were even a couple of marten tracks. Could be because the sun shines on the ridge along the west side of the lake whereas the ridge along the eastern side remains in shadow until late in the day. We've noticed before that there always seems to be more fur sign along the sunny sides of slopes and valleys. On our way back, we also noticed two depressions in the snow where moose had bedded down. Nice to see we have neighbors.

Friday – Dec. 23rd -14C   What a pleasant change from the minus thirty-five temperature we'd been having. I was up about five and discovered it was snowing lightly. Our bright full moon and stars were obscured by cloud. It's still cloudy this morning. A bit of snow is falling and a light wind is blowing.

At breakfast we decided to stay in and work on furs. Which we did!! There were quite a few marten to remove from stretchers and brush out. While Gordon was working on them, I washed another fourteen marten. We don't have enough pins to do more than that at one time. Anyway, working on the furs kept us busy all day. Just after we'd placed the last marten on a stretcher, a radio-call came in from Don Taylor advising that a friend of ours, Joe Corcoran, will be flying out tomorrow for a visit – weather permitting. We're looking forward to seeing Joe. Will be nice to have company.

Saturday – Dec. 24th -23C   Clear out so should be a nice day but since the sky has cleared, temperature will probably drop to the minus forties that the weathermen are forecasting.

Shortly after breakfast we heard, through Jackpine portable, that Joe was on his way and expected to arrive at approximately twelve forty-five. We had originally planned on closing Crisco line today. Hopefully the temperature won't be so cold that it'll keep us from going there tomorrow. Joe arrived just around one o'clock for a very brief visit and a cup of coffee. He brought a case of oranges from Jamie and the mail. Will have our fill of oranges before we leave. It was good to have company, even for such a short spell. Joe wanted to get back to Watson Lake well before dark and was also concerned about his aircraft engine cooling off too much. It's hard to start when it's cold.

After Joe left, I decided to make a pineapple/carrot jellied salad to go with a large, plump chicken that Jamie had brought out to us when he flew out here. Will be a nice, tasty addition to tomorrow's Christmas dinner. Just as I finished the salad, Don Taylor called to let us know that Patti had phoned to wish us a Merry Christmas from Jamie, Debbie and herself. Will seem odd not having Christmas at home with the kids.

Sunday – Dec. 25th -28C   Merry Christmas at Ridge Lake. The sky is overcast and fog patches are lying along the lakeshore. Not the nicest looking day!!

During breakfast we decided to check one short line today, Crisco, and close it down. So right after breakfast, I made the dressing for the chicken, washed the bird and left it to drain while I made a "Mile High" lemon-meringue pie. As soon as that was done, dressed in my outdoor clothes, I was out the door and climbed aboard the skimmer. About a minute later we were on our way down the trail for Crisco. A short while later when we reached Swan Lake, Gordon checked the snares he'd set around our old moose kill but found nothing. A wolf had gone by one of the snares, shoving it aside without getting caught – lucky!! The wolf trap he'd set beside the moose head was sprung and signs indicated that a wolverine had been caught but was held for only a short time. Too bad!! The wolverine can be a very destructive animal on a trapline and once caught in a trap, never forgets what a trap is . It's almost impossible to catch a wolverine the second time. The only possible way to get him now is with a deadfall.

As we were going along the trail to the top of the ridge leading to Crisco, I spotted a couple of black objects in the snow near the skidoo trail. Turned out to be the heads of a pair of curious grouse. Grouse fly into deep snow where they'll remain buried for considerable lengths of time. The snow protects them from the cold and they're also invisible to most predators. It's unusual to see just their heads though – they're usually kept beneath the snow. These birds must have been getting ready to fly out. It was pretty neat seeing them. We only caught one marten on the Run. Not so great!! We took the trap boxes down from the trees and then, along with the traps, hauled them to a location further along the ridge where they'll be handy for next year. We don't plan on using this trail through the valley anymore. Instead, we'll reroute it up along the ridge.

After returning home, I prepared dinner while Gordon worked on a few outside chores. We had a very nice dinner – chicken with dressing, mashed potatoes with gravy, asparagus, jellied pineapple salad and dilled carrots. All topped off with a bottle of wine. Later for dessert, a lemon pie. A typical trapper's Christmas dinner!! Later in the evening there were a lot of radio communications with other trappers. It was great having good radio signals so we could wish everyone a Merry Christmas.

Monday – Dec. 26th -26C   Broken conditions early morning but by mid-morning the sky had cleared and temperature had dropped to minus twenty-eight. By two in the afternoon the sky had clouded over and temperature was only minus twenty-four. Hopefully, it won't get too cold.

We'd thought about going to Rose Lake to close up that part of our trapline but decided it would be best to first finish washing the furs we have here. That way they'll be drying while we're away. Gordon removed quite a few more from the stretchers, brushed them out and hung them in the cache. While he was looking after furs, I was sorting and packing the groceries we'll take to Rose Lake. Also was making a list of the supplies we'll have left over. A bit of an inventory so there won't be a last minute rush when we're leaving.

Tuesday – Dec. 27ᵗʰ -18C   Cloudy. The dogs acted up for the longest time during the night. We don't know what set them off, possibly wolves howling.

We left Ridge Lake cabin about eleven-thirty and skidooed down to the river. Picked up one marten along the way. Going was very good along the hard-packed trail. Then it was on to our cabin at Rose Lake. Not really a nice day. Very dull out, overcast sky with patches of fog along the river. Mountains pretty well obscured, wrapped in blankets of fog. When we reached the cabin, the first thing I did was check on the groceries we'd left behind from our trip before Christmas. Since then we'd had some very cold days. I'd placed eight eggs, quarter bottle of gingerale and a couple of other freezable items – all well wrapped, in our little storage cellar under the bed. Couldn't believe it!! Nothing had frozen but, as soon as I pulled the gingerale out, it formed a slush inside the bottle. The cabin was cold and the gingerale must have been near to freezing. After lunch we skidooed up to Rose Lake. Nothing in the traps. Gordon dumped me out of the skimmer twice – the turkey!! But it was a rough trail.

Wednesday – Dec. 28ᵗʰ -26C   Broken sky condition this morning. No fog.

We're going trap checking today. Shortly after breakfast we skidoo'd up river past our airstrip and onwards to the Lynx/Twin Runs. The sun came out from behind the cloud just as we made the last river crossing. Must have been an omen – not a trace of overflow on the river !! Hard to believe!! The trail was packed hard, super going. Sure nice skidooing when you're not worried about getting stuck in slush. After leaving the river, we followed our trail through the big meadow and onwards to Lynx Creek. No new snow had fallen since we were last over the trail. Lynx Creek was frozen hard, no overflow, so we had no trouble at that crossing. From there on, right up to where we joined our Twin Run, the trail was great. We picked up a marten and a mink from the traps along the way. After we joined onto Twin Run, we picked up two more marten. We also noticed a lot of marten sign as we traveled along the trail, right up to the high meadow – our turn-around point.

We left the skidoo and continued on snowshoes up to the top of the hill, about half a mile away, to check on the two traps we'd set there. As we approached the second set, Gordon exclaimed "Oh No". The trap box was hanging in the tree, face down, rather than sitting crosswise. Approaching closer, we noticed the trap was missing. We looked around, studying the snow for any indications of what might have happened.. Nothing!! There weren't any signs to indicate that a larger animal might have taken the trap. About two to three feet from the set, I noticed a depression under the willows where a rabbit or some other bird or animal had buried itself. Gordon started digging in the snow, hoping the trap and whatever animal was in it would be there. Nothing!! He'd just finished checking around the trap box when I called out, "I've found the trap". Anyway, about six feet off to the side of our trail, I'd spotted a trap-spring sticking out of the snow. I literally flung myself at it, practically disappearing in the snow!! Then I noticed a patch of fur to the side. I was sure it would be the remains of a partially eaten marten. Anyway, I pulled on the trap and found a marten in it, not damaged at all. Then I had a problem!! I couldn't get out of the snow.

I, without thinking when I'd spotted the trap, had flung myself into snow that was over five feet deep (way past my waist). Now I found myself lying lengthwise in it, unable to get up. What a dumb thing to do. I'd been so pleased at finding the trap, especially with the marten intact, that I'd just never thought. Gordon had to give me a hand and a pull to get me out. He thought it wasn't very smart, jumping into the depression as I had. Right beneath the snow where I'd landed, a thin crust of ice covered a very deep, narrow creek. I could have had a rather chilly bath!! Later when we checked the trap we found the wire, that we'd tied the trap to the tree with, was broken. If we'd thought to check the tree when we first noticed the trap was missing, we'd have seen the broken end hanging from it. Guess when the marten was first caught, another animal had come along, pulled it down and partially buried it. A trace of fresh snow had covered any tracks so we have no idea if our supposition is right or not.

On the way back, it was still early, we put on our snowshoes and did some scouting. We found more meadows and potholes. The number of marten tracks around them was unreal. Marten love mice and mice live in the meadows. Next year we'll branch off our trail and put a spur line out through them. What we'd been scouting for was a large lake that was shown on a map of the area. We finally found it on our way back to the skidoo. We want to find out if we can reach Kettle Creek by following through a series of sloughs and swamps that head that way. It looks very interesting but needs more scouting. On our way back to Rose Lake we closed down the traps along the Run. Rather sad knowing we won't see this part of our trapline again until next year.

Thursday – Dec. 29th -31C   High broken conditions. Mountains look majestic with the sun shining on their peaks.

We checked and closed down the traps along the ridge to Jamie Lake. Picked up one marten. Was nice to see fresh marten tracks in a few places, also wolverine tracks followed our trail for quite a ways. After we returned, Gordon went and closed the traps around Rose Lake while I stayed behind preparing lunch.

After lunch he took the skidoo and packed the runway again. Should be good and solid for the Beaver aircraft when it arrives with our supplies. Afterwards, Gordon took the chainsaw and cut down a big spruce that was growing on the edge of the riverbank in front of the cabin. The tree was leaning way out over the river. We were worried that, if it should fall, it would take a lot of the riverbank with it. The side of the cabin facing the river is only about twenty feet from the edge of the riverbank. If high water took the spruce out, it would likely rip away a good portion of the riverbank out front. This had happened at our Kettle Creek cabin a couple of years before. Besides, we now have a better view with the tree removed.

Friday – Dec. 30th -27C   Overcast this morning.

    It got a wee bit chilly in the cabin this morning so I got up, put more wood on the fire and bounced back into bed for awhile. Then after the cabin warmed, got up and made coffee and did a bit of packing. We're closing up our Rose Lake cabin for this season and moving back to Ridge Lake. We'll stay there until we fly home to Watson Lake. Last night Gordon mentioned that he felt so sad about closing down our trapline. He loves it out here. Wouldn't surprise me if he suggested moving to the trapline permanently.

    It only took us a little over two hours to return to Ridge Lake. Travel along the rock hard trail was so easy and enjoyable that I almost wished the trip was longer. Along the way we closed our traps but left them hanging in the tree – ready for next year. The dogs sure know when we're returning to Ridge Lake. They're all excited knowing they'll soon be back to their home and the moose bones they have buried there. Everything was fine at the cabin. Fresh tracks showed where a couple of neighborly marten had come up and inspected the porch.

    After lunch Gordon took the skidoo and repacked the runway. It's now in first class shape for any aircraft that decides to land here. Just like Edmonton International Airport!! Our water hole down at the lake had frozen over so Gordon had to chop through the ice to get water. The creek that runs out of the lake is still open, not even ice along its banks. Must be some mineralization in the water that keeps it from freezing.

Saturday – Dec. 31st -26C   Broken cloud conditions – looks like it'll be a nice day.

    After breakfast we headed up Swan Run to Wolf Run. Travel along the packed trail in brilliant sunshine was very enjoyable – even though we only picked up one marten through the timbered section. We'd only spotted a single marten track through the timber but once we hit the open meadow country, tracks were all over. It looked as if a bunch of marten had migrated through the area. Anyway, we had three traps set along about half a mile or less of the trail and found a marten in each one. It was sure a great way to close down that part of the line. After such good results in that section of meadow, we figured that when we reached the next section there'd be marten tracks all over and we'd have a couple more in the traps. A real surprise!! Not a single track and nothing in the traps. Quite a letdown!!

On the way home, we decided to explore some of the country to the east of our trail. We snowshoed for about an hour – gradually climbing uphill to the plateau above. When flying in to the trapline, we'd spotted a fair-sized lake on the plateau we were heading up to. Anyway, after finally reaching the plateau, we couldn't locate the lake. However, on our return down the other side of the plateau, we did find another fair-sized meadow – covered with lots of marten tracks. Gordon was very pleased with our find and thinks it has good potential. Another year, we can make a loop around the higher country and come out somewhere towards the end of Wolf Run. It'll be another area to explore and cut trail to. By the time we got back to the skidoo, light snow was falling.

When we checked, just before going to bed, we found it still snowing – heavier. Jamie called this evening to wish us a Happy New Year.

Sunday – Jan.1st -20C   Happy New Year to All. Broken conditions again. We received about an inch and a half of snow overnight.

We skidoo'd up Lake/Twin Run, checking and closing traps. We found just one marten, in a set we had along the first ridge. Along the second ridge, where we had a wolverine trap, we found a rabbit but only bits of fur remained. Birds or other animals had eaten it. In another ground set we had along the second ridge, we found another rabbit. It wasn't eaten so the dogs will have a treat tonight. Where the trail came down from the ridge, Gordon had set out a wolf snare. A wolverine had come by but had gone underneath it. Too bad!! The snare had been set higher for a wolf instead of lower for a wolverine. Wolf snares are set much higher above the ground than those for wolverine. If it'd been set lower, we'd have had a wolverine. As it was, he'd just kept sauntering along the trail – passing beneath the snare. We did pick up another marten shortly before we came to Twin Lakes Creek. Where we crossed the creek atop our log bridge, we had set out a mink trap. No mink today but we did have a rabbit. A marten was still feeding on the rabbit when we came to the creek. He ran off. Gordon decided to reset the trap and will check it again tomorrow. We hoped the marten would be back before we returned from checking the rest of Twin Run. The sky had clouded over completely by the time we finished checking the rest of the line. It was really enjoyable being out, quite warm. We picked up four marten on Twin Run today so it was a good way to close the line. No marten in the trap at the creek when we returned. Gordon wants to do more exploring up this way tomorrow so will check and close the trap then..

This evening after supper we drew up a rough blueprint of the cabin we plan on building this spring. We're not going to add onto this cabin but will build a new one. It'll be built on the hill overlooking the south end of the lake. The view from there is just so spectacular. Lake, meadow and mountains all spread before you!!

Monday – Jan.2nd -23C   Clear sky and not a trace of fog along the hills and mountains. Beautiful!!

At eleven the sky was still clear. Not even a trace of cloud. Will be one of the nicest days we've had here. We can already notice the increase in our daylight. Gordon says it's even nicer out here later in January and February with the longer daylight hours. As a result, we're already considering staying here until at least mid-February when we return next year. I just can't believe that we're talking and considering doing that but it is so nice and peaceful here. My back feels stiff and sore today for some reason so I decided not to go exploring with Gordon. He went to close the trap we'd left set at the creek yesterday. After checking and closing the trap, he's going to do some exploring on snowshoes further up the valley. Exploring new country on snowshoes would bother my back so I stayed home. While he was away I started packing the supplies that remained on the storage shelves in the porch.

Gordon returned around two-thirty bringing home a marten. He reported that the wolverine set, where we'd found the remains of a rabbit yesterday, had so many fresh marten tracks around it that he just had to set a trap there. The set is only about a half hour's walk from here or ten minutes by skidoo. Will have lots of time to check it since we still have two full days before the Beaver comes for us. The area he snowshoed over to explore, two to three miles east of our trail, just about floored him!! After reaching the little valley east of our trail and following up it for a short distance, he started seeing marten tracks. All over the place!! Anyway, he continued seeing tracks, very many, as far as he went. The valley opens up wider the further you go. Looks tremendous!! Next fall we'll cut a trail into it, very little clearing required.

Cooling off tonight. At nine o'clock, temperature was down to minus thirty-two.

Tuesday – Jan. 3rd -25C Cloudy. Temperature didn't go down as much as was forecast. Forecast was for minus thirty-seven. I'm spoiling Gordon. I've been up two mornings in a row to get the fire going, warm the cabin and then make coffee. That will never do!!

After breakfast we skidoo'd up Lake Run to check our trap at the wolverine set. Nothing!! But, we saw so many tracks that we decided to leave the trap, still set. After we'd turned around and were heading for home, we re-opened all the sets (four) on the way back. We'll close them tomorrow. After we reached home and had a cup of coffee, we snowshoed up to the knoll where we're planning on building our new cabin. During the next hour, the floor plan was decided on and marked out with posts driven into the frozen ground. The view from the knoll is great!! A wonderful place for our new home.

After lunch we packed up most of the remaining groceries and put them in the cache. Nearly everything is done. Just a few odds and ends to pack at the last moment. Our furs have all been placed in sacks, ready for shipping.

Wednesday – Jan. 4th -38C   Clear and cold.

Can't believe it!! I again got up first – a new record. Even though it's cold, it's so beautiful outside with the sun shining down from a deep blue sky. After breakfast we bundled up, strapped on our snowshoes and headed up the trail to close the traps we'd left set yesterday. It's about a three mile return trip. Nothing in the traps but, snowshoeing along through the trees, enjoying the scenery made it very worthwhile. The spruce were all white under their covers of snow. When you looked upwards to the bright, blue sky above, tree tops appeared to be shimmering in the sunlight – white, silver and multi-shades of yellow. Unbelievably beautiful!!

After we got back to the cabin, we finished packing and storing our gear. Furs, all sacked, were hung in the porch ready for loading on the aircraft. After supper Don called to tell us that chances aren't good for a flight in the morning because of extremely cold temperatures.

Thursday – Jan. 5th -42C   Clear and cold. Doesn't look as though we'll get away today.

Again, I got up first. Not a good habit to get into. During breakfast we made a list of the groceries we have left over – ten dozen eggs, one case of oranges, one and a half heads of cabbage, twenty pounds of potatoes, one turnip, plus all the other canned goods stored in the cache. Figure we could stay for another two months at least.

The day sure dragged by. Waited for that radio message advising us the plane was on its way but it didn't come. Anyway, Gordon decided to dig the snow away from the area where he's planning on building the new cabin. If we do go ahead and build another cabin, we'll use this cozy cabin as a guest home and a place where we'll work on furs. Temperature was minus forty-two at bedtime!!

Friday – Jan. 6th -44C Another cold day and again – No flying!! Gordon will have to go up in the cache and bring down a few supplies, coffee, tea, etc.

Just as we finished breakfast we heard via the radio that J.B. Fitzgerald had passed away. He was the Yukon Game Director when we started our Big Game Outfitting business and it was also through him that we got our trapline. He was a grand gentleman and will be sorely missed by so very many people. Also learned that John Anderson, the trapper whose cabin had burned, will have to have his big toe plus the two toes next to it amputated. Not sure which foot is involved. Anyway, he is in very bad shape.

It didn't warm up above minus forty today. Even so, it was so nice out in the sunshine that Gordon just had to work outside for most of the day. He dug snow away from the area where our new cabin will be built. Time goes so slowly while reading, waiting for news of the plane.

Saturday – Jan. 7th -42C Clear. Guess we won't get away today.   Gordon did more shoveling. Said he's about three-quarters done. I piled a bit of wood in the front porch and then knitted. Running low on propane.

Sunday – Jan. 8th -38C Clear but a little warmer.

!!HURRAY!! Just after ten, we heard from Watson Lake Flying Service that they plan on coming in for us today. A rush after that, putting everything away in the cupboards and cache, emptying water pails and burning the trash. Gordon packed the furs and all our other gear, that's going to Watson Lake, down to the flight strip on the lake. I've got mixed feelings, I'm looking forward to returning to our home at Watson Lake but I don't really want to leave Ridge Lake. I have so many good memories. I also keep thinking – next fall really isn't so terribly far away!!

About the Author

Rose had been quite content with her life as a city girl living in Edmonton, Alberta until the summer of 1948. Then it abruptly changed! Her brother Louis, a member of the RCAF stationed at Snag, Yukon, arrived home on leave and brought along his buddy, Gordon.

After meeting Gordon, her life was changed forever. They found they greatly enjoyed being together and, after a whirlwind courtship, were married.

Shortly afterwards Gordon, employed by the Canadian Meteorological Service, was transferred to Watson Lake, Yukon. Rose agreed to come north for a two year period. She stayed a little longer!!

They built their log home on the shore of Watson Lake and still live there. Over the years Rose, besides raising their family of six children, has assisted Gordon in a number of ventures – Big Game Outfitting, a Fly-in Fishing Camp, clearing land for their hay farm and others. Life was always a challenge and enjoyable.

Gordon also had a trapline in the mountains a hundred miles north of Watson Lake. Rose, realizing how much he enjoyed being on the trapline, promised that once the children had all left home she would spend a month out there with him to find out why he enjoyed being there so much. She too fell in love with life in the wilderness and kept a diary of her experiences.

This book is composed of the diary she kept during her first four years on the trapline.

Her diary for the next eight years will follow.

ISBN 141202055-7

9 781412 020558